Xiang Shi

The Evolution of the Vampire, Book I

Shawn Boyd

Printed in the United States of America

Prologue
Bloody Beginnings

With peasant origins, the family known as the Liu Clan took control of China in 206 BC, ushering in one of the greatest periods in China, the Han Dynasty. China became a Confucian state and saw a time of great prosperity and expansion. During the rule of the Han, paper was invented, the idea of acupuncture (Feng Shua) appeared, as well as the first instrument to track earthquakes the world had seen. With its military prowess the Han extended their influence and territory over parts of Korea, Mongolia, Vietnam and Central Asia. Military expeditions took them west beyond the Caspian Sea. This produced a safe route for trade across Central Asia that would become known as the Silk Road.

Unfortunately, internal strife, corruption and political power struggles failed to improve the harsh lives of the peasants. Invading Taoist ideals of equal rights and fair land distribution spread through the peasantry leading to the Yellow Turban Rebellion that swarmed the Northern China Plain. When the chaos subsided three overlords had seized control of China proper.

Civil war erupted. The period that followed would be known as the Era of Disunity. The first sixty years would see the rule of the Three Kingdoms (Wei, Shu and Wu). This short-lived era was one of the bloodiest in Chinese history. In 263 AD Wei conquered the Shu. Wei victory was cut short as the Jin overthrew Wei in 265 AD. By 280 AD the Jin had also seen to the destruction of the Wu.

The western Jin Dynasty, founded by the Sima family, had made China whole once more. However, this union would be brief because the Jin couldn't withstand the constant invasions by the nomadic tribes in the north for long. In 317 AD the Jin court had to flee to the southern city of Nanjing and re-establish there because they could no longer hold their capitol in Luoyang. This move would mark the beginning of the Eastern Jin Dynasty. China was divided with the Jin holding control of the south, while the north was split into thirteen barbarian states. The south continued to prosper during these troubled times. Yet, even with the success the Jin experienced, internal conflicts plagued them. Fights between the Taoists, Confucionists and growing number of Buddhists exploded across the land.

The north had its own problems to deal with. The ruling tribes such as the Xiongma, She Le and Fu Jian not only had to defend their lands from one another, but also from incessant raids by the nomadic Ruan Ruan and Xia people. These times would be known as the Dark Ages in China.

To go with the increasing turmoil it experienced among its own people, China would face the emergence of a new enemy. Rearing its ugly head for the first time in the war-torn north, it would soon threaten to sweep all of China and beyond. No one would be safe from its wrath. Every man, woman and child would be affected by its emanation. The differing religious factions would point blame at each other. Resentment between these groups would harden into hatred.

Evil was about to take a new, more absolute form. Its fierce hunger would be like nothing mankind had ever known. The mere mention of its name would strike terror into the heart of any man who heard it. Its name was Xiang Shi.

VAMPIRE.

CHAPTER 1

Zhan's sleep was not restful. Often one of his brothers would hear his cries and wake him, ending the recurring nightmare that had afflicted him since two days after the New Year. He realized as he got ready to lie down that it had been weeks since he had slept well. He felt tired, worn out and very old. In fact he was an old man, relatively speaking. For seventy-seven years he had dreamed the dreams that told of the future. Never in all those years had anything troubled him so deeply. Not even the dreams that told him of his father's imminent death, followed by his mother's passing last spring, caused such an ache in his heart. However the pain and sorrow the visions brought were minuscule when compared to the sheer terror these new dreams delivered.

Zhan walked to the table by the window and took the half-full wineskin. He proceeded back to his bed and sat. Zhan had always liked strong drink, but as of late he had been taking more and more of it. Just a little he always told himself. He needed just a little to calm his nerves. Almost always a little turned into a little more, then a little more, until he finally passed out.

Zhan opened the flask and took a long draw.

He began to recall his childhood. Those memories always served as gentler ones to go to sleep by. He remembered a time when, at the tender age of six, his parents began to realize that their son had a special gift. Zhan had foreseen the deaths of both his maternal grandmother and aunt. His father was disturbed by this of course and immediately sheltered his son from others. Zhan was their only son and they feared for his safety. The people of their village might see his gift as born of evil. They could conceivably panic in their ignorance and call for his sacrifice. Perhaps they would see that as the only way to prevent the anger of the gods, who might punish the entire village with famine and disease.

It did not help matters that Deshi Li, Zhan's father, was the only Buddhist in their village. Their Taoist neighbors shunned Deshi and his wife Mei-Hua more than once for their beliefs. Deshi's brother Jing was a Buddhist monk. Jing Li lived in the nearest predominately Buddhist village some two days ride west of where they lived.

Deshi was perplexed by, and somewhat frightened of, his son's unusual abilities. Not knowing where else to turn, he wrote a letter the best he could to his brother. He and Jing had not spoken in years. He was not sure whether his brother would be able to, or even want to come.

Jing did come. He journeyed from the monastery to their home to witness firsthand what his brother had spoken of in his letter. He stayed with them for a full cycle of the moon. Jing declared that, "There is nothing evil about this child or the gifts that the gods have bestowed on him. You should move your family to the village near the monastery. The elders should see the boy. Little Zhan should be formally trained in the ways of Buddha. It's possible that Zhan might actually be an incarnation of Buddha himself. At the least he was an enlightened one."

Zhan's father resisted, and said only that, "I need time to contemplate these things."

Mei-Hua pleaded with him to take them from this place. They had no real friends here and she no longer felt safe for any of them. Zhan was her only child.

Deshi would certainly agree that this village was not the best place in all of China to raise their son, especially under the circumstances, but at least here their son had choices. Having choices mattered to Deshi. Deshi had fled his family's village, left it behind with the monastery. He had done so many years ago and with good reason, at least in his mind. He had not been like his older brother. His parents had always been so proud of Jing. Deshi did not show the same devotion as his brother in the study and practice of Buddhism, and he certainly had no desire to become a monk. Rather than embracing the enlightenment, Deshi had rebelled against it.

The teachings had been forced on him, especially after Jing had joined the monastery. When he got old enough he left a note, went out one morning and never came back. He traveled living off the land, meeting new people, learning more about himself and taking his lumps along the way. He had studied Taoism, animism, learned from a shaman, and discussed the teachings of Confucius. None of it worked for him. He did like some of the Confucianism philosophy, but in the end he found he agreed more with the teachings of Buddha he had been raised with. If asked, yes Deshi Li was a Buddhist, though in what many would consider a loose definition of the word. Everybody had to be something.

Deshi did not want his son to have religion forced on him. If he returned to the site of his youth now, that would be Zhan's fate. Whatever path his son chose, Deshi wanted to make sure it was a choice. If Buddha's way was the one he followed, then let him discover it in his own right.

"You know mother misses you. Had she been able to make the journey she would have come. Your sisters miss you. I miss you, Deshi." Jing said, a tear welling.

"And what about father, Jing? Does he not miss me?"

Jing's head bowed. Deshi could see the pain on his face as he looked up again. "Father passed on three summers ago. I sent you a letter. Did you not receive it?"

"I did not." Deshi answered as his lip began to quiver.

"We thought maybe the last argument you had with him, before you left, had something to do with you not coming."

"That argument was forgotten long ago. Had I known, I would have come. I wouldn't have stayed, but I would have been there to pay my respects. I still loved him, you know." Then it was time for a tear to roll down Deshi's cheek.

Mei-Hua hugged him, and held on as he quietly sobbed on her shoulder. "Won't you come with me Deshi? Just for a little while, if not to stay. It would do everyone good to see you."

"Someday. Maybe. Not right now. Give them my love, Jing. I thank you for coming." Jing left without another word of argument. The couple spent the next few days in sorrow. Mei-Hua knew Deshi had no intentions of moving. Deshi's grief led him to drinking more than usual. A lot more than usual.

So many things weighed on Deshi's mind. He and his wife had been blessed with this wonderful son, but only the one. They had tried so hard to have another. It was not meant to be. Deshi thought there was something physically wrong with him. Mei-Hua blamed herself the same way. She cried every time they talked about it. She even had suggested that he take another wife because she could only bear him the one son.

One night, in a drunken stupor, Deshi roamed the streets of his village crying over his father's passing. Slurring his words out loud, Deshi wondered why his son had not been able to see the passing of his father. He had not had a chance to say goodbye. Several of his neighbors overheard his wails and cries and took hold of Deshi, leading him back to Mei-Hua to sleep it off. His ranting had not gone unnoticed by his fellow villagers, and talk slowly started to spread through the village. People became concerned about this reclusive man and his strange family, who did not share their Taoist beliefs.

Young Zhan was troubled by his parents' grief as well. That night his dreams spoke to him. They delivered a glorious message. He awoke from his slumber and stirred his mother and father from their own rest. "Zhan, it is too early for you to be up. Lay back down." his father said with a yawn.

"Please father, I have great news! My dreams—they have spoken to me!"

"In the morning, Zhan." Deshi rolled onto his side pulling the blanket up around his neck—his head pounding from the earlier consumption of too much wine.

"What is it little one?" his mother asked. Deshi let out a groan.

"You carry my brother in your belly!"

"What?" Deshi shot up. "Say that again." he rubbed his temples, trying to stop the pain and clear his head.

"She is going to have a baby father."

Deshi looked over at his wife. "Is it possible?" Mei-Hua smiled. "Really!"

"I was going to tell you, but I wanted to be sure first. I have thought myself to be with child since shortly before your brother came. We have had so many false hopes before."

"This is wonderful! I am so happy!" Deshi stood, scooped Zhan up in his arms and danced around the room. "You were right to wake me for such glorious news!" The excitement had momentarily helped clear his head, but not brought back his balance. Deshi tripped over backwards, falling to the floor with his son clutched to his chest. He let out a moan on impact, and then broke out in laughter, something his wife and son had not heard since his brother had left.

"That is not all father! There is more!"

"Tell me, son. Tell me all about it." Deshi worked his way slowly back to his feet, Zhan still held in one arm. Mei-Hua was on her feet now as well. He hugged his wife to them and laid a gentle kiss on her cheek.

"He will be born on my birthday. All my brothers will be."

"Brothers? There will be more?"

"Yes, father. You will be blessed with seven sons." *Seven sons!* Tears came to Deshi's eyes. The people of the village would laugh behind his back no more. "They will be born seven years apart exactly."

Deshi stopped dancing and frowned. He lowered his son to the floor. "Seven years apart? It is not possible, Zhan. You must be mistaken." The pain and dizziness swirled back in.

"Seven years, father. My dreams have told me."

"Then your dreams are wrong! Your mother will be too old to bear children by the time the fourth one arrives. We will be long passed before the seventh is due!"

"But father, it is true! You and mother will both have long lives. Long enough to see all your children grown to adulthood. Please believe me."

"I cannot believe that which is not possible! Your dreams deceive you!"

"But father—"

"Enough, Zhan! I have heard enough. If you have made up this tale to make me feel better it has failed. I only feel worse now."

Zhan tried to fight back the tears, but his eyes welled over just the same.

"Deshi, what is wrong with you? Look at our son," said Mei-Hua.

"I will have no more talk of this tonight woman!"

Mei-Hua cradled Zhan in her arms, wiping the tears from his cheeks with her gown.

"Why don't you two believe me, mama?"

"I believe you little one. I believe you."

"You will not encourage him, Mei-Hua. You know what he speaks cannot be."

"I know that his dreams have come true twice before. And I know that I am pregnant now. Why cannot the rest be just as true? Dao-ming gave birth to Enlai last year, and she is twice my age."

"But you will be twenty years older than she is now when you have our last! And you know how sick Enlai has been. His father tells me he fears his son will not make it till the New Year."

Mei-Hua glared at him. "And you would not love a son just because he is ill?"

"I did not say that. Do not put words in my mouth, Mei-Hua. You know I would love my child no matter what."

"Father, may I speak?" Zhan asked, wiping his nose on his sleeve.

"What? More lies? I do not have the patience for any more tonight!" If it wasn't for the nausea in his stomach, Deshi thought a drink would serve him well at the moment.

"Let him speak. You need not be so rough with him. He is but a child." Mei-Hua said. "Look at him. He cries for you are angry with him. He needs your love—not your anger."

"Speak, Zhan. Say what you must and be done." Deshi relented.

"You two were given a gift. You will be given six more. All of your sons will be gifted. I promise that it is true."

Deshi stopped pacing. His anger cooled as he remembered just how blessed he was to have Zhan. This was why he left the monastery behind. He wanted a family of his own. A son to raise without the pressures of religion, politics, or a father who believed only his way was correct. "You are right, little one. You are a gift." He reached down and hoisted his son in his arms once more. "You are a precious gift. I treasure you and your mother above all things." Deshi beckoned his wife to join them. "I am so sorry. Please forgive my anger." A tear trailed down his face.

"Then you believe me father?"

"It will be hard, but I will try."

It wasn't until after Zhan's brother Wei was born that his father began to believe these things were possible. When Wei was four, events took place that erased any remaining doubt Deshi held. Zhan remembered, taking another sip from his flask, one day in particular that stood out among the others. He could still picture it like it was yesterday.

Zhan got out of bed early that morning to find his father getting ready to go fishing. "Good morning, Zhan. Come fishing with me?"

"I would love to. May we take Wei as well?"

"Little Zhan, I will be happy to take you, but Wei is too small. He will not like fishing. He will only get in our way. I cannot be worried about both of you and still catch fish. I will let Wei come when he is a little older. I didn't even take you until you were almost seven."

"Please, father, I will look after him."

"And how will you learn to fish from me if you must watch Wei? There are things I still need to show you." Deshi paused. He was almost ready to give in to the plea in his older son's eyes, and then thought better of it. "No. Wei will come when he is bigger. There is no need for him to go now."

"But father, there is."

"What, Zhan? What purpose will it serve to take him? He is too little to be of help. He will only get in the way."

"I will tell you, if you promise not to get mad at me."

"I'm already annoyed by your insistence in taking him," Deshi answered, crossing his arms. "But go ahead. I will listen, and I will hold my temper."

"It is my dreams. They are what woke me. They said we must take Wei fishing with us."

"Why, Zhan?"

"I am not sure. It was not a vision this time. It was like somebody talking. The voice said that Wei will protect us."

Deshi frowned. How ridiculous that a child as small as Wei could offer any protection. Zhan's eyes held no doubt when he looked into them though. There was a conviction there that made Deshi give in. "Hmmm. Then wake him—but I warn you now, Zhan, if Wei is too much trouble I will not hold my anger. Your backside will suffer my bamboo stick."

It was a long walk to the lake. Wei had actually been good for most of the trip. Zhan worried that his younger sibling might get tired, and he would have to carry him piggyback. Much to the surprise of Zhan and their father, Wei showed no signs of slowing. Deshi led his boys down a narrow pass to his favorite fishing spot. It was the safest, fastest way down to the lake from the cliffs. The pass could be treacherous when it rained, however. The trail was steep and straight down. It was lined with large smooth rocks that became extremely slippery when wet. The sides of the pass rose sharply, almost five meters on either side. The descent, while dangerous if you became careless, was worth the effort. Of the countless times Deshi had come to this place, he had never had to spend more than a couple of hours there to catch all the fish he could carry.

Deshi was pleased at how well behaved both his sons were. He even started to show Wei a few fishing tricks. Deshi helped Wei bring one in, and Zhan caught two on his own. In a short while both of Deshi's bags were brimming with fish. He was proud of his sons and felt good about the day's catch. He could hardly wait to tell his wife how quickly their little men were learning the art of angling.

"It is time to head back home now boys."

"Aw, but papa."

"Sorry, Wei. We did have fun though, didn't we?"

"Yes, sir!" The brothers exclaimed in unison.

"I will carry the bags, Zhan. I need you to go up behind Wei and help him if he needs it." Deshi said. "Now go on. I will be there in a moment."

Zhan led Wei over to the passage. This was the part of the trip that he did not look forward to. The long assent was excruciating. His legs would be wobbly by the time they reached the top and there would still be the long trek home ahead of them. Zhan also worried about Wei. The climb might prove more than his little brother could handle. Zhan would have to carry him part of the way home if that were the case. Wei started up the pass. "Race ya!"

"No, Wei! It's too dangerous!" Zhan's words fell on deaf ears. Wei was on the move. "Wei, no!" Zhan hurried after his brother, who giggled as he climbed steadily upward. It wasn't that Wei moved fast, but that his pace did not slow. Zhan's legs were already cramping, but he raced forward. If Wei got hurt, he would be blamed. Their father always threatened the bamboo stick, though he never used it. Zhan didn't wish to have it broken in on his bottom.

At this pace they would reach the top in no time. The two were halfway there already, with Wei still holding a sizable lead. Zhan looked back to see his father just starting up—a load of fish over each shoulder. Their father would be tired from lugging the added weight of the fish up the incline. They would all get to rest by the big round boulder at the top. That was something Zhan did look forward to. That big beautiful rock was his salvation. It signaled the end of the climb.

Zhan turned his eyes back to Wei. The little monster had put more distance between them. Zhan could see the summit and the large round boulder. *Something was not right.* Zhan had been here many times with his father. You could not see that rock until you actually came out of the pass—the grade was too steep before then. "Father, I think the rock has moved. I can see it already."

"What?"

"The rock, father. The big one up there—it has moved."

"Impossible."

"Look, father, there are several men around it!"

Deshi dropped his bags of fish. His jaw hung agape and terror rolled over him like a tidal wave. "Zhan, come back! Get behind me!"

"What about Wei?"

"I will get him! You get back down here as fast as you can. When you reach the bottom move as far away from the mouth of the pass as you can! Now, Zhan!" Deshi rushed by his older son, chasing after Wei. "Wei! Stop! Come back! Daddy needs you! Come back to me, Wei! Wei!"

One of the men at the top of the hill shouted down at them. "Today Deshi-Li, we will send you and your demon spawn back to the level of hell from which you came!"

Wei did not slow down. "Wei! Stop now! Daddy is not playing with you! Stop!" Deshi realized that already it was too late. Wei finally stopped, but he was only four meters from the top. Deshi could hear the men grunting. They had disappeared behind the rock again. Once they moved it that last little bit, it would come crashing down upon them. Deshi rushed by his son. He knew that both of them would never be able to beat the boulder back to the bottom. It was inches away from steam-rolling downward to the lake. The sides were too steep and high to climb—there was no time.

If he could wedge his feet against the rock trail and brace the boulder with his back— maybe—just maybe he could hold it long enough for Wei to reach safety. He turned and placed his back against the boulder and planted his feet against two of the rocks embedded in the pass that stuck out just a little bit higher than the others. Deshi locked his legs and strained against the tremendous weight of the stone and the force of the men pushing it.

"Get back down the hill, Wei! Find Zhan and go with him." Why had he ever brought Wei? Had it only been Zhan with him they might all still live. That didn't seem important now. His life meant little to him at this point with the safety of his boys in jeopardy. He must save his sons. "Daddy will hold the rock back until you get down! Hurry, Wei!"

Deshi could feel the men increase their effort. His knees began to buckle as his body cried out in pain. "No!" he screamed. *I must hang on for my sons! I will not fail them! I will not fail Mei-Hua!* He tilted his head back and pushed against the rock with everything he had. His legs wobbled and bent a little further. Tears rolled down his face. The strain was overwhelming. Blood rushed to his head and he longed to pass out. If he could just let go, allow the rock to roll swiftly over him and end the agony. "No! Not yet! I will not let you have my sons! Damn you!" He pleaded with his body to fight.

For a moment he wasn't sure if the rock had lightened or if he had finally fainted from exhaustion. Then he felt his legs straighten. The boulder moved back. *The gods are with me!* Or maybe the men had grown tired and given up. More likely they rested a moment and were going to regroup for another try. *I must work fast!* If he could keep it rolling back maybe he could push it far enough to escape. First he had to make sure Wei had made it to safety. He glanced down the trail and did not see his son.

The boulder moved backward quickly and Deshi scrambled and tried desperately to keep his feet. He fell flat on his back, but quickly rolled over expecting the rock to crush him immediately. He saw two little feet. *Wei's feet!* He looked up and watched his son push the rock as easily as one might push an empty wheelbarrow. Deshi could not believe his eyes. He lay there in astonishment for a moment until screams came from the other side of the rock and snapped him back to reality. He gathered himself, got to his feet, and took up position beside his son.

They pushed the great stone forward—and suddenly Deshi could see the meadow around it. There were still screams that echoed from beyond. A cry for help rang out, followed by a sound like the snap of dry twigs underfoot. The screams died. Father and son continued to push. Deshi stumbled over something and nearly fell. He looked down to see a crumpled leg jutting out from under the boulder. Wei stopped and the rock stopped with him. "Wei help daddy, good?"

"Wei is very good." Deshi tried to catch his breath.

Wei glanced down at the leg. "One of the bad men. He shouldda moved."

"Yes, son." Deshi moved around the rock. He could see five men racing back across the field in retreat. Deshi limped over to the top of the pass. "Zhan! Zhan! It is safe now. Come up, son." He stared down until he could see his elder son wade in the water at the bottom of the trail. *Why did I ever doubt?* The adrenaline rush left his body and fatigue swept over him. Deshi watched Wei for a moment. His little one was picking flowers three meters away from the boulder and the dead man underneath. For his younger son it was as if nothing significant had happened here at all.

Zhan struggled to the top, carrying one of the bags of fish. He had tried to manage both, but the second proved to be too much for his thin frame to handle. His father lie sprawled out on the ground. At first Zhan feared the worst as he rushed to his father's side, tears glistening in his eyes. He laid his head against his father's chest. The thud of a heartbeat and the rise and fall of his father's chest came to his relief.

"For mama, Zhan!" Wei said as he held a handful of flowers. Zhan hugged his little brother. "Where's other bag of fish?"

"I couldn't carry them both."

"Wei will get it."

"No, Wei."

"Gotta get fish. I think my fish in other bag anyway."

Zhan looked over his shoulder and watched as Wei disappeared down the pass. He was too tired to argue and much too tired to give chase.

Later that day, in great haste, Zhan's family left the village for good. Few were sad to see them go. They journeyed to the village outside the monastery where his Uncle Jing lived. Zhan and his brothers would become apprentices—then monks there. The training they received and later taught conditioned the mind, body and inner soul.

Zhan remembered those times with great fondness as he took another drink. The village they lived in was far enough to the south that it had not felt the trouble caused by the raids of the nomadic tribes in the north. Everyone around them followed the way of Buddha, so there was no conflict over religion. The village and the monastery were a safe place in a troubled world.

That was then—now was different. The dreams were all bad. An evil greater than he had ever known was about to be born. His brothers and his country would all experience its wrath, of that part he was sure. Zhan just couldn't see what it was, or when or where it would make itself known. Its time drew near. He could sense it. He prayed and meditated for ways to stop it. There was no answer. There were only the nightmares. He dreaded his sleep this night for six of the seven beds in his room would remain empty. His brothers had journeyed to a neighboring monastery to see an old friend off to the next existence. Zhan had stayed behind to watch over their monastery and continue the training of the younger monks.

Zhan had seen many a friend, his age or younger, pass on. He knew he would see many more before his time to transcend came. At seventy-seven, not a single gray hair touched his head. In the way of the Buddhist monks, he and his brothers of course kept their head shaved. However, the stubble when left to grow came in as thick and dark as when he was a child. His skin was soft, without a blemish. There were no spots as other men his age had, and only the slightest trace of smile wrinkles broke the smoothness of his face. That was until the nightmares began. Now bags and dark rings circled his eyes and his face was more drawn from a combination of too much drink and an often-poor appetite. While his general appearance and physical ability suggested that of a much younger man his mind felt—especially since the nightmares had come—all seventy-seven years and then some.

Zhan drained the last bit of wine from the flask. He offered a slurred prayer for his brothers' safety, and a speedy journey for his departed friend into the next existence. Zhan laid his head down groggily. The thought of being alone, no one to hear his cries when the nightmares came, saddened him. Then the drink took over and Zhan fell fast asleep.

CHAPTER 2

Night fell upon the land and its band of travelers. The clear skies that let the stars and full moon shine through were more than enough light to travel by. The small army, numbering near five hundred, would stay on the move. They were driven by a ruthless leader who was eager to spill the blood of his enemies, or anyone else that got in his way. Ju-Long's men were hunted and hated by even their own people. However, these men were completely loyal. If not from admiration of their leader's great physical prowess and cunning in battle, than by sheer fear of his terrible wrath. The latter had been brought upon many an unfortunate soul that dared to question his authority.

As his army swept across the north they took over small villages, robbing them of their resources. They raped the women and left their calling card, beheading the men and mounting their heads on wooden spears driven into the ground. This type of action was one of the milder atrocities they committed, and led to their exile from the Xia tribe. They had become a rogue army, and that suited Ju-Long just fine. The Xia tribe, considered barbaric by all others in their own right, still held a loose code of conduct. Ju-Long and his band of murderers had disobeyed orders more than once and gone so far in their cruel treatment of those they conquered that even previously allied tribes began to make a push against the Xia.

Ju-Long was the one behind it all. He was a man who held nothing sacred. He believed himself to be above all others. The Xia council saw him as an outcast. How they had ever allowed him to lead men was beyond any of them. While his results were guaranteed, his methods were abominable. They exiled any man who chose to remain at his side and placed a death sentence on Ju-Long himself. He was to be executed immediately if captured. They forbid any aid be given to him or his followers.

When Ju-Long heard those words he swore to feast on the bodies of his former leaders. They were the ones who had bought themselves a death sentence. His rage toward them became focused on every village he and his men encountered from that moment on. They slaughtered all they met—regardless of age or sex. Now he had set his sights on the city of Dulan. From there he would build a kingdom, then an empire. He would recruit all those intelligent enough to recognize his natural leadership abilities and lay waste to the rest. Dulan was a large enough city to accommodate his men, yet poorly defended by those whom dwelled there. The city relied too much on its natural defenses. The terrain of the mountain passes to the north and west was too rough for any sizable threat to overcome. There was little threat from elsewhere, because it lay too far away from the lands fought over by the northern tribes and the Jin to have any strategic significance. Ju-Long wanted it for those exact reasons. It would allow him the sanctuary he needed to begin his plans to rule all of China. Life in Dulan had been easy for its people for long enough.

His army was only a day's march from the city. There he would gather unto him all those who sought a god-like leader to end their woes. Then he would crush his enemies, unite the north, and use it to overrun what was left of the south. The Jin and their people were like a fat, overripe fruit waiting to be plucked. One-day China would be his. The studies he did on the past allowed him to see the weaknesses of his predecessors. China demanded an iron hand to rule it, and he knew his grip would fit her perfectly.

There would be no more of this Buddha or ranting of Confucius. There would only be Ju-Long's law. China's ways would be his ways. To him it was the perfect union of a mighty country with a ruler strong enough to tame her. He and he alone could make her a power that the whole world would fear. The west, Japan—all of them would have to bow to China.

Ju-Long was lost in the thoughts of his own grandeur when the earth began to tremble under his horse. He rode quickly to the front of his army, ordering his men to stand fast. "Kong! What is happening?" Ju-Long demanded as he approached his cousin and second in command. Kong was at the front leading the soldiers through the mountain pass.

"I do not know my master. The ground seems to be opening up just ahead of us. We must fall back! Our whole army might be swallowed up by the earth!"

Kong was pathetic. No matter how long he stayed with Ju-Long, and how hard Ju-Long tried to mold him into a brave warrior, it would not be. Kong was a weak coward. Ju-Long would have killed him for it had it not been for Kong's father. He had been the only man Ju-Long looked up to as a child. Kong's father was his uncle—his mother's brother. Ju-Long had never known his father. His father was a thief. Exactly which one of the thieves that had kidnapped and raped his mother repeatedly for two nights—until his uncle had tracked them down and killed them single-handedly—he would never know.

"Damn this! We are so close to Dulan. Damn this delay!" Ju-Long roared his disapproval. "Have the men fall back and set up camp as soon as the earth stops shaking."

Kong bowed and turned to carry out his orders just as fire exploded out of the crevice in the ground. Ju-Long's horse bucked wildly, throwing him to the ground. "You will pay with your life for that beast." As he stood up, brushing himself off, he noticed that the ground had quit shaking. The fire from the large crack in the earth had receded, leaving a thick billow of smoke behind. He turned to watch his troops almost running over each other as they fled down the pass. "Cowards! You run scared! Fall back like men!"

Ju-Long knew no fear. He felt himself invincible. By his sword and strength he had survived certain death so many times he almost believed himself immortal. At the age of nineteen he had achieved the rank of warlord in the Xia tribe on the merit of his skill in battle and knowledge of warfare. Now, eight years later, he was on the verge of establishing his own kingdom.

Ju-Long turned back to the crevice and decided to take a closer look. He had covered half the distance to it when he saw a large man-like creature coming out of the smoke. Ju-Long drew his sword and took up a fighting stance. "That is far enough. Come any closer and you will taste my blade creature!"

The beast did not even slow its pace. Ju-Long tightened his grip on the sword and got ready to strike. "Do not anger me with your disobedience—whatever you are." He found himself staring up at a dark form with the head of an ox and hollow eyes. Ju-Long was six feet five—taller than most of his own people. This aberration was easily over ten feet tall. It wore no garments, and huge corded muscles covered its body. "I will kill you where you stand beast! This I swear!" Ju-Long brushed his jet black, waist-length braid behind his back. His eyes, almost as dark as his hair, gleamed with rage.

The dark figure stopped just out of the reach of Ju-Long's blade. "If I had come here to harm you, you would already be dead, mortal." The figure snarled. Ju-Long eased back a pace, eyes still locked on the hollow sockets of his enemy.

"Then why have you come? Who are you to dare interrupt me in my quest for my kingdom?"

"To offer you power like you have never dreamed."

"And all I have to do is follow you, right demon?" Ju-Long spat. "I follow no one. I have no gods. I recognize no higher power. Ju-Long is master! I require no one and nothing else. I do not know who or what you are, but I strongly suggest that you crawl back into the hole from which you came or suffer my wrath. I will not repeat myself. You have been warned."

The creature moved faster than Ju-Long's eyes could perceive. Instantly the demon covered the distance and was upon him. Ju-long found himself dangling in mid-air, supported by the large, strong hand that the creature had wrapped around his neck. Ju-Long raised his sword planning to deliver a severing strike to the beast's arm. The creature sensed his movement and tightened its grip. He couldn't breathe. The sword dropped from his hand.

The demon's eyes blazed to life, burning red like a magical fire. "My time above ground is limited. I do not have time to play games with you, mortal. I will not repeat that again. You will accept what I am about to offer you, or you will perish by a mere clenching of my fist!"

"I offer you immortality, strength ten times what you now possess, speed and agility greater than the cheetah or the tiger. I offer you what you already believe yourself to be—a deity in human form. I offer this to you and your entire army. With the power I shall share with you and your men, you will be able to crush any opponent. You want revenge on the ones who dared to exile their greatest warrior? I have it here for you."

Ju-Long felt helpless in the beast's clutch. The demon had him, and for the first time in his life he realized that he couldn't win. For the first time in his life, Ju-Long felt fear. A mystical power flowed through the creature's hand and into his body. He could feel his heart pounding—feel the rush of his own blood as it coursed through his veins. The demon loosened the hold it had on his throat. Ju-Long gulped in the night air. "What is the catch creature?" he rasped.

"Your repayment, mortal? You will crush the faith of all men in their so-called gods. They will believe in you and your power alone. Isn't that what you dream of already? You will enslave mortal men, farming them and using them as you wish. Those who outlive their usefulness you shall consume and send their souls to us. Is that so much to ask?"

"What do you mean, consume?"

"You shall feed on human blood and human blood alone. Only it will sustain you." The thought of that did not bother Ju-Long. He had drunk the blood of powerful men before, believing he could consume their power and strengthen his own.

"How will I control my army if they possess the same power as I?"

"A kiss from my lips will mark you as master. The power I unleash upon them through my hands will make them subordinate to you. What you destroy shall stay destroyed, but what you kiss shall become like you. As long as you feed regularly on human blood you shall live eternaly. Mind you, there are things on this earth and beyond that can destroy you, but they are few. I cannot tell you what they are—so you will not know—but neither shall your enemies. The power you possess will make it hard for any mortal to implement the things that would threaten your immortality. As time goes on you will become more and more powerful. The longer you avoid what would destroy you, the more difficult it will be to stop you."

"What good is immortality if you can still meet demise?"

"There are only a handful of true immortals. Do not flatter yourself with thoughts that you should rank among them. Even I could face death at the hands of those who created me."

"Then you hold not the power which I seek. Be gone and send one of them in your place."

"I almost admire your arrogance. Unfortunately, you must die now. You were warned." The demon, almost taunting him, began to slowly reassert his grip.

"Wait!" Ju-Long gasped. "I only meant to test your res-o-lu-tion."

"No more games."

"Pleeaase. You have my word." The beast loosened his hold. Ju-Long gulped in another breath. "Would you want someone so weak they don't at least attempt to negotiate a better offer?"

"So sure of your own worth." The beast laughed and it echoed like thunder. "You don't even realize how unnecessary you are. We will have what we want, whether you are the chosen one or not. Do you really believe you are the only one on the list? Yet I suppose, your presumption of greatness along with your manner of life is probably why they sent me to you in the first place. Number one on the list—that I'll give you—but there are a number to take your place should you refuse."

"I have not refused. I can hardly believe there would be any other among man who would serve you as well." The word serve tasted bitter in his mouth.

"You had better hope you are right. You are not the only player on the battlefield."

"Can you offer me nothing more? Why must so many things be secret?"

"My little pawn, he whose life is at our disposal no matter how this night ends, your true fate was sealed long ago. Alas, I can offer you this—you will operate only at night. The sun can and will destroy you. Should you be foolhardy enough to step into its light, you will burn to ash. However, by night you will know no equal. You will rule in a kingdom of darkness. By day you will be vulnerable, but you may mark chosen individuals who will protect your daily rest. With your mark, your bond, they will share some of your power. Their loyalty to you will be complete. They will carry out any order that you give and watch over you as well as those you enslave. As you go, so shall they."

The vagueness of this entire interlude troubled him. Ju-Long was a man who demanded concise answers. Unfortunately he was in no position to make ultimatums. This demon would deal with him again, but it would be another day. "Who are you creature? Who has chosen me? What game is it they play?"

"That matters not. My master, who your people refer to as Yen-Lo, sent me to offer you the honor of being his ambassador on earth. I myself am known to you as Niu T'ou." The demon observed the blank gaze on his captive's face. "You know not that name? No matter, you have asked and I have answered. My ability to sustain myself on this plane dwindles. If you accept our offer, you and your army shall travel to the large cave that lies just ahead and stay there until tomorrow's nightfall. Then, you will take the city as you planned and turn it into a fortress against your enemies, including the sun. I will ask only once, and for you there is only one answer. I must return to my place. Do you accept?"

There was no time to think. He had felt the beast's power and realized that it must be his. So many questions, but his options were only two. The power was all that mattered. "Yes."

With the utterance of that single syllable the creature drew Ju-Long's lips to his. Ju-Long could feel, actually see his own life force being drawn. It was not physically painful, but the thought of his life being sucked from him was terrifying. He struggled against the demon, pummeling its head and shoulders with his fists to no avail. His body became limp—for a moment the world faded to black. Then suddenly a rush of power coursed through his veins. Life was restored, only in a different form. It was like the height of ecstasy, bringing more pleasure than he had ever known. *The power! Yes! Yes!*

Abruptly the demon released him, and Ju-Long fell to the ground. His head swam in the wake of the magical energy that had been transferred. He was reborn. Born to rule all of China and eventually the world. Still, a look at the beast made him realize that in order to achieve his final goal even the ones that created him must be made to serve him.

The creature raised its arms and reached outward, extending its hands toward the army below. With a roar ten times louder than a lion, a flow of power rushed from each palm. Bright bolts of energy flashed down the mountain, expanding as they descended. They slammed into his men and he could hear their cries of agony. The energy burned even brighter as it returned to the creature. It carried the screams of his warriors with it, as if their very life forces were captured. The creature's mouth opened to devour the surge of power. Its body began to glow like a flame as it consumed their mortal lives—their souls. When the beast finished, it bellowed again, its once dark body now burning red.

"I must leave now, Ju-Long. Go to your men and lead them to the cave. There you shall relay to them what I have told you." With that, the demon turned and walked back toward the crevice.

"Wait!" Ju-Long cried. The creature ignored him. It walked steadily back to the opening and disappeared into the smoke. A moment later the ground began to tremble once more. As the smoke dissipated Ju-Long noticed that the land before him had sealed. There was no trace that there had ever been a crack in it.

***

Zhan tossed and turned in his bed. His body was covered in a cold sweat. The sheets were saturated. Images of an army of man-like beasts invading a small city ran through his dreams. Men with long fingernails as strong and as sharp as daggers and teeth like the fangs of a tiger were ripping people apart as if their flesh were mere paper. There was blood everywhere. The beasts tore out the throats of their helpless victims and consumed the blood that flowed.

Some of the monsters pulled the hearts from the chests of their victims, plunging their hands through muscle and bone and plucking them as easily as one might pick fruit from a tree. They held the still beating heart in their hands for their prey to see. Zhan saw the terror on their faces before they collapsed in death. The wicked howl of the demons as they destroyed life after life without conscience sent shivers throughout his body.

He saw a mother and her three-year-old son. They hid in the back of a small hut. The child cried as they watched the demons slaughter four men, one of them her brother, through a crack in the outer wall of the hut. She turned the boy's head away from the gruesome scene and cradled him to her bosom, desperately trying to muffle his sobs. Two of the horrible creatures crashed through the flimsy front door. They swept the room with their eyes. They had not seen the pair huddled behind a pile of empty crates. Zhan breathed a sigh of relief when the two exited.

The woman began to cry. She tried to comfort her son between her own sobs. "It is all right little one. The bad ones have missed us. It's all right." she said as she brushed tears from his face.

A fist punched through the wall beside her. The hand latched onto the boy's hair and tore him from her. It pulled the child right through the wall, shattering the old bamboo. She desperately reached for his foot. Her screams of terror were cut off when a second hand shot through the opening and clamped around her throat.

"Master Zhan! Master Zhan! You must wake up! Your wailing has awakened all of us down the hall! You must wake up! The younger boys are afraid! Please, Master Zhan!" Gan pleaded, shaking Zhan roughly. Zhan stirred slowly as if trapped somewhere between the dream and reality. He babbled incoherently for a moment, speaking frantically, then sat strait up in one swift motion.

"Gan, it has begun! All of us must fear! The nightmare has become real! My brothers return tomorrow and I must be ready to council with them."

"Master, your brothers return today."

"What?" Zhan asked, getting to his feet.

"Yes, master, today. You have been asleep for two nights and a day. We tried to wake you many times. You would not stir. We feared you might never wake."

"Have I been wailing the entire time?"

"No, master, only for the last few hours. I have been trying to wake you for the last two."

"Gather everyone into the courtyard, Gan. I will be there momentarily. I must talk to everyone. A great evil has emerged and we must prepare for it!"

"Yes, master."

Zhan stumbled over to the large bowl Gan had already filled with water for him. He dipped his hands into the cool liquid and rubbed some on his face. It felt good, but he needed more to bring him back to life. He submerged his face, letting the water come up to his ears. He breathed out and the bubbles escaped from around his cheeks as he tried to clear his head. He drew back, lifting his face out and sucked in a huge breath of air through his mouth. Zhan grabbed the rag next to the bowl and patted his head and face dry, then blew his nose into it and discarded it on the floor. He took in another long, deep breath—this time through his nose. The sour smell of sweat and urine made him want to gag. He stumbled back, almost falling onto the bed. Zhan steadied himself and saw the flask on the floor. He slowly bent down to retrieve it, falling to his hands and knees in the process, but found it empty. Zhan needed a drink. He crawled across the floor to the doorway, working his way back to his feet by using the frame to steady himself. Down the hallway, nearly tripping on the steps at the end, Zhan made his way to the first floor and then the kitchen. He knew what cupboard to look in. He opened it and found four fresh flasks. He grabbed one of them, opened it, and tipped it to his lips. He took long draws without a breath until the container was empty.

He knew Gan would carry out his orders quickly. Gan was still young—only thirteen—but he showed great maturity and knowledge for a boy his age. He was Zhan's finest pupil. For one without a special gift, Gan showed good speed, strength, and tactics in his physical training with Wei. What was most impressive about him though was how far beyond even the older boys he was in his studies. Gan was anxious to learn and always willing to perform any task given to him. Zhan, without any child of his own, treated Gan like a son. He cared for all the young men at the monastery, but Gan was by far his favorite.

As he grabbed a second flask and began pouring it down his throat, Zhan could not help but worry for Gan and the others. The evil was still far off, but certainly it would find its way to their doorstep. *When?* That was the question. Zhan hoped he and his brothers could find a way to stop it before that occurred.

He finished the second flask and tossed it aside. Zhan felt light-headed. He needed to get to the bath and change clothes before he addressed the others. He leaned against the cabinet and tried to shake off the effects of the alcohol. The sight of the mother and her child being slaughtered by the demons flashed through his head. He grabbed the remaining two flasks, one in each hand, and staggered back out to the hallway.

Gan ran from room to room, looking for his teacher. The others had been waiting for over an hour in the hot sun. He rounded a corner and went to the bath. *Surely Master Zhan is finished cleaning up by now,* he thought. As he entered the small chamber he found Zhan passed out on the floor, naked, two empty flasks at his side. "Master Zhan, no." He had seen his teacher drunk more than once, but never in this condition. He checked to be sure Zhan was still breathing, then dashed back to the courtyard and instructed the others that the meeting would have to wait until Master Wei and the others returned. He told them Zhan was meditating on some important matters and could not be disturbed until then.

Gan then raced back to the bath and closed the door. Zhan was still out and snoring loudly. "Master Zhan, why must you drink so much?" Gan walked over to the water barrels and found that three of the five were still full. It usually took at least two of the boys to push them over to the in-ground pool and tip them over into it. This time Gan was on his own. He could not let the others see Master Zhan like this.

He strained and struggled and got two of them over and emptied into it. He was sweaty and tired and wanted to lie down. Instead he scooped a little water from the third barrel into a small pot, wetted a rag, and began ringing it out slowly over Zhan's face. Zhan opened his eyes as Gan applied the cloth to his forehead. "Master Zhan. You look terrible. Why do you do this to yourself?"

Zhan raised a hand to Gan's cheek. "Good boy. You're the finest of all the other fine finers," Zhan murmured. Gan was frustrated and sad at the same time. If only the nightmares would stop for Zhan, he would go back to his old self. "Have-did I tell you? I mean did I ever said that to you before? You make me very proud of being proud. But don't you fret one bits, cause my brothers and I gonna take care of them demonmons. Won't let them head a hair on your harm."

"Master Zhan! You are drunk. We must get you into the bath and back on your feet as soon as possible. If your brothers come home and find you like this they will not be happy."

"Ah yes, my brothers be here sooon. Got to get ready. Bad things coming tooo. Gonna be a fight. Can't be long for they come to us in then we gonna have trouble. Bad, bad things." Zhan began to cry softly.

"This is just great. With all due respect master, you must quit babbling and blubbering and help me get you cleaned up. Now come on Master Zhan, please work with me. Master Zhan?" Zhan had passed out again. Gan struggled to pull him over and into the pool, resting his teacher's head on the edge. At one-hundred ninety pounds, his master wasn't that heavy, but his six-foot-seven frame—a foot and a half taller that Gan—made it awkward. He washed Zhan as best he could, who thanked him by peeing into the water. When he was finished, he dragged Zhan back out, dried him, and went to get fresh clothes for the both of them.

CHAPTER 3

Ju-Long awakened with a fierce hunger. He needed to feed. He stumbled across the room trying not to trip over his still sleeping soldiers. Pain racked his body hard and he fell to his knees, landing on one of his slumbering men. He found the warrior's body to be as stiff as a board. Stiff like a corpse. Quickly he felt another, then another. *They were all dead!* He could sense no sign of life in any of their bodies. Ju-Long jumped to his feet, fighting the hunger pangs. He moved over to Kong's body, reached down and touched him. There was no life there either.

Rage consumed him and the hunger quelled for a moment. They had taken the city without losing a single man. *How can this be?* They were all dead. Ju-Long wondered how soon he would suffer the same fate. The demon had tricked him. Niu T'ou would pay dearly for this treachery. Somehow he would find him and destroy him.

Only a handful of his men had even been wounded. *How could they have died?* Their injuries did not slow them in the least during the battle last night. He remembered Kong taking a sword through the stomach. He raised his cousin's shirt and found no sign of any wound where the blade had sunk in. *Why if it healed completely was Kong dead? Why are any of them dead?*

The thirst for blood overwhelmed him again and his knees buckled. His head felt dizzy and his stomach rebelled against him. He doubled over and began dry heaving over and over until he thought he would pass out. Finally he regained enough composure to stand. He had to get to the stronghold. There were other men in separate buildings, but he had no time to check on them. He must feed before the hunger drove him to madness.

Ju-Long raced for the door, nearly tripping over the bodies that lie in his path. He burst through it and fell to the ground, covering his head with his hands. It was dusk outside, but not yet true dark. He hesitated as he waited to burst into flames in the sun's last light. Nothing happened. The sun was out of sight. Maybe that was the only thing that had saved him.

He jumped to his feet, his body pleading with him to remain still, but the thirst calling even louder. He made his way across the courtyard and climbed the few steps to the door. Like they were nothing, Ju-Long tossed aside the two large boards that secured the doors and flung them aside. As he entered the holding area he could hear women screaming. Their cries grew louder as he approached and men were shouting some unintelligible words, a warning perhaps. The hunger now consumed him completely. He could smell the sweet scent of what he needed. He strode with purpose to the very first bamboo cage and vaguely noticed that a few of the thinner pieces of bamboo were cracked. There were droplets of blood everywhere, spattered all over the door of the cage and the floor.

One man stood in front of the door, a dozen or more woman huddled behind him. The man cursed at him, blood covering his lips and chin. Ju-Long could understand none of it. Blood also covered the man's forearms, hands, shins and feet. He grabbed the ropes that held the door shut. They were frayed as if a rodent had chewed them. Ju-Long noticed a human-size tooth stuck in the rope's fibers. Doubtless it belonged to the man that faced him. Ju-long tore the rope as if it were mere thread and swung open the gate. The man moved into a fighting stance, hobbled by feet that were so swollen and bruised, they must be broken.

Ju-Long moved on him quickly, biting into the large vein on the side of the man's neck. While his victim screamed and beat him with closed fists, warm blood filled his mouth and ran down his throat. He swallowed hard again and again as a rush of power flowed through his body. It was a feeling better than any woman had ever brought him. He drank until the man became limp. Ju-Long felt his prey's heartbeat fade. One of the women tried to bolt by him to the open doorway. Ju-Long snatched her by the hair and tossed her back into the others. He had jerked her so hard that her hair ripped away from the scalp and he was left holding a handful of it.

The women screamed even louder as the door to the building flung open once more. Ju-long dropped the man's lifeless body to the floor and whirled around. Kong and a score of others filed in. Confusion and delight filled his mind at once. More poured in after them and his warriors rushed to the cages making short work of the ropes. *My men are alive!*

The feeding frenzy that ensued consumed the lives of every human prisoner they held. Ju-Long tried to control his men, ordering them to take just enough to renew their strength and sate their thirst. It was futile. There were far too many soldiers to watch. The food supply that should have lasted a week was decimated in a single night. Body parts littered the cage floors. It was a reckless feeding that produced too much waste.

It also presented a dilemma. They must capture more humans at once, and repair the damage to the cages done by both the prisoners trying to break free and his men trying to get to them. He had hoped to fortify more of the buildings against the light of the sun so his army would not be housed in such cramped quarters. He also wanted to prepare a more private chamber for himself. There were a million things Ju-Long wanted to accomplish, but only food mattered right now. He knew his reaction would be horrible—let alone that of his men—if they awoke tomorrow night and had no blood to drink.

There were several villages close by and with his army's newfound speed they could make them easily. Herding the humans back to Dulan would take time. He would have to split his army. Half would remain here to repair the damage and reinforce other structures, while the others went on the hunt. Ju-Long called Kong over to him.

"Yes, master?"

"I must take half the men to search for food," Ju-Long replied. *Food*, he thought to himself. Yes, that is all humans were to him now. Other than their life-giving blood they held no purpose to him. "You will remain here. Repair the cages and start the work I have planned for our new home."

"Yes, master."

"If we do not beat the rise of the sun back, we will find somewhere to hold up. Pray that is not the case. I shudder at how the men will react if they awaken tomorrow night with nothing to eat if I am not here to calm them."

"I will do my best in your absence, Master," Kong said with a bow.

Ju-Long hated leaving Kong in charge of anything. Whatever his cousin touched turned bad. "I am sure you will." Ju-Long paused and thought for a moment. "One other thing. Something strange I noticed when I woke up. You and all the others in our building were as cold and stiff as a corpse. Everyone appears fine now, but I was troubled by it. I wonder just what it is that happens to us between sun-up and sun down."

***

A fierce storm delayed his brothers' return. It was the middle of the night when they finally made it home. Zhan's brothers were tired, wet and hungry. The boys quickly prepared a meal as the men bathed and changed out of their rain-soaked clothes into dry robes. When they had gathered around and the food was set before them, Zhan began to brief them on the events his dreams had shown him.

"What is it that troubles you so much that you would keep us from much needed rest? Our journey was hard and the ill weather only made for more horrid travel," Te said as he took his seat next to Cai.

Zhan, hands trembling, took a sip of water from his cup. "My brothers, we have trouble like we have never known. It has begun. The nightmares I have suffered in my dreams are now a reality. A small army of demons has emerged. They are alive, yet dead. I can sense no soul among any of them. Their speed is like Ling's, their strength like Wei's." Ling, the second shortest of the brothers at five feet seven, possessed a gift of speed and agility unequaled by any other creature on earth. "They walk like men, talk like men and look like men—but when they attack they have fangs like wild beasts and drink human blood. It is as if they have been sent by Yen-Lo himself."

"Where, eldest one? In which direction do these creatures lie?" Cai asked. Cai was the shortest at five foot six, the same height as their father. He was muscular, but strength was not his gift as it might appear. Cai's gift lay with animals.

"They are north. Exact location I am not sure of. I don't even know the name of the city. It lies somewhere in the foothills of the Himalayas, not too far from the Great Wall. They took it without losing a single one of their number. The demons seemed oblivious to the counter attacks of the defending army. These creatures walked through sword strikes that would have delivered mortal wounds to any man. The beasts did not even unsheath their own weapons. They ripped apart their victims with their bare hands and crushed through bones with brute strength. It was the most horrible thing I have ever witnessed." The brothers all looked at Zhan, who was shaking so badly they could see the tremors from head to foot.

"If they possess my great speed and Wei's super strength—and they cannot be killed by the sword—how do we fight such creatures? Only Xiong could match up with them, as he possesses both quickness and strength, yet he still would have no way to kill them. Not to mention, he is but a single man and you speak of an army of demons." Ling said, rising from the lotus position and pacing the floor. Xiong, the youngest of the brothers, was six feet tall and built like his gifts suggested—strong, yet graceful.

"These creatures sound invincible. How can you be so sure there is a balance left now?" Wei asked, frustrated. "What if there isn't a way?"

"That kind of talk, even thinking such thoughts will not help. Negativity closes the mind to the light that guides the way," Zhan said, leaning over in Wei's face. Wei shoved him back firmly with one hand.

"And wine impairs the thought process completely. You reek of it, Zhan."

"You watch your tongue! What I do Is my business, damn you!"

"What is wrong with you, Zhan?" Xiong asked. "Certainly these dreams have taken a toll on you since they began, but until now not so much as to make you curse at one of us."

Zhan rose to his feet. "I am afraid! I have always been the one to have the answers! Before my dreams have shown me that which will come to pass and how to deal with it! Now, I stand before you without a clue as to what to do or where to turn. It is as if something stops the answers before they reach me. Maybe my gift falters as I grow older. Maybe the drink does affect me adversely. I don't know! For the first time in my life I really don't know. Everyone has always come to me for answers. Now when we need them the most I have none!"

Te reached up and grabbed Zhan's arm. "Be at ease brother. Together we will find the answer." Zhan could feel the rush of Te's healing power wash over him. His heartbeat slowed and the pressure he felt building inside him subsided. "We have not lost faith in you. You need never worry about that. Do not lose faith in yourself. Just as Wei cannot crush them all by himself, Ling cannot catch them all at once, and Xiong can match himself evenly to one—but not an entire army of them. We do not expect you to foresee how this foe must be conquered all by yourself either. We are together. We are family. Our individual gifts are strongest when we are in unison, each talent complimenting the other." Te was second tallest of the brothers, an inch taller than Zhan yet shorter than the enormous Wei. His gentle face and easy smile represented his talent well. His mere presence could soothe, but his touch could truly heal.

"Te is right, and so is Zhan," Cai said as he rose from his seat. "We have each known from an early age that we were born for a purpose. This mission is obviously the greater purpose the gods intended us for. Everything until now has just been practice. Now we face the challenge we were put here for. There is a way. Yin-yang says so. Together we will face these demons. Together we will defeat them. Now is not the time to bicker, but the time to work as one. In the words of Guatama Buddha, *When you fix your mind at one point, nothing is impossible for you.* We all must focus. One mind. One body. Only then will we find the path to victory over our enemy."

The room fell silent. The seven brothers quietly finished their meal. When they were done and the boys had cleared away the dishes, Zhan stood and spoke once more. "Tonight we shall rest. Our minds will be clearer and our tempers more even after a night's sleep. I shall pay close attention to my dreams tonight, and you Xiong should do so as well, for in the past you have shown your own gift of sight. Focus your energy on tapping into this problem. I do not wish these nightmares on any man, but I fear these troubled times make it necessary. Tomorrow we will re-open our discussion. For now I bid you all a good night."

His brothers all retreated to their beds. When the boys were finished cleaning up, Zhan joined them. They were already asleep when he laid his weary head down and drifted off praying for the answers.

***

Ju-long and his men reached the first village quicker than he anticipated. After putting down a token resistance of fifty warriors, they captured two hundred villagers alive. Even out-numbered and out-classed, the village men had put up a short but courageous fight. Ju-Long enjoyed the taste of the brave men's blood. The adrenaline pumping through them coupled with the fact that they fought him with every fabric of their bodies made the liquid meal that much sweeter. Even though their greatest efforts had proved futile in the end, he respected the spirit of the warrior they had all possessed. To him it was an honor to have fed on men of such great will.

Ju-Long sent a third of the men he had with him back to the city. They would escort their prisoners to the stronghold in Dulan, while he led the others onto the second village that lay to the east. It took them only an hour to reach the next village. Ju-Long knew he still had a good while before dawn. As they entered they found the village quiet. There wasn't a single sentry standing guard. His army swooped down upon the dwellings, kicking in doors and racing into the huts. It took only a few moments to realize that they were empty. They were all empty. Ju-Long punched the closest of his warriors in frustration. "Where are they?"

"Master! Master! There are fresh tracks leading north. They must have fled," Dong-Feng yelled.

"Really? You think so?" Ju-long said, the sarcasm thick in his voice. "Don't just stand there! After them! Run them down like animals!" His men chased behind Dong-Feng. How had these people known they were coming? Had someone escaped from the last village unseen and warned them? This created an unforeseen delay in his plans. It would push their return to Dulan too close to dawn. He considered calling his men back and returning to the city immediately. However, the two-hundred they had collected earlier would not be enough. They needed more humans to feed upon, so Ju-Long could spend a couple nights planning their next move. It was clear they would not be able to do this every night. Soon there wouldn't be enough food nearby to hunt during the night and still make it back to the safety of their stronghold by dawn.

No, they could not return yet. They must track down the villagers and take them back with them. Ju-Long followed the howls of his men down the trail.

A chill ran down Huang-Fu's spine. The howls were getting closer. He and forty of the other warriors guarded the rear of the fleeing villagers. Soon the enemy would be upon them. No matter how fast they traveled their pursuers seemed to gain ground. *What if our small band can't hold the enemy off long enough for the others to escape? What will become of my family? I will gladly sacrifice my own life for their well being, but what if that isn't enough?*

Anger grew inside him as he pictured his wife being raped by the men that followed them. He heard a howl just behind him. Huang-Fu whirled and raised his sword. The others continued to run. He could see a dozen or so men coming up the trail. "You will not have her!" he screamed as he charged into the oncoming force. At over six feet tall and chiseled like stone, he was one of the strongest of his village's men. His face, at twenty-three was still boyish, but not particularly handsome. *How did I manage to capture the heart of the most beautiful woman in our village?* His wife was three years younger, but they had been together for over five years. She was his entire world and had just bore him a son to go with his beautiful daughter

The first man dodged his blade with ease. A fist slammed into Huang-Fu's jaw and he thought he felt a snap. His head swam and his eyes began to water as a second man snatched him off his feet and tossed him through the air. He saw the tree just before his head smashed into its trunk. He was going out without even taking the life of one of his enemies.

Ju-Long reached the place where his men had the humans surrounded. He noticed a few dozen of the village warriors scattered about on the ground. The rest were all huddled together, women and children screaming and crying. Ju-Long waded through his men toward the humans. *There must be around three-hundred of them,* he thought to himself. He was glad they had given chase. If he forced his men to control their feeding habits the five hundred they captured tonight might last them three or four days.

"Silence!" he shouted, his voice exploding through the forest like the roar of a tiger. The villagers became quiet, mothers muffling their children's sobs against their bosom. "I am Ju-Long. You are all now my prisoners. We will march to Dulan tonight. You will cooperate fully. Any of you who try to escape or disobey my men or I will be killed. Anyone who lags behind or slows our journey will be killed. In Dulan you will be held captive, but will not be harmed. I have spoken. Now move!"

Ju-Long's men started herding the humans towards the city. There was no need to let these mortals know that their destiny was now that of a meal. They were merely a part of the food chain and their thoughts were unimportant. What was important was getting them to the stronghold before dawn. If leading them to believe they would be safe there ensured their cooperation, then so be it.

***

The light of the sun hurt Huang-Fu's eyes as he opened them. His head pounded and his jaw ached. His vision was blurred and his entire body ached, but he was alive. He felt a huge knot on top of his head and winced at the tenderness of it. Dried blood surrounded a cut in the middle of it, matting his short dark hair. He felt his jaw. It hurt to even touch it but it did not feel broken. He rolled his tongue around and felt two of his lower teeth missing.

Slowly he got to his feet. *Thank the gods my legs still work.* He thought about his wife and children. *Where are they? Are they safe?* He could only hope they were still alive.

Huang-Fu looked around and found his sword. He picked it up and slid it back into its sheath. He had been launched some twenty feet off the trail. He walked back to it and headed in the direction his people had been running last night. He must find his wife. Slowly his vision came into focus. He breathed deeply in an attempt to clear his head as he traveled.

About half an hour later he entered a clearing. The bodies of some of his fellow warriors were on the ground. It bothered him to do it, to take the items of his late friends, but he needed food. He went from body to body gathering all he could carry and still move quickly. He came upon the remains of his brother. Tears filled his eyes, spilling down his cheeks and splashing onto his brother's face as he cradled him in his arms. "I will avenge you, Zhong. You were a brave warrior and I know you fought hard to protect our people. I will return to see that you and the others have a proper burial after I have made the men who did this pay. I am sorry, but I have to go. My family and yours need me. Please accept my apology for leaving you like this for now. May the gods show you mercy in your next existence."

Huang-Fu lowered his brother to the ground and stood up. Rage filled every fiber of his being. He spotted many tracks heading northwest toward Dulan. "I will find you Lin-Yao. I will search all of China if I must to find you and our children. Hang on for me. I am coming!" he yelled into the quiet of the forest around him. With a fire in his heart he ignored the pain in his body and followed the tracks in front of him.

***

Zhan and his brothers slept til mid-morning. After finishing breakfast they gathered in a circle, each seated in the lotus position, and began to meditate. Zhan's dreams had been filled with terror again. He saw death come to many at the hands of the demons, yet he made some interesting observations as well. The latter might prove to be a key to the solving of the riddle this new enemy presented.

Zhan opened his eyes and noticed that his brothers had already broken from their meditation and sat staring at him. He let a smile creep across his face. His brothers could not resist the temptation to follow his lead. When he saw them smile back he knew that this day would be a good day to start finding the solution to the problem they now faced. He could feel the solidarity of their brotherhood fill the air around them.

"May I first say that no great revelations have come to me personally. However, certain items of interest have been revealed to me in my dreams," Zhan said, meeting the gaze of each of his brothers in turn. "Our enemy seems to develop a strong sense of urgency with the approach of the sun rising in the east. It is as if they must avoid its light at all costs. This, coupled with the fact that I have witnessed them only by night in all my dreams, leads me to believe that they are strictly nocturnal. It is quite possible that due to their demonic nature they may be unable to tolerate the sun's warm rays and the goodness it represents. If this be so, then we need worry about them only during the hours between dusk and dawn."

"Secondly, I believe that these creatures sustain themselves on the blood of man. Without it, I think they would perish. I have felt their hunger before they have fed. It drives them—gnaws at them until they have satisfied it. When they feed, it is as if life rushes into them. I can feel the exhilaration that flows through their bodies from the moment that first drop of human blood touches their lips."

"If they do hide from the sun, where do they go during the day?" Wel asked.

"I do not know yet, Wei. It is as if their aura disappears with the rising sun. I cannot detect their existence at all between sun-up and sun-down."

"I know the name of the city in which they dwell. It is called Dulan," Xiong said.

"Then you have dreamed of them as well?"

"Not exactly, eldest one. I had no image of them as you have. It was merely a voice that repeated, *Dulan is the city of your enemy,* several times during my sleep."

"Where exactly is Dulan?" Cai asked.

"It is north, near the foothills of the Himalayas. It is outside the boundries controlled by the Jin in the barbaric lands of the north," Biao answered.

"How do you know?" Wei asked.

"He remembers the story of Buddhist monks who tried to establish our religion there. They were killed by others who do not share our beliefs," Zhan responded.

"Is there any other relevant information you can provide us, Zhan?" Te asked.

"They took two more villages last night. They hold many of the people from those places prisoner. Those poor people are going to become food for their captors."

"If we fail to find a way to stop them all of China will be consumed by these demons," Ling spoke up. "I say we travel to Dulan and spy on these creatures first hand. Maybe that would reveal some weakness."

"I agree," Xiong added.

"You are right, Ling, it might provide us useful information, but it would be dangerous. Too dangerous. Should we be discovered before we found their weakness we would be destroyed. We cannot save China in death," Zhan said.

The brothers fell silent, each one locked in deep thought. Then Cai had an idea. "What if we could observe them first hand from a safe enough distance? Well, I mean, what if I could?"

"Go on," Zhan said, and motioned for him to continue.

"If I can travel close to there and commune with the animals in the area I can use their vision to watch our enemy."

"It is not a bad idea," Zhan said.

"Are you kidding? It is a great plan!" Ling shouted. "We could obtain a fast horse for Cai, and with our speed Xiong and I could provide escort for him in case there was trouble."

"I think it will work," Wei said. "Meanwhile we could still learn from your dreams here and begin to make up a plan for defeating our enemy. I need to step up the training of the younger boys fighting skills. I hope they are never made to fight these beasts, but I want them to be ready to defend themselves if they have to."

Zhan thought for a moment. He stretched, rubbed his eyes, and then scratched his head. "Then it is settled. Cai, Ling, and Xiong will travel toward Dulan. The rest of us will remain here and prepare the best we can."

"What about me?" Biao asked. "I am tired of being ignored. Ever since Xiong was born and his gifts showed themselves I have felt lost in the shuffle. My speed and strength are near his, yet I seem to get no credit for even having gifts. A fourth could not hurt their mission. I can travel as fast as any horse Cai may ride." Biao, seven years older, slightly taller and much bulkier than Xiong, hung his head. He was shamed not so much by his brother's lack of acknowledgement, but his inability to remain humble.

"Forgive us, Biao. You have suffered in relative silence while we ignored your abilities. You would be a great help to them. You should go as well," Zhan said.

"I apologize to you as well," Xiong said. "I do not mean to have my existence overshadow yours. While my abilities may be slightly more, you still possess hand to hand fighting skills that are superior to mine. Wei has trained you well and you have been far more vigilant than I in your study and practice."

"I do not begrudge your existence, Xiong—I merely wish that mine be acknowledged." For a short while no one spoke again. The others all felt guilty for they realized they had overlooked Biao for quite some time.

"I believe I can arrange a swift mount for Cai," Te said. "Xing-Fu owns the fastest steeds around. He would lend me one. He constantly attempts to find manners in which to repay me for saving his daughter from her infirmities last autumn. I have let him know that repayment was not necessary, but if loaning us a horse will ease his conscience then I will beseech him for the best of his stock. I know how it does trouble him to feel indebted to another."

"Thank you, Te." Cai bowed his head.

"I shall have the boys pack some food for your trip," Wei said.

"Not too much," Xiong said. "We don't want to carry so much that it slows our travel. We will be able to find food on our journey as well. The growing season is alive everywhere."

"And not all of us eat as much as you big boy." Ling chuckled, looking at Wei. The others, including Wei, joined in the laughter. The large man's belly shook and Ling gave it a little pat as he walked by. At nearly eight feet tall and well over four-hundred pounds, his brothers often teased that it must have been he that modeled for the statue of Buddha himself.

CHAPTER 4

Huang-Fu could see the gate of the city ahead. It was mid-afternoon and he had traveled hard and fast to reach Dulan. Unfortunately he hadn't come up with a single idea on what to do once he got there. He reached into his pouch and fished out a few nuts to curb his growing hunger. He scanned the walls and towers for guards. The tracks led right up to the city. They had to have come here. *Where is everybody?* Moving quietly among the trees he made his way to the wall near the gate. He listened and heard only the songs of the birds in the woods behind him.

Carefully he began scaling the rock wall seeking out finger and toe-holds among the jagged stonework. As he neared the top he felt queasiness in his stomach, intensified by the smell of death. He peeked over the wall and saw no one. *Something is not right.* He had to find his family if they were somewhere in the city, so whether it was right or not he was going in. He checked his gut. His nerves were in overdrive. He took a deep breath and over the wall he went.

When he hit the ground he scurried behind a building and listened. There was nothing but the pounding of his heart in his ears. If someone had spotted his entry the guards would be converging on him by now. *Maybe it was a trap.* How would they know he was coming? *Had someone seen him on the trail and raced back to tell the others? No.* If all the soldiers were as fast, strong and skilled as the ones he faced last night they wouldn't bother laying a trap for a single man. They would have simply killed him on sight.

Huang-Fu worked his way between buildings, cautiously listening at each turn. Then as he moved by a small shed he stared across an open space and saw a large building with a double brace across the doors. *There!* he thought to himself. *If I were holding a large number of prisoners I would lock them away in there.* He scanned the courtyard. Nothing stirred. He took off, sprinting for the door. Huang-Fu leaped up the three steps that led to it, then glanced back and saw that there was no one chasing him. He put his ear to the door and listened. He could hear the soft cries of women and children beyond as the voices of men that tried to console them. *They were in there. His people were alive and they were in there. My family must be among them!* He wanted to throw aside the wood that held the doors shut and rush in. *You have made it this far, Huang-Fu, don't get stupid now. There must be some manner of guard locked in with them.*

His heart pounded, pulse racing and sweat dripping from his brow. He eased the first brace out of its holders and carefully set it aside. The next one was wedged in tight. He worked at it, prying at the wood with his sword. It moved a little, but not enough. Huang-Fu glanced around and saw a rock large enough to try to pound it up and out with. He knew that the noise it would create might alert any guards waiting inside but he had little choice. He moved down the steps and picked up the stone. He walked back up, positioned his body and began to swing upward under the brace. He did so gently at first, but when the wood refused to move he came up hard and fast.It slid up a little, but the loud crack that seemed to echo forever made him stop and listen again. There was only the continued plea of those trapped inside. He swung again and again, frantic in his effort. Each hit caused a loud bang, but moved the board a little more. No guard came from anywhere to investigate. No sentry issued a verbal challenge from the other side of the door. Finally the brace broke free from its holders. Huang-Fu tossed the rock aside and moved the brace out of the way. He drew his sword as the left door began to swing open on its own. No one charged out to meet him. He peered inside, then jumped back behind the still closed right door. Three guards lie on the floor asleep. *How did they not hear me pounding?*

He brought his sword in front of him and moved into the building. He rushed over to the guard closest to him and brought his blade down on the neck, severing the head. The other guards did not stir, nor did blood flow from the man's severed neck. Huang-Fu squatted down to get a closer look at the wound. A small trickle of dark blood ran slowly from a larger vein in the neck. He moved between the other two men, his sword at the ready. The people called for him to come free them. He leaned over and touched one of the guards. The body was cold and stiff. He was already dead. "I will make sure you stay that way." He said as he crashed the sword down through the man's throat. He kicked the head across the room, turned and did the same to the last guard. "For my brother!"

The cries from his people grew louder. He turned and yelled for them to be silent. If there were any guards in the city he did not want his own people to alert them and foil his rescue. Huang-Fu moved to the first cage. At least thirty people were crammed inside a space that was made to hold twenty at the most. He sheathed his sword and took out a dagger. He sawed at the thick ropes. It was taking too long. There had to be a faster way. He scanned the room for something, anything. There was a dozen or so battle axes in a rack by the doors. He ran over and pulled one down. "Move as far back as you can. I am going to chop the rope." He swung hard and the rope split in two. He worked the ax free from the bamboo bar it was stuck in and opened the cage door. The prisoners poured out. "Grab the other axes! Hurry!" He yelled, watching each woman and child as they exited. None belonged to him. There were twenty cages in all. His family had to be in one of them.

He moved down to the next cage, chopped the rope and opened it. No wife. No children. Other men were working on getting some of the cages open. He raced past four of them and chopped open another. The people funneled out. A small figure clamped its arms around his legs. "Daddy!" He looked down and saw his daughter. He could not stop the tears that fell as he dropped the ax and reached down scooping her up into his arms. "Daddy, I missed you!" Her sweet little voice was like music to his ears. "I missed you too, little one."

"Oh, Huang-Fu, I cannot believe it! I thought the demon men had killed you!" Lin Yao threw an arm around her husband. She held their tiny newborn son in her other arm. Huang-Fu looked into his wife's face and gorgeous green eyes. Even with tear and dirt streaked cheeks her beauty could not hide itself. Joy filled him as they all stood there hugging and sobbing in each other's arms.

"We need to get out of here, Lin Yao. All the villagers are free, but who knows when that army will return. I cannot believe I was lucky enough to find you again."

"I knew you would come for us, daddy. Mommy cried every time I told her you would save us, but I knew you would come!"

"I would always come for you. Always." Huang-Fu ushered his family toward the door. As they stepped out they found the courtyard filled with people. It was as if they were waiting for someone to tell them what to do next. Some were seeking out other family members in the crowd. Huang-Fu knew they could not afford to stand around for long. They needed to put as much distance between themselves and this place as possible. When the army returned and found out their prisoners had escaped they would surely send out search parties to find and recapture them.

From the top of the steps that led up to the stronghold Huang-Fu pleaded with the crowd. "Good people we must flee from here quickly. Follow me and I shall lead you to the exit. Once we are outside Dulan we should split into smaller groups and travel separate paths. If we remain together we will be too easy to track down. Run to the lands of your relatives or friends, but do not return to the villages yet. That will be the first place our enemy checks. What is there is lost!" All eyes were upon him. "Please make a way for me and my family through this crowd. I will show you all to the gate."

The crowd parted and Huang-Fu, his wife and children moved through the mass of people. As they walked his two remaining brothers, sister, mother, nieces, nephews and Lin Yao's family joined them. They made their way to the gate only to find a huge timber braced across its double doors holding it shut. It took a score of men to lift it from its holders and lug it out of the way. It took another four men on each heavy door to swing them open.

As Huang-Fu had suggested, the people began to split up into family groups and head off in separate directions. He did notice a group of about fifty people headed down the trail to his former village. He had saved them—

but he could not force them to follow sensible advice. Huang-Fu took his extended family and headed south. No one else joined them.

***

Ju-Long opened his eyes. No one else had risen yet. This was good. He could get to the stronghold before any of them, feed, and then allow only a few dozen or so of his men in at a time. There would be no wild feeding frenzy this night. They would get enough to sustain them and quell their hunger, but they would not drink recklessly.

As he stepped out he saw that it was almost dark. He could feel the hunger inside himself, yet it was not near as bad as it had been the night before. He made his way across the courtyard and saw that the boards that secured the stronghold had been removed and the doors were standing wide open. He ran the rest of the way and dashed inside. The cages were open and empty. His three warriors, who had slept inside, were decomposing in the summer heat. Their heads had been severed from their bodies. *How could this be? Who freed the prisoners?* he asked himself as he walked back and checked the cages. There wasn't a single human left. He raced back outside and sprinted to the gate only to find its brace removed and the huge doors wide open. He moved through it and saw footprints leading off in all directions. Anger rose within him.

Ju-Long stumbled back toward his resting-place, enraged. His thirst beckoned to him and he knew it would grow far more intense before he could sate it. He found Kong and some of the others gathered in the courtyard. "Kong! The prisoners have escaped!"

"Oh no, master! How? I have only just risen and already my hunger is driving me mad."

"We must gather everyone. We will head for the village east of here. If any have dared to return there they will be our meal tonight. We shall leave Dulan behind from there and find a new home."

"Master, what if some of us cannot make it that far before feeding?"

47

"There is no choice, Kong! You must make it! Bring these men to the gate," Ju-Long ordered. "I will get the others." His remaining men in the other buildings were already filing out and heading to the stronghold. "Stop!" He yelled. "It is empty. The prisoners have been set free and escaped. We will have to hunt for our food this night."

Grumbles came from many of his warriors. They complained that the hunger would consume them if they had to wait. Their frustration grew louder and curses of protest swept through the crowd of soldiers. "Silence you fools! I have heard enough! There is no choice but to hunt. We will not return here tonight. We will stay on the move if we must until I can develop a plan that will allow us to establish our kingdom and still maintain enough human captives to keep us fed."

A single warrior stepped forward. "You are the one who allowed us to be turned into the creatures that we are. We did not possess the power we have now but it seemed as if we fared better when we were merely human. Nevertheless—we are what we are—and so far your plans have turned out to be shit. Maybe it is time for a new leader! We all possess the same power, so why should we follow your obvious incompetence?"

"Did you just issue a challenge? You did, didn't you?" Before the warrior could utter another word Ju-Long drew his sword and delivered a single severing blow to the man's neck. As the head flew into the air Ju-Long sheathed his weapon and watched as it hit the ground. He then took a quick side-step to avoid the headless body as it fell forward. "Allow this to be a two-fold lesson, gentleman. One, you must protect the head. Should it become detached from your body you will be finished. There are three of our number lying within the stronghold that have lost theirs and will rise no more."

"Second, and this is a far more important message than the first, none of you are my equal. It is the same as when we were mere mortals. Your powers will never match mine. If any of you find a further demonstration of this fact necessary please feel free to step forward." The men stood where they were, some rubbing their fingers along their neck. "Very well then, we can move on. We head to the village in the east. If any were foolhardy enough to return there they will be ours. With haste! Allow your hunger to become your driving force."

***

Tung awakened to the rancid smell of decaying flesh and darkness. He could feel the weight of many bodies piled atop his own. He remembered being trapped in a cage with some of the women of Dulan. He had beaten the bamboo bars with his fists and feet until they were a raw, broken, bloody mess. He had even attempted to chew his way like a rat through the ropes that bound the door shut. Then a tall, strong demon-like man had come and ripped the rope from the cage as if it were mere thread and attacked him. The demon had sunk teeth into his neck and he had fought against the creature violently. As the blood was sucked from his body the life drained from him as well.

Tung struggled to move under the weight of the dead bodies. He shifted, squirmed, and clawed his way upward. *How many bodies are there?* Tung thought. *How did I manage to not be crushed beneath all of them?* It didn't matter, he was alive and he intended to stay that way. He pushed body after body aside until finally he could see the stars in the night sky above him. Tung stood on top of a pile of dead that must have numbered over a hundred. He sucked in the night air and nearly gagged from the smell of rot. He was alone. There was niether man nor demon in sight. A strange feeling hung in his gut. Unsure if it was hunger or nausea from the wicked stench, he began his dissent. He stepped on bodies he recognized, both family members and friends. Oddly, he felt no sorrow for their loss. The queasiness in his stomach was turning to pain. A strange craving came over him and he tried to dismiss it, but it demanded to be filled. He needed blood. Human blood.

***

Ju-Long and his army took the village by storm. Just as he had suspected some of the villagers had returned to their homes. Ignorance ran amok through the mortals, especially the peasants. He realized the fifty or so humans would not be nearly enough to satisfy his ravenous men and there would be no controlling them. It would be strictly first come, first served. He remained near the rear as his men ransacked the huts. He would forgo his own urge to feed until they found a more abundant crop of humans to harvest. The hunger pained him, but he would not allow it to rule him. He was not sure if the one who created them meant that they must feed every night, but it mattered not. The others might perish under the strain of an evening without blood—but it would not end him. Ju-Long would not die until he was damned good and ready—and that day would never come.

His men fell upon the villagers like a pack of wolves. Their hunger had put them at the brink of insanity. They fought over the humans, ripping them apart. The scene was a chaotic one as his warriors punched, kicked and clawed each other over the smallest scrap of human flesh they could put to their lips and suckle blood from. If he did not take control of the situation soon they would tear each other to pieces. Ju-Long rushed into the village, throwing his soldiers this way and that as he made his way to the middle of the fray. "I command you to stop! Control yourselves! Be strong!" He yelled. The humans had been devoured entirely and his men had begun sinking fangs into one another. Some had even brought their blades into play, attempting to behead one another in their madness.

Ju-Long climbed atop one of the huts. *Damn them all*, he thought. *Let them kill each other. They are more of a hassle than they are worth!* Kong and a few others were trying to break up the melee. *Perhaps they are not all imbeciles.* He summoned energy from deep inside him and let out a roar louder than thunder. "Cease this madness you ignorant fools!" His warriors stopped and looked up to him. "You ignorant bastards can kill each other if that is what you wish. Or stay here and die of starvation. It matters not to me. However, if you desire to feed, follow me. There is blood to be had east of us and I travel to it. I will waste no more time on fools who wish to die. I have not fed, nor will I until all of you have sated your thirst. I feel the hunger—but it shall not be quenched among these empty huts." Ju-Long leapt from the rooftop. "Kong, lead all those who will follow east. To hell with the rest!"

***

Tung picked up tracks heading west and followed them until they disappeared into the rocks of the mountains. The terrain was rough all around and he knew that any sizable group would have to travel the trail he was on. He found that he moved with more speed and grace than ever before. His reflexes were sharp and his night vision incredible. Other than the pain of hunger that tied his stomach in knots, he felt powerful. It was almost as if he had been transformed into some supernatural being. The bones that he thought had been broken were healed, and the tooth that had been missing was there along with the others, as well as two that seemed more pointed than before. He felt invincible, as if no one and nothing could stand in his way. He would catch this little band of travelers and steal one from their number. Half repulsed by his own thoughts, he knew that what he needed flowed through their veins.

***

The watchers sounded the alarm. An army was fast approaching from the west on foot. Fanzhou would soon be under siege. Yun-Qi, chief warlord and member of the council in Fanzhou, wondered if this was the army the half-crazy peasant who rode into town ranted about yesterday afternoon. He begged for shelter and cried as he told the tale of how a minion of demons had attacked his village the night before. Yun-Qi had personally seen that the ill man was properly locked up in a holding cell. He had also, however, placed extra sentries in the towers and archers on the walls should this idiot be telling a legitimate tale. His entire guard was on the alert, with every able-bodied male in the city sleeping next to their sword.

Yun-Qi climbed to the highest tower on the west wall to witness his enemy's approach first hand. He watched as the oncoming force covered the ground between them as if they were mounted. He gave the signal for his archers to ready their bows. At the speed they were traveling his men would do well to get off one round, maybe two, before the army was upon them. He looked down to see his soldiers gathering behind the gate. It was time. "Fire!" he commanded. The first wave of arrows whistled through the night in unison.

With cat-like reflexes the advancing troops dodged the majority of the missiles as they imbedded in the ground harmlessly. "Recharge your bows and fire at will!" Yun-Qi shouted. While he was impressed by his opponents' abilities, a few of the arrows had indeed found their mark. The warriors they struck howled like nothing he had ever heard before. It reminded him of neither man nor beast, but of what some hellish ghoul might sound like. Shivers ran down his spine. Maybe the peasant had not been crazy after all. He watched as the second wave of bolts missed the mark completely, his archers unable to compensate for the speed of their targets.

Ju-long saw a score of his men who had been hit by arrows limp to the sides of the charge. The three warriors who had taken shots straight through the chest had fallen dead in their tracks. A second volley was launched at them and he could see it was going to pass over his men, but was headed straight at him. He ducked behind a large rock until they flew past. Part of his army quickly scaled the walls while the others rammed the gates at full speed, using their bodies to batter it open. They had a few hours before dawn. It would give them enough time to accomplish their mission. Ju-Long's mouth watered with the thought of a meal. He would drink his fill of blood this night after all.

"Master, please, it hurts! You must help me." One of his stricken men cried out. Ju-Long went to him. "The pain is so much that it feels as if I am mortal again." He didn't want to lose any more soldiers than he had to, so the hunger would have to wait. More importantly, he had to discover what made these arrows so special they caused pain such as this to one of his kind. The sharp metal point had driven all the way through the warrior's thigh. Its wood shaft stuck out both sides of the leg.

"Please, master, I beg you remove it." Ju-Long looked into the man's eyes. The face was contorted in a most hideous fashion. Ju-Long grabbed the shaft just above the metal point and pulled it the rest of the way through.

"It is not a fatal wound. Stop sniveling and go join the others. A quick bloodletting will be cure enough." Ju-Long examined the arrow. It appeared quite ordinary. The warrior stumbled toward the city. He wondered if the wound would heal as the others they received in the past had. One by one he removed the bolts from the warriors who had absorbed them. The ones who had been hit in the chest looked as if they had been dead for days. He removed the arrows from them but it changed nothing. He let them lie, to be dragged in later and sheltered from the sun should by chance they be able to rise again tomorrow.

By the time he strode through the gates the people of Fanzhou had already surrendered. There would be a bounty of prisoners to sustain them for nights to come. Right now he just needed one of them.

***

Tung was quite pleased with himself. He had caught up to the little group and stolen a young woman from their number while most of them were asleep. He thought about how tender and soft her skin was. She was beautiful. Two days ago his thought would have been to bed her. That thought hadn't crossed his mind tonight. He wanted the treasure she offered, that was for certain, but it had nothing to do with her body. Rather he had wanted, no, needed, what she carried inside it.

He tapped the pulsing vein in her neck and drank in her sweet, salty blood. It made him feel better than any sex he had ever experienced. He consumed her until his head soared and his belly felt like it would burst if indulged even a single drop more. When the rush finally calmed he sat looking at her lifeless body, realizing she had served her purpose and no longer held any use for him.

The sun would be up soon. *It will be nice to travel by the light of day*, he thought. The feel of the sun's warm rays as they caressed his body while he frolicked about brought a smile to his face. He knew he had been given a second chance in this life, probably granted by the gods for his acts of bravery in the face of mortal danger. He was transformed into an improved version, and he would make sure he did not squander what he had been blessed with. So what if the gods had put a funny little quirk like a thirst for blood in with the powers they had bestowed upon him?

He went to stand, but felt a tiredness in his bones that kept him seated. The day held so much promise, and he didn't want to waste a minute of it. However, the blood must have had an effect like taking in too much strong wine. The power that had given him the ultimate high had now turned into the equivalent hangover. All he wanted to do was curl up and drift off to sleep in the little cavern he had drug the girl into before feeding from her. "A short nap will cure this," he mumbled as he laid his head back and sank into a deep slumber.

***

Zhan awoke to find that his brothers were already up and out of the room. He washed his face and threw on a fresh robe. He prayed four of his siblings had not made their departure yet. Zhan rushed down the hall and into the courtyard. *Thank the heavens,* he thought as he spotted Cai and Xiong.

"Good morning, Zhan," Cai said, waving a greeting to his eldest brother.

"More like afternoon." Ling smiled as he walked out of an opposite hall.

"We are almost prepared to leave, eldest one," Xiong said.

"We must speak first. The situation has changed. Our enemy has moved to a new city. It is called Fanzhou. It is not far from the border between the Jin lands and the northern barbarian states. They departed Dulan last night in haste, after discovering someone had set their captives free. They took Fanzhou, a much larger place than Dulan, with relative ease. Something of note, however, though I am not sure why. Arrows through the heart took down three of their number last night. Beheadings claimed another four. I would suggest that in the event an accidental encounter is made you have a healthy supply of arrows on hand. Take your swords, but carry both long bows and crossbows with you."

"Who rescued the prisoners?" Xiong asked.

"I am not sure, but I mean to find out. I have no idea if it was one of them who found their way out and freed the others, or if it was an outsider."

"The weapons you speak of are already with our gear. However, I will add to our supply of bolts before we depart," Biao said.

"Xiong, you must keep your mind open to me throughout this journey. I do not know how long our foe will remain in Fanzhou. Should they go on the move again I want to be able to let you know when and in what direction. It would not be good to learn this after they are right on top of you."

"I will keep an ear strictly for your call."

"And without sounding like the condescending older brother, let me say to all that there will be no heroics on this mission. You are to gather what information you may and report back in one piece. We can ill afford to face these demons before we are fully prepared."

CHAPTER 5

Fanzhou turned out to be quite the prize. They had taken nearly three-thousand prisoners. It had required a mad rush to rig together that many makeshift strongholds by dawn. Tonight, after awakening to find their captives still subdued, Ju-Long gave the order for reinforcement of the holding structures. The city itself was ten times the size of Dulan. As humans his army would have stood little chance against the defending army, especially when hunkered behind the walls of their own fortress.

Ju-Long managed to oversee a controlled feeding. They used up just a little over two-hundred-fifty humans, one for every two of his men. Except for himself of course, which was the exact opposite. Half a human's blood would quench their thirst and return their power. None grumbled over the fact, happy their need was met without a long hunt beforehand.

As he had suspected, the three who had died last night from arrow wounds to the chest, remained just as dead even after true dark had fallen. Their bodies continued to decompose and he had them burned with the victims of the night's feeding. He pondered what it was exactly about the arrows that had caused three of his men to die. *Was it the weapon itself or the fact that it penetrated their hearts?* There were questions to be answered. Maybe it was a combination of the two.

"Kong!"

"Yes, master?"

"Fetch me four of our men. I have a few experiments I must conduct for the future of our army."

"As you wish, master." Kong bowed and ran to the gate where many of the men were repairing the damage they had caused to it during the assault last night. He motioned to a group of them, and then sent one man back to work before leading the rest to Ju-Long. "Per your request, master."

"I asked for four, not seven you idiot. You three on the end, back to work."

"Excuse me, master, I only wished you to have enough."

"Can you count to four? One, two, three, four. How hard is that?" Ju-Long snarled. "Fetch me a sword and a wooden staff. Do you think you could accomplish that without screwing up?"

"A staff and a sword. I will get them master."

"A wood staff."

"I know of no other kind, master."

"I believe that if I were not explicit in my instructions you would find one made of some other substance."

"I don't believe I would know where to locate such a thing," Kong answered innocently.

"Can you locate your neck?"

"Of course, master. It is right here."

"Good, then you are not a complete dolt. When you have finished, use that knowledge to choke yourself."

"Choke myself, master?"

"Go now, Kong, before I loose your head from the neck you are able to locate!" The others laughed for a moment until Ju-Long turned his attention to them. "I require your assistance as well. I must test a few things. Some things I will do may cause you pain, but it will pass. Others of our number suffered the same wounds last night. It is imperative that we learn more about those things that may harm us. Your sacrifice will be duly noted and your efforts rewarded," he said, twirling an arrow in his hand.

"Yes, master," they replied in unison.

"You, step forward," Ju-Long commanded. He took the tip of the arrow and shoved it into the man's arm. "Tell me what you feel."

"A slight tingle, master. I know it is there, but it is only a minor bother." Ju-Long nodded. He grasped the man's wrist tighter and shoved the arrow in until it came out the other side. The warrior howled in pain and convulsed as he tried to pull away from Ju-Long with all his might. His face contorted, changing from almost human to vile beast as the others had last night. Ju-Long reached under the forearm and pulled the arrow the rest of the way through. He released the soldier's wrist and the man stepped away clutching his wounded arm. Whimpers continued to emit from his throat.

Kong returned with a sword and a wood staff. "You, come here." He pointed to the next man. Ju-Long grasped the long blade in his hand.

"No master, please. What have I done to dishonor thee?" The man pleaded, cowering back and raising his hands to protect his neck.

"Do not fear. It is not my intention to behead you. Stand tall and be brave," Ju-Long assured him. The man immediately lowered his arms and straightened to full height. Ju-Long thrust the sword through the man's chest, penetrating the heart and coming out the other side.

"Damn you!' The man cried as Ju-Long withdrew his blade. The warrior staggered, but remained upright. He considered what he had just said and knew it was a mistake. He dropped to his knees. "Forgive me, master. I did not mean to curse at thee. The pain was just so intense."

"It is all right. Your apology is accepted," Ju-long said. "Hand me the staff, Kong, then take these two men to the stronghold and see that they have a human each to feed upon. You have done well."

"Yes, master." Kong bowed before he led the men off to the stronghold. Ju-Long cast aside the sword and drew a small dagger from his belt. He began to sharpen one end of the staff into a point.

"You men, come here." He motioned to his remaining soldiers. They both stepped forward, anxious to get whatever Ju-Long had in store for them over with. Ju-Long shoved the staff through the chest cavity of the shorter of the two men. The soldier clutched his hands around it and screamed. Within seconds he lay on the ground, dead. The taller man backed away, hands in front of him in a defensive posture. "Relax. I am finished. I know what I need to."

Ju-Long studied the decaying corpse In front of him, the wood spear still imbedded in the body. "Wood is bad for our diet." He stared at the last soldier. "Avoid consuming it, especially in this manner. Go and gather everyone. It is best we get this information out as soon as possible." Kong had returned. Help him, Kong. Bring our men here to me."

Tung had overslept. It was night again. *I must have really been exhausted*, he thought. He left the dead women in the cave and ran along the trail in an attempt to close in upon the travelers once more. The hunger cried out to him. It was a thirst for blood, and as he thought about this strange new need he began to realize that it was what the demon that had attacked him had been after. Maybe this transformation was not a work of the gods. *Have I somehow become like it?*

It took only about an hour for him to catch up. The group had not traveled far. *They probably wasted most of the day searching for the missing woman,* Tung thought. They would never find her. Then the fools had made the mistake of setting only one sentry to guard them while they slept. If they only knew what went bump in the night, they would have thought better of it. *I'm here,* he laughed to himself. Tung circled the camp, staying out of sight. The watchman was posted on the far side. He was larger than average and would make for a very filling meal. Tung crept up behind him. Simultaneously he wrapped his right hand around the man's barrel chest and clamped the other hand over the watcher's mouth. The guard struggled violently as Tung drug him backward. Tung felt a slight but sharp pain in his abdomen. The sentry had pulled a dagger and was plunging it into his stomach again and again. Tung twisted the man's neck until he felt the pop of bones under his grip. He pulled the lifeless body back behind several large rocks and bit into the soft tissue of the nape. Tung sucked hard, but got little in return for his effort. Without the heart pumping the meal had become a chore. *Surely a stout man such as this holds more.* He bit in deeper and tried again.

The exertion caused as much pain in his head as it did pleasure. When at last he was full he used the man's sleeve to wipe the droplets of blood from his lips. Quietly he slipped back toward the camp, perching himself on a large boulder. He looked over the sleeping people and realized he had been just like them. He did not miss that life. He was now superior to them. He was a predator and they were his prey. No longer would he work long hours for a little amount of food and even less appreciation for the benefit of some fat, wealthy, lazy nobleman. He would never again face the wrath of soldiers who often picked on him simply because he was young, handsome, and popular with the women. With his new strength and speed he would crush such men.

Movement interrupted his thoughts. One of the other men in the camp was up and walking toward a line of trees. Tung climbed down and started to make his way in the man's direction, circling the camp once more. If the man noticed the guard not on duty he might alert the others and spoil the little game Tung was playing with them. He intended to keep following this little band, feeding off them until he reached a city where he could operate until someone figured out what he was. *And just what are you now, Tung?* he asked himself. *I'm a bloodsucker.* He smiled, realizing he was the top of the food chain.

Tung slipped into the outer edge of the tree line. The man was urinating on a rock. He prepared to cover the last twenty paces between them when movement once again caught his attention. A female form approached from the other side. It looked like the woman he had fed on last night. *How?* he wondered. He had left her in the cave, stiff with death.

"Yue-Yan! You have returned!" the man said. "We feared you were dead." The man pulled his pants back up, tucking himself away. The woman placed a single finger to her lips, encouraging him to be quiet. She strode to him confidently and placed her hands under his shirt, running her fingers along his bare skin. "Yue-Yan, one of the others may wake up and catch us. Your husband is awake, keeping watch over us as we sleep." The man whispered as he glanced over his shoulder. He could not see the camp through the trees.

She lifted his shirt over his head, then gently pushed him down to the ground until he lie on his back and she straddled over him. Yue-Yan ran her wet tongue up his stomach, over his chest, and stopped at his nipple. She bit it gently and looked up into his eyes giving him a teasing smile. He ran his hands through her long black hair. He had often fantasized about mounting Yue-Yan. For a moment he wondered if he were still asleep and this only a dream. He reached up and caressed her cheek. He could feel his flesh growing hot and his groin stiffen as the excitement built. She ran her palm over his mouth and stopped. He parted his lips and painted across it with his tongue.

Then her hand clamped down. She pinned his head to the ground so hard he thought his head would cave in under the pressure. He let out a muffled scream as she lowered her head to his flesh. He felt sharp teeth tear hard into his neck. He tried to knock her off, but each blow grew weaker as he felt the life drain from him. He was still conscious when she raised her head, her mouth dripping with blood. Yue-Yan wiped the back of her hand across her lips, smearing blood onto her cheek. Her fist came down hard and he could feel it break through his ribs. The world went dark as he saw her holding his heart over her head, squeezing the last remaining droplets of blood from it.

Tung found himself fully aroused as he watched the woman feed. He crouched down, concealing himself among the lower limbs of the trees. He wanted her. It was not a feeling like the hunger, but one of pure sexual desire. He reached into his pants and gripped his length. He must have her. Before he could satisfy himself, she was on her feet. She lifted the dead man easily, draped him over her shoulder and moved back up the trail. Tung quietly followed her.

***

The reconstruction of Fanzhou was coming along well. His men worked tirelessly and with great speed. The strongholds were reinforced and booby traps were set for any man who might try to enter the city by day and free the prisoners. What happened in Dulan could never be allowed to occur again.

Each building was sealed from the sun's light. Soon Ju-Long would have the impenetrable fortress he had envisioned. By day they would still be vulnerable to a clever party who knew their weaknesses even with the scattered pitfalls they created for unwanted guests. He needed the daytime guardians Niu T'ou had spoken of. *"You will mark chosen individuals…they will share some of your power…they will protect you by day,"* he had said. Ju-Long considered those words. *What did he mean by mark them? How can I share my power with another?* Then there was the question of creating his own. The losses thus far had been minimal, but they would occur and continue, until one day he was faced with the dilemma of being short-handed. Besides, if he could bring down this great city with five-hundred, what could he do with a thousand? Ten thousand? Once he figured out the key to the mystery, the sky was the limit. *"What you destroy will stay destroyed, but what you kiss will become like you."*

What is the kiss? Is it like the one the demon gave me? Ju-Long asked himself. He had tried that with several women in Dulan that first night. He kissed them with all the passion and energy he could muster, but nothing special had occurred. He placed them in that very first cage with the man who had tried to beat and chew his way out. When he arose that next night, they were still merely human. The kiss therefore was not a kiss, but something else.

Frustration was setting in. *Damn Niu T'ou and his riddles!* There was still time before dawn, and he would find out what it was if he had to use up every mortal in the strongholds to do it. "Kong! Kong! Blast you fool! Where are you when I need you! KONG!"

"Y-yes, master?"

"Are my private quarters prepared yet?"

"Yes, master. The men finished up a little while ago. I was inspecting them when you called. The men are skilled workers, but I wanted to ensure everything was up to your standards."

"As if you could live up to, let alone judge my standards. Bring a pair of women to my chamber. I have work to do and questions to find answers for. Quickly, Kong, I will meet you there."

"As you wish, master."

Ju-Long wasn't sure where to begin. Maybe he just needed to focus, bring the energy within him somehow and unleash it into his human subjects. Why he had asked for females he did not know. He found that mortals were no longer a source of attraction to him in a sexual manner, regardless of how beautiful they might be. Just more natural to have women in his chambers he imagined. If the marking of a human turned out to be a very intimate event, he'd rather perform such an act on a woman rather than a man. He wasn't sure how he would arouse himself to perform intercourse if that was what it took, for the sight of a naked female form since the change had not remotely stirred his groin. Feeding was ecstasy, but of a different kind. It made him feel a hundred times better than any sex he had ever had, but did nothing in the way of bringing his manhood to full length. If sex was the key he'd find a way, but with a woman, never a man. If sex were the only way, he'd have an army of females.

As he entered his private quarters he was more than pleased at the look of it. Kong didn't have a clue, but some of his men understood exactly what he liked. Its luxurious interior was balanced by concealment and reinforcement on the outside. In the event that the city was attacked by day it would be quite a feat to locate and penetrate his personal resting-place.

There was a knock at the door.

"I have brought the women you requested, master."

"Enter."

"Is the chamber to your liking?"

"The men have done well, Kong."

"I have brought the two fairest I could find. I hope they are to your liking as well, master."

"You two women get on the bed. Resistance will bring death, so don't try anything foolish." The women, wrists bound in front of them, did as ordered. There was fear in their eyes and well there should be. They were in the lair of the one whom ruled those things that go bump in the night. Ju-Long pulled Kong close to him. "Do you ever get excited when you see a beautiful woman anymore? You know, down there."

"No, master, I don't believe I do."

"I wonder why?"

"I was always nervous when approaching women before. I imagine it has merely carried over to this existence."

"Well I never had much trouble with that, yet I am no longer aroused by the feel of their soft flesh against me. I am willing to bet not one of our number is either."

"That is odd. I hadn't really thought about it before now."

"Oh well, beauty is only skin deep. It is what's inside that counts." Ju-Long laughed. It took Kong a moment but he finally caught the joke.

"What's on the inside master! Very funny!"

"Kong."

"Yes, master?"

"Leave."

Kong bowed and exited, securing the door as he went. The two women huddled next to each other. "Do not fear. I do not intend to kill you. I merely seek to find answers. As long as you cooperate fully you will not be harmed. Any defiance of my orders will result in your death. Do we understand each other?" The women slowly nodded their heads. "That pleases me." Ju-Long cut their bonds with a dagger. "Now remove your clothes."

***

Tung watched as Yue-Yan dropped the body she carried over a small cliff. He followed her as she moved off the main trail and made her way across less traveled terrain. The thought of lying with her made his blood boil. She moved elegantly over the rocks and around obstacles. There was a sheer cliff face ahead that she was obviously headed for. With the ease of a spider she scaled the rock. Tung waited as she climbed, not wanting to give himself away yet. Halfway up Yue-Yan came to an opening and slipped into it, disappearing from sight. Tung began his own ascent. He could not lose her.

What appeared to be a small hole from ground level was actually a large opening. Tung made his way in, then stopped to listen. He saw only one way to travel, so there was only one way she could have gone. Tung quickly but quietly eased down the passage. Farther down the pass opened up into a large chamber. He hid in the shadows and scanned across it. In the far corner he could see the outline of the woman he pursued. He watched as she pulled her loose dress over her head and cast it aside. Even though she was in the shadows herself, Tung could make out long muscular legs that led up to firm round buttocks. Her hips were more shapely than most of the women of his city. They were usually either flat or flabby in that area. The curve of her breasts showed ample size and there was no sign of sagging. Tung once again felt the ache in his groin and rubbed it gently.

Yue-Yan stepped into a pool of water and immediately plunged to her waist. Tung removed his top and slid his pants off. Methodically he worked his way across the chamber toward her, hoping to join her in the water. Yue-Yan spotted his approach and was out of the pool in a shot. She rushed strait at him, bearing her fangs. Tung bared his in return and moved to intercept her progress. The two circled each other like feral cats preparing to fight. He could feel the energy between them. Yue–Yan lunged at him and he dodged right. He delivered a blow across her back as she passed. It sent her sprawling to the floor. Instantly Yue-Yan was on her feet again and on the attack. He caught her by the arms and the two rolled head over heels. Tung landed on top, their bodies pressed close together. He pinned her arms over her head, his stiffness pressed into her stomach. Yue-Yan raised her head and bit firmly into his shoulder. Tung howled in pleasure. He slid his body down, prying her thighs apart with his knees. She twisted and turned, trying to deny his entry. Yue-Yan released her bite and growled at him. Tung buried his head in her breasts and gave her nipple a playful bite of his own. She broke free of his grip on her wrists and clamped her hands around his back digging in deep with her nails. Yue-Yan wrapped her legs around him and forced his length inside her.

Tung's body exploded in pleasure as he thrust himself in deep again and again. She cooed and moaned under him, but just as he thought he would climax she shoved him hard and sent his body flying off her. Tung landed on his back and she was on her feet racing toward his prone body. He caught her with a foot and sent her sailing over him. Tung leapt to his feet and turned to give chase. Yue-Yan had scrambled up and was running away from him. However, she hadn't moved fast enough and Tung caught her and tackled her face first to the floor. She got to her knees and attempted to break free. He clamped his hands firmly on her hips and plunged into her from behind.

Yue-Yan bucked wildly against him as he felt the pressure build once more, begging for release. She arched her body and curled her back against his chest, wrapping her hands behind his head. They slowed their pace and moved together in rhythm. Tung moved his hands slowly up her abdomen, circling his fingers around her navel. Her flesh was burning up. He climbed his hands higher, cupping her soft breasts. Tung pinched her nipples between his thumbs and forefingers as he pounded harder inside her.

Yue-Yan shifted her weight and drove her elbow into his face. The move knocked him over. "You tease me, woman! Tung cried. "Stop this playing and satisfy me!" Yue-Yan let out a laugh. She fully enjoyed this game and her new-found powers. It was nice to be in control for once. She was the dominant she had always dreamed of being. Yue-Yan pushed Tung on his back and straddled him, her thighs hovering above his groin. With a smile she slid down the length of his shaft. Tung wrapped his hands around her and grasped her buttocks as he drove her down onto him. She lowered her upper body and Tung opened his mouth to receive her breast. He slid one hand up her back and pulled her closer, then sank his fangs into her neck. The energy exploded between them as she bit into his shoulder in return. They trembled together as one another's power transferred in a cycle from their groins to their lips. Tung shuddered and released his bite as he erupted inside Yue-Yan.

The pair tingled from head to toe. He had never experienced such ecstasy. Yue-Yan licked gently at the twin imprints she had left on his shoulder like a cat licking its paw. She didn't stop there, but instead made her way down his chest, across his stomach and onto his groin. She took him between her lips and circled his manhood with her tongue. He moaned loudly as she drew him fully into her wet mouth and worked her hand and lips up and down his manhood. He hadn't realized it last night, but he had created the perfect mate. This beautiful woman shared both his thirst for blood and his voracious sexual appetite.

CHAPTER 6

Ju-Long grew tired and angry. For three nights he tried everything he could think of, but had neither marked nor transformed a single human subject. There remained plenty of prisoner's left to work with, but he had run out of ideas. He needed something to take his mind off the mounting frustration. Running through the wilderness tracking humans and robbing them of their precious blood might do the trick. Certainly it would serve to take his mind off his failed problem solving. Ju-Long decided to gather a small group and venture away from Fanzhou for a night or more of hunting. The rest of his men would remain in Fanzhou to complete the moat that needed to be dug around the city to further improve their defenses. Surely Kong, as inept as he was, could oversee the accomplishing of such a task.

"Kong, you know well my wishes. I'll ride out for a while, a night, maybe more. I need time to free my mind so that I am able to seek the answers we must find in order to succeed in our ultimate goals. Control the feeding while I am gone and see to it the work assigned is completed. When I return I will take a larger force with me to the nearby cities and villages we come in contact with so that we may replenish our livestock."

"Yes, master."

Ju-Long mounted his steed and joined the five warriors that awaited him at the front gate. It would feel good to be out again. The six rode to the edge of the perimeter wall and then spurred their stallions to a full gallop. They raced into the woods and followed a well-traveled trail north. Ju-Long realized that one-day he would follow this very trail even further up the line and exact revenge on the people who had exiled him. With every brutal method he could dream up he would torture the Xia council, each one in turn. Afterward he would drain their blood, the only worth they held, then feed their remains to wild dogs. *Dogs? Why didn't I think of that before?* He could capture and bring back dogs to help guard Fanzhou. Mastiffs were notoriously good watchdogs. They would definitely bring a valued service, at least until he could make some human servants. Ju-Long smiled at his own brilliance. He steered his men northwest through a pass that cut between some foothills.

"Master, there are tracks that appear fresh." Ju-Long raised a hand as he brought his steed to a halt. The others reigned in their mounts. Ju-Long studied the prints and saw that they scattered just ahead into the tree line on either side of the pass.

"Shhh," he whispered as he listened. There was movement in the hills to the left and right. *A band of thieves,* he thought to himself. "I know you are there. Come out and play with us if you dare," Ju-Long challenged the men in hiding. For a moment there was silence, followed by the sound of many hooves descending upon his position. "Remember to protect your heads and hearts gentleman, especially beware of weapons fashioned from wood," he whispered to his men.

Within moments, fifty thieves, all on horseback, surrounded them. The enemy formed a tight circle around his small band. Escape was impossible, yet the furthest thing from his current agenda. A man dressed in clothes he had obviously stolen from a noble broke rank and rode a few paces forward. "We will have your weapons and anything of value you hold, including the fine studs you are perched upon. Surrender those items now and I may show mercy, sparing your lives," the man said as if he were quite confident his demands would be met without question.

Ju-Long laughed, a hideous sound that startled the horses, including his own. The one dressed as royalty brought his steed back under control and frowned. "You are a foolish one. You face numbers you cannot defeat and laugh in the face of the one who was generous enough to offer you a way to exit with your lives. Men, bring them death! Spill their blood until this little valley becomes a river of it!"

The sound of swords being drawn from their scabbards echoed in the night. Ju-Long's men dismounted and flew into the ranks of their enemy. They tore with their claws at men and mount alike. Ju-Long leapt from his saddle and ripped the leader from his horse. He sank his fangs through the man's skull. The man wailed as Ju-Long tore a chunk of flesh and blood from his scalp and spat it into the air. Blood gushed from the wound like a fountain. Ju-Long ripped his throat out, then discarded the body and grabbed the next closest man. He punched through the man's ribs and tore his heart out, shoving it into the screaming mouth before casting him aside. A sword came sweeping toward Ju-Long's neck. He ducked it, grasped the arm as it moved away from him and spun the man around, then grabbed the man's jaw with his free hand and snapped the neck with a powerful jerk. The corpse crumpled to the ground.

With a single blow he knocked a mare off her feet and the rider spilled into his arms. He cracked the man's spine like a twig then launched him through the air into two more oncoming riders. He stomped the neck of a fallen thief, crushing the man's windpipe, and then caught another by the hair and drew the thief to him. Ju-Long sucked the life from him ferociously, then let out a roar as he dropped the lifeless body and searched for his next victim. Several thieves rode up the trail screaming, "Xiang-shi! Xiang-shi!" Two of his warriors gave chase. A third fed on the last man standing. He did not see his other two soldiers. He walked through the mangled debris of ravaged corpses that littered the narrow battle field and found one, then the other, both with a spear jutting out of their chest.

He called his warriors back and they picked through the bodies, taking coins and the more exotic weapons, as well as any jewelry they came across. He had lost two more of his minion tonight and it enraged him. He wasn't mourning the men in particular, but more the fact that he still had no idea how to create their replacements. He wished not to dwell on the matter, so he led the remaining three up the trail. Their mounts had fled during the skirmish and all the others had been killed. He had no intention of trying to track them down—though he was sure they could do it with a minimal loss of time. They were a luxury, not a necessity. He and his men could move faster without them.

The four walked up the trail, discussing the brief battle. Despite the losses suffered it had been a good night. It was far more thrilling to feed during the heat of battle than to drag a prisoner from a cell and suck the life from him. It had already become a dull routine after only three nights in Fanzhou. They were predators, meant for the hunt. They could make some sport of it by ripping the limbs from a captive as you drained them, but that led to wastefulness. Besides, the fate of one in a cage was certain, while even with their powers the outcome of a fight was never guaranteed. That added to the thrill of the feast.

By the time the war stories were exchanged, full dawn was not so far off that they could ignore the need for shelter from the sun. They trekked as far as the Great Wall and made camp there inside the bottom of one of the old abandoned towers. It wasn't the most secure of environments, but it would do. Ju-Long planned to move west into Tibet. They raised mastiffs there that were known for their fierceness.

***

The brothers traveled almost non-stop, day and night, for four days. They rested only long enough for the horse Cai rode to be fed, watered, and rested to regather its strength. From their best estimate they were within half a day's trek of Fanzhou. It was closer than Zhan wanted them, but Cai needed to be as near as possible to be effective in using his gift. The others agreed it would be safe enough.

Depending upon the animal, Cai could operate over a vast distance. However he was unsure what creatures would be available to him and which would be most efficient to use for their purposes. Through the larger mammals and birds of prey distance was rarely a problem. With small birds, rodents or snakes he had to be as near as possible. This expanse should work, but it was pushing it.

Xiong was at work communing over a great distance as well. He heard Zhan's call shortly after they made camp. Xiong went off on his own, finding a peaceful plot of high ground to answer his eldest brother. He sat lotus-style and took several deep breaths, exhaled the last very slowly, then reached out with his own mind. They had traveled many miles from the city near the monastery, Guilin. Zhan's power crossed it so easily that when Xiong closed his eyes he felt as if his brother was seated directly across from him speaking. *I am here, eldest one.*

Xiong, I have much to tell you. I believe I have uncovered a way to destroy these creatures. I told you before you left that arrows had been effective in slaying several of their number. It is not the arrow itself, but the wood of the shaft. It appears any wooden weapon would do damage, and when delivered to the heart it causes death among the xiang shi.

Xiang-shi?

It is a name dubbed upon them by the native people of the northern lands. It is an ancient word meaning drinkers of blood. I have spent time within the minds of several of the warriors, most often entering the mind of a simpleton named Kong. I believe he is a second in command within their army due to blood relation to Ju-Long, a wicked demon who is their true leader. I have seen his face through the eyes of Kong and others, but I am hesitant to attempt to enter his mind. He is stronger than the others are in every way and I fear he would detect my presence should I link my mind with his. I have felt his power with several gentle probes. He has walls that guard his thoughts unlike any other I have dealt with. The others have been quite easy to intrude upon without their knowledge. Beware of this Ju-Long, for his speed, strength, and cunning in battle are unequaled. Even without his army it would take much to defeat him personally.

But wood will kill him as well?

I see no reason to believe otherwise. I do not wish to make it seem easy to bring death to any of them. Wood will destroy them, but delivering the fatal strike is no easy task. Their speed and strength make it extremely difficult to accomplish this. They know what wood will do to them, and if they see it coming they will simply move out of the way or block it and deliver a lethal strike of their own. There are five hundred of them Xiong. Do not delusion yourselves with the thought that knowing how to destroy them is enough. The knowledge we have gained is of great importance, but realize it would take an enormous army to defeat them and you are a mere foursome.

Your mission is to gather information. There are to be no heroics, Xiong. Make sure you and the others return to us safely.

You have my word.

I know that already you are closer to Fanzhou than I warned you to go. Please be careful. Avoid any direct contact with the xiang-shi. Soon we will fight these creatures, as you so desperately desire now. But not yet. It is not time. Be patient and we will overcome them.

I will control myself, eldest one. I will not jeopardize my brothers because of my desire to do battle with these demons. I promise you that.

I am confident you will make the right choices. I must go for now, but I shall call often. The energy I have spent these past days tapping into our enemies' minds and the atrocities I have witnessed therein have taxed me heavily. I must rest before I attempt contact with them this evening.

Rest well, Zhan. We will not fail or disappoint you in our actions.

You could never disappoint me, young one.

CHAPTER 7

Ju-Long's trip to Tibet got sidetracked by a couple of wonderful skirmishes and a storm that rained so heavy it forced even him to seek shelter from it. He rose the next evening inside the cave they made camp in to the sound of someone humming. It came from deep within the bowels of the cavern, but echoed through the chamber as if the person doing it was within the same room. The others were still at rest. Ju-Long could not wait for them to arise before investigating the source of the melody. To think a human had been in their vulnerable presence during the day disturbed him. He would leave his men a clue as to his whereabouts should they awaken before his return. Ju-Long drew his sword and placed it at the entrance to the tunnel that led further in, pointing the tip down its path. He hoped they would be smart enough to figure it out and travel that direction. Ju-Long descended into the cave, following the sound of the humming.

He came upon a huge chamber at the end of the tunnel. Torches hung from the wall and illuminated the entire room. As he neared the entrance the humming stopped. Quietly Ju-Long stepped in. There was a large pool of water near the center. In the middle of it a tree grew, its branches reaching the top of the cave. Ju-Long scanned every nook and cranny for any sign of movement. There weren't any other visible passages leading out. *What form of witchery is this?* he thought. *A cave that hums, torches that burn unattended, and a tree that grows where there is no sun?* Ju-Long moved toward the water. Maybe whoever had been doing the humming had submerged just as he entered. *You cannot hold your breath forever.*

The water was crystal clear and only waist deep. He moved around it, scanning the bottom, but saw no one. Perhaps it was his hunger playing tricks on him, but his hunger would wait. Ju-Long had not bathed in quite some time and the pool looked inviting. He stripped and waded into the cool water. The rains had washed away the blood of battle, but it did not serve to refresh him. The water itself seemed mystical, as if it had an energy all its own. He lowered himself down, submerging completely. His thirst for blood was all but removed for the moment. Ju-Long came up, tossing his long mane of hair behind him. A noise interrupted his bath. He turned to see his three warriors enter the chamber.

"Master, behind you!"one shouted. Ju-Long whirled around to see an old man standing behind him where the tree had been. Ju-Long took two steps back.

"Who are you old man? What trickery do you dare play?"

"You have invaded my home and soiled my inner sanctum with your foul odor. I believe it is I that should be asking who you are." The old man drew in a deep breath through his nose. "You bathe in my waters, but still you smell of blood and death."

"I am Ju-Long. I am death."

"Well if it is my treasure that you seek, I am afraid you have traveled here foolishly. It is hidden on another plane, guarded by my servants, where no mortal can ever reach it."

"I am no mere mortal. I do not seek your pathetic little treasure. The only thing you could offer me of value is the liquid that pulses through your veins. I am Xiang Shi, beware my wrath!" Ju-Long yelled as he lunged through the water at the old man, who leapt straight into the air, making him miss. Ju-Long sprawled face first into the pool, then rolled to his back. The old man hovered near the top of the chamber. "Come down and face me! Do not worry for suffering—I will make your death quick."

"A blood drinker? A long time since I have seen one of those, and never in such an entirely human form." The old man laughed. "You shall not drink my blood tonight demon!"

A bright blue light filled the room, blinding Ju-Long and his men. Wind began to whirl, whipping around them with the strength of a typhoon. As they fought to keep their balance, the torches went out and they were immersed in complete darkness.

It took only a second for Ju-Long's eyes to adjust to where he could make out some shapes and forms in the dark. The wind stopped as suddenly as it had started. Ju-Long looked all around, but could not find a single trace of the old man's form.

"What was he master?"

"I do not know." They all watched as one by one the torches re-lit. "But I believe we are about to find out." Ju-Long glanced around, but the room appeared empty. His senses told him otherwise. "I can feel your magic in the air! I know you are still among us! Come out and fight ancient one!" In the far corner Ju-Long could see the shadow of a large creature cast on the wall. "Make yourself visible coward! Or are you so afraid of me that you must hide yourself in the shadows?"

The shadow slid along the ceiling, a form slowly materializing as it neared Ju-Long's position. The beast was monstrous in size, over seven meters long. Ju-Long's men drew their swords and eased backward. The creature was almost completely visible now. It had the head of a camel with the horns of a stag. Its eyes were not unlike those of the demon who had created Ju-Long, and its body whipped snakelike back and forth as it appeared to slither through the air. Large scales covered the length of it— while short, thick legs with oversized paws hung below. Ju-Long noted the five long sharp claws each foot contained.

"It is you that should fear, Ju-Long! I am K'iu-lung, horned dragon, the god of both sky and wind!"

"Then you shall be a worthy opponent. I will take great honor in sucking the life from you." Ju-Long charged out of the water and rushed toward the dragon. Reluctantly, his men followed him into battle. The dragon drew back its head and unleashed a mighty wind. Ju-Long was slowed by it, but continued to fight forward. His men were not as strong, especially before feeding, and the gust picked them up and sent them hurling across the chamber.

Ducked down low, Ju-Long was able to spring from his crouch and jump onto the beast's belly. He found the creature's abdomen to be covered with a hard, turtle-like shell. He grasped for finger holds with one hand and punched hard against its armored underbelly with the other. His knuckles exploded in pain and Ju-Long lost his grip and plummeted to the floor below.

The dragon bellowed out a last gasp of wind, then chuckled at his puny assailant. "You will break every bone in your body before you penetrate my armor, little man." The beast soared upward, circled, and dove toward Ju-long's men. The three warriors had been stunned by the impact of the hard collision they had made with the stone wall behind them. With the dragon racing toward them, they tried desperately to scramble to their feet. The great horned beast opened its wide mouth and caught one of them in its jaws. As it bit down into the helpless warrior's body, its immense crushing power turned bone into dust. Ju-Long's servant called out his name.

"Release him, beast! Stop playing with the boys and face the man!" Ju-Long bellowed. The dragon snapped its head to the side, slinging the warrior's limp body across the room. "Do not worry Ju-Long—I will do you the same courtesy you promised me. I will make your death quick."

"You dare mock me, monster? No one mocks me! I will rip you apart with my bare hands."

The dragon swiftly rose to ceiling height, then coiled around and swooped down on Ju-Long. Its jaws opened to receive its next victim. Ju-Long timed his jump, launching himself straight up, narrowly avoiding the gaping jaws. He landed on the creature's back, holding on for dear life with one hand while he clawed away at the scales with the other. The beast twisted and turned its body in an attempt to dislodge its unwelcome rider. The dragon slammed its body lengthwise against the wall and Ju-Long's head bounced off the rock. The world went fuzzy as he lost his grip and slid off to one side, barely catching hold of the creature's foot. As he tried to climb back up, fighting against the beast's constant attempts to throw him, Ju-Long made a discovery. The bottoms of the dragon's paws were padded like a tiger's. *A chink in the armor,* he thought, pulling himself up until his mouth met the dragon's heel. He bit hard into it, tearing a piece of the padding out with his teeth. He spit it aside and saw bone, meat and a strange blue liquid that looked nothing like the red that ran from the human body. One lick of it and he knew without a doubt what it was. Ju-Long sank his fangs deep into the exposed tissue and drew in the creature's mystical blood.

Power rushed through his body as the dragon let out a roar. The blood was amazing. As it ran down his throat in great rivers he could see the millennia that the dragon had existed flash through his mind. His head swam in the magical properties it held. The lightheadedness reminded him of a good drunk from some very potent wine. Even when all sense of himself abandoned him, Ju-Long continued to consume steadily, until he was so sated he thought he would burst. He withdrew his fangs and let out a satisfied moan. The dragon sailed sideways along the ceiling and moved into the wall again, knocking its parasitic rider off.

Ju-Long skidded along the wall, the jagged rock tearing the flesh on his back open. When the adjoining wall stopped his slide, he did all he could to find something to hold onto. He was near ceiling height, and while he was sure he would survive the fall, he didn't feel like going through the agony of a crash landing. Only he wasn't falling.

The dragon's blood spewed from its injured paw, dropping to the floor like rain. The enormous beast spiraled downward. With its strength diminished, the creature crashed to the ground. One of Ju-Long's warriors sprang upon it, driving his sword up to the hilt into the dragon's body. The beast let out a wail as its tremendous body writhed in pain. The remaining warrior slashed his sword near the creature's head, loping off an ear. Blood shot from the creature's wounds like great fountains, drenching the two men.

The dragon snapped its head from side to side, trying to fend off its assailants. The warriors dodged its sweeping jaws and continued their assault. The dragon staggered against its injuries and the loss of copious amounts of blood. Gasping in ragged breaths, the beast came to rest, all the fight gone out of it. The warriors could taste the power in its blood, and when the last of the creature's writhing had stopped, they drank heavily from it.

Ju-Long, coming out of his dream-like state of ecstasy, gathered his senses and realized that he was hanging in mid air. He shook his head and rubbed his eyes in disbelief. The floor, the dragon, and his feeding men were at least twelve meters below him. Has *the dragon's blood altered my perception of reality?* he thought. He watched as his warriors stumbled back from the huge carcass, drunk on its blood as well. They called his name with panicked voices as they slowly began to levitate off the ground. "Master, help us. Help us master, please."

Ju-Long tried to move. As soon as he did he plunged downward, the floor coming up faster than he liked. Then, as if by some magical instinct, his body righted itself and he soared upward, sailing across the room. *I'm flying!* he thought as he glided over the dragon's body. The beast groggily lifted its head as he passed. Its breaths came in short, fast pants.

"Ju-Long." The beast called to him.

"How does it feel to taste defeat, oh god of sky and wind? It would appear that I have become your replacement in the air!" Ju-Long laughed as he circled back over the dragon.

"Ju-Long . . . please . . ." the dragon moaned. "You made a promise."

Ju-Long attempted to land, thudding and rolling across the floor as he did. With a quick movement—as he skidded to a stop—he was on his feet again. He wanted to look the beast in the eye so that its dying image of him victoriously standing in front of it would be the image it carried through all eternity. "Speak, ancient one. Do you have some last request before I finish you? Would you grovel at my feet? Beg for my mercy?'

"You have won. I will not grovel. I will not beg. All I will ask is that you fulfill your promise and finish me now. Do not leave me to suffer. I am beyond recovery, and true death might take days. I have not the strength to take myself to the one place where I could possibly nurse myself back to health—so end it. Take the sword one of your men left lodged in my side and drive it straight through my eye socket. That should do it."

"You have fought well, dragon. However, you have learned to your demise that Ju-Long cannot be defeated." Ju-Long stepped around the creature, withdrew the needed sword, then moved right up to the beast's face. "I honor my promises. May hell receive you with open arms." With those words Ju-Long thrust the sword into the dragon's left eye driving it as deep as he could. The creature twitched for a moment, let out one last breath, then expired.

"Master! What is happening? Please help us down from here."

"Quon, Yun-Qi, do not fear my young warriors. Think like the bird, for you can fly." Ju-Long said as he bounded into the air.

"How, master? How is this possible?" Quon asked, his tall thin frame flattened against the ceiling. His fingers were white to the knuckle from trying to obtain some sort of grip on the stone canopy above him.

"That creature's blood has delivered more than a meal, my friend. It has brought power to us! By drinking from the beast, we have stolen its power. I don't know if it is only for the moment or ours forever. However, tonight gentleman we ride the sky!"

***

Xiong played the role of sentry while Biao and Ling slept. Deep down, as he swiveled to face any sound of movement in the night, Xiong hoped it would be one of his new adversaries come to call. He longed to face his enemy and defeat them, spoiling for the fight. Standing back while innocents suffered was not something he enjoyed.

Cai sat by the fire meditating. Xiong had seen him in this deep trance before, yet only briefly in passing. This was the first time he had ever really watched his brother for such a long period. As stoic as Cai's face had remained this past hour, it was hard to read whether or not he had touched minds with a member of the animal kingdom, or simply fallen asleep. Xiong had observed his eldest brother, Zhan, many times in a deepened state such as this. Zhan's face was always filled with whatever emotion he was feeling at the time. Zhan laughed, cried, convulsed, spoke in panicked murmuring and occasionally screamed in terror. Not Cai. Were it not for the slight rise and fall of his chest when he breathed, one might mistake him for a statue.

It took complete concentration on his part for Cai to establish the initial contact with an animal. Once a link was established, maintaining it and later contacting the animal when needed was easy. Tonight would be the roughest night. The energy it took to locate a suitable bird or mammal was taxing by itself. Now he needed to engage with several because he couldn't be sure what type of creature would be best used in penetrating the city of Fanzhou and spying on his enemy.

Tree branches surrounded him, and his mind constantly had to dodge tiny limbs that jutted out into his path of flight. He rode the slight breeze, seeing through the eyes of an owl, his first contact of the night. His bird companion was hungry. Cai had disrupted the owl's hunt when he linked his mind with its. The owl knew he was there, but made no protest toward the outsider who had taken control of him, save the ones coming from its stomach. Cai was satisfied with his new friend and released him to find his meal before taking control again and flying the bird of prey to Fanzhou.

Cai reached out once more seeking his next contact. He brushed minds with numerous small creatures as he searched for a large mammal, preferably a predatory one that could defend itself if need be. Then his mind melded with that of a tiger. She was a large one, full grown and mother of several litters, though presently without cub. She roared when she sensed his foreign presence.

Easy there, girl. I mean you no harm. I request your assistance, if you will excuse my intrusion, he told it, feeling the beast's uneasiness. *I will be in your debt and eternally grateful if you will lend me yourself for a little while.* Cai stroked its mind gently, as one might pet a tamed animal. The tiger purred softly, relaxing a bit. *Dear friend, I ask that you follow the trail of man north to his great walled city. Do you know of the place of which I speak?* Cai felt her nervousness rise again. She knew the place and had no interest in going anywhere near it. He could see the memory of being hunted last time she ventured near that city. Men with spears and bows had nearly surrounded her. They almost had her trapped, but a narrow escape had been made. Not without injury though. There was still a scar from a spear had grazed her hind leg as she fled.

Just travel close to there, but not too close. I will guide you from danger should I need you to go nearer its walls. Please trust me. I would not lead you into death, great one. Reluctantly, she growled in agreement. Thankfully, this magnificent creature would carry out his request voluntarily. Cai could take over her mind forcibly if he had too, but he always got better results when he used the willing. Besides, he didn't like or believe it was fair to operate that way. A hostile takeover could do permanent damage to the psyche of an animal. If such an invasion were prolonged it might drive the animal mad in which case it would have to be destroyed.

Cai stretched out further, working his way through mice, fowl, and several grumpy boars as he moved himself closer to Fanzhou. He touched literally hundreds of minds in various states of sleep or activity. Once able to see and identify the outer wall of the city he sought out the eyes of a small songbird. Cai used it to fly right into the heart of city. As his new little friend swept over the wall, Cai could immediately sense hundreds of tiny minds throughout the city below him. He communed with several adolescent creatures in his search to find the right one. The young ones were receptive to his presence, but had not the knowledge or experience he sought.

Finally he came upon one that displayed the wisdom of having survived several years. The rat was large, possibly the largest he had ever encountered. The creature went about its business, feeding on grain in what appeared to be a storehouse of sorts. The rat acknowledged Cai's presence, but kept right on eating.

Cai was almost certain that he was in fact adjoined with a rodent resident of Fanzhou. However, never having been there before he was not totally sure. *Could I have found my way into a different city by mistake?* He should not have left the bird behind so soon. It would have been very simple to scout the city and determine if this was Fanzhou itself, and if the demons were here.

He thought about leaving the rat and seeking out another bird, but he liked this particular creature and didn't want to have to invade its mind twice in the same night. Better to establish the bond with the rat now and let it tell him where they were.

"Aid me friend. I will trouble you only for a short while. Take me out into this city of yours so that I might know where you are." The rat finished chewing its snack, and then scurried out of a hole in the back of the hut. Cai's power drew animals to him. Rarely did he run across a creature that totally rebuked his presence. Almost always they accepted him as a kind spirit to which they willingly lent their assistance. The rat was no exception.

Once out in the open the rat swept the area with his eyes and sniffed the night air for danger. It darted behind the cover of an adjacent building. It moved quickly along the outer walls going from building to building. The rat never remained in the open for more than a few seconds. Cai watched patiently through the rat's mind as it kept an eye out for predators. So far, Cai hadn't seen any, nor had he seen a single human being. The city seemed deserted.

Can you take me to the entrance to this city, my friend? Cai asked, hoping the rat understood. The creature stopped, looked around, and then took off to the right. The rat led him through a maze of buildings. Despite its obesity it moved swiftly—things passing by in a blur. Cai thought it had slowed to rest then realized that he was looking at a huge gate less than twenty meters away. There was a set of steps to the right of the gate that led up to a guard tower at the top of the perimeter wall. *There. Take me there. Climb the steps so that I may look over the city from atop the wall.*

The rat sniffed the air and checked its path for potential threats, then raced toward the steps. It leapt up the first two, then stopped to sniff the air again. Cai could hear voices coming from above. *Go on friend, but carefully.* The rat started his assent, creeping up each step. Its body was tensed to turn and run at the first sight of danger. As it eased up the last step it stopped, carefully peering around the corner. There were two men engaged in a test of strength. They stood on opposite sides of a waist high stone partition— their hands locked together, elbows bent, biceps bulging as one tried to pull the other's arm over.

Cai could see the strain on their faces, teeth gritted together—and fangs. They had fangs. *Turn and leave my friend. You dwell in the city I was searching for. Be mindful of the men you share this place with. They are not human. These creatures live on the blood of others. Take us back down into the city. The people who once ran this city must be imprisoned here somewhere. Help me find them.*

The rat didn't hesitate. It flew down the steps hardly touching them. *I didn't like being that close to those things either, little one.* The rat scurried back into the cover of the labyrinth of buildings and then came to an abrupt halt. A picture of a building came into Cai's thoughts. The rat was remembering. It had heard the people trapped in that building, smelled their human scent. *That's the one, my friend. Can you find it again?*

The rat sniffed then took off at a full sprint. It turned so many corners as it weaved between buildings that Cai was sure they were running around in a circle. *Where are you going my friend? Slow down and really think about it. Take a whiff of the air.* The rat ignored Cai's remarks and kept going full tilt. Finally it stopped next to a large building. Its eyes darted to and fro, checking all around. Then Cai heard them. The soft moans of people came faintly through the walls. He could smell them as well—and a foul stench it was. They had to be living in their own excrement. *Can we get inside?*

The rat made its way along the outside of the building. Every time it came to a spot where there used to be a hole the rats used to gain access to the building through, they found it had been boarded up or otherwise closed-off. *We will have to make a new entrance. Are you up to it?* The rat turned and stood on its hind legs emitting a series of high-pitched squeaks. *A call to arms. Good thinking, little one.* They waited several moments, then it seemed as if rats were flooding in from everywhere. Cai's companion began to dig and several others joined in. The rest formed a perimeter around them, guarding against danger. As one rat grew tired another would take its place. They worked fast and furiously, until there was room for one then two to slip through to the inside. There were already four other rats in the room before Cai and his friend entered. Some women had spotted them and were attempting to scream through parched lips. A few men were desperately reaching out to try to grab them through the bars of the cages. The people were crammed so tightly together that there wasn't room to lie down or even sit.

Tell your comrades that they may go now. I think it would be safer for all if we explored the rest of this building on our own. The rat rose up and let out a few squeaks. The others began crawling back out through the opening.

Let us proceed, but with due caution. There may be guards lurking about.
The rat squeaked several times. *Yes, you're right. Maybe a cat, a snake or a dog as well.*

The interior of the room was huge, looming even larger through the eyes of a rat. They had no choice but to walk right down the middle of the aisle between the cages. Human hands reached through the bars trying to catch hold of the furry rodent. They were starving. Catching glimpses of gaunt faces, the stench of human waste, and the reek of urine and sweat made this the most horrid sight Cai had ever witnessed. An old man lay on the floor of one of the cages dead. His hollow eyes stared right at Cai's little friend. People were standing on his back—a woman had one foot on his head, the other on the ground beside it. They had no choice. The slightest movement in the cage made everyone shift. One moment they were pressed hard up against the bamboo bars, the next they were falling back slightly, only to be caught again and shoved forward once more.

Cai's heart ached. These people needed help and soon or they would all be dead, one way or another. As if the scene could become any more grim— a little further down Cai saw something that almost made him withdrawal back into his own body immediately. The little face of a child no more than two years stared at him, its head hanging awkwardly out of the bars. The child had bruises, cuts and scrapes all over him. Part of his left ear was torn away from the side of his head. A woman, most likely the child's mother, stood behind him. The period of weeping for her dead son, apparent from her tear-stained cheeks, had passed. A haunted look now filled her every feature, her eyes staring straight ahead, but seeing nothing. It was at this point that Cai realized he couldn't take it anymore. He had to go back, figure out some plan. They couldn't just be left to die.

Let us depart my friend. I have seen enough. I will stay with you until you are safely back feeding once more in the place where I found you, but then I must go. I may call on you again very soon my friend. You have risked much for me tonight, compromising your own safety for my benefit. Thank you.

***

Ju-Long reveled in his newfound power. He and his men sailed over the treetops searching for any sign of the Xia Army rumored to be marching through this area. The threesome passed over two men on horseback. They were indeed wearing the colors of Ju-Long's former tribe. They dropped down on the riders through the forest canopy, startling the men's steeds. The riders had no time to react as Ju-Long's warriors knocked them from their mounts and pounced on top of them, pinning them to the ground.

"Easy gentlemen. Do not rip their throats out just yet. Right now these men may be worth more to me alive than dead." Ju-Long landed softly right beside them. Both faces were unfamiliar to him. One was a short but stout older man, still fit for battle even though he was visibly past his prime. The younger one, a large man-boy, was even taller than Ju-Long. He was a physical specimen. "Do either of you know who I am?"

"You're demons! You're come to rob us of our souls!" The younger one yelled, fear evident from the quivering in his voice. Tears welled in his eyes as he stared into the slightly parted lips that revealed the fangs of the one who held him down.

'You are partially correct. You could call me a demon, but what happens to your soul means little to me. It is blood that I feed on, and if I wish it yours will be mine tonight. Your soul can go to whatever god you pray to, or whichever devil you owe. I was not always this blood-drinker, this xiang shi that I have become. Once I was one of your own people. I am . . ."

"You are the cursed Ju-Long!" The older man interrupted. "The wretched scum sentenced to exile by the Xia council—to be killed on sight if ever you were to pass our way. You are a madman who respects no one— holds nothing sacred. If it is your plan to kill us then be done with it. Our people will avenge our deaths"

"Flattery will get you nowhere, old man." Ju-Long sneered. "So you do remember my name. Touching. I do not recall you in particular, but then again you are one of the thousands of pawn that serve the Xia Council." The old man just stared directly into Ju-Longs eyes without any sense of fear about him. "I would guess the idiot—yet a hardened warrior who would run from nothing—regardless of the odds against him. You show great bravery or foolishness tonight. The two are often the same in the end. I therefore will grant your request. Kill him."

As Ju-Long's soldier tore into his flesh the old man did not flinch but merely kept his cold stare fixed on Ju-Long. The elderly warrior's eyes held the lifeless gaze of a man who had killed many and seen many killed. His feelings were deadened to the sensitivity of life and death a civilian possessed. It was a quality Ju-Long could relate to.

The younger man quaked with fear as his captor licked his lips. Ju-Long stepped toward him and knelt down. "You are disgusted to watch my soldier feed? It is blood that gives us power, makes us strong. Not so much different than what a good meal would do for you, and judging from your size you have had a great many of those." The young man shut his eyes, trying to block out the nightmare happening around him. "Open your eyes and look at me, boy. You can decide your own fate tonight. Will you be a good little boy and answer all my questions? Or will you become a source of power like your friend for the demon that holds you?" *Power* Ju-Long thought. A revelation was trying to make itself known. *The blood of humans gives me power. The dragon's blood gave me power. To share that power? To let them feed how we feed!* Ju-Long rejoiced. "That's it. That is the secret. I know how to make our servants! Quon, force the boy to drink from the neck wound Yun-Qui has opened on the old man."

"No, please don't. I will answer any question. Please, I beg you. I . . . I can't."

"I didn't leave much master. I did not know you would require it."

"I don't think it will take much Yun-Qui. Just get it flowing again." Ju-Long turned back to the man-boy. "And when he shoves your mouth down to that wound— you'd better suck like your life depended on it—because it does."

Yun-Qui got the blood flowing again, though with great effort. With the old man's heart stopped, the pleasure of feeding became a chore. By the time he withdrew and Quon forced the boy's head over the wound, Yun-Qui had quite a headache.

The young man drank in some of the coppery tasting liquid, gagged, then spit it out. "Drink it! Drink it or my friend will snap your neck with the mere flick of his wrist. Drink now!" The boy placed his lips back over the wound and sucked hard. He took small gulps, trying to keep the blood in his mouth for as short a time as possible. After a few minutes Ju-Long nodded to Quon to let him up. The boy coughed, then puked blood and remnants of a meal he had eaten earlier all over the old man's face. "Idiot. Now look what you've done."

"I'm sorry. The blood made me sick. I did not mean to defile my comrade's body by throwing up on him."

"Who cares about the body? You wasted the blood! Did you not feel its power as it flowed into your body?"

"No. It made me feel weak, nauseous."

"Stand up. Take my hand." The boy reluctantly did as Ju-Long bid. "Now pull with everything you got. Pull me to you." The young man slowly began to tug on Ju-Long's arm. "Don't hold back boy. I want to feel your strength." The young one bent his knees, tensed his muscles, and leaned back as hard as he could. Ju-Long yawned. "Is that all?" He flung his arm and sent the boy flying. "Pathetically human. Damn." The young man's head narrowly missed a tree trunk as he sprawled to the ground.

Ju-Long paced toward him. "What is your name child?"

"Kai."

"You were to be the first. Too bad the method didn't produce the desired effect. I'm afraid you are useless to me. But I'm sure my friend Quon will be able to find some worth in you."

"No. Please, I can help you. I can tell you anything you want to know about the Xia. I can show you where they are—lead you to the council's camp if you wish. I will share any information you want. Please let me live."

Share. Ju-Long had a thought, but held it in check for a moment. He could mull it over while the boy spilled his guts about exactly what Ju-Long's former tribe had been up to recently. "Very well then, prove your worth. How many does their army number in this area?"

"The entire army, as well as all of our women and children are on the move. Our leaders plan to take the lands the She Le now occupies. We are being driven from our lands by an enemy force too large for us to defeat. Besides, the She Le are weak right now, too many fights with the Jin at the border between their two lands. Their territory is far more abundant than ours as well."

"If I were still with the Xia, there could be no force large enough to drive them from their homes. Fools."

"There are nearly five thousand soldiers camped in a village near here. There are a dozen camps like it all along the southern border of our domain, gathering for the battle against the She Le. Another ten thousand are not far behind with the Council itself. Those figures do not include women and boys too young to fight.

"Has there been mention of taking a city named Fanzhou?"

"I have not heard of it. If it lies within the land of the She Le, than it will be subject to attack, I am sure."

"The north is so split, I'm not sure whose territory it sits in, but the city itself is mine. They will perish if they come anywhere near it." Beneath the concern that his kingdom might soon be in jeopardy from a large force, an idea was formulating. The words of the demon spoke to him. *Share your power.* The humans gave him power through their blood. If he wanted to share his power . . . they would have to drink his blood! Now Ju-Long was sure he had it right. He let out an evil laugh. "You still want to live child?"

"Yes. I'll do anything. Anything you ask."

"Really?" Ju-Long raked his nails across his wrist deep enough to start blood welling in the cut. "Drink this." Kai gasped, still feeling the ill effects of the blood he had already consumed. His face went pale and he put his hands up in front of him as if to say no. "I think you will find this more to your liking, young one. Besides, your choices are limited, extremely limited." Kai lowered his shaking hands and closed his eyes as tight as he could. He tasted the coppery blood as Ju-Long pressed his wrist to Kai's mouth. "Part your lips boy and drink from me. I shall not repeat myself." With a whimper Kai opened his mouth and licked tentatively from the wound. "That's a good boy. Keep going."

As the minuscule amounts of blood that Kai took in ran to the back of his throat and into his belly, Kai began to feel something. This was different. He wanted more.

Ju-Long looked on wide-eyed as Kai grasped his arm tightly, bit down around the wound and began sucking furiously. "Yes, it's working. Feed my child. Feed!" Ju-Long flipped his head back and laughed. "We have found the key and unlocked the gate! There will be no stopping us now." Kai continued to feed until Ju-Long began to feel dizzy. "That will do." He said, trying to pull away from Kai. Kai continued to drink, clutching his arm even harder. "Enough!" Ju-Long ripped his arm away from Kai and knocked him backward using a heavy open palm strike from his free hand.

Quon and Yun Qui seized Kai by the arms and held him. Kai slung the unsuspecting Yun Qui off, but Quon held fast. Ju-Long staggered against a tree, the movements around him a blur. Kai launched a punch at Quon, who ducked it and delivered two quick knee strikes to the man-boy's abdomen. Kai doubled over and fell to his knees. Back on his feet, Yun Qui came down hard with an elbow to Kai's back that flattened him against the ground. "Stop!" Ju-Long shouted, regaining most of his vision. "Let him be. I will take it from here."

"But master, he nearly killed you. We only tried to hold him off until we were sure of your safety."

"I—as you can see—am fine. Kai, come to me." Kai picked himself up off the ground and walked over to Ju-Long, kneeling at his feet once directly in front of him.

"Master, what would you have of me?"

"Stand boy, and turn to face the others. Gentleman, meet our first daytime protector."

"Protector, master? He threw me off trying to get back at you." Yun Qui said.

"And he took a swipe at my head. Just weren't quite quick enough though were you?"

"They tried to keep me from you master. I had to get to you."

"Yeah, so you could finish him."

"I would never hurt the master." Kai said looking at Ju-Long.

"Well you didn't mind giving us a fight."

"You and you are not master." Kai pointed in disgust at Yun Qui and Quon.

"Very true." Ju-Long grinned. "And they never will be. But master wants you to watch over them also. There are many more that need looking after as well, and I hold you responsible for them all. I will make more like you, but you shall be leader over them."

"As the master wishes, Kai does."

"And how does Kai feel?"

"Strong master. Nothing will hurt the master while Kai watches over him."

"We are running out of moonlight. We shall find a place to hole up for now, and our servant shall put in his first day's work, guarding our rest. Tomorrow we return to Fanzhou and create an army of protectors. We will make enough to watch us by day, and gather dinner so that it is waiting as we rise."

CHAPTER 8

Biao stood watch over the camp and the sleeping Cai while Ling and Xiong explored their surroundings in search of breakfast. The sun had only been up for an hour, but already the day was growing hot and humid. By afternoon Biao was sure the temperature would be close to unbearable.

Like Xiong, Biao spoiled for a fight. Every day they waited more innocents lost their lives. His patience with the waiting game grew thin. He could not see the future. He could not look through the eyes of an animal like Cai and observe the enemy up close. Not only was he becoming restless, he was beginning to feel useless.

He needed something, anything to provide relief to the day's monotony. He should have told Xiong to stay behind and watch the camp. Gathering food wasn't exactly what he would consider exhilarating, but at least it was something to do.

Biao became lost in his thoughts for a moment. They knew how to kill the xiang shi. So why weren't they doing it? How long before Zhan let them fight? How many more had to die before it was safe for the heroes to enter the battle? Biao crouched down and took out his knife. He began whittling the bark off several appropriately sized limbs he had cut earlier and began to make spears. Wooden weapons killed the demons, especially when placed through the heart, Zhan had said. If they killed those foul creatures, then he would make them, and plenty of them.

Cai opened his eyes to the bright morning sun. He stared up at its position in the sky and realized he had slept longer than he intended. Cai reached over into his pouch and took out a handful of nuts and dried berries. He would curb his hunger with a quick meal of these and then contact his friends in the animal world one by one. Cai stood, taking a look around. Xiong and Ling were nowhere in sight. Biao was sitting on a stump next to a pile of long wood. "Morning brother," Cai said with a yawn. "Where are the others?"

"Gathering fruit and berries for breakfast. They should be back soon. I trust you slept well?"

"I'm afraid I have overslept. I am going to find a comfortable spot and get to work. I have made the animal contacts I need for now. It will not take me long, but there are certain things I would like to know. Zhan said these demons seem to disappear with the rising of the sun. They have to be holed up somewhere in that city I suspect. I mean to find out where." Cai stretched toward the sky and took in a deep breath. "What's that you're making? Spears?"

"Yeah, not much work for a warrior here today. Just trying to pass the time."

"Well, off I go. See you in a couple of hours."

"Not too far off now, Cai. Stay within sight."

"I will."

***

Huang Fu had pushed his family south. They stood on the outskirts of a small village. They had little to barter with, but certainly someone would help them. Their clothes were heavily soiled and tattered, and his wife needed a meal desperately. Soon her breast milk would run dry and their baby would suffer. Already his tiny son struggled to suckle anything from her.

"Find a comfortable spot to rest. I will go down to the village alone and see if I can gain someone's help and find a place to stay for the night. We will continue to travel southeast when we leave here. Hopefully we can find the city your mother's brother lives in," Huang Fu told his wife, giving her and the baby a gentle hug.

"Please be careful, Huang. These people may not take well to strangers."

"I have no fear of anything human after facing those demons," Huang Fu said with a half smile. "But for you, my love, I will be cautious. Do not worry so much. These are common people like us, not greedy nobles who only give aid to those who can offer them something great in return."

"Just come back to me in one piece, Huang."

"Don't I always, Lin?" Huang Fu kissed his wife and turned to the village. If the natives weren't friendly, he would back out and wait for nightfall. He would sneak back after dark and steal food for his family if he had to. Theft of any nature would normally be against his moral code, but he had not struggled to save his family from the monsters to turn around and watch them starve in the wilderness. They had managed to gather some food along the way, but a meager amount at best. Had they not been preoccupied with running as far away from Dulan as possible, they would have had opportunity to gather far more. Not knowing if they were being pursued put distance at a premium. It was better for them to skip a few meals than become a meal themselves.

***

The tiger had made a kill and the hunt had slowed down her progress. When Cai found her, she was resting, allowing the deer to spoil a bit in the hot sun. With this development, the tiger would not even begin to trek toward Fanzhou again until tomorrow. Once she did fill her belly with meat, she would rest through the evening. He could make her move, but there wasn't really any need. Tomorrow would be soon enough. He had others he could link with for now.

Stretching out further he found the owl. The owl, rarely a day flier, did as Cai asked and made several passes over the city of Fanzhou. Cai studied the layout, memorizing as much as he could. It was a much different view from up here than it had been at ground level with the rat last night. He believed he recognized the building the prisoners had been locked in, but he wasn't positive. What he was sure of was the absence of anyone, human or demon on the streets or in any of the guard towers. Had the xiang shi deserted the place completely, or were they just in hiding? Cai was betting on the latter. Maybe the rat could help him. Cai released the owl and went in search of his rodent friend.

He found the rat nestled with a score of other rats, all enjoying a mid-morning nap. Cai gently brushed the rodent's mind. *Wake my friend. I must request your services once again.* The rat stirred slowly, stretching its four legs as it got to its feet. *I apologize for waking you, but there are questions I must find the answers to.*

The rat gave a squeak in protest. *I know, I know. We humans have not always been the kindest of creatures toward your species. I for one appreciate and realize your worth, and treasure you like a brother as well.* Cai filled the rat's mind with warm thoughts.

The pair made their way outside. The bright light of day made the rat squint. It did not hate the sun, but preferred to operate under the moon's gentler, more concealing light. Besides, humans were much more active during the day and that made it far more dangerous for his species. Several weeks ago, when he last had to journey out during the morning the streets had been crawling with people. Today there was no one. There was something wonderful about the absence of humans. That made one less predator to watch out for. Yet if there were no more humans, the easy meals he stole from their storehouses would eventually be gone. He might someday have to venture out into the forest and forage for his food. Maybe helping this human save the rest of them did have an upside.

I'm not sure where to start looking, but I need to find out where the ones like those guards in the tower go during the day. Do you remember them? The rat let him know that he not only remembered them, but also knew the location of a building he had seen some of them go into just before dawn this morning. *You amaze me, friend. This is definitely your city. Nothing gets by you. Take me to that place.*

As they drew next to a large building, Cai could smell the stench of death. *This must be it.* The rat searched diligently, but couldn't find a single crack to crawl through. The building was sealed up tight. *What are the odds we could call on some of your brethren to help us dig our way in?* The rat emitted several squeaks of protest. *Please. I need to know if they are in there right now. I can't rescue the ones in the cages until I find out the status of their captors.*

Through the surrounding alleys the rat ran, ducking into little hiding places and calling to his sleeping comrades. By the time they had made a full circle and were back to where they had started, hundreds of rats were behind them. Cai's friend had even peeked into his own hiding spot and called his pack into action. He told them the same thing that he had told the others— *Come quick! I have found the mother of all storehouses! A feast awaits us all!* Cai wondered how much of a problem it would be for his friend when the others found out it was a lie.

He didn't have long to dwell on that, as the rats were off again, racing to the building where Cai believed the xiang shi were hiding. When they reached it, only a handful of them stood watch while the rest dug, gnawed and scratched their way through. By the time Cai and his companion made their way in, scores of other rats were already inside searching for the feast. Cai was in shock. The rats were crawling over what must have been a hundred bodies or more, laid out in perfect rows across the floor. Cai took a little more control of the rat's mind and led it over to the nearest body. The man he looked upon was definitely dead. There was no sign of injury to the body, but there was the familiar bruising that seemed to occur in all dead men. *This guy had some long, long nails*, Cai said to the rat. He looked closer and used the rat's nose to sniff. *Smells like blood caked under his nails. Zhan said the demons had nails like claws. I wonder?* Cai moved his friend up by the man's face. *Only one way to find out.* Cai reached out with one of the rat's paws and pried the man's stubborn lower lip down. The rat immediately lurched backward when it saw the fangs. *It's one of them!* Cai yelled in the rat's head, which responded with an irritated squeak. *Sorry, my friend. I was as startled as you were. How it could be them and why they are dead is a mystery to me.* Cai looked around. Several rats were actually chewing on the flesh of these creatures. *That is very odd. Do you see what some of your comrades are doing? I did not think your kind would eat anything rotten.* He wondered if maybe the flesh was more than it appeared. *Let's not taste it and find out. What we really need to do is get you and your brethren out of here and get over to that stronghold.*

The rat rose up on his hind legs and began communicating with the others. It pleaded for them to follow. The ones that were feeding, and that number seemed to be growing, didn't even bother to look up. The rest weren't responding either, save a sarcastic squeak here and there. Cai couldn't wait for them to be convinced by his friend, whose word was probably mud among his brethren now. They had to get to those prisoners and figure out a way to free them. He stayed based in his friend's mind, but branched out to as many of the others as he could and took control of them. The ones who were eating put up heavy resistance, so he let them go. It was going to sap what little energy he had left just to control the more willing. In a moment they were out of the holes and racing to the stronghold. As they ran straight across a large open courtyard, the rat instinctively checked the sky for any sign of trouble. Cai used the moment to note the position of the sun. It was early afternoon and they needed to hurry. The people needed to get out before sundown in case any living xiang shi were still around.

As eighty or more rats scooted through the entrance they had made in the stronghold last night, women and children started screaming in terror. Cai wasn't sure how this was going to work, and he hated losing a member of one species trying to save another, but there was no way to communicate to the people that the rats were there to help them. Focusing solely on saving the people, he used his control to make the rats ignore their instincts and the threat that the human's presented, and ordered them to start chewing through the thick ropes that tied the cage doors shut. The women tried to press themselves as far from the doors as possible, while men tried to grab the rats. Whether they intended to try to eat the rats, or just kill an animal they considered a menace wasn't clear to Cai. What was clear, and disheartening, was the sorrow he felt for four of the rodents who were killed within the first minute of the rescue attempt, by the very people they were trying to save. *If only I had the power to touch the mind of humans I could let them know why the rats are here. Damn it!* Cai thought as he felt the pain of two more rats lose their lives.

"Leave the rats alone! They are chewing through the ropes that hold us in! They have been sent by the gods to save us! L-Let them do their work," Cai heard a male voice shout from a couple of cages down. The room went silent, except for the squeaking and gnawing of the rats as people took a moment to try to ascertain what was really going on.

"What if they are chewing through the ropes so they can eat us?" A female voice this time echoed through the room.

"Are you serious? They are merely rats, woman. I'll wage we have a lot better shot against them than the d-ddemons! Let the rats free us, we'll worry about the rest la-later." Cai had moved down toward the sound of the male voice and caught a glimpse of the young man who was speaking. *Thank the gods that someone understands,* Cai thought as he watched the young man wrestle the remains of one of the rats that had given his life in this effort away from a short, older man. "You cannot eat it!" The young man yelled, trying to keep the rat's body away from the smaller man, who was still fighting him for it. "Do you wish to of-offend the gods who have sent them? Fool!"

"You watch your tongue when speaking to me, Jie! Who are you, a common soldier, to interpret the work of the gods! I say they sent the rats to save us from starvation." The older man retorted.

"It is just like you Cheng-gong to think of yourself, and with your fa-fat belly. If we were to die of starvation, you would be the one who held out the longest. Your face is still full! Look around you at the gaunt faces of our women! Our ch-children! Were these rats here to feed us, there are those in much greater need than ya-you!"

"How dare you! How dare you speak to one of the council like that? The last remaining member of the council at that!"

"And the most useless. The others are dead because they fought alongside their men. Not like you, our fa-fearless leader, found hiding in the sh-shadows!"

"Well, well, well, then explain to all of us how you, a big strong soldier in his prime, escaped death when so many of our fine warriors are now dead? You must have found yourself a hole to crawl into. You are not a warrior, you are a coward!"

"I will kill you for that old man!" Jie clasped his huge hand around Cheng-gong's throat. *Great, now they are going to kill each other,* Cai thought. His rat companion let out a couple of squeaks. *I know my friend. There are moments when we humans show very little intelligence.*

"Jie, the door is open! We are free! We are free!" A woman yelled. Jie released Cheng-gong's throat and the heavy-set man coughed as he tried to learn how to breathe again. "We will finish this later," Jie said in a low voice. "Right now killing you is not nearly as important to me as ss-saving what is la-left of our people."

A crowd had already formed by the exit. The huge doors were secured from the outside and would not budge no matter how many bodies pressed against it. "I told you!" Cheng-gong said, still wheezing. "See what those foolish rats have done! We are free from our cages, but still trapped in the building. When the demons find us like this they shall kill us even quicker. It is as I said, the rats were sent by the gods to nourish us! Had this been a rescue they would have sent something capable of opening the great doors as well."

Jie strode over to Cheng-gong. "This has been a long time ca-coming." He growled as he leveled the smaller man with a hard blow across the face. "If you can't think of anything positive to say, then just keep that fat mouth shut!"

Get yourself and the others out of here before somebody listens to that fool and the people turn on your kind for a second time, Cai told the rat. *Thank you for your help, I am forever in your debt.* Cai withdrew his presence from the rats and went in search of the owl. He found it quickly, resting in the forest just south of Fanzhou.

No time to explain, my friend. I apologize for this and ask that you just trust me. With that Cai took over the owl's mind and body flew toward the city. It seemed like forever before he was able to locate the stronghold. The doors were secured on the outside by two rows of braces, each holding a large log to prevent anyone from getting out, or getting in for that matter. It would take a small army to lift those logs. He wasn't even sure Wei could have done it. *There must be another way in.*

Cai used the owl to quickly scan the outside of the building. There was no windows, no other doors, and the sun had sunk even lower in the sky. *We are running out of time, my friend.* It was hard to tell how late the hour was in that dark building. *Wait a minute—it wasn't pitch black in there. There were a few rays of light sneaking in from overhead.* Cai flew higher, skimming the rooftop now. After a moment of circling, he spotted it. An entry hatch had been cut into the roof. *This must have been done recently. These cuts look fresh, not weathered like the rest of the roof.* A thin rope tied to a metal ring secured the hatch. *Not very secure when one considers the effort put into making sure nothing could get through the front doors.* The owl gave a couple of hoots. *You're right. Not many things could even get up this high. I guess if the demons made this they probably figured they didn't have to worry about humans breaking in or getting out this way. This building would be a tough climb.*

Cai stared at the rope for a minute. It was half the diameter of the ones that tied the cages shut. *It would be easy to chew through, if you had teeth.* The knot was a simple one. *It would be even easier to untie, if you had hands.* The owl protested. *I didn't mean to offend. You have been more than useful thus far. I am just going to need to use a couple of other friends to complete this mission. Let me think. First, we have to take care of the rope. The rat can do that.* The owl made a small noise. *What? No you may not eat him afterward. Second, we have to get the hatch up. I can use you and possibly a couple of your flying pals for that. Huh? No my friend, not a sparrow or a wren. I was thinking a lot bigger than that. Stop thinking with your stomach. Now be quiet and let me think. Then we are going to need a rope to drop down to them so they can climb out, and something big and strong enough to hold it. If the right species are around, this should only take a moment.*

Cai called to the rat once more, finding its location in a close by alleyway. *Do not fear my friend, I am the owl and I will not hurt you.* He said as he swooped down upon his furry friend out of nowhere and gently lifted its heavy body from the ground. It took everything the owl had to carry its heavy load back to the rooftop. *Stay and rest, my friend.* Cai said as he released the exhausted owl. He entered the rat's mind and led it to the hatch. *Chew through this rope. I shall return in a moment.*

Cai stretched out, searching for horses. *Surely a city this large has horses.* He was right, for within a nearby stable he found a number of large mares. Without time for pleasantries, he leapt into the mind of a beautiful black horse and took over. He used its mouth to reach over top of the gate and manipulate the simple latch. Once free he searched for a rope, finding one lying on the ground that appeared to be long enough. He scooped it up into the mare's mouth and hurried out into the street, racing back to the stronghold with much of the rope trailing behind.

Once in position he let the rope drop and nosed around for one end of it. Catching it securely between the horse's teeth, he reassured her all was well and asked her to stand fast and hold tight to the rope with all her strength. He ran his mind skyward, looking for another large bird. A great eagle was circling over the city, looking for a meal. *Sorry about this,* Cai said as he slammed himself into the eagle's mind and directed it to the ground beside the horse. He sought out the other end of the rope, running awkwardly along the ground until he found it a ways back up the street. Snatching it up into the eagle's beak he rocketed skyward heading for the roof. The rat, spotting the eagle as it crested the edge of the roof, scurried as far away as it could. Cai looked at the hatch and found the rope securing it had been chewed through. "Excellent." Keeping the other rope firmly in the eagle's beak, he clasped one of the iron handles in its talons and furiously beat its wings in an attempt to lift the hatch. It moved slightly, but was too heavy. He felt the owl land beside him. Though he had not prompted it too, it grasped the other handle and joined in the effort. It was all that was needed. The hatch lifted back on its hinges and the birds released it, allowing it to fall all the way open.

Screams came from inside. "The demons are coming!" Cai flew above the opening, judged its size to the great bird's wingspan, then swooped in through it. People scurried away, hands covering their faces. He let the end of the rope drop to the ground, let out a screech, then shot back out through the roof.

"The gods send marvels once more. It is a rope from th-the heavens," Jie said.

"It might be a trap!" A woman yelled.

"If it is death that awaits me at the other end of this rope, than I shall not keep it waiting long." Jie tugged on the rope, which gave a little, then started his climb.

Cai had released the eagle back to the hunt, used the owl to lower his rat friend back to the ground, and then reached back out to the horse. He reinforced its mind as it struggled to hold the rope in its mouth with the weight of a climber on the other end. *Just hold on for a little bit longer, old girl.* The horse whinnied and snorted through gritted teeth, until finally Cai felt the weight ease. *One must have reached the roof.* Within seconds he could see a large man peering over the edge. *No wonder you had to fight so hard, girl. They could have had a lighter man climb up first.*

The man disappeared from the edge, and Cai heard him shout. "Secure the rope to one of the cages. I have to climb down and find what is blocking the doors." Cai could hear yells from inside, but couldn't make out what they were saying. "Just do it! There isn't anything out here but a horse holding the other end of the rope." Cai waited a few moments until he saw the man come over the edge of the roof and start his dissent. He allowed the horse to drop the rope, then ran back for the stables. Sunset was near and if he didn't hurry all this effort would end with him watching these people being slaughtered.

As quickly as he could he touched the mind of the fifty or so horses in the stable. He flipped latch after latch until they were all free. Concentrating hard he led them to the stronghold. The large man was on the ground and had secured the end of the rope the horse had held to a post. Another man was already on the ground with him, and another was coming down the side as Cai and the horses came to a stop.

"The gods smile upon us today! We need more rope, but with these horses we can pull those logs free." Jie ran off in one direction, while the other man went the other. Four more had made it to the ground by the time they returned, carrying all the rope they could. Cai aided by keeping the horses relaxed and cooperative as the men tied the ropes to the top log, and secured the other ends to several of the horses. It seemed to take forever, but the first was finally pulled free. Almost twenty people were out now, but hundreds remained inside as the sun sank lower. The men quickly secured ropes to the second log and a fresh set of horses.

A scream came from somewhere behind them, followed by the sound of crashes and curses. Cai led his mare around a couple of corners and found demons crashing through the walls of the building he had seen them in. Several of them were engulfed in flames while others, limbs on fire, dove back into the safety of the building. Rats scurried out of the building running in all directions. "What in the world?" Cai couldn't make sense out of it. The demons had been dead earlier, now they were alive but bursting into flames. Cai watched as the building itself began to ignite. "Those people have to get out of here fast."

By the time he got back to the stronghold the doors were open and people were flooding out, heading for the gate. As Cai approached the entrance he saw the large man and several others lowering the drawbridge. Sunlight remained. Hopefully they could put enough distance between themselves and the demons to be safe before nightfall.

Once the bridge was lowered, Jie took up position in front of it. "We are not safe yet."

"Get out of my way!" Cheng-gong yelled as he rode a steed past Jie and out the gate. A score of others, also on mounts, followed his lead and tore out behind him. A mass of people on foot began to follow.

"Wait." Jie watched as Cheng-gong and his followers turned northward and headed off. "Put the elderly on the remaining horses and follow me south. There are th-thieves and enemies to our north."

"And the Jin to our south. Are you mad?"

"No. We are safer heading to them than anywhere else. To be captured by their army would be a blessing at this point. They are at least united and may be the only army strong enough to defeat these da-demons. Those who are with me may follow. The rest can do as you please."

Jie turned and walked over the bridge. Most followed him south, but a few ran north and a dozen rode east on mounts they hadn't relinquished to their elders. Jie dropped back to the end of those that followed him and urged them on as fast as they could go. He would watch the rear and be the first in line to fight or die if the demons caught them.

Cai stayed with the larger group that headed south via the horse he controlled, bearing an old woman and a toddler-aged boy. The owl flew ahead, taking breaks here and there but staying close to the band of travelers. Cai, just like his flighted friend needed rest. *Relax, my friend. You have done well. I will visit you again soon. Thank you*, Cai said as he brushed the owl's mind.

Back inside his own body, Cai could sense the presence of Ling and Xiong. He had no idea how long they had been back. Hunger and mental fatigue gnawed at him. The group he left traveling south had the safety of a few more hours before true dark. One of the groups, the north bound or south bound, would surely be caught. The one that convinced the group to go south had been smart, urging the group to travel no more than three or four abreast as they exited Fanzhou. This would hide their numbers to some extent, making the group headed north seem larger, as they ran scattered on the path they had chosen. He offered a prayer for the group headed north, then went to grab something to eat and speak to his brothers about the group headed south, toward them, and what might soon be following.

***

Kong awoke with the same maddening hunger he felt each night as he rose. The others around him were stirring as well. This was the largest of the three resting places that housed the army during the day. Over half the men slept here. He was sure men in the other two buildings were on the rise as well. He must get to the stronghold quickly to oversee the feeding. Kong pushed his own hunger down and leapt to his feet.

The other men did not fear Kong, only the fact that if any disobeyed the instructions Ju-Long had left for them, Kong would report it and they would suffer for their transgression. So far the punishment for disobedience in their new form had not changed from when they were human. It was death.

The smell of smoke, burnt flesh, and death filled the night air. It was stronger and closer than in days past. Traditionally, at least since in Fanzhou, they carried their prey outside the city and burned them on a nightly basis, scattering the bones later along the moat Ju-Long had them dig around the fortress shortly after they arrived. It was a warning to trespassers, especially those that might happen upon the city by day, that bad things lived here. Ju-Long's hope was that soon enough bones would stack high enough around the city to act as a second perimeter wall, making anybody think twice before trying entry.

Kong raced for the stronghold, fearing the worst. He could see a dark cloud above the area where the stronghold laid. He could hear the crackling of wood still burning. *The stronghold was on fire!*

Kong panicked as he ran around the corner onto the street that ran behind the prisoner confine. To his amazement, and relief, he could see it still stood. *One of the other buildings must have caught fire! Not good, but better a vacant building than one that housed their food!*

Kong turned up the alley that ran beside the stronghold and stopped dead in his tracks. His mouth dropped open as he noticed that the smoke was coming from the direction where one of the other buildings that housed their army lay. The smoke had just drifted over the stronghold. He took off, sprinting in that direction, blowing by the side of the stronghold, not noticing the two logs that lay in the street in front of the building as he passed, nor the fact that the doors were wide open. He rounded a couple of corners between other buildings, the smoke and smell becoming thicker. The building where his comrades rested came into view, and he saw that it had burned nearly to the ground. The roof had completely collapsed, with only a small portion of the far wall remaining, yet still on fire.

Skeletal remains littered the street, as if his fellow soldiers had tried to escape the fire inside the building. *Why had they been unable to?* He thought for a moment, mostly about how pissed Ju-Long would be at him. He was left in charge, and without a doubt Ju-Long would hold him responsible for this. Even if it happened during their daily rest, when he would have been unable to do anything about it anyway. That must have been what happened to the men, this fire started before sundown for sure, and as they tried to escape the fire inside, the sun wouldn't allow it. They were burned alive either way.

At least a hundred men lay in that building. Ju-Long would be more than a little displeased that he had lost so many, especially since the master had not yet figured out how to reproduce their kind. He would have no problem making the loss one hundred and one when he returned. Kong knew he was a dead man walking, both figuratively as well as literally.

Kong decided he must act swiftly. He raced to the stronghold hoping to catch a quick meal and decide what to do next. As he approached the front of the stronghold, he was stopped in his tracks for the second time. The front doors were swung wide open. Piao, one of the largest and strongest warriors when they were human, stood in the doorway.

"They are all gone, Kong. All of them! The prisoners have escaped. You are in charge. You are responsible!" Piao rushed him, and Kong knew that he wasn't going to have to wait for Ju-Long to bring him death. He was no match for Piao in a fight, he knew that, but thankfully he was a little faster. He turned and bolted in the other direction, then cut down the first alley he came to. He could hear Piao shouting after him. "Stand and fight, coward! You have failed. Face your punishment."

Kong could also hear the roars of others as they also found the stronghold empty. Kong dashed by the smoldering building, cut down another alley, and doubled back toward the main gate and its drawbridge. He could hear Piao let out a thunderous roar. He must have seen the burnt building and the skeletal remains of the fallen warriors. Kong kept running.

As he rounded a corner onto the main street he could see the drawbridge was down. Piao was nowhere in sight, but there was a large group of men running down the main street behind him. He wasn't sure if they were after him as well, or simply pursuing the tracks the humans had left on their way out. He wasn't going to stop and ask. He headed north once outside of the city, quickly realizing that it was the same direction Ju-Long had departed in. *He might be heading back this way! No good!* He glanced back and saw no one else had made it out yet. He reached the north edge of the moat and turned east. He heard his name being roared again. "Kong!" It was Piao, and he sounded as if he were still inside the city walls. Kong could see a tree line to the east. If he could make it he might escape. But it was too far, somebody would round the corner and see him before he made it. He dove into the moat and submerged himself, carefully but quickly swimming east. When he got to the easternmost edge he stopped, peeking his head out of the water just enough to see a large group running north. He swan the rest of the perimeter until he came up on the southwest edge. Kong poked his head up again and ducked immediately back under. Piao and several others were on the drawbridge walking out.

Kong slipped back around to where the outer wall would block any chance of them seeing him. He listened intently, thinking he would make his escape once they left. He hoped they headed north after the others. If they headed south, then he would go east. That would not be good, though, because he knew he needed to feed soon, and he had seen a smaller number of tracks headed south as he cleared the drawbridge earlier. He could surely catch that group and steal one of them. If he had to head east, he had no idea when he would come across humans again.

"Looks like the others headed north. We'd better catch up, Piao."

"I don't want to catch up. I want to catch Kong!"

"He is gone, maybe even headed north with the others."

"That coward isn't with them. He knows what his fate is."

"Kong will pay eventually, but not tonight. We must feed, and our brothers and our prey are headed north. We should get there before the others leave nothing for us."

"Yeah, yeah, I'm coming," Piao said. Kong wasn't sure what other soldiers had been talking with Piao, but he heard them all roar a battle cry and listened closely as their light but quick footsteps faded north. Once he could no longer hear them, and was certain they had made their way into the wood line to the north, Kong pulled himself from the water and started south.

"There you are." Kong froze. Glancing back he saw Piao step out from around the corner of the wall on his side of the drawbridge. Piao leaped from the bridge at an angle that allowed him to clear the moat and land on the grass, cutting the distance between them by half. Kong bolted like a rabbit running from a predator. An owl flew over his head as he raced into the woods. It startled him, but he kept his balance. There was no time to stop, no time to stumble, no time to fall. The chase was back on.

***

Cai knew many in the northbound group would be doomed, that was certain. He had hoped that the demons would have picked one direction as a whole, but an apparent dispute between two of them had one of them chasing the other south. They were going to catch up with the humans soon enough, but they were also headed right for him and his brothers. When he opened his eyes, Xiong, Ling and Biao were all staring at him.

"So what's new?" Ling asked

"Most of the army is headed north, but there are two that headed south."

"How long before they catch the group?" Xiong asked.

"As fast as they are? Not long. They will certainly overtake them well before dawn."

"Can we get to the group before they do?" Biao asked, a gleam in his eye.

"I like the way you think, brother," Xiong said, giving Biao a nod.

"Zhan said specifically we were to avoid contact with these creatures," Cai reminded them both.

"Cai's right." Ling added

"What?" Xiong and Biao said in unison, giving Ling a surprised look.

Ling's face finally broke a smile. "Just kidding! Let's go kick their ass!"

"We can't!" Cai insisted.

"Really?" Biao asked. "All those in favor?" The three raised their hands. "Those opposed?" They all stared at Cai. After an uneasy moment, Cai gave in.

"Oh, all right! I guess I have to back my brothers. I had to try. I promised Zhan. He knows that I am the most level-headed of this foursome."

"We are all breaking that promise tonight," Xiong added.

"Yeah, but don't you worry. We'll take the fall on this one. You tried to talk some sense into us, we out-voted you, and you were powerless to stop us. Zhan will accept that," Ling said.

"Damn." Xiong sighed.

"What is it?" Biao asked.

"I was so wrapped up in the thought of facing these demons, I didn't notice Zhan in my head. He heard most if not all of our conversation."

"Uh-oh. Big brother is watching." Ling chuckled.

"I'll be right back. He wants to talk." Xiong stood and looked for a spot where he would be far enough away from the others to concentrate. Cai closed his eyes as his brother departed and resumed a trance of his own.

***

Piao had lost sight of Kong. They were both following a path some of the escapees from Fanzhou had traveled. The hunger must be gnawing at Kong as well. *Lead me to the humans Kong.*

The thirst was becoming unbearable. Piao could feel himself fading in and out, the world around him a blur. Only the thought of killing Kong and the faint scent of the humans carried by the breeze kept him upright

Kong was weary. The blood of the humans called to him. Piao was out of sight, but still chasing behind. He could sense that. Kong found himself stuck between the need to feed and the need to escape. He wondered if he had enough of a lead to capture his prey, feed, and escape from Piao all at

110

the same time? If he just kept running, could he live a night without blood? Would the hunger drive him insane?

Kong could hear Piao in the distance as the larger man crashed through the forest. The art of stealth was not with his pursuer, no doubt the hunger hindering his progress. Unfortunately the heart of the warrior was something Kong did not possess, and Piao did. He would not stop until Kong was dead.

The dilemma. If he reached the humans, Kong could feed. However, if Piao caught him he would die. He could not defeat Piao in a fight. That he knew. Would he die if he did not feed? Too many ifs.

If he turned east now, and Piao's assumptions and thirst kept him on the trail of the humans, Kong might be able to escape. There had to be more humans to the east. Could he get to them soon enough? More questions, more ifs. Not good. It was better to take his chances without blood tonight than it was to face a starving, raving mad Piao in mortal combat. Kong spun on a dime and headed east, being ever careful to disturb as little of the brush as possible so as not to leave Piao a clear trail to follow.

* * *

Cai, reunited with the owl, swept over the forest just under the canopy. He caught a glimpse of one of the demons turning east, off the trail and into the heart of the tree and underbrush laden landscape. A moment later Cai heard a loud crash and a booming scream that he was sure could only be heard in nightmares. As he urged the owl to travel further north in the direction of the frightening howls now echoing through the forest, Cai eventually began to see a human form through the sharp eyes of his flying companion.

His winged friend perched on a limb just above the human-like monster. The beast's face was contorted in pain, its fangs showing as it yelled into the night. A hand, with talon like fingernails, attached to a huge arm with a bicep that bulged in the faint moonlight peering through the leaves, gripped a

111

branch that was at least an inch in diameter. The branch had driven itself into one side of the demon's thigh and was protruding out the other.

***

Piao pulled furiously at the wood lodged in and through his right thigh. He felt weak—sick—as if he were merely human once again. The missed meal upon rising, coupled with this excruciating pain was almost too much to bear. The lack of feeding had caused this in the first place. Had he been at full strength, he wouldn't have stumbled off the path and crashed into the fallen tree and its nasty limbs.

With a monstrous last yank he managed to free the injurious object from his leg. The effort had taxed him heavily, and Piao lay on the forest floor, trying to gather himself. With great pain and a menace in his voice he screamed into the dark. "I will find you, Kong! I will kill you! Do you hear me? I am your death!" After a moment Piao rose to his feet. His thirst for blood and hatred for Kong was stronger than ever. "I am coming for you, Kong! I will not be stopped!" As if he were uninjured, Piao raced back onto the trail.

***

Cai wondered who Kong was. He must be the smaller demon that had darted east moments ago. Yes, that was it, the larger beast had screamed it as he started pursuing the other from Fanzhou. Cai slipped back into his own body and opened his eyes.

Xiong had returned and was discussing things with Ling and Biao. From the gist of the conversation, Cai caught that Zhan was in agreement with their plan to take on the two demons that pursued the escaped prisoners heading toward them. They were to immediately escort the group, along with themselves, back home if all went well.

"We must hurry, my brothers. The beast nears the humans even faster than I had imagined," Cai said, startling his brothers who had not noticed that he had come out of his trance. Ling, always joking around for the most part, but deadly serious when he needed to be, caught the lack of plural in the word beast.

"You mean beasts?" Ling asked.

"There is only one now," Cai answered.

"And the other?" Biao asked.

"He turned east. I believe he was trying to avoid any contact with the other. His fear of the larger demon chasing him seemed to outweigh his thirst."

"Cai and Ling, when we reach the villagers you will stay with them and guide them toward our home," Biao stated.

"Why don't I get to come?" Ling asked in disgust.

"In case the other demon changes course and tries to grab one of the humans. No one is faster, or more accurate with a bow than you. I don't think Cai's skills will be of much use if the other one decides to change his route," Biao said, understanding Ling's yearning to fight, but knowing that his being left behind was for the best.

"Oh, alright! Come back alive will ya. I don't like it, but you have a point," Ling answered, clearly disappointed.

"Cai, mount up! We have people to save!" Biao yelled.

"And garbage to take out!" Xiong added.

Xiong and Biao crouched down, scanning the path and surrounding tree line for any sign of the demon. Ling and Cai were with the former citizens of Fanzhou, leading them further south toward the village next to their monastery. Xiong and Biao would join them as soon as an unwanted parasite had been eradicated.

Xiong and Biao could hear the heavy footfalls of the demon coming. The beast made no attempt to conceal his pursuit, as if he believed he had nothing to fear. Biao gave Xiong some hand signals letting him know to keep an eye out for the other demon, then the older brother stepped out onto the path to ready himself to greet the enemy. Biao tightened his grip on the spear he held and confronted the fast approaching form.

Piao slowed his pace, believing his starved, crazed mind was playing tricks on him. The figure ahead was clearly too large to be Kong. It must be a human from the pack that had headed south. *How convenient. Apparently, dinner is served.* "You should not have stopped! I will end this quickly for you though, brave, yet foolish one." Piao saw the man, nearly his size, heft a spear into throwing position. He remembered Ju-Long stating to him and the other warriors that wood was their enemy, and winced at the memory the tree limb had just caused him. Along with the fact that this man stood his ground with such confidence, made Piao pause.

Biao stared into the demon's eyes as the beast stopped. A standoff. He had no worries about what else was around—his younger brother had his back. "You are doomed, mortal. That pathetic weapon will not save you from me! Did you fashion it yourself, hoping it would bring favor from your people if you brought down a monster such as I?" the demon challenged. "I will feast on your blood, use the point to clean your flesh from my teeth, then impale your head upon it and carry it with me as I slaughter your people one by one!"

"We shall see," Biao answered. "Come now, you promised to be quick about it!" The creature launched itself at him, flying though the air just beneath the tree limbs and covering the thirty odd feet between them in a single bound. Caught by the surprise of how fast the creature actually was, Biao didn't have time to take aim and throw, so he quickly went to a two hand grip and caught the beast as it came down upon him.

The demon let out a blood curdling yell as Biao's spear sank through its right shoulder and ripped out the other side. The weight and force of the demon made Biao stagger backward, but he managed to stay on his feet. The creature writhed in pain, its feet still off the ground, suspended in the air by Biao's spear and awesome strength. "Gotcha! Does it hurt? It sure looks painful to me!" Biao's words seemed to gain the demon's attention as its hands collapsed on the spear and snapped it in half. The two fell backward away from each other and crashed to the ground simultaneously. Biao rolled almost instantly to his feet, his back to the demon, just in time to see a blur leap over his head. As he whirled around to face the beast again, he saw Xiong standing over the creature gripping a spear that was buried deep into the monsters chest and beyond.

The demon grasped at the spear Xiong held for a moment, let out a gurgled cry, then went limp. "You killed it!" Biao said, sarcastically.

"Sorry. I didn't mean to spoil your fun, but you had your chance, so I took the opening." Xiong answered, releasing the spear, but leaving it buried in the creature's chest.

"My fault. Next time I won't try to showboat. I underestimated the enemy. It won't happen again."

"I know. Believe me, I had no idea they were that fast, or that strong. Thank the gods it was only the one." Xiong said.

"Good work, little bro. Let's see if we can catch the others," Biao said, giving Xiong a slight bow.

"Yeah, Ling will want all the details! Race ya?" Xiong exclaimed.

"Sure, why not!" Biao answered. He stuck out a foot and tripped Xiong as he tried to rush by. While his little brother sprawled to the ground, Biao raced ahead. He could hear his younger sibling yelling after him as he sped down the trail.

"That was dirty! It's on now, big bro!"

CHAPTER 9

The water from the rains had seeped in to fill the low lying spot in the forest that Kong had made his resting place just before dawn. He had hoped that the cover from the trees above as well as the foliage he had uprooted and pulled over him would be enough to protect him from the sun. Apparently, coupled with the overcast day, it had. The water was nearly up to his ears. Kong struggled to move, his whole body felt cold and stiff. It took several tries and great effort for him to achieve a sitting position. It was if his joints had locked up, he could hear the bones grinding against one another. Kong had effectively escaped Piao, but had failed to find food last night. He knew he was close to a village, but he had run out of time as the sun trapped him just a short distance from the blood he so desperately needed.

Kong struggled to his feet, fighting more than just the hunger, but his pain racked body. Using small trees for balance, he stumbled east. Kong realized that he was not anywhere near full speed and strength, and his head felt light and dizzy. He would have to find a weak victim, and remain undetected by any others until he fed. An old, feeble woman or a small child would be all he could handle until then.

Kong slipped down into a clearing, huts lined up and down the valley below him. Struggling with every movement, he took cover behind some bushes and scanned the area for an easy kill. The village was quiet. He must have been out longer than usual, for in the early hours of darkness, most villages were still active. This one was dead, though he could smell humans, probably in their homes for the night.

The rain had stopped, and the moon, almost full, was starting to peak out from behind the clouds. Maybe it had been the rain that had kept everyone inside? Kong hoped someone would emerge soon or he would be forced to risk entering one of the dwellings in search of food.

As he waited impatiently, Kong ran his hands through his hair, trying to remove some of the wetness caused by the rain. It felt as if he had rubbed his head with tree bark. He drew his hands in front of his face and found them covered with hair. His hair was falling out! He wiped his hands off on his garments and looked again. His hands appeared withered and bruised. The skin on his knuckles was cracked and laid open. He had seen this on humans who had been dead for a while, the flesh beginning to rot off the bones. He was dying.

Something large and furry slammed into him. He could feel the bone in his upper left arm snap from the impact and hear his ribs crack under the weight of his assailant. Huge jaws applied tremendous pressure to his throat, huge teeth ripping into his flesh. Sharp claws slashed across his abdomen, shredding meat and skin. Kong beat the beast with his right fist, having little to no impact other than to cause the beast to tear out half his throat in one powerful bite.

His spine was splintered, and his body trembled, unable to move no matter how hard he tried. The tiger struck again, taking what was left of his neck into its jaws, cleaving his head from his body with a second bite.

Several armed men from the village ran out of the huts. They had heard the roar of the tiger and came to drive it away or destroy it. They rushed toward the giant animal, yelling and screaming, hoping to scare it off without a fight. It was dark, not the best time to tangle with such a huge and deadly beast, whose night vision was far superior to theirs. Better to drive it away and hunt it down after the sun came up.

They watched the creature crouch into a defensive stance over its prey. It had taken a victim already tonight. They were too late. It was too dark and too far away to make out who it was lying on the ground beneath the tiger, but it had to be one of theirs, just a matter of who.

The tiger roared again as more men emerged from their huts. It seemed to assess the odds and didn't like them. It backed away reluctantly before turning and bounding up the small hill into the tree line.

***

Xiong took command over the second watch. They had traveled through the night and all day. The escaped prisoners had been on the run for over twenty-four hours, and they were exhausted. With Zhan letting him know that there seemed to be no present danger they had made camp and gotten some overdue rest.

Biao relayed to him that all had been quiet during the first watch. The sun rose. Ling was helping some early risers gather food. "Holy and mighty one, would it be safe enough now to light a fire? We need to heat water and I know you forbid fire during the night so that we would not attract attention to ourselves. But the sun now rises." A frail middle-aged woman asked, bowed before him.

"I think a fire would be good now. You can call me Xiong, and you don't have to kneel when you speak to me."

The woman did not rise or look up. "You are obviously a monk, and if the story I hear about you and your brother beating one of those demons is true, than you are more than mighty. You—you are all our saviors."

"I appreciate your high praise, but we are not saviors. We will do all we can to help you and your people, but the demons are still out there. They still number in the hundreds. We did manage to slay one of them when we came to you that first night, but my brothers and I will not be enough to stand alone and stop them when they come in force."

"I know. I know maybe better than you the death and destruction they will bring. I watched as they massacred my husband, all six of my sons, and two of my daughters." She looked up at him with haunted eyes. Xiong reached out a hand and helped her to her feet, pulling her into a protective hug. She sobbed against his chest.

"We are still alive, so there is still a chance. I will not concede defeat to these creatures until I have drawn my last breath," Xiong said. "I only wish I could have done something to stop them before they took your family from you. I am sure they fought like the brave warriors they were."

The woman drew back and looked into his eyes, tears flowing down her cheeks. "We must eradicate them, so my lost loved ones will not have to know them in their next existence." She lowered her head against his chest and continued to weep. Xiong held her until she drew back. "I suppose that will be enough of that. I will go help the others start the fires. Thank you. Even if we don't make it, thank you for your help and kindness."

As she walked away, Biao approached. "Up already?" Xiong asked.

"Couldn't really sleep. Had you not been there, my stupid toying with that demon could have meant my end."

"I will always be there. Just like you would for me." Xiong stretched and yawned.

"Still tired?" Biao asked.

"Nope, just bored. After the thrill of two nights ago, pulling watch was almost painfully boring."

"No sign of the other demon then?"

"None. And that was the worst part. I was hoping to go two up on you last night."

"Hey, I at least get credit for half that first one. I did soften him up for you."

Xiong laughed. "Sorry, cheaters never prosper."

"You talking about the race last night? You still caught up and beat me!"

"And I also am taking full credit for the kill." Xiong smiled. Biao lowered his head, shaking it from side to side. "Hey, ease up. I was only joking."

"You are hanging out with Ling too much. His smart ass is starting to rub off on ya."

"Look who's talking, Mr. let's tease the demon on the stick." They both laughed. Xiong shot out a hand. "Together."

"Together." Biao clasped his hand around Xiong's.

"It's not a competition. The only goal is to make sure we keep each other alive."

"Thanks, Xiong. Thanks for having my back that night."

"Always." The two let go of each other and gave a slight bow.

"Cai is awake as well. He has gone to meditate and commune with the animals. He wants us to get him when food is available."

"I think I will find a quiet place myself and reach out to Zhan. Fetch me when breakfast is ready." Xiong headed off across their makeshift camp.

***

The owl had flown him back and forth down the trail toward Fanzhou. All was quiet. He needed his flying friend to take him into Fanzhou now, because when the group he was helping escort traveled further south after breakfast, he was sure he would be unable to commune with his rodent friend one last time. He left his winged companion as they crossed over the outer wall of the city and quickly found his companion. The rat was both terrified and in mourning at the same time. Cai just observed for a moment as the rat sniffed and nudged at dead body after dead body, many of his companions mutilated and ripped apart. Something or someone had destroyed well over half the rat population in Fanzhou. Had the demons attempted to feed on their blood before they departed? Or had they figured out that the rats chewed through the ropes and set their captives free, deciding to exact a cruel revenge on the only creatures left in Fanzhou?

Who did this, friend? The demon-like men? The rat did not respond, but stayed on the search for any of his kind that were left alive. *I am so sorry. I did not think the demons would come after you. Please accept my apology.*

The rat opened himself up to Cai now. It was not the demons who had done this. They had fled almost instantly when they found their cupboards dry of human blood. No human or beast had re-entered the city since then. It had been the rat's own kind that caused this atrocity. The rats that had eaten the flesh of the sleeping demons did this. They had gone into convulsions a few hours after they escaped the burning building. When they came out of it they were crazed, attacking the other rats and anything in their path without mercy. Only Cai's companion and about thirty others had survived the ensuing onslaught. The maddened rats had fled the city a couple hours after true dark. Cai's friend was the only survivor not still in hiding. He had led those he could to safety, but now felt an obligation as pack leader to search for any others that remained alive.

Cai reached out with his mind. Save a few snakes, the only remaining life forms in the area were a pack of rats huddled together in the place his friend had left them. Cai relayed this information to his furry companion and implored him to return to the others and lead them as far away from Fanzhou as possible.

***

Hu and Kun were paired together. They had been best friends since childhood and had been on many hunts together. There had only been a couple like this. Tigers, for some, were sacred creatures. Gods if you will. The two young men had always held the majestic beasts in high regard themselves. For the most part among their people, these huge cats were revered and left alone. Unfortunately, this particular one had killed a human. Though it turned out the tiger's victim was not one of their own, the attack could not go unanswered. The elder men of the village, their council, felt that it would only be a matter of time before it struck one of their own. It had a taste for human flesh now.

The man's body, left where it lay when no one claimed it until it could be burned during the day, had been stolen before they arose. Even with sentries posted, it was clear the tiger had come back to claim her prize.

Hu hoped that the tiger had moved on beyond the lands that surrounded them. He did not want to face the tiger for many reasons. His very name, Hu, meant tiger in their language. His father and brothers had always respected the beast's majesty. Three of the village elders who had lost small children to the last tiger that plagued their village did not feel the same way, and via a vote the hunters were in the woods.

There were a total of twelve men in the forest searching in pairs for the tiger. Once the beast was spotted, the men that found it were to alert the others through a series of whistles.

"Kun, not so close to that thick brush," Hu whispered. "Wide circle around it." Hu drew a circle in the air with his index finger. Both men were tall, over six feet each, but Hu was bulkier by twenty pounds, all of it muscle. They had faced many an opponent together, but Hu's size as well as experience made him the leader of the two.

Kun turned back toward Hu, and Kun's eyes grew wide. The sudden look of shock and terror on his face could only mean something bad. Hu whirled around, spear at the ready, and spotted the tiger. Kun regained himself and let out a series of whistles. The tiger had silently crept up on them and was ready to pounce. It stood on a small knoll, just eight feet from Hu. Hu tried to whistle himself, but no sound came from his suddenly dry lips.

The tiger's body coiled before it sprang right at him. Its powerful legs allowed the beast to cover the short distance in a single bound. Kun drove his shoulder into Hu. Hu was thrown to one side, out of harm's way for the moment. The move kept Hu from being leveled by the mighty beast, but left Kun exposed to bear the full weight of the tiger coming down on him.

Kun's move to protect his friend had put his sword in an ineffective position. As the mighty beast landed upon him, one gigantic paw on his face, the other ripping claws into his chest, Kun's sword fell uselessly to the ground. Kun was defenseless as he and the huge predator slammed onto the forest floor. Hu watched in awe as he quickly scooted backward on his hands and bottom. He watched the tiger rip his friend's face and torso apart.

Hu's spear had been knocked from his hand when Kun shoved him out of the way. Scrambling to his feet, Hu managed to work his sword from its sheath and discovered the voice he had momentarily lost. "Help! Over here! Tiger! Tiger! Help us!" The tiger let out a low growl and turned its head toward Hu. The beast's face was dripping with blood, a hunk of his friends flesh hanging from its jaws. Hu rolled to the left as the tiger sprang toward him. The beast seemed to turn in midair, catching the back of Hu's leg with its right front paw. Hu cried out in agony as the big cat's claws' shredded his calf muscle.

More by instinct, from years of training and play fighting with Kun and his brothers, than from actual thought process, Hu rolled up into a hobbled standing position as the tiger moved on him again. He brought the sword around in line with the tiger's head. His defense was too late. The tiger caught Hu's sword arm in its powerful mandibles, and with what seemed like a simple flip of its neck muscles, sent the young man flying into the trees to the right.

Hu's back slammed into a large tree, stopping his flight and leaving him crumpled on the ground. He nearly passed out as he saw his arm hanging from his body in an unnatural position. The bone from his wrist to his elbow was cleanly snapped in two. Blood flowed freely from the wound the tiger's bite had caused, a large portion of tissue missing from his forearm.

Hu heard the thud of several arrows as they pierced the tiger's side. The tiger roared and staggered a moment, but recovered quickly and turned in the direction from which the projectiles had come. A second volley of shafts hurtled through the air, two sailing by the beast harmlessly, one striking the tiger's shoulder, and the fourth hitting home in the creature's breast just below its massive neck. A spear, launched from the tiger's right side, found its mark. The beast roared again, breathing heavy and falling to its left. As it lay there unable to regain its feet, one last arrow struck home sinking deeply into its eye socket. The tiger stopped moving, stopped breathing.

Hu began to lose focus. He could see several men standing over him, but could not make out their faces. He was either dying or going into shock. The voices of the men seemed distant, but he could feel their hands on him, lifting him, carrying him. "We must get him back to the village quickly!" was the last thing Hu heard as the world faded from grey to black.

***

I hear you, Xiong. I am here.

I bring news that all is well with us. We have not, to our knowledge, lost a single member of the group. We are still a week or so away from the monastery traveling at this pace. Is there anything new on your end?

Since we last communicated I have tried to further investigate our foes with the information Cai was able to obtain. From what I can tell these creatures do in fact die in a sense, with the break of dawn, rising again as darkness falls over the land. During daylight they seem to be completely vulnerable.

There was a long pause, as if Zhan was giving his younger brother a chance to speak. Xiong knew that was not the case. He could sense something was troubling his eldest brother. The silence seemed to grow deeper and deeper. It went on for so long that for a moment Xiong thought he must have lost contact.

What is it, Zhan? Xiong whispered through their minds. Slowly, Zhan began to explain what else he had discovered.

Xiong, as you know, my ability to see things, see into other peoples' minds, is limited to the living. I do not have the knowledge or power to communicate with the dead. That is why I could never be certain as to what happened to these demons at sunrise. They disappeared from me because they died. Now, I have found that I can walk among them during the day, see them first hand as they rest. I can do this because they are now joined by humans who have been bent to do their will. In exchange for their cooperation, the humans are given strength and speed beyond normal human levels. They are not demons themselves, yet they aren't truly human either. It seems as we attempt to solve the riddle of how to extinguish these creatures, they uncover secrets to their survival.

The first night only one of these servants was created. I call them servants, but they are more like slaves. They follow the orders of the one called Ju-Long without question. The second night he created a dozen more. I have yet to make contact with them today, but I am sure that number will continue to grow. The demon army has reunited with their leader in the north. They are holding up in a large cave by day and attacking a nomadic people, the Xia tribe, by night.

But Zhan, I do not understand why humans would freely join these demons.

In some humans, evil is as thick as a demon's. The choice, never the less, is more of an ultimatum. They may either partake in the ritual that transforms them, or simply be killed.

You said ritual that transforms? What ritual?

The humans are forced to drink the blood of the one called Ju-Long. It is as if there is a power transfer, with the strength and speed of the humans increasing. They do not become as powerful, or exactly like their creator. They possess no fangs or thirst for blood. They eat as normal humans eat, however they seem to require no sleep. I believe they can be killed in the same manner as any man, yet their powers would certainly make it more difficult. On this part I am not so sure, for I have yet to see them in combat. It appears that they are merely daytime guardians at this point.

Have they figured out how to make their own yet?" Xiong asked, hoping the answer was no.

Not exactly. It has happened accidently once, but they have no knowledge of its existence. It happened in Dulan. The new demon is nowhere near them, but he accidently created another as well. A female.

It is good that they do not know yet, especially the one called Ju-Long. However, it bothers me that this plague has still found some small way to spread. The new ones will have to be dealt with as well if we are to end this.

Yes, but at another time. Ju-Long and his army is our only agenda now.

I agree. I am troubled by how far this will eventually spread before we can stop it.

As am I. They both were silent for a moment. *Also, the other demon that chased you, Kong, is dead. He was attempting to escape the demon named Piao that you and Biao killed. Kong was terrified of him, so he turned east as Cai had noticed while communing with the owl. He failed to find blood to feed on, but still rose the next night, though in a weekend condition. As he looked over a small village trying to pick out an easy target, he became a meal himself. A large female tiger attacked and destroyed him.*

Interesting. Xiong paused, taking the new information in. *I will relay this to our brothers before we break camp today. Is there anything else before I go?*

The demons are not near you now, but you are still far from home. It would not be hard for them to catch the group before you reach us. Don't let your guard down. Travel safely, but hastily. Call on me when you reach your next stop. If I need you before then, I will initiate contact.

Xiong rounded up his brothers and relayed what Zhan had told him as they ate breakfast. Xiong allowed several of the men from Fanzhou to listen in on the conversation. The men had numerous questions. Xiong answered most of them before kindly letting them know that in time he would answer all their inquiries, but for now it was time to run. Within the hour they were on the move again.

***

Tung and Yue-Yan reached civilization. They followed and fed off Yue-Yan's people for over a week. The apir had learned a lesson or two along the way, the most important one being that they had to stay out of the sun in this new form they possessed. Feeling exhausted as dawn approached one morning, they decided to lie down under the cover of a large clump of trees. As the sun rose, small rays shot here and there through the leaves. One of the beams hit Tung's arm and he woke, howling at the burning sensation. Yue-Yan woke to the sound of his screams. Tung rolled over on his side, grabbing his arm. A second ray of light hit his cheek, the flesh charring black as his screams intensified. He raised his hand to his face, only to feel it start to burn.

Yue-Yan first stared in disbelief. "What's happening, Tung?" He continued to howl like a banshee. His skin seemed to be smoldering in spots. She reached a hand over to place it on the one he had covering his face. Before she could touch him, her hand started to burn. Screaming, she yanked it back, the pain still there but easing. She looked at the charred skin, then looked at Tung's hand, which was almost completely black and smoking. "What the . . . " She stopped midsentence, noticing that the only place he was burning was where the sun peeked through and hit him. She used her uninjured hand to grab him by the shirt and drag him deeper under cover until they were both completely out of its rays. Tung was marked in all the places the sun's light had touched him. He had stopped wailing and now gently moaned into her chest as she cradled him to her.

She thought about what had happened and realized that they would never walk in the sun again. Somehow the change had affected them in such a way that while they were more powerful than ever before, they were now punished by the sun for what they were. As she pondered this she found herself unable to keep her eyes open, and slept until the sun had once again gone down.

When they arose, Tung's skin on his hand, arm, and face were scarred from the earlier injuries. While they no longer hurt, they were both worried that his face, once so perfect, would be permanently ruined. After feeding that night, however, his wounds started to heal, and now, as she looked at him, his skin was back to its flawless perfection.

They stared at each other for a moment as they awoke from their resting place on the outskirts of the city. The thought of sex was heavy on both of their minds, but they had something else to deal with first. The thirst. Quickly, they stood and went on the prowl for the one thing they craved even more than each other . . . blood.

They had slipped into the city shortly after rising and quickly found a target. A lone guard stood in front of a building that must have housed something or someone of importance. Yue-Yan, her black, silky, waist length hair pulled back in a loose ponytail acted as the bait. The guard, a young, ruggedly handsome man, stood motionless at his post. His eyes darted back and forth as he continuously scanned the dark for any sign of trouble.

Tung and Yue-Yan entered the back of a storehouse across from the building where the guard was posted. Yue-Yan started to giggle like a young child, giddy with the thought of the plan. Tung spun her around and placed his index finger to her dry lips. She fell silent, but a devious, sexy smile crossed her face. Tung moved his finger and pressed his mouth to hers. The kiss was rough, not from the force of it, but from the cold, hard feel of their unfed bodies. They broke from the lifeless kiss knowing something was wrong, but also how to fix it.

"Go and fetch our young man, my love. We shall pick back up where we left off after we have sated our hunger," Tung whispered.

Yue-Yan turned around slowly and moved to the front entrance. She slid off her clothes and draped them over a large crate. Tung slid into the shadows not far from the door. Yue-Yan carefully eased the door open just enough to peek out, and scanned the street in search of any unwanted company. The area was quiet, and satisfied they were safe from witnesses, she fixed her gaze upon her prey.

Pushing the door open further, less carefully this time allowing it to let out a whispering creak, she drew the man's attention. He snapped into a defensive stance, drawing his sword in one swift motion. Even over the ten meters that separated them, Yue-Yan could sense the man's pulse quicken. Her body yearned to embrace that pulse, feel that heartbeat fast in her mouth.

Yue-Yan pulled her hair free from the ponytail, letting it spill over her shoulder and around part of her face as she edged a little more of herself out the door. The man took two steps closer, lowering his sword, but keeping it out and ready. Yue Yan let a smooth, shapely leg curl around the door, exposing enough of her hip to let him know there was nothing covering her lower body. The man paced closer, his eyes going from her to the surrounding area, checking for others as well. When his eyes met her again they found a smile on her face. She winked at him and moved out just enough to let the outer curve of her ample breast show. He stopped just feet from her, looking around quickly once more. She eased out a little further, until her navel, small and perfect lying on a flat, firm stomach showed. She saw his eyes grow wide and wild with excitement as he took in the beauty of her nakedness. She put her hand out and coaxed him forward with a finger. She could sense the blood that now flowed into lower parts of his body.

Slowly she backed into the storehouse, never taking her eyes off her prey. He stopped just inside, one foot in and one foot out of the doorway. Yue-Yan stroked her hand over her breasts, lingering there for a moment untll slowly gliding them down her body. She buried one hand into her thick, shiny pubic halr until she found the right spot and began stroking her fingers up and down. "Come to me," she whispered. "I need you. Come inside me."

Tung moved further into the shadows and listened, still undetected by their victim. He could hear the sound of a sword going back into its sheath. Yue-Yan gave a very quick glance in his direction, accompanied with a smile to let him know the game was approaching its thrilling climax.

Yue-Yan knelt down on the floor. "Close the door and let me help you out of those clothes." She smiled. The young guard did her bidding. "I want to feel you, taste your manhood in my mouth," she pleaded as he obeyed her request. "Come to me."

The guard stepped closer, looking to and fro in the room to make sure there wasn't a trap. He had never seen a woman so forward, and this left him wary. The young man eased toward her, until the cloth surrounding his groin nearly touched her face. Yue-yan could see that he was hard and ready underneath it.

"I am going to make you forget every trouble you ever had," she said as she tugged his pants down around his ankles. He casually stepped out of them and widened his stance. His manhood stuck straight out begging for whatever part of her would take in his length.

Yue-Yan nuzzled the side of her head into his thigh allowing her long soft hair to swim around his groin. "Yes," he sighed. "Put me in your mouth and let me feel its wet warmth."

Tung quietly slipped behind him. The young sentry was too occupied by what he felt was his greatest conquest to date. Tung watched as he saw Yue-Yan flick her tongue at the tip of the guard's growth. He could feel a stirring begin below his waist. They would feed and then he would take her.

Yue-Yan forced the guard's legs further apart. Dropping her head lower she started kissing just above the man's knee, then slowly glided her wet tongue upward toward his groin, the pulse in his inner thigh making her salivate heavily. She traced circles inside his inner thigh until she found the place where the pulse was strongest. Like music, it called to her as if it was actually singing her name.

"Stop teasing me, woman. You wanted me. Please me," the young man growled, slapping his hand across her face. Tung, now directly behind the guard, clamped one hand over the guard's mouth to stifle any screams and used the other hand to tilt the man's head, exposing the sweet, soft flesh of the neck. Simultaneously Yue-Yan sunk her fangs into the man's thigh as Tung bit firmly into his neck. They both gulped in the salty sweetness like a hungry infant suckling from its mother's breast. The guard futilely struggled against them, driving his fist into the side of Yue-Yan's face again and again to no avail. When Tung noticed this he reached down and caught the young man's arm, snapping it instantly.

The pair continued to feed, each feeling their lover's pull as they fed. Tung glanced down and caught Yue-Yan's gaze as she stared up into his eyes. They both began to suck at their meal harder as if it were now a contest. Who would get the most blood? Yue-Yan had proved herself his equal, if not his dominant already in the short time they had been together. It was important that she kept that edge, so she drank furiously. Yue-Yan had spent her previous life being dominated and pushed around by men. From her father, who had raped her since she was just a child, to her brothers and the husband she was forced to marry by family arrangement. She would never again allow that to happen. She resented her past, she hated being ordered around as if she didn't matter, and she refused to ever be subjected to that kind of treatment again.

It wasn't that she wanted to dominate Tung, or attempt to make him submissive, but to make sure he saw her as an equal and not an object. Tung was easily the most beautifully handsome man she had ever met, and even though their relationship was not yet two weeks old, she loved him. Even feeling the way she did about him she wanted to be at his side, not a servant at his feet.

Yue-Yan drank faster and faster until she thought she would choke. Her stomach was full, the thirst quenched, but she kept drinking. Her head began to swim in a dizzying rush and she felt nauseated. Yue-Yan was caught between agony and ecstasy, but she was winning.

Tung withdrew his fangs from the man's neck. Fresh blood coursed through his veins and even though he felt light headed, he knew life and strength had returned to him in the fullest. He was drunk on the power in the same way he had felt when he had consumed too much rice wine in his previous existence, only better. He felt as if he could make love all night, or beat two dozen men single handedly with ease.

Tung punched through the man's back, stealing the heart from its place as his arm protruded through the other side. "For you my love." He smiled as he let the blood from it drip onto Yue-Yan's face. She rose up on her knees, licking greedily along his forearm and working her way slowly, meticulously to his hand. She nibbled and lapped at the guard's heart until Tung pulled his arm back through the man's body and shoved him to the side. With his other hand Tung drew Yue-Yan to her feet and into his now warm embrace.

The two locked into a kiss with their blood stained lips and tongue's exploring each other's eagerly. Yue-Yan took the heart from his hand and stepped away from him. "Now I have something for you." She traced the heart along her neck and gave it a gentle squeeze. The remaining blood slipped through her fingers as she rubbed it over her breasts, coating her nipples. She glided the organ down over her navel, circling around it, and into her nether region, allowing the last of the blood to spill over her womanhood before dropping it to the floor.

"Dinner was nice. Come taste the dessert," she cooed. She was always beautiful, but with fresh blood coursing through her veins she was gorgeous. Her skin, once again soft and silky, was without blemish. Tung sucked at the blood on her neck, taking her flesh gently between his lips as he took in the slowly drying blood. He carefully worked his way down, cleaning the blood completely from her breasts and spending extra time as he sucked at her nipples. When he had finished his journey downward he clasped his hands behind her thighs and lifted her off the ground. She instinctively wrapped her legs around his neck and let them hang over his shoulders as he buried his face into her. He slid his hands up and let them encircle her buttocks as he ran his tongue along her wet pussy, bringing soft moans from her throat. Her breathing increased as he continued to play his mouth and lips around her clit. Yue-Yan gripped the hair behind his head and rode him as his tongue flicked in, out and over her vagina.

With ease Tung stood, still working his mouth over her as she bowed over him, her hands shifting to claw her nails into his back. He lowered her onto a short stack of bags filled with rice and withdrew his tongue from her.

From her back Yue-Yan looked up at him and smiled. Tung returned a smile of his own, before burying his face between her legs again with renewed vigor. She shuddered as he took her lips between his teeth and gave them a gentle bite. She ran her hands through his hair frantically, beckoning him upward.

"Take me. Take me now!" she pleaded.

Tung walked his body up hers on his hands and toes, nibbling here and there over her chest as her breath came in pants. With just his lips he sucked at a small pool of coagulating blood that he had previously missed and sat clinging to her chin. Finally their mouths met and she eagerly accepted his tongue. Once again their kiss was warm, soft, wet and full of life.

Tung raised his hips and positioned himself over her, the tip of his manhood rubbing along her opening. Yue-Yan let out a moan and wrapped her legs around his waist. With a heavy sigh she pulled his body towards her forcing the length of him all the way in. Working together they found their rhythm, her hips rising to meet his downward stroke perfectly. Within moments both could feel the ecstasy rise between them. Yue-Yan clawed and raked her nails along his back as she felt him swell even larger inside her. Tung could feel the pressure building as she squealed under him, riding wave after wave of pleasure. Yue-Yan found a spot just below his nipple and sank her fangs in. Her entire body shook as he erupted into her with the first of many orgasms.

***

Ju-Long was still infuriated by the fact that he had lost over a hundred of his men. He felt no compassion for the ones who had fallen, but anger because his army dwindled without him knowing the secret of how to create more of his own kind. Kong was a failure, worthless in every way. He hoped Piao had found the miserable little wretch and removed the weak link in the chain.

Whatever happened in Fangzhou would never happen again. Ju-Long did know how to turn the humans into his own personal servants, slaves that would watch over them during the hours of daylight. He had converted twenty-five from among the ranks of the army of his former people. What a delicious irony. He turned those who were sworn and under orders by the

Xia council to kill him on sight into men that would protect him from that very fate.

Ju-Long watched his warriors storm the latest camp of Xia soldiers to fall victim to their blood cravings. Recently, he had given up on trying to hold a large number of prisoners. His men were on the move constantly now, with no city to return to. Fangzhou was compromised, just as Dulan had been. There were plenty of humans to feed on in the surrounding area, and with their daytime guards they only needed to find a place—a cave, cavern, or building—large enough for them to hide from the sun.

Ju-Long willed his body upward, rising into the air with the slightest of effort. He rode the night sky, observing the chaos below. Women screaming, crying, men drawing their swords, only to have them, and the arms that held them, ripped from their bodies. All the sounds of terror, the howls of his men, the pleading of their victims were a symphony in his honor. As Ju-Long loomed high above them, he realized he was a god. He was a god and below stood his subjects, even the humans. Some would be chosen to become like his soldiers, once he solved the mystery of their creation, others would become servants and guardians. Many would be enslaved in time, doing the work he considered to be beneath his warriors. Most, however, would provide the ultimate sacrifice, the blood that brought them life would be consumed to ensure the survival of Ju-Long and his minions.

Ju-Long scanned the surrounding area for any stray Xia soldiers that might have slipped through the loop and were attempting to escape. Quon and Yun-Qui, the two that had been with him when they defeated the dragon, were already airborne and on the lookout. It was extremely important that they keep everyone in the camp they were invading contained. If even a single man evaded their net and warned other camps, it would not be long until the entire Xia army was breathing down their necks. He knew that with his decreased numbers his warriors could ill afford to confront such a large host. Even worse was the thought of the Xia army stumbling across their daytime lair and destroying them while they lie defenseless. His servants would sacrifice their lives trying to protect him, but they would hardly be enough to stop an entire army.

Ju-Long intended to take out as many camps as he could before the Xia council learned of his work. If all went well, their army would be devastated, their full number cut in half, before he made his assault on them personally. He also hoped to discover the means by which he could create more xiang shi before he faced them.

***

Fa lay on his side, hiding in the thick underbrush, hiding from the world and the demons who had found their way into it. His camp had been raided by these creatures last night. Fa had been wounded, but not fatally. He had played dead, and when no one was watching, he dragged the remains of another dead soldier over his chest and face to hide his breathing.

After the battle the beast had come back through checking for any survivors. By the grace of the gods he was not discovered. Fa lay under the bloody remains of his fallen comrade even after they left. Too frightened to move, he just waited and waited. He finally passed out, and awoke around mid-day. As Fa sat up he could feel excruciating pain in his ribs. There were broken ones on his right side, that he was sure of. His hair was matted with blood, some his own, some from the dead man he had hidden beneath.

As he walked, each step brought tears to his eyes. Along with his ribs, he could see the swelling in his left ankle, and feel the grinding of bones therein. He ignored the pain and traveled as fast as he could, desperate to reach another camp. He needed to sound the alarm, alert all of his people to the threat of these demons, who, if he heard correctly, were being led by the one the Xia council had exiled and ordered to be put to death if captured.

Unfortunately, his injuries had slowed him down enough that he hadn't reached anyone. If only he had a steed, but the demons had either destroyed or driven off every horse in his camp. Just after nightfall he heard the demons coming from behind him. Fa dove under some heavy brush that had grown up around a fallen tree and lay as still as possible as the beastly army stormed by him. With amazing speed and agility they were jumping rocks and dodging tress like a fast animal that knew the forest well from living in it all its life.

They had sailed past him several hours ago, but he had no intention of moving from this spot yet. He was severely fatigued, and while terrified by the thought of being discovered if they came back this way, Fa closed his eyes and tried to sleep. Tomorrow he could travel again, and hopefully find someone soon. Someone with a horse, who would listen to his warnings and help him alert as many of the Xia as they could. He might even be able to deliver the message as far as the Xia council camped to the north.

CHAPTER 10

Huang-Fu led his family, and his wife, Lin Yao's, parents, southeast without much success of finding a place to call home. Every village they had come to only allowed them to stay a night, his big-mouthed in-laws unable to keep their mouths shut about the demons. The villages sent them packing, calling them lunatics in some places. They shooed them away, afraid that if the demons did exist they would invade the village in search of these wayward travelers.

For the past week they had been following the trail of a large group, easily numbering in the hundreds. It was not a bloody trail, ravaged with bodies of victims, so Huang-Fu assumed the band to be human. He thought they might be like him, a people fleeing their northern homes after escaping the demons. If they were, then they would understand, and hopefully together they could find a way to stop these beasts. Huang-Fu had killed three of them, three that quite possibly were already dead. He would not forget his promise to his late brother. He would not rest, once his family was safe, until he hunted down and killed them all. He wasn't sure how he would do it, but he would see them destroyed. The one thing he was almost certain of was that sooner or later, the demons would come south. Then he would not have to hunt them, for once again he would become the hunted.

***

Hu's wounds from the tiger attack had healed remarkably well in a short period of time. Last night he had felt strange, though. He was restless, especially after sundown. He had horrid night sweats, accompanied with nightmares of the tiger. Both his wife and his mother had been awake most of the night with him, trying to curb his fever. His mother said it must be infection. The wounds were hardly noticeable, but she feared something was tainted inside him, below the surface of the skin. Hu told them not to bother over him. He felt fine. The sweating and dreams were merely post anxiety from the attack. Truth was, physically he felt strong and healthy, but something was indeed wrong. *Strange.*

As darkness fell over the valley, Hu heeded a call to walk alone through the surrounding woods. His wife begged him to stay home, while his brothers offered to go with him. Hu insisted he was fine, that he just needed some time to himself. His mother tried to stop him, but his father intervened. "Woman, your child is no longer a boy, but a man. He has a right to chose his own path, make his own decisions, now leave him be."

The forest seemed cool, with a slight breeze whispering in the trees. Above, through the forest canopy, he could see the stars and clear night skies. The moon loomed overhead, not yet full but shining. As a matter of fact, he had never seen it as bright as it seemed now.

The forest looked more alive than ever before. He could hear everything, amazing sounds he had never before taken time to listen to. He could smell things, too. There was a burrow of rabbits close, hidden from view, but nonetheless there. He could smell them just as plainly as if he were holding one to his nose right now.

Hu took careful steps, moving in near silence. It was the way he had always tried to move when he was on the hunt, though never with as much success as he had now. Hu continued deeper into the woods. He could smell a large animal not too far away. It was feeding on some vegetation, a couple of smaller animals with it. Hu stopped and breathed in deeper through his nostrils. It was a female boar with two offspring. *Prey.*

Hu followed the scent, slipping through the trees quietly, effortlessly. He was downwind of the trio, and he was betting he could get close enough to touch them before they even knew he was there. Hu peeked around a tree and could see them not more than four meters away. He drew in another breath of the night air. There were more boars within the area, a little further off. In numbers, the boar could be dangerous. The males with their tusks were formidable by themselves. Hu was without a weapon. It mattered not, he must have one of the boars. The pull was strong, his hunger insatiable. He wasn't sure how he would kill one of them without a weapon, or how he would elude the males if they decided to give chase. He wasn't sure how, yet he was confident he could.

One of the young would be physically easiest, but if the mother tried to protect her offspring, like she most certainly would, she could sound an alarm that would bring the whole pack of them down on him. The mother, he would take the mother. Hu crept closer, and the large female ventured a little nearer to him. The two young were turned away, playing. Hu sprung over a fallen log that separated them and pounced on the boar's back. She squealed and tried to break free, but with amazing speed and strength he latched onto her head, and with a violent thrust snapped the boar's neck.

The little ones let out a series of high squeals and bolted off into the woods. Hu could hear the rustle of underbrush and the snorts of males moving toward the young. Hu hoisted the female over his shoulder and ran. It was incredible. In the past it would have taken him and another to slowly drag such a large beast out of the forest. Now he moved through the woods at tremendous speeds for a human, carrying a load it would normally require two people to acquire, while navigating the forest's natural obstacles as gracefully as a big cat.

The boars were not giving chase. They had opted to protect the young and accept the loss of one without jeopardizing others. Hu slowed his pace, but kept going until he was certain none had followed.

He covered over half the distance back to the village before he stopped. He tossed the pig near a large rock and sat down, resting his back against a tree. Sweat poured off him, and he was a little out of breath. He sat there in disbelief of what had just happened. There was definitely something strange happening to him.

Hu looked at the pig, a prize kill. His entire family could eat off it and then some. The pig's scent made his saliva glands go crazy, and he began to realize that he had no desire to take it back to the village and prepare it. Hu wanted it now, just like it was, fresh, raw meat. He had no means by which to cut it open, no way to get to the wonderful meat inside. Hu looked around for a sharp rock, anything to tear open the flesh and get to the meal the pig contained for him.

***

Hu's mother pleaded, then argued, and finally demanded that someone go look for Hu. His father finally gave in when she got ready to go herself. Hu's father gathered his brothers and several other friends and relatives to go and search for him. It was nearing dawn, and Hu had been gone since just a short while after nightfall.

They scoured the woods. The sun reached its zenith and still no Hu. Now his father began to worry that his wife had been right. Maybe he should have gone out sooner, or even prevented Hu from going. Guilt overwhelmed him. Hu. His son. Survivor of an attack by a great tiger, lost because his father had not cared enough to prevent him from doing something as foolish as hiking through the woods alone after nightfall.

"Over here, come quickly!" his father heard one of the others yell. Everyone rushed in the direction of the voice. When they arrived, Hu's cousin had his sword drawn, holding it out defensively. Across from him was Hu, with a wild look in his eyes. Hu was covered in blood, snarling at them, as he crouched over the partially eaten remains of a wild pig.

"My, God!" Hu's father gasped as he looked at the horrible sight that was his son. "Hu! What has happened?"

"Go away! The kill is mine, I will not share it with you scavengers!"

"Hu! It is me, your father. Do you not recognize me? These are your brothers, your friends. We mean you no harm. What is wrong, son? Your mother and wife have sent us to find you. They are worried sick. We are worried sick."

Hu scanned the faces of each of the men. They were recognizable. Their scent was familiar. Something inside him began to reside, and the need he had felt to protect his prey just moments ago died down. He looked at his hands, covered in blood, and down at the pigs grisly remains. What had he done? He could remember, but it didn't seem real. His head began to swim and he could see the world fade to black.

Hu's father covered the distance between them quickly, but not near in time to catch his son as he fell to the forest floor. "Quickly, help me! We must get Hu home!"

***

Zhan sat cross-legged in the middle of the monastery's main courtyard. Gan watched his master, teacher, and father figure sit almost motionless for the last sixteen hours in a meditative trance. Zhan had chosen Gan to be with him, keeping all others out of the courtyard in order to prevent unnecessary distractions. Gan himself had been both awake and nearly motionless since late last evening when they had begun. He knew that if he were too loud he might break Zhan's concentration at a critical moment and cause him to miss out on an important piece of information about their opponent.

Zhan had chosen Gan for just that reason. Zhan knew he could count on Gan to manage himself appropriately during this long period of meditation while quietly keeping others from disturbing the work at hand. Gan himself for the majority of the time sat watching his teacher, fascinated by Zhan's patience and discipline. He longed to be like him, to be able to set aside his own hunger, thirst, and personal needs and focus in—giving strict attention to accomplishing his goals.

Zhan was amazed himself by the discipline showed by the young Gan. Most adolescent boys would not have the patience to sit through such a long, boring, and seemingly menial task. While Gan might not have a supernatural gift, he was definitely proving he could focus and accomplish any goals he set for himself.

Zhan had spent most of the night tracking the demons. They had spent their nights as of late attacking and invading nomadic tribes from the north. Over the past ten nights they had slaughtered thousands of soldiers while only losing a dozen of their own men. They still numbered well over three hundred, but as of yet, their numbers were not on the rise.

The one thing that was rising rapidly, however, was their number of daytime guardians. Zhan had watched them increase from one to a dozen, and on up to their current number of fifty-seven. Soon they would have to fight one army just to get to the other.

Zhan had also been keeping an eye on a single man fortunate enough to have escaped the demons onslaught. Fa had wisely given up trying to reach his comrades to the east, who were in the line of camps the demons were attacking night after night. Fa headed north, and during the day yesterday had reached a larger Xia camp, riding a horse that he had stolen from a small band of travelers who had been left homeless by the war that was being waged throughout northern China. If the whole of the Xia army were to flood the area the demons were in all at once, the beasts might be defeated once and for all. The Xia people easily numbered near a million. Unfortunately they were currently spread so thin above The Great Wall that any sizable or smart opponent could rack up victory after victory against them, never having to face the full brunt of the Xia's huge military. This was obviously Ju-Long's plan. Chip away at the huge rock— pounding away at its weakest points, until the rock was small enough to crumble with one single mighty blow.

Zhan knew he could not rely on the refugee making his way to the largest Xia camps. It would take a long time for the message to reach the Xia council, and the separate camps to mobilize and converge on the location of Ju-Long's army, which seemed to change by quite a distance every night. No, that action might never come to pass.

Zhan also realized that there was nothing he and his brothers could do about the situation but wait, study, and prepare for their enemy. The trek north to where the demons were would be a foolhardy one. They still numbered too many to be taken by any small force they could mount, and they currently resided in a war zone. Zhan and his brothers might be wiped out by the Xia people or another faction who did not take kindly to any outsiders. In the north everyone saw the world as us and them, and you killed them every opportunity you got.

"Master Zhan."

Zhan could hear a voice whispering in his ear, yet seemingly a million miles away. He recognized the voice instantly and began to draw his mind back from the far places it reached out to.

"Master Zhan, I am sorry, but it is important," Gan repeated.

"I am here, Gan."

"Master, Cai, Xiong, Biao, and Ling have returned with the large band they traveled with."

"I know, Gan. But thank you, it will be good to see them in person again. I believe we have both put forth our best effort for today."

"Yes, master. Thank you."

"Come, let's go and welcome my brothers home."

***

Feng and Jin slept in a makeshift tent, having become tired from the strong drink they had all been sharing. Kang, Dong, and Jin were still awake, drinking and laughing like mad-men. They failed to hear the soft patter of little feet moving through the undergrowth around them. Nor did they notice the shining, beady little eyes as the rats closed in.

Kang reached his hand across and snatched the flask from Dong's hand. "I tell you this. If I never run into one of those blood suckers again it will be too soon," he said as he took in a huge draw from the flask. "We need to move south, as far away from here as possible. These lands are dead for us now. The demons own it. It's an evil place."

"Feng won't leave until he finds his brother. He wasn't among the dead when we went back two days after the attack," Shen said, beckoning Kang to pass the wineskin.

"Could we please not talk of this tonight? The thought of the smell of the rotting corpses we had to look through, the sight of our fallen comrades dismembered and mutilated makes me sick in my stomach," Dong complained, his face pale from the memory of the horror they had been through.

"Feng's brother has probably already headed south. He was always smarter than Feng, and a much better thief and warrior. I'll bet one of the dead xiang shi was his doing," Kang stated.

"I'm with Kang, to hell with Feng. Tomorrow we head south with or without him. I ain't ashamed to tell you I am terrified staying in these parts. If it weren't for the strong rice wine we drink almost constantly, I'd probably be out of my mind by now." Dong said, grabbing the flask from Shen and putting it to his lips. "It's empty!"

"Then I'll just have to grab another one," Shen said, staggering to his feet.

"There's only two left. Then what are we gonna do?" Dong cried.

"I'm with you two. Tomorrow we pack up and ride out of here, with or without Feng," Shen said as he stood.

"That's three of us then. I know Jin wants out of here too. I hope Feng comes with us, but if not, to hell with him," Kong said, tilting his head back and taking a deep breath. "Man, that's some good stuff. Hurry up, Shen!"

"I'm goin'. I just got to take a piss first." Shen stumbled over some rocks, woozily righted himself, and loosened the rope that held his pants up. It was pure bliss as the warm stream poured from his body. A few paces away the horses were starting to prance and stomp nervously.

"Now what's the matter with you? Calm down, I ain't aiming it in your direction!" Shen laughed. Then he saw some small, furry animals darting around the horses as he looked more closely. "What the hell?"

Out of the darkness leapt over a dozen rats. Large rats. No, huge rats! Shen pulled up his pants and turned to run. "Kang! Rats! Rats!" Shen screamed as he felt the first one jump up onto his back. He nearly fell as a second rat joined the first, clinging to his clothing. "Wake the others! Help me! They're on me!"

A third, then a fourth rat caught his right leg, both sinking their teeth into his fleshy calf. Shen screamed in agony as his forward momentum sent him sprawling face down onto the ground.

Dong ran toward the tent. "Feng! Jin! Wake up!" Dong tossed aside the cloth that draped over the entrance to the tent. Feng was gone through a large hole in the back of the tent. Jin was most certainly dead. He lay there, soaked in blood, one rat gnawing on his neck, two more burrowing into his chest and abdomen.

The rat on Jin's neck looked up with its blood-drenched mouth, bits of flesh clinging to its whiskers. All of it was just too much, combined with the amount of wine Dong had consumed. Hot putrid liquid poured out of his throat as his stomach emptied its contents onto the dirt floor of the tent. Dong fell to his knees as he heaved again, his eyes watering, a thick line of snot dripping from his nose.

Dong felt something bite into the back of his leg. He let out a squeal and tried to shake it off. Two rats jumped on his back and Dong rolled over twice, hearing the rats squeal themselves as they scrambled to get out from under the weight of his body. Three, then four, then the gods only know how many rats poured over him, tearing into his arms, legs, and torso. "Kang! Help! Shen! Help me, please!"

Feng was bleeding, but not too badly. He had managed to kill the two rats that clung to him as he bolted out of the back of the tent. They had bitten a nice size chunk out of his right forearm and scratched up his right thigh. The rats had gone right for Jin's throat. He didn't even have a chance to cry out before his neck was torn apart and spurting blood as high as the roof of the tent.

Feng crept through the tree line to where three of the horses were tied. There were no rats near them, but the horses more than felt their presence. The mounts were trying to break free from the ropes that tied them to one of the larger tree trunks.

"Easy now, boys," Feng said as he worked on the ropes. The horses calmed a bit with his familiarity. "Just relax. We're getting out of here."

Feng glanced across the clearing their camp was in. Shen and Kang were fighting for their lives, and apparently losing. A little further behind them Feng could see the other two horses under the attack of even more rats. Feng held the ropes of all three horses as he jumped onto the back of his own. "C'mon, let's get the others," he whispered, talking more to himself than the horses.

"Kang, Shen! I'm coming! Let's get out of here!" Feng yelled as he led the reluctant horses toward his friends.

Kang and Shen had almost a dozen rats clawing and biting at them. Kang had killed three, but the situation was bad. Shen was bleeding from a multitude of scratches and puncture wounds. He could see his partner becoming weary from the massive loss of blood and knew he wouldn't last much longer.

Kang heard Feng's shout as he threw a rat off Shen's shoulder. The rat took half of Shen's ear with it. "Hang on, Shen! We're getting the hell out of here!" Kang hoisted Shen onto his shoulders and ran toward the horses the best he could, the rats biting at his heels. "Grab him, Feng!" Kang yelled, as he pushed Shen upward into Feng's arms. Feng swung Shen's body across the horse's back. Shen helped as much as he could, kicking his leg over and holding onto Feng's arm.

Shen slipped as Kang released his hold and ran for another horse. "Hold on Shen! I got you." Feng's body was twisted almost completely around, and his horse stomping at the rats didn't help the matter.

"Leave me, I'm dying. I can feel it!" Shen said, blood running from his mouth. No you're not, damnit! Now climb! Climb up and let's ride! Don't give up on me Shen! If you fall, I fall with you! We'll both be dead."

As Kang went to mount his horse, a rat clamped its teeth into his ankle and he let out a pain-filled cry. The horse bucked and moved sideways. Kang stumbled and fell flat on his stomach. He pulled a small dagger from his belt and struggled to get up. The rat on his ankle was chewing right through to the bone. Kang stabbed at it, and the oversized rodent squealed and backed away. Kang stood and ran for his horse, which had moved several feet away. Shen was sitting upright behind Feng, leaning into him, with both arms wrapped around Feng's waist. Feng still had the other two horses in some small semblance of control, but he wouldn't be able to hold them much longer without being ripped from his own steed.

Kang could see more rats heading for him out of the corner of his eye. Kang ran harder, ignoring the pain in his ankle. He nearly fell again as he grabbed onto the horse's mane and flung himself onto its back. The horse jumped and he struggled to stay atop it. "Ride, Feng! Ride!"

***

Huang-Fu and his family saw the huge monastery and the surrounding village just ahead. He knew this was where the large band of travelers had gone. Hopefully they would grant him and his family refuge. Huang-Fu stopped, and begged his in-laws to let him do most of the talking, and not to mention the demons until later, much later. His mother-in-law shrugged her shoulders, complaining that it was the right of everyone to know that these demons were loosed upon China.

"Huang-Fu! Look! Men on horses!" Lin Yao exclaimed, pointing over his shoulder.

Huang-Fu turned to see five riders heading their way. "Everybody stay calm, but be ready. Men up front, women and children to the rear." Huang-Fu said, wondering if friend or foe approached. The riders came from the direction of the village. Maybe a lookout had spotted them and a welcoming committee was sent out. Huang-Fu fought the urge to draw his sword. An opponent on horseback was formidable enough if you were completely ready for them. Once they were in close enough, the riders could wipe out half his family before Huang-Fu and the other men drew their weapons.

The riders slowed their pace as they neared Huang-Fu's group. As far as he could tell, none had weapons out and in hand. It was a good sign. The five horsemen stopped and dismounted. They were all dressed in the traditional robes of monks. Not fancy, ceremonial robes, but more practical, everyday attire.

The tallest and possibly oldest one, though all of them looked young, healthy, and strong, gave a bow that the others followed. "Huang-Fu, I am Zhan, and these are four of my brothers, Ling, Biao, Cai and Te." Each brother gave a quick bow as he was introduced. "We have been expecting you. You and your family are welcome in our village."

Huang-Fu stood there silently. *How do they know my name? They have been expecting us? What have I led my family into? Have the demons spread this far already? These men do not look like demons.*

"I assure you, Huang-Fu, that we are not a part of the evil you run from. Please believe this. We mean you no harm. We hold the same goals that you hold in your heart. We too want to protect your family, see to their safety, and rid the world of these demons that afflict China."

"How do you know me? You speak so kindly, and yet you know things that you couldn't possibly know," Huang-Fu said, sizing up each of his possible opponents.

"I have visions, Huang-Fu, a gift given to me from birth. I saw you try to fight the demons, and when you failed, I watched you bravely follow them and rescue your family and many others from certain death. You are a hero, and should be honored for your actions."

"I know that you are apprehensive, and I know of your troubles in every village during your long journey here. I promise that you need not fear, you are as welcome and as safe here as anyone can be in these troubled times."

Huang-Fu wasn't sure if he should believe them and follow them into the city, or depart for another place.

"How can I prove to you that we are sincere in our speech and pure in our hearts, Huang-Fu?" Zhan said, "Please come with us. I am sure that you and your family could use a place to rest and a good meal to eat."

Zhan turned to Cai. "Lead the horses back in. The rest of us will walk in from here. Hopefully, our friends will walk with us."

Cai climbed on his mount and spoke softly to the other horses. They all turned at his command and trotted back toward the village.

"Walk with us, Huang-Fu. I will answer all your questions on the way in. If you will allow my brother Te, he will heal your sister's leg. I can see her pain just standing on it."

"Lin-Yao, talk to me? You are the sensible one when it comes to strangers. Do we trust these men?"

"Yes, Huang-Fu. I believe we should. When we were driven to Dulan by the demons and locked up in those cages, I could feel the evil they emitted. I cannot feel any such thing now."

Huang-Fu nodded to his wife, and looked at the rest of their combined family. "Does anyone here have a reason we should not follow them?" No one voiced, or made any gesture of disapproval. They just stood motionless. Huang-Fu could see the tired, worn-out look in their eyes. They needed rest, and food, and there would be plenty of that in the village.

Huang-Fu's daughter stepped forward and tugged at his belt. "I trust them, daddy. They are nice men. I don't believe they would hurt us." Huang-Fu lifted his daughter in a huge hug. "It is a beautiful thing to see that with all you have seen, my dear little one, you have not lost faith in your fellow man."

Huang-Fu turned, still holding his daughter in his arms. "We accept your offer, and are grateful for your kindness. If you will lead, we will follow."

"You will not regret your decision." Zhan said with a smile. Te stepped forward. "May, I?" he asked. Huang-Fu nodded and Te walked over to the beautiful young woman who was clearly in pain, supporting most of her weight on her good leg. Te knelt down in front of her, taking her right hand in his and placing it on his shoulder.

"For balance." Te smiled. "I assure you that you will feel no pain in what I am about to do." Te leaned over, bending slightly at the waist, and raised her foot, cradling it between his hands. He closed his eyes and let his healing powers wash over the young woman. She could feel the warmth of his touch as the pain in her ankle faded. Te continued his healing power sweeping through her body and pouring outward over the rest of the group. They all felt his touch as little scrapes, and cuts healed all over them. The fatigue they all felt seemed to float away, as they felt strength renew in their tired bodies.

"That was the most incredible thing I have ever felt. How did you do that?" the woman asked as Te gently released her foot. "I don't think I've ever felt this good before."

Te smiled at her and stood. "We all have gifts. This one is mine. I think my brother Zhan puts it best. We are the yin to the demon's yang."

"Come, now, let us finish your journey. A fitting meal for a hero and his family is being prepared as we speak," Zhan said, laying his hand on Huang-Fu's shoulder. "Come, we have much to talk about, my friend."

***

Fa reached a large camp. He left out the part about the demons for fear they would think he had gone mad, and simply told them that Ju-Long had put together a great army that was claiming victory after victory over their armies further south. The war-chief immediately sent word to other camps and the Xia council itself by horseback. He might be promoted to council status himself if he was responsible for the capture and death of Ju-Long. Fa was given food, and attention to his wounds.

"We shall wait for the others to meet here with us, Fa, and when they do, we shall find and crush Ju-Long and his so-called army. If they make me council, I will see you have your reward. I personally believe you would make a fine war-chief."

Fa listened to him, and hoped that there would be an army left to lead after the battle. Part of him wanted revenge on Ju-Long and his demonic horde. The other part wanted to jump on a horse and be nowhere in sight when they faced the beasts that were out there.

***

Hu's family allowed him freedom during the day, but the last three nights they tied Hu down forcibly. After the episode in the woods, and his attempts to journey into the forest each night thereafter, they had decided it was best to just restrain him for his own safety. In reality, Hu had been acting so strangely lately that they had began to fear for their own safety even more than his.

All the village elders talked to him, trying to find a rational explanation for the apparent illness of such a healthy and bright young man. Every remedy they could think of had been tried. There was a lot of talk in the village that the tiger they had killed might have forced his spirit upon Hu and was seeking revenge against them all.

Hu was tied with several thick, heavy ropes to a large wooden post they had put into the ground inside his hut. He pleaded with his brother and his wife to untie him. Both of them stood watch over him, but ignored his pleas.

Hu couldn't see outside, but somehow he knew the moon was bright and full overhead. Something inside him could feel its draw, beckoning him to break free and run wild under its light. Hu had ceased his struggle against the ropes that bound him, but sweat still rolled down his body. His wife laid a damp cloth on his forehead and Hu flung his head, flipping the rag onto the floor.

"Hu, you're burning alive, please let me help you."

"I am fine, woman, let me be!"

"Go and get your mother and father. Maybe they can talk sense to him. He will die if we don't cool his fever!" Hu's wife said, nearly in tears.

"I am not to leave him," Hu's brother replied sternly.

"Damn it! Can't you see he's dying? If you do nothing to prevent it, his blood will be on your hands! How can you just stand there and let your brother die!"

Hu's brother looked at him. Hu was drenched in sweat and his body had started convulsing involuntarily. "I will go, but stand away from him while I am gone."

Hu could see the great tiger he had fought in his mind. It was right in front of him, but he was not afraid. He realized that they were inside his hut. He was standing there looking at it, not afraid, but sobbing as if sad. It was as if he was feeling some sort of pity or loss for the tiger itself.

The vision he had playing inside his head panned around, as he became the tiger and he now faced not himself, but his wife. He had been looking at the tiger through her eyes, which meant, yes, he realized the tiger was him. The tiger was fighting the urge to take the easy meal in front of it. He had to get out of here, leave before he took the life of the only woman he ever loved.

"Hu, I love you. Please fight whatever this is for me. Don't leave me, Hu. Don't die on me."

Hu opened his eyes and looked up to see his wife. She stepped back, startled by his gaze. His eyes were like that of a jungle cat. "No, Hu. Oh no." She didn't scream, Hu could smell her fear, and even more so her pain. She looked into her husband's eyes and knew he would never be the same again. Tears flowed down her checks as her heart broke, realizing she had lost her husband forever.

"Run! Run as far from me as you can, Niu! The tiger is coming and I cannot stop it! Run, Niu! Run now!" Hu begged.

"I will not leave you, Hu. I would sooner die than live without you. Hu jerked and twisted, he could no longer control his body, nor contain the beast rising inside him. The ropes that held him snapped one by one as his bones and muscles expanded, shifting and changing into a new form.

Hu cried out, and his voice echoed like a roar. "Get out!" He pleaded with his wife one last time. Hu's brothers and father appeared in the doorway. They could see Hu free from his restraints, down on all fours and rapidly becoming something else. Orange and black fur grew out of his skin. His muscles and bones rippled underneath. His limbs grew thick and elongated. A great tiger was taking over Hu's body. This was a curse! The tiger returned to have his revenge.

"Niu, we must get out of here!" Hu's father yelled. "Grab her if she will not come willingly."

Hu's brothers gave a wide berth to the emerging tiger and took Niu by the arms. "No! No, no, no!" she cried as they dragged her out of the hut. Hu's mother was sobbing behind the men. "Go with her! She needs the comfort of another woman right now!"

Hu's father watched his wife scurry off after their sons and daughter-in-law, crying hysterically. He turned to his eldest son and three cousins that remained with him. They could hear the popping of bones as Hu's face contorted, then pushed outward, turning his human mouth into the powerful jaws of a tiger. There was no time left, the transformation was almost complete.

"We must kill him, now! He is no longer Hu, but an evil spirit sent to kill us all!" One of his cousins yelled.

"I cannot kill my own son!"

"Then leave so that we may!"

Even Hu's older brother was in agreement. "Go, father. We will do what must be done. Do not stay and have your heart broken worse by watching it."

Hu's father turned and ran out into the darkness.

"Let's finish this."

Hu looked up at the foursome, the shift from man to tiger physically complete. Only a small portion of the mind was still his, the rest belonged to the raging beast, and it needed fed.

With the small grasp of control over the tiger that Hu clung to, he charged toward the doorway. He hoped his kin would dive out of the way, clearing a path for his escape. "Look out!" Hu's brother yelled as he rolled out of the tiger's path. Three of the four men reacted quickly enough to avoid the tiger's charge. The fourth found himself bearing the full weight of the tiger as it bore down on him.

Huge claws ripped into his chest as the tiger bounded over him. His wounds were not mortal, but still painful. His shirt quickly soaked with blood as he lay screaming in the doorway.

Hu was outside, the moon illuminating the village. He turned the beast and raced toward the woods. He needed to run away, for his safety and the safety of his loved ones. *What have I become? Why me? Why had life cursed me?* He hadn't actually killed the tiger, the others had.

The tiger bounded into the trees, as Hu was pushed further and further back by the beast, whose only desire was to feed. *May the gods have mercy on my soul?*

***

The entire village was awake. Hu's mother and aunt were tending to his cousin's wounds. Niu calmed herself down, and slipped away from the others, gathering some food and water.

"Don't help me like this. The tiger has marked me. I will share Hu's curse. Kill me now!"

"Everyone out. Now!" Hu's brother yelled, shoving people out the door. "He is right. If we don't kill him now, there will be two tigers to deal with!"

"No! No! Not my son! He will be alright. His heart is pure, his soul clean! He will not be cursed."

"So was Hu's! The tiger seeks vengeance! He will see us all cursed or dead if he can!"

"Please, mother, go. It is best this be done now. Do not make me submit to the curse's power! Please, please!"

Hu's eldest brother, with the help of his other siblings, got everyone else out. "Block the doorway. I will usher our cousin into his next existence." He turned and walked back to where his cousin lay. "We have been friends as well as relatives since we were boys. You were always there, teaching me and protecting me as my elder cousin. I am so sorry for what I am about to do."

His cousin fought back his fear. "Just do it, quickly. Take my head and hide it from my body. Remove my heart and separate it also. Leave no chance that I might return."

"I will see to it that your wife and children remain safe from this tiger and its curse."

"I know you will. Begin that promise right here, right now." His cousin closed his eyes and tilted his head back, exposing his neck in full.

***

Niu crept to the stable where the horses were held. She found Hu's mount and led it out the back way. She took a quick look around. Most of the people of her village were all crowded together near her father-in-laws hut. She struggled onto the horse's back and quietly rode into the darkness toward the woods. *Wait for me Hu, I am coming,* she whispered, as she started her search for the man she loved.

***

Ju-Long walked along the banks of the Huang River, contemplating their next move. They had taken thirteen camps in all since they started their mission of Xia destruction. He hesitated to move north, for he knew the farther they went, the greater numbers they would run into.

He was losing soldiers slowly, but steadily. The last three camps had been larger and he had lost a score of men in each of the battles. His guardians had, however, grown to seventy in number. Soon he would have to use them in battle if he could not discover the *kiss* required to create more like him. He had tried numerous methods without success. Ju-Long was no closer now than when he was in Fangzhou. The only thing he had discovered was a thousand ways that didn't work.

There were plenty of humans in the area, more than just the Xia tribe. There were cities, large cities. Larger than Fanzhou. Those places were within a day, maybe two, of their present position. So many options, but which one to choose? Finding food was not a problem now, it was the cost of the meal.

The thought of facing a massive Xia army if they turned north seemed suicidal. Ju-Long was realizing that his army was not as invincible as he had been told. Losing men was just a fact of war, and losing such few men even in the more epic battles, was a sign of a well disciplined and powerful army. However, even the greatest army will not stand for long without reinforcements to take the places of the fallen.

Ju-Long's entire dilemma revolved around reproducing his own kind. It was the missing piece, the key to him accomplishing his goals. He had no fear, that like a number of his less fortunate warriors, his own immortality would be extinguished. It was his plan to conquer, control and rule China that was in jeopardy. He must find the means by which to procreate.

No, they would not go north, nor would they attempt to take a large city to make their fortress. Staying on the move made them less vulnerable to attack. With the guardians to watch them by day, all they had to do was keep any large force from pinpointing their position or finding their daytime lair. Movement would see to that. If a great army got too close, they could put enough distance between them and the enemy with their superior speed. That would ensure their daytime safety.

Retreat? That was what it amounted to. Backing down, running because you no longer had the ability to win. The mere thought, the word itself made Ju-Long's temper reach its boiling point. He had never retreated. *How would his men react when he called retreat for the first time?*

They would lose faith in his ability to lead, see him as weak. A man could not lead men for long if they did not believe he was truly in control. He had to find a way to preserve his army while convincing his warriors that it was all part of a greater plan. Ju-Long sat down on a large rock that was firmly embedded in the river bank, but jutted slightly over the water itself. He could not let them know that they were on the run. That for the first time Ju-Long was hiding from his enemy.

Since he was old enough to understand, Ju-Long had listened to every story he could that dealt with great battles and the strategies of the most legendary military leaders. He had decided way back then that one day people would be telling stories of the greatest military leader of all. Ju-Long.

As he sat watching the Huang River flow just beneath him, Ju-Long went over those stories of war. Somewhere, in those tales, would be the information he needed. One story in particular came to mind. He could not remember the man's name, but he had been one of the master warlords of the Xia tribe.

The man had led a force of only four hundred men through hostile territories to an ancient and sacred place where legend told the Xia tribe first came from. There, in that land, lost for over two-hundred years, was a small statue laden with jewels. The statue was in the image of the god of war, and worshipped by the Xia people before battle. If the god was happy with the offering, and satisfied with the reverence shown him by his people, then the Xia would have victory on the battlefield.

Ju-Long did not believe in such things. He had been taught early on about the gods and the beliefs of the Xia. He had refused to believe any of it. Such rubbish was a waste of time, meant only to control the weak minded. No god controlled him, or had anything to do with his success in combat.

While he did not have any interest in gods, or see the point in anyone wanting to retrieve some ridiculous statue that obviously had not done any good when they were driven from their homes and turned into the nomadic people they now were, the story told was truly a great one. The tale of the mighty warlord, and his betrayal by a member of the council, fascinated the young Ju-Long. The warlord himself was being considered for a position as a member of the council. One weak, sniveling council member stood against the others and their desire to make him one of them.

As the story was told, the dissenting councilman argued that while the man was indeed a great military leader, he knew little of the ways and traditions of the Xia tribe itself. How could they make one council strictly on his knowledge of war alone?

The others disagreed, and planned to go ahead with the ceremony that would make the warlord council. In a desperate effort to prevent this, the coward, who feared that he would lose his once strong voice within the council if this man were allowed into the circle, offered a challenge to the warlord.

"If this man be as great as you all believe him to be, let him go on a quest to find the statue of the great god of war. Let him make the journey to the place that we once called home, and retrieve this relic. If he succeeds, I will no longer try to stop his candidacy, but will accept him with open arms into the council."

The coward had known the mission would be suicide. The council told him no sane man would take on such an impossible task. Yet the challenge had been made, and the challenge must be presented to the warlord. If he accepted the challenge, then he must complete the mission before becoming council. If he rejected the challenge, even though it would be the logical thing to do, his appointment to council would be delayed indefinitely. Refusing a challenge was a sign of weakness, and unless you were council by birthright, then you must accept the challenge of any council member before being brought into the fold.

The warlord was brought before the council and the challenge explained. The great warrior knew that the odds of finding the statue were slim. He also realized that the challenge wasn't really about finding the statue. It was about sentencing him to death. Only a fool would travel the road to the original homeland. There were five armies between here and there, and a sixth that occupied the territory directly surrounding the sacred place where the statue was supposedly hid.

Only a fool would accept, a fool or a man with a point to prove. He would take a small force of the best men under his command. He wouldn't go storming into each army, but skirt them, sneaking by undetected. He would reach the homeland and recover the relic. If that was not possible, then some other item to prove he had indeed been there. He was a master of confrontation, but also knew that sometimes you won by avoiding it.

He would accept and complete this challenge, but one detail would be added. If he successfully completed this mission that was quite obviously created to see him meet his end, then upon his return the coward issuing the challenge would face him in combat. Sure that the warlord could not possibly return alive, and knowing that his refusal to accept the counter-challenge would nullify his own, the coward agreed.

The warlord headed off with his small army, making the trek to the homeland in three full cycles of the moon. They had quietly crept through each territory without even a small skirmish. He actually found the statue, along with many other lost items.

In the meantime, the coward had sent some of his loyal followers to inform the different armies that a rogue detachment of the Xia tribe was wandering through their territories stealing anything and everything of value that they could.

When the warlord and his men began their return trip, they quickly discovered that they were actively being hunted. During their original trek, they had been very careful to cover their tracks, taking special care to leave no signs of their presence in the places they had chosen to camp. The mission had been jeopardized by someone. The warlord knew it must be the treacherous work of the pathetic coward who had challenged him.

The first attack they came under wiped out almost half of his small army. Their pursuers chased them all the way to the border of the next territory, where yet another army awaited them. They were trapped, and the warlord realized that the game was up. Unless he could pull off the impossible, all was lost.

One of his scouts informed him that a small regiment of the pursing army was encircling them from the north. Another smaller band from the awaiting army watched them if they turned south. The group to the south consisted of almost three hundred soldiers on horseback.

They were surrounded. To the east and west hid two large armies. To the north and south were two other formidable opponents. True panic would have set in at this point, except a small idea began to be realized. They might die trying to act it out, but if they remained where they were they were dead men anyway. He would not just sit and wait for them to come to him. There was too much warrior in him. If this were the end, he would go out fighting.

He took his men south, sneaking into the camp there after dark, surprising the soldiers as most of them slept. He lost another fifty odd men in the ensuing battle, but now he had an escape route and a means by which to do it more quickly.

The wise warlord had his men change into the outfits of their defeated foe. Then they mounted the horses and rode southeast, away from both armies.

They had nearly a full days ride on the army whose colors they now dawned. The other army could not give chase without starting a war. They successfully escaped one pursuer and were well on their way to eluding a second.

To make a long, but worthy tale shorter, the warlord used this hit and run, disguise yourself as your enemy technique all the way back to the Xia

Council. Once there, the coward of the council, learning of their successful return, escaped. The warlord took great pleasure in his next quest, as he hunted down and killed his challenger, then returned to take his spot on the council.

Ju-Long had made the elders tell him that story over and over again. Now, one of his favorite childhood tales could be used as a guide to make his next move. This strategy would serve a twofold purpose. They could feed, and also fuel the already existing flames between his enemies into a raging fire. It would also keep some of the building heat off his own men, and buy him time to try and unlock the secret of their creation.

Ju-Long delighted in this wonderful plan. He gazed over the steadily flowing water and laughed out loud. Ju-Long's tales would be legendary, and being the immortal god that he now truly was, he would be around to both tell them, and hear them told.

Something splashed in the water upriver. It had been a long time since Ju-Long paid attention to the animal life that surrounded him. At one time, hunting and fishing had been quite an enjoyable necessity to him. Now, the hunt was still enjoyable and quite necessary, but the wildlife no longer need have any fear from him. Humans were the only game-animal on his list.

Ju-Long studied the river more closely, watching for the next big fish to jump. Closer now, one did, but it was no fish. It was a man with the lower half of his body resembling a serpent.

What manner of creature is this? Ju-Long asked himself. He levitated upward, trying to penetrate the cover provided the creature by the dark waters. The man-snake surfaced again briefly, and Ju-Long rushed toward it, narrowly losing it again in the black current. He followed along flying just above the course it seemed to be taking.

The creature surfaced again, and like a hawk plucking an unsuspecting fish from the water, Ju-Long snatched it around the waist and scooped the oddity up. "Greetings, snake-man. I am Ju-Long, bloodsucker, walking death, and god eternal. And you would be?"

"Put me down, demon, or I will be forced to fight you," the snake-man yelled as he tried to break Ju-Long's hold.

"Oh, now, is that any way to treat a superior being? You may fight me, but like all others you shall lose." Ju-Long laughed mockingly. He could tell that the creature possessed supernatural strength, but did not feel threatened in the least by it.

"What do you want from me, Ju-Long?"

"Just a little taste of that sweet liquid flowing in the veins just beneath the surface of your skin."

"Never, demon!" the creature yelled. Before Ju-Long realized what was happening, the man completed his change into a massive snake form. The serpent slid through his arms and dove for the water.

Ju-Long gave chase, catching its tail just before the snake completely submerged. His downward momentum and the serpent's desperate escape attempt pulled both of them under the fast currents.

Using lighting speed the snake turned under water, striking Ju-Long's shoulder with its own set of fangs. He could feel it release its venom into him. Ju-Long released the tail and grasped the serpent just below the neck. The snake coiled its body around him quickly, dragging him downward as it attempted to crush him.

Ju-Long struggled against the beast, sinking his claws into its scaled body. The snake released its bite and drew back slightly for another strike at his neck. Ju-Long slid one hand up, blocking the attack and gaining control of its head. He pulled it in and delivered a bite of his own.

The serpent fought hard, but couldn't break free. The waters around them began to swirl rapidly, and Ju-Long wasn't sure if it was really happening or if it was just the dizzying effects of the wonderful blood he now consumed from the beast's body.

The currents pulled them both further down as they spun around and around. Ju-Long felt no need for air, but at the same time was not positive he wouldn't actually drown. The serpent was weakening, he could feel it. It was time to end the fun. Ju-Long tore into the snake viciously with claws and fangs, ripping chunks of meat from the bone. Finally satisfied that his opponent lived no more, Ju-Long released its remains and tried to find his bearings in the whirlpool the snake-man had most certainly created.

He wasn't sure which way was up until he felt his back scrape the river bottom. Ju-Long swam like mad away from the river's bed, fighting the water as it spun him in its circular pattern. It seemed an eternity before his head surfaced. Ju-Long drew in a breath, not certain if he needed it or not. He continued to struggle away from the whirlpool, swimming for the nearby shore.

He reached the bank and climbed out of the water. His body was tingling as the power rushed over him. Ju-Long leapt into the air flying at top speed, feeling the exhilaration of both the flight and the mystical blood that pumped through his veins.

Whatever that creature was, he hadn't felt this alive, this strong since he had feasted on the dragon. He searched his mind, trying to remember the name of a snake-like creature he had heard about in legends. *Naga,* he thought. *You were a Naga. Pleased to meet you. You were quite delicious.*

CHAPTER 11

Huang-Fu and about three hundred other men stood in columns, being given a crash course in how to use a weapon, the one called Wei thought would be most effective against their enemy. The long staff, over almost meters in length, took a lot of getting used to. It also required room to work, or you'd be taking out your allies along with your opponents.

The long sticks of wood were blunt on both ends for the sake of training. Once familiar with them, the ends would be sharpened to a point, making them capable of delivering lethal strikes to the demons.

Ling, Biao, and the monstrous-sized one named Wei led the drills. Many younger monks, most of them mere boys, assisted them. While they looked like mere children, they acted with a level of maturity well beyond their years. As they helped the men with proper grip and strike techniques, it was plain to see that these boys had spent a lot of time developing their skills with the staff themselves.

Zhan, Xiong and Cai walked thru the village, watching as new huts were being built to help house the influx of people. Everyone was working hard in harmony with each other to accomplish the mission. One problem had arisen. It was the answer to that question they now discussed.

"Xiong, with the addition of this group you have brought to us, how long will our current food supply last?"

"Zahn, our storehouses will be empty before the next harvest. I would say we have a month, month and a half, if we cut rations."

"Ah, so we will have to visit with our neighbors to see if trade arrangements can be made to acquire more rations. Our new friends need to eat well to regain and maintain the strength needed for the battle we might face at any given moment. We must get busy. Get the boys and have them gather up whatever we can spare for barter. Tell Biao to gather some warriors from the new groups and take them for security. Have him get Te. He'll be in charge of negotiations on this trip. You two will take some of the women and go gather anything edible growing wild around us. We will need to put together a fishing group as well to go each morning just after sun-up to catch all they can."

"I will go and pass the word," Cai said as he headed back toward the monastery. Zhan and Xiong continued to walk in silence for a few moments. When they finally spoke it was through the link between their minds.

I know what troubles you, Xiong. I fear for these people as well. But do not fret, we will gather the food necessary. I have already reached out to the elders of several of the surrounding villages. They will trade their excess stores for a reasonable exchange. We shall have enough. You'll see.

My thoughts are on more than the food shortage, eldest one. When these demons come many of these fine folks are going to die. The training Wei and Ling are providing is tremendous, but I fear hardly enough. They can't match the speed and strength of the creatures we will face. It is suicide for them to join in this fight.

There is always hope. If we dwell in the negative, we can only achieve the negative. We have been able to keep our village safe for all these years on our own. We cannot do it this time. Some of us might also perish. Alone we all will perish. We need our friends as much if not more than they need us. While I have reached out with my mind to the leaders of the surrounding villages and tried to warn them of what may soon be on all our doorsteps, some are reluctant, but a good many are preparing as well. I have also had Gan write letters to all of them that Te and Cai will deliver on their journey.

I am also working on a plan to decrease their numbers before they even arrive here. As far as when they do, your brother Wei, along with Biao have been quietly working on a battle plan that includes every man able to fight. And I know I don't need to remind you of the bravery these people have already shown.

My apologies. Of course I have faith in your words. I do not mean to be negative.

Xiang Shi

Xiong, we are gifted but still human. Doubt and negativity enter us all. I have seen this battle in my dreams. The outcome is different each time. The actual outcome will not be known until it happens. Some mornings I awake with renewed hope.

And other mornings eldest one?

As I said, doubt creeps into all of us. Better to focus on hope. What else troubles you, Xiong? I can feel it, but I'd rather hear it from you.

The two had walked away from the village. *I die a little each day and am tormented by the thought of all of the innocent people who will die tonight and every night that these demons exist, while we wait for them to come for us.*

What are you suggesting, Xiong? That we hunt the hunters?

Well, you said they are defenseless, save these guardians you speak of during the day. With our powers I am sure we can locate their hiding place and destroy them all. Before so many more people perish at their hands.

What you speak would be a great idea if we knew where they are going to be every night. I even pondered the idea myself when they seemed to be in Fanzhou to stay. Unfortunately they are constantly on the move now. Learning their hiding place one night would do little good. By the time we reached it they could be gone, off to another place too far to reach before the next sundown. It would be like chasing the wind.

On the other hand, Xiong, I do not think it will be long before our enemy turns this way. The messenger I told you about, Fa, has reached the northern camps of his Xia people. They are listening to him. As we speak their numbers are gathering together. Ju-Long does not wish to face such a large force just yet. That is why he has not gone further north, but has remained along the Huang River and Great Wall. Ju-Long realizes that his men are hard to kill, but that it can be done. He faces that fact almost daily. It's not even the fact that his opponents know how to stop them, because they haven't a clue. It has been sheer luck and larger numbers that have caused some of his men to fall. Ju-Long knows how to create servant guardians, but has yet to solve the pro-creation puzzle to make more of his own.

165

So, eldest one, if that is the case and Ju-Long knows he is cut off at this point from going north or south, how do you figure he will head our way soon? He will not risk challenging the great Jin armies between us and them.

Soon, Xiong, he will have no choice. To the east lies the sea. The west he has made barren. The Xia will converge from the north with an army numbering in the hundreds of thousands. He will be driven south, and his only option will be to tip-toe past the Jin, or risk losing his army completely. Once he slips by the Jin he will continue south to where the land is not as occupied by the Jin military. He will come to us. There is an ample food supply in our area, and he has no idea what awaits him.

By food supply you mean humans? And by what awaits him you mean us?

Yes, Xiong. That is why I feel confident that very soon, maybe too soon, we shall meet our enemy on the battlefield. Between then and now there is much to be done, so we had better keep busy.

I will begin gathering those for my part of the mission.

Very good, little brother. And I shall return to the courtyard with Gan and attempt to check up on our enemies.

* * *

Tung and Yue Yan had entered the city by night, but returned to their hidden nest before sunup the first three days. On the fourth night, a festival began in the city. The place was alive with activity well into the early morning hours. They were caught up in the celebration, enamored by the fact that they could party along with the people. This city turned out to be a wicked place even without their own blood-thirsty presence. Debauchery. It was a dream come true.

The town thrived on the business brought in by travelling mercenaries, bandits, and other nomads. A large group of rough men had arrived in the city earlier in the afternoon, and the townspeople knew how to throw a party. There was drinking and dancing, betting on cock fights and men engaged in tests of strength. There were fights here and there, typically started by drinking, and ending with more drinking. Sex was for sale and happened right in the street.

Once fed, the couple could pass for humans. Very beautiful humans. It drew a lot of attention, and the pair ate it up. Apparently the festival lasted until the travelers decided to move on. By the third night of the festival, Yue-Yan and Tung moved easily through the crowds and found a room for rent. They still returned to their hidden lair before dawn, but the room came in handy. They discovered that individually they could not perform sexually. Some of the humans were attractive, but only arousing when they needed to feed. Make it a three or more some with both of them involved and it was let the good times roll.

All had been going well until the fifth night. Tonight the hunters became the hunted. Yue Yan, in her typical seductive manner, had lured a man away from his friends and the cock fights they were gambling on, with the promise of the most fulfilling sexual experience of his life. The couple had already had several sexual interludes with each other and a dozen others. The wild night had brought the thirst back on. This man was the snack before bedtime.

He was among the group that arrived that first night of the festival. He was exceptionally tall and muscular. Not huge, but strong and finely chiseled. His long hair was braided into a tight pony tail. His moustache and unkempt goatee were as jet black as his hair. His face was handsome, but scarred and battle worn. Actually handsome didn't really describe him, but exotic would do. He wore the garments of a leader. Not the top man, maybe a second or third or even the chief's enforcer. He carried a long, broad, double-edged sword on one hip, an oversized dagger on the other. A two-headed battle axe was strapped crossway on his back. Smaller knives lined the rest of his waist, with at least two more strapped to his boots. A necklace, made of various teeth—some human, some animal—loosely circled his neck.

Everything about him said dangerous. He was a man you didn't poke or prod. Most stepped out of his way when they saw him, others wished they had. Yue-Yan was certain he liked his sex rough. He had no idea how rough it was gonna get.

Tung was hidden in their room, but could smell and hear them coming before they even entered the main building. As they entered and began the ascent up the steps he could sense that the man was large, his loud heavy steps almost completely covering Yue's soft, light ones. It had not taken her long, and as they entered, Tung took in the height of the man she had chosen. From his hiding spot he smiled. She hadn't just brought a snack, but a hearty breakfast. They would both be blood drunk after this meal.

Yue-Yan slipped her clothes off as she paraded across the room. Slipping onto the cheap straw bed covered with stolen furs from a couple of nights ago, she spread her legs and began to caress herself with one hand, beckoning the large man with the other.

"Such long, beautiful sharp nails," the man said, standing just inside the closed door.

"Afraid of a little girl? Come over here. I promise I don't bite. Hard." She giggled. The man slid off his belt and carefully laid it on the only table in the room. The battle axe came off next. "My, what large weapons you have."

"Little woman, you haven't seen the largest one yet."

Outside the room four of the man's friends had gathered. This woman would service them all before her night was over. Let the big man have his fun, then they would take what was left.

As the man moved onto the bed, his huge member sticking straight out, begging to impale her, Yue let out a gasp. "My, my, my . . . that is quite the specimen."

He pushed his way in and Yue let out a deep moan. He rammed in and out of her, each stroke rough and fast. She was dry, and he was enormous. It was painful, even for her. After a couple of minutes he hesitated. He had withdrawn himself until only the tip remained. He looked around, puzzled. "What is it?" Yue asked, wondering if he had somehow sensed Tung's presence.

"I forgot something."

"What?"

He smiled down at her. "The other half," he said, and grunted as he shoved his full length inside her.

Yue screamed out, "Tung!" Tung flew across the room, shoulder tackling the man, sending both men rolling off the bed and onto the floor. Tung was stronger and faster, but not a seasoned warrior. The man used their momentum to toss Tung off him and into the wall next to the door. His boots still on, he drew a knife from each. Yue-Yan was on him in a second, wrapping her body around his back and sinking fangs into his neck.

With a loud roar the man belted out "Get off me bitch!" as he reached across his body and drove the knife in his left hand into her eye. She screamed, face contorting into that of the demon she actually was. Tung was on his feet again and lunged, hitting the tall warrior at waist level, driving the three of them back on the bed. Tung could feel the sting of a knife plunging in and out of his lower back, stabbing his left kidney, his spine, then back to his kidney. The man was strong, fast, and skilled. A crash from behind and suddenly there was more pain in several areas of his back.

Yue-Yan freed the knife from her eye and drove it into the larger man's neck, over and over again. Tung turned his head, the look of the demon now on his face. He saw four men yelling and driving various blades into his body. When they gazed into his bright red eyes they let out a collective gasp of horror and stumbled backward. Tung staggered to his feet, one blade still stuck in his back. He let out a blood curdling yell that shook the room. Yue-Yan shoved the large man's limp body off her. The other men had backed out the door and were screaming "Demons, demons! Xiang shi!" She knew what a demon was, but xiang shi she was unfamiliar with. One of the men tripped and fell on his back as the others took off down the hall. Yue snatched him by the feet and drug him back into the room. The couple were both covered in blood, some their own, the rest from the large man that now lay dead on the floor.

"Feed, Tung! Quickly!" Yue-Yan yelled as she straddled the man, holding the man's arms down.

"The sword in my back, Yue! Take it out!"

"Let me go, demon bitch!" the man shouted.

"You're the second person to call me a bitch tonight. Must be something to it." Yue drew back her fist and smashed it into his jaw, leaving the man unconscious. She got up, pulled the sword from her lover's back and watched him immediately crumple to the floor. "Get up! We have to get out of here."

"I can't. I can't feel my body."

Yue grabbed his arm and pulled him over to the man, putting his face right up next to the neck. She leaned down and put her face near his. Can you bite, or do I need to help?"

"I can do it. Your eye is gone!"

"Just eat. I got another one. I'm gonna check the hall." Yue returned to the room a moment later. Tung was on his hands and knees, body parts working again, but he was still swallowing blood as fast as he could. "They are coming back, and from the sound of it, with a lot of reinforcements."

Tung looked up, still coated in blood, but looking better. "Out the back, Yue-Yan!"

"There's no door or window!"

"There will be!" Tung leapt up and ran full force into the back wall. He broke through easily and soared through the air until he met the wall of the building behind theirs. With a thud and a grunt he slid downward until he hit the ground. Yue sailed out the opening at a tremendous speed. She too hit the same spot, only Tung's impact had busted a board and it impaled her gut. She screamed like nothing he had ever heard. Then the board gave way and she plummeted to the ground. She was on her back wailing when he got to her. "What is wrong?"

"Part of that board is still in my stomach!" She said with a ragged breath. "It burns!" Tung immediately grabbed for it, then jerked his hand back in pain as a splinter lodged itself into his palm. "Damn it!" He used his other hand to carefully pull the piece stuck inside Yue out, then with a roar freed the splinter from his own hand.

"Down there!" A man yelled from the opening Tung had made in their bedroom wall.

"I'm dying, Tung. The pain is better, but I am so weak! Save yourself!"

"Not tonight, my love." Tung scooped her up and threw her over his left shoulder. As he began to run down the alley an arrow imbedded itself into his right arm. He screamed and stumbled, nearly falling. He grimaced through the pain, righted himself and kept going. He could hear the whistle of another, then another quarrel as they sailed through the air but missed their mark. He turned up and down alleys, going left then right, then left again. He became lost, but kept running. He passed a window and saw a dim light burning inside. He doubled back and saw the shadow of a woman sitting in a chair eating a piece of bread. He burst through the door next to the window and dropped Yue-Yan into the older woman's lap. "Help her!"

"I no medicine! I no healer!" Before the old woman could utter another syllable, Yue grabbed her by the head and sank fangs into her neck. Tung yanked the arrow from his arm with a howl. An older man walked in from another room, probably the women's husband. All Tung saw was food.

"What's go--" Tung stopped him mid sentence, biting hard into his throat. When they had both finished, other than their blood-soaked bodies, they felt strong again. Outside they could hear yelling in the distance. The hunt was still on. "I believe we may have out-stayed our welcome, Yue."

"And dawn approaches." She sighed.

"Time to leave. Oh, and honey, next time we need to feed in the middle of the night, I'll do the cooking."

"Agreed." She laughed. They slipped back out the door and into the darkness that was their domain. The pair stuck to the shadows and the unfamiliar alleys. Most of their time here had been spent on the main streets in the center of the city where the action was. They were lost. Halfway down the alley they were in Yue-Yan stopped. "What is it?"

"This is the third time we have passed this spot."

"You sure?"

"Yep. We are running around in circles." She looked at Tung. "You got any bright ideas?"

"Just one."

"Go ahead."

"We shouldn't run that way." Tung pointed behind her, where a sizeable group of men had rounded a corner and were coming at them. "Is there no end to this night?" They dashed in the other direction, reaching a cross alley that had a score of men coming from the right. From the left approached another dozen.

"Looks like we keep going straight." They ran to the next intersecting alley and went right until yet another group spilled into the alley in front of them. Yue looked around and up. On the left was a taller building, at least four stories high. "In there." She pointed to a door.

"I don't like this," Tung said as he followed her. Yue busted through the door. A middle-aged man, completely naked with a younger woman kneeling in front of him, shouted, "What the--" The couple ignored him and ran through the room and down a hallway.

"We have to find a way up! Once we reach the roof this building is tall enough that we should be able to see a way to exit this city." They entered another room and met a Mastiff. The dog latched onto Tung's arm and bit down furiously.Tung flung the large dog across the room, feeling the bone in his forearm crack as he did. The beast had also taken a chunk of flesh with it. "Damn vile creature!"

"Over here, in the corner! Rungs that lead up!" Tung saw his forearm hanging at a strange angle. The thought of getting a little blood to heal it seemed like a good idea until he heard the sound of men in the other room.

"Where are they?"

Yue-Yan scaled the ladder with great speed. She reached the top floor, Tung a second or two behind with his injured arm.

The two found themselves in a room, a woman holding an infant with three other young children asleep on the floor. "You leave now! You no belong!"

Yue grabbed the woman by her throat. "The roof. How do we get there?"

The woman screamed in response. Yue clamped a hand over her mouth. "You want to die?" The children woke crying. "You want these kids to die? The roof. Now!" The woman nodded nervously.

"Lead!" Tung grabbed the eldest child, an eight or nine-year-old boy. He had already taken a moment to pop the bone in his arm back in place.

"Sorry, kid. I just need a little. You'll live." He bit into the boys arm, found a vein, and took five long gulps. He laid the child, who had passed out, down on the floor and ran toward the next room where Yue-Yan had gone.

Tung flew by the woman huddled along the wall and joined Yue-Yan on the roof. "C'mon, hurry!" she yelled as she sprinted to the far edge of the roof. "This way." She peeked over the edge and saw more men down on the ground. "And we might want to travel by roof top."

Tung caught up and could see the edge of the city. Yue-Yan moved back several steps. "Let's see if we can fly." She got a running start and launched herself toward the shorter building next door. Tung watched her land—do a half roll—and come immediately back to her feet. He jogged back a bit and followed her lead. The next roof top was closer and even with the one they were currently on. Eight jumps later they made the last building. All that remained was the outer city wall and the ground in between. It was crowded down there, but more with partiers than soldiers or mercenaries.

"I guess we leap as far as we can, then knock people out of the way till we get to the wall," Tung said. "Ready?"

"On three. One, two . . ." Yue-Yan didn't even say three, but took a running leap into the air.

"Cheater!" Tung laughed as he chased after her. They hit the ground close to each other and in between two groups of people, who moved backward and let out yells and screams. Yue-Yan's naked, dried blood covered body more than startled them. The pair let out a roar and charged toward the wall, knocking those who didn't move out of the way. Tung reached the wall first and jumped high enough to catch the top of it and pull himself up. He rested atop it on his stomach and reached his hand down for Yue. She jumped, landing her feet on the shoulders of a surprised, drunk man, then leapt again easily, clearing the wall to the left of Tung.

"Show-off!"Tung said as he landed on the ground beside her. They both heard, "Crazy bitch!" come from the other side of the wall, presumably the drunk Yue had used to propel herself over. Then the sound of horses echoed through the night air. This wasn't over yet.

"Damn it! Do these people ever quit?" Tung spat. The two took off into the night in the opposite direction of the sound of the horses. A quick look at the sky let Tung know dawn was soon approaching. They had to get a safe distance away and find a resting place. "Run Yue. Don't look back or up! Just run!"

"Tung, am I a bitch?"

"Never. You are my beautiful, deadly flower. I'm your bitch."

***

The three large rats feasted on the horse, gorging themselves. They would eat a gluttonous amount, then find a place to curl up and sleep. If they could have only caught the other two steeds they would have had meat for another couple of nights. In retrospect they were lucky to have captured this one. The horses had all run when the transformation began, but this one had not run far enough.

It was just after sundown when it hit. Kang had been first. They were riding south, hoping to reach a village by dawn. None of them had eaten or really slept since the night the rats attacked their camp. They had been fortunate to escape with their lives.

All three had been wounded, Shen the most severely. Had it not been for Feng reaching the horses, the feral rodents would have finished them. They were alive, but maybe it would have been better if they had died. The rats had marked them, placed a curse on their existence. They were now something that should not be.

Kang slowed his horse, complaining of severe abdominal cramps. He was pale and sweaty. Feng stopped and dismounted, going to his friend's aid. Kang slumped in his saddle, sliding off the horse and falling head first onto the ground. Feng quickly covered the last few steps, knelt by his side, and called Kang's name. Kang just lay there in the fetal position, his entire body trembling. "Shen, help me lift him!" Feng yelled, trying to get Kang to his feet. "Shen!"

It was too late. Shen was on the ground also, writhing in pain, his skin seeming to bubble. Suddenly Feng was no longer on his feet, but hurling through the air. Kang, in his seizure-like state, had tossed him off like he weighed nothing.

That's when Feng felt something stir inside him. Once he hit the ground and the shock of the impact subsided, a warm sensation began to ripple throughout his body. He raised his head, looking for Kang. What he saw could not possibly be real. His friend had hair growing from his body like a wild animal. Kang's nose and jaw pushed outward. In a huge burst his clothes ripped to shreds and where there was Kang now crouched a huge, black beast.

Feng saw the horses running. He struggled to his feet and began to run after them, calling his horse by name, hoping it would wait for him. He was also trying to escape the creature Kang had turned into. He got about five steps in before pain racked his own body sending him to his knees. Feng saw an enormous grey rat scurry by him in a blaze of speed. A second salt and pepper colored one sprang by him an instant later.

Feng screamed in terror as he felt his own bones sliding underneath his skin. He tried to stand, but fell once more. He could feel his skull shifting, the cracking of bone as it morphed into a new form. He could see his hands, now covered in jet black fur with long sharp nails extending from his fingers. Fang had seen his friends and knew what he was becoming. They were rats now. The size of mules. Perfectly enlarged replicas. His body had transformed. His senses were enhanced, yet his mind still thought like a human. However it contained the impulses, wants, and needs of his physical being. He had been hungry, now he was starving. There was no thought to it, just instinct. He needed food, and he needed to join the others. He needed his pack.

Maybe because he was the youngest, maybe because he had always been the fastest, but for whatever reason he caught up to the others in a short time. They could all hear the whine of one of the horses in the near distance. It was injured and struggling. All reacting as one unit they raced toward its cries. Feng could smell it long before he actually saw it. There was no trace of the other two.

As the threesome navigated a large log, the injured horse came into view. It had landed wrong on a small pile of medium-sized stones. One of its front legs hung twisted and bleeding, bone sticking out from the skin. It rolled desperately to get upright as it looked into the beady eyes of death.

Careful to avoid the powerful kicks of its hind legs, the rat trio moved in. Blood and flesh flew as the rats tore into him, biting at his throat and belly. Claws ripped away large chunks of hide as sharp teeth gnawed into the exposed meat. The horse's kicks became mere twitches as the rats bored into him, seeking out vital organs. In a matter of moments the horse was fully subdued. Kang released the hold on its throat and acknowledged the power that coursed through him. Then he went greedily back to work, gulping down morsel after morsel as he ripped it from the horse.

Whatever had happened to them, whatever the rats had caused, he was starting to enjoy. Kang, as a man, had been on many, many hunts as well as his fair share of battles with the numerous people they had robbed over the years. None of it compared to this. Nothing had been nearly as exhilarating. His instincts and senses were sharper, his bond with his comrades was true, simple. Feng would lead them. He was younger, but had always been wiser, more dominant. Now, however, there was no jealousy of that.

***

Ju-Long and his army had taken a smaller Xia camp right after dark. They had fed, but almost as importantly they had dressed themselves in the clothes of their former people. They were mounted on steeds atop the crest of a small hill, carrying the standard of the Xia. Ju-Long wanted to be sure everyone below knew who the attack was coming from.

Below was a mid-sized settlement of the She Le. It was more of a farming community, only now there was a sizeable military presence. The She Le had already fended off one offensive gesture by the Xia, and were preparing for an even larger attack. They realized the first move by the Xia was not about conquering, but about getting a feel for the strength of their opposition. It had been the power and numbers of the She Le that had left the Xia camped outside their borders.

Had the She Le retreated, the Xia would have continued their advance. However the She Le repelled the first force so convincingly, the Xia had been the ones to fall back and wait on the larger armies still further north. It was the smaller Xia camps that Ju-Long and his band of demons had been pummeling night after night.

The She Le had moved more units to its northern border. They were preparing for a massive strike from the Xia and the enormous army they wielded. So they dug in and waited. No major attack. Still they waited. Talk was beginning among the She Le ranks that the Xia had reconsidered and were going after other territories, that their quick response had made the Xia think twice. Ju-Long needed to stir the pot. That was the plan tonight.

The soldiers below appeared relaxed, but Ju-Long knew better. He had made sure the outer sentries had seen them move in. He had watched them quietly work their way around the camp alerting the others. Ju-Long had given his men strict orders that death would come to these people the old fashioned way. No claws, no fangs, and no feeding. Swords, quarrels and axes were to be used. This had to look like a legitimate assault by the Xia. The survivors, who would be allowed to run screaming to neighboring camps and villages about how the Xia are coming, were to be left to do so. Save a few to make it look good, the rest would make their destination, and set up the next stage of Ju-Long's plan. If they ran screaming of a demon attack on the settlement it would not help his cause.

Then the weapons, clothes and standards of the fallen She Le would be gathered. They would strike another small village for feeding purposes tomorrow, then hit another Xia encampment guised as the She Le. Ju-Long knew his small army could not conquer the She Le or Xia on their own. So, as the heralded warlord had done, he would give due cause for the two sides to massacre each other. He and his men would feed from both sides as they waged their war and he spent his time on procreation, and unlocking the mystery of it.

Ju-Long smiled widely at his own brilliance. "Tonight we fight like we once did as humans. Use your speed and strength to your advantage, but don't overdo it. Do not make a meal of any of these people. I assure you that anyone caught sinking fangs into a single one of them will answer to me!" Ju-Long looked around. "Now let us have some fun. Quon!"

"Yes, master?"

"Take half the men and circle east," Ju-Long ordered. "Yun Qui!"

"Here, master."

"You shall lead the others straight down into the valley below. When the two of you hear my command you will stop fighting and allow any retreating men to do so."

Quon asked, "And what will be the command sir?"

Ju-Long rode his mount straight up to Quon's until they were side by side facing opposite directions. "How about halt? That should be sufficient for you to understand." He back-handed Quon, knocking him from his steed. "Are you Kong? Are you an idiot? I don't know what happened to my simpleton cousin, but your fate will be far worse than his if you ask another stupid question. Now everyone get going. The night won't last forever."

***

Hu awoke to the sound of a horse tramping through the forest. He was naked and human once again. Time passed like a blur. He wasn't sure how long he had been asleep. He knew he had left the village two nights ago, or was it three? Or four? He remembered tracking a pack of wild pigs, feeding off their number at least twice. He had spent a full day in human form after the first change. He couldn't remember how many times he switched back and forth since then. He slept a lot, usually in tiger form until the huge meal the tiger consumed was broken down enough for his much smaller human stomach to hold.

The last thing he remembered was eating some leftovers from a boar he had taken down at some point, then prowling through the woods in tiger form. He was now hidden in a thicket near a brook. He couldn't see it, but he could hear it running. He could also hear the horse's hooves as it splashed through the water about ten meters away. It had a rider. She smelled familiar. *Why is she here? She shouldn't come anywhere near me.*

The horse hit dry ground and stopped. It let out a gruff snort. It had caught his scent and it smelled danger. "What's wrong, boy?" He heard her voice and a tear started to well up in his eye. He rose up enough to see the horse, and her. Her eyes were red, bloodshot from lack of sleep and a thousand tears. She was covered in dirt, her hair a mess, and her frail body looking malnourished and dehydrated. She wearily slid off the side of the horse and knelt down by the water. Despite her current physical state, none could deny her beauty. He could not deny his love for her. Hu flashed back to making love to her. They both wanted a child so bad, but it had not happened. He knew there was something wrong with him. There was no way, as perfect as she was, it was her.

He couldn't think of a single thing that was wrong with her. From her small but delicious breasts, to the soft, round mound of her ass. Her womanhood held the scent of beauty, and when he was inside her it felt like heaven. Her eyes were like a flame that burned only for him. She deserved better. She deserved a man that could make her with child. She was better off without him.

A part of him wanted to remain still, waiting for the horse and her to move on. A much stronger urge begged him to stand, reveal himself, and rush into Niu's loving arms. He longed to hold her, touch her smooth, soft skin, and cry into her bosoms like a baby.

"Hu? Hu, are you there? Please, Hu, come to me. I love you. I can't live without you." Niu cried into her hands. Her sweet sobbing voice was too much. Hu got to his feet, carefully trying not to spook the horse, and gently called to her.

"Here, my love. I am here." The horse reared up on its back legs, startled by the emergence of a predator this close. "No!" Hu yelled, fearful the horse would trample his wife. He headed to her side, but was blocked by the steed as it snorted and kicked wildly. Hu let out an unhuman roar and swooped by the beast snatching Niu up with one arm and running across the brook. The horse gave chase. Hu darted around some trees and laid Niu aside, then turned to face his pursuer. He met its head as the horse lowered it and rammed into him, launching Hu into the air. Five meters later a tree stopped his flight.

"No! It is Hu! It's ok!" Niu pleaded with her mount. Hu could hear her, but she seemed so far away. He saw enough to know the horse had reared back and was about to land its front hooves on his chest. He rolled right, barely avoiding its attack as he made it to his feet. He could feel something changing inside him. Hu staggered sideways falling over a bush and into some brush. The horse had moved close again and was snorting and stamping on the other side of the bush. "Easy, boy. It's ok," Niu said.

Hu knew it wasn't ok. The change was coming fast this time. The tiger emerged from the bush leaping straight toward the horse. Hu dug his fore claws into the horse and clamped huge jaws around its neck. "Don't kill him! He was your favorite horse! Hu, please!" Hu could hear her, but the tiger was on its own mission. The horse fell on its side, and Hu clamped down on the throat harder, suffocating it. It twitched a few more times, then relaxed and took a final breath. Niu was crying. "Hu! Hu where have you gone?"

The tiger released its bite and turned to the sound of her voice. It had its meal, so she wasn't on the 'I'm hungry' list. Part of it wanted to run her off, protecting his food. Another part recognized Hu's memory of her and her scent. It was curious about how it could mount and mate with her. Hu's voice came out in a boom "Run, Niu!"

"Kill me if you wish, tiger, but my husband is still in there and I will not leave him!" Niu stood defiantly. "Hu, I have searched for you for almost a full cycle of the moon. Come back to me, Hu! Come back now!" Hu paused and so did the tiger. *A full cycle of the moon?* He thought it had been a matter of days, not weeks. The tiger refocused quickly. Hu tried to fight through its instincts and urges. What it wanted would not be good for Niu. Dealing with the basics, the tiger would not choose flight. Food was already covered. Fight, though it knew its opponent was no match, was a slim possibility. The fourth primal instinct, fornication, was moving to the top of the list.

"Niu, please run. The tiger wants to do unspeakable things to you. To your body."

"Then let it, if it will bring me back to you." The tiger took a step forward. It drew in the scent of her womanhood and began to grow rigid. It pictured her on her hands and knees. It mounting her from behind. The tiger edged closer.

"No beast!" Hu screamed. He forced the tiger, with great effort, to turn its gaze from her. "If you will not run, I will!" Hu bolted down the brook as fast as he could, hoping to make it far enough away that Niu would be safe from what he had become. He began to tire after making it a fair distance away and he slowed to a trot. He smelled it a moment before it attacked. Another tiger landed on his back and they both rolled into the shallow water. From there the fight was on.

***

Niu stood watch over her husband, as she had for the last three days. His breathing was better, but his many wounds were slow to heal. She talked to him and tried to wake him every hour. Today she had brought him food, hoping if he could eat, he could heal. She squeezed the meat over his face, dripping blood into his mouth. He stirred in his sleep. She dripped a bit more and he began to lick his lips. "That's right. Come back to me, Hu." She lifted his upper body and moved a decent size rock under his head. She had already cut up some smaller pieces and she began to feed one to him. At first it just lay on his tongue. "Chew for me, Hu."

He started slowly. Then the tiger awoke inside him, recognizing the taste of what it needed. Hu's eyes popped open, and while still in human form, his eyes were not. And they looked hungry. Hu tried to sit up, but Niu pushed him back down. He must be really weak. His body protested in pain. The tiger however did not make an effort to resist, but instead greedily took the next morsel and gulped it down, followed by another and another. His sweet Niu could even tame the beast inside him.

The meat couldn't come in fast enough in this form. The tiger was ravenous. Hu felt the change coming. He barely got the word "Run!" out when his body exploded from one form into the next. Niu stood back, but stayed her ground. The half-eaten carcass she was feeding him from was just to her right. The tiger gazed at her for a moment, then tore into the animal as if it hadn't eaten in weeks.

The tiger gorged itself, filling its body with the rest of the meat, then began looking for more. There was another tiger laying ten meters from him. Dead for days, with a sword still sticking out of its neck. It wasn't fresh, but the tiger did not care. It fed on the spoiled meat until its brain caught up to its stomach, and by then it was too late. The tiger had forgotten about Niu and moseyed into the trees, found a quiet space, and laid down to sleep. It didn't even protest when the familiar scent of Niu lay next to it and stroked its fur. She smelled and felt like home. Add that to the sedation of a large meal, and the beast went out.

***

Hu woke to the sounds of the forest at night. He was naked, and there was a bare arm wrapped around his waist attached to a naked female body pressed firmly against his back. Niu. *Where ate we? How did she get here? Has everything been a dream? Is this still delirium from the night I got attacked by the tiger?* He just didn't seem to know anything anymore. He certainly couldn't separate reality from fantasy at this point. Surely he was going mad. He laid his hand on top of Niu's and gently began to move it. He didn't want to wake her, but he needed to get up. He needed to pee. Bad.

Niu tightened her hold and nuzzled her face into the back of his neck. "Don't go."

"I'll only be a moment, love. I promise."

"Hurry. I'll be here waiting." She released him and rolled onto her back. Hu did not look at her as he got up. He was confused and afraid. He went about fifteen meters away and began to relieve himself. It felt amazing, but his mind was traveling in a million different directions. *What was real? Have*

I really become a tiger? Why are we in the middle of nowhere? He could hear the babble of the brook and knew some of what happened was real, but how had Niu stayed and lived with the beast he had become? The thought of running, as far and as fast as he could, crossed his mind. But Niu was here. She loved him, and he her. Somehow she had found him. Somehow he knew she would find him again. He didn't want to leave, but he knew it wouldn't work out. Eventually the tiger would hurt her. Kill her. He could not let that happen.

He remembered killing his horse. He remembered the tiger wanting Niu. He remembered that and then the image of the beast killing her during the unnatural sex they were having. Not on purpose, but by the act itself. It had even tried to lick her face to wake her, but she would never wake again. The tiger began to awaken inside him and he finished urinating through a full erection. There was no time to waste. He had to run, and run now.

Hu took off, not looking back. That would only weaken the tiny bit of resolve he had in this decision. Before he got up to speed, a naked figure, Niu, stepped out from behind a tree several meters in front of him. "Going somewhere?" Hu stopped abruptly, knowing he would run right over her if he didn't. He skidded to a halt, losing his footing and sliding onto his back. Niu stepped over him, one foot on either side of his thighs.

"Niu, no! You must let me leave!"

"Why leave when I am apparently what you want?" She smiled, staring at his stiff groin.

"It's the tiger! He will hurt you!"

She went to her knees, her opening hovering over his manhood. Hu went to move her off him as gently as he could. With tremendous speed and strength she grabbed his wrists and pinned then on each side of his head. With the movement the tip of his manhood was touching her. "I'm a big girl. I can take care of myself." She whirled her head like she always did before she mounted him, throwing her long, silky black hair behind her. When their eyes next met, Hu saw the eyes of a tiger staring back at him. Niu let a wicked smile cross her face, then she slid all the way down his length, letting out a purr.

CHAPTER 12

For over a week Ju-Long and his army had masterfully carried out his plans. They had managed to feed, successfully play hit and run, and turn the attentions of the Xia and the She-Le toward each other and away from his own men. The Xia were gathering in large numbers near the northern border. More units arrived each day. The She-Le in turn were sending support to the war front. As of yet no major battles had occurred, merely a few small skirmishes.

Ju-Long planned to change that tonight. Disguised as the She-Le his small force would attack the Xia, goading them into driving southward in retaliation for the assault. Once the invisible boundaries were crossed, the war would be on.

Ju-Long had picked a smaller force of merely four hundred She-Le to feed upon They were camped a little further north than they should have been, and Ju-Long intended to take advantage of that. Once his men had fed, they would take the clothes of the fallen She-Le, then take the battle to a large force of Xia and attack mostly by way of arrow. Hopefully that would get them charging. His own retreating men would then lead them to a sizeable force of She-Le southeast of them and let the onslaught begin.

For the first time ever his human servants, who had swollen in numbers, would travel on horseback and fight alongside them. He was anxious to see how they would fare in battle should he ever have to rely on them for defense by day or night.

Thus far he had still fallen short in his attempts to create more like himself. His actual army still numbered just above two-hundred and fifty. This number was insufficient to accomplish his ultimate goals. If he could just protect them until he found the key to replicating humans into demons like his men, he would gladly sacrifice his human servants. He knew how to replace their numbers, and while clearly lesser beings they were still a cut above mere humans.

Ju-Long and his men traveled east, finding the small encampment of She-Le right where he had observed them just before dawn. He left half his human servants to guard over the horses as he and his men moved quietly and quickly through the trees and closer to the camp. From there it was forty meters of tall grass to the clearing where the She-Le were gathered. Only a few guards stood watch as the majority of the She-Le had turned in for the night.

Ju-Long motioned to Quon and Yun-Qui to fan the men out encircling the camp. No sooner than he gave the silent command, the dozen or so guards were yelling an alarm and running for their horses. "Now! Converge on them and allow no one to escape!" he ordered. Quon and Yun-Qui took to the air, flying furiously towards the riders. His men rushed toward the tents, yet there were no soldiers emerging from anywhere.

The sounds of hundreds, maybe thousands of arrows whistled through the air. He looked up to see quarrels filling the night sky. His men howled and screamed in agony as the deadly missiles hit home. They tore into flesh and muscle, sending his men writhing in pain. Others of his number just dropped where they stood. Quon and Yun-Qui soared higher into the air, getting above the carpet of bolts that endlessly flew from both the north and south.

A trap? But how? Ju-Long thought. He watched half his men fall with the first two waves of arrows. He had to yell the word he hated the most. The word he planned to use on his own terms later that night. This wasn't supposed to be happening now. "Retreat! Find cover! Retreat!" A third wave of arrows was on its way, only half as many this time. He could hear the sound of horses moving in from the north. His servants, what was left of them, were heading to him with the remaining steeds. The third wave of arrows landed, mostly missing their mark as his men found cover or narrowly evaded them. The skies fell silent.

Then came the thunder of a huge number of horses from either direction. *What had gone wrong? How had both sides known his next move?* Ju-Long saw his men fall and his dreams of conquest falling with them. He must escape. Preserve what he had left, but foremost save himself. Fifty or so of his men followed him towards their horses. Looking north Ju-Long could see an enormous wall of mounted Xia emerging from the trees. Ju-Long glanced back to see an equal number of She-Le heading toward them from the other side of the camp. More arrows flew in as the Xia targeted his human servants and the horses.

The mounts bucked and kicked wildly as the bolts found their marks. Many of his human servants fell to the ground as they also became victims to the incoming projectiles. Ju-Long shot straight up into the air. He had to find a route to escape. Looking right and left he saw a chance to the west. The line of She-Le was shortest that way. The line of Xia seemed endless in either direction. "West! Run west! Then south! Save yourselves! West!" Ju-Long roared through the night. Another bevy of arrows, this time traveling in more of a straight line and coming from the mounted Xia, slammed into his men. Many more fell, and those that remained ran with total abandon. He looked behind the riders and saw foot soldiers kneeling, preparing to send missiles his way. It was time to go.

Ju-Long climbed higher as he sped west. His survival was paramount. If others survived he would gather them once they had escaped. His arrogance had cost him. He should have had Quon and Yun-Qui recon the area before he charged his men into the encampment. They could have spotted the awaiting armies and prevented them from running into this well laid death trap. Ju-Long had reached the end of the She-Le line to the south, his men not far behind him on foot. That's when he spotted several hundred riders coming in from the west, dressed in both the garments of the She-Le and the Xia. There was still distance between the approaching riders and the line of the She-Le to the south. He hovered in place and bellowed to his men "South! Now!"

As his men heeded his order, a group of nearly a hundred, a score of them mounted, moved out of the tree line to the south and leveled arrows at his troops. "Down!" His men dropped and evaded the assault. "Up! Charge them!" It may not have been the best idea, but it was the only idea. "Push past them to the tree line! Do not feed! Just get through and keep moving!"

Ju-Long flew lower, just above his men. One of his warriors tossed both horse and rider into the air as they broke through the enemy line. Ju-Long dodged them both, but felt a sharp pain in his right calf. An arrow from the riders approaching from the west found home. The pain was more intense than he had imagined. He crashed to the ground and immediately ripped the arrow out. Then he had to roll away from the end of a spear being driven down upon him by a She-Le soldier. Most of his men had made it through the gauntlet and were within the refuge of the forest. Ju-long rolled to his feet. He found himself surrounded by eight men. They all held pointed wooden staffs. Their swords and axes were sheathed. Strange to choose a stick over a sword when it is available. Not only did they know his moves, his plan, but also what worked best against his kind. Somebody had been talking. He immediately thought of Kong. *I'll kill him if he's not already dead!*

Ju-Long knew he could just leap into the air and fly away, but first he would take vengeance on this lot. In the blink of an eye, Ju-Long drew his sword, decapitated his would be captors, then leapt skyward. Hungry, wounded, and filled with rage he screamed into the dark. As his anger grew, so did the winds around him. Lightning lit up the sky and storm clouds gathered. The angrier he became, the worse it got. "Yes! Let it rain! Let it monsoon on the Xia and the She-Le as we make our escape. Let their armies suffer as mine has suffered. Bring the ultimate storm!" Ju-Long laughed as he willed the weather as if it were his to command. And apparently it was. "Seek out my enemies and what you don't destroy—make scurry for their worthless lives!"

***

Zhan emerged from the tent sweating profusely, but with a grin that ran from ear to ear. Xiong was talking with a group of men when he saw his brother approach. "Zhan, you look like you just went through three hours of hand to hand combat training with Wei, and came out smiling about it."

"I have great news. I told you before I had been tracking our demonic foes. Well I have also been planting thoughts, ideas, and the ever changing

188

location of our enemy into the minds of warlords from both the She-Le and Xia armies. Two days ago the Xia formed a pact with the She-Le. They promised to withdraw from the She-Le borders if they would help the Xia trap and defeat Ju-Long and his small band of trouble makers. With a little mental coaxing on my part, the two tribes managed to reach an uneasy truce."

"Tonight the two forces laid the trap, which Ju-Long and his men fell right into."

"That is wonderful plan, eldest one! So our enemy has been defeated!"

"Not quite, Xiong, but his numbers were truly devastated, and the hunters have become the hunted."

"Then the war is not over?"

"No. However the tide has turned in our favor. Ju-Long's army is now a mere forty or so, with a handful of human servants that also survived."

"Then we should put together our own force and find them and destroy them."

"I do not believe that will be necessary, young one. They have two large armies that are hunting them. I am certain they are heading to the Wall and into the Jin. The number along the Wall will be too much for them to tarry there for long, they will come further south."

"And so we wait for them?"

"Yes. For now. We gather and prepare for our enemy. They will have to come to us. The Jin are strong along the wall."

"We depart for home in the morning?"

"No. We leave now. We have what we need from here, and time Is of the essence."

***

Ju-Long was on foot again, continuing to lead his men south. This area had become too hot to stay in. South, over the Great Wall laid new opportunities. They would have to move to a more central location, for the wall was well guarded for the same reasons they were on the run. No one in the land of the Jin had a clue to their existence. They could re-group and rebuild. That is when he would figure out the damned kiss the demon spoke of.

With the small band that remained, they could lose themselves in the south, remaining in total obscurity to their enemies. This was not about taking over anything, not for a while yet. For now things were going to be about preservation and discovery. Survival was all that mattered. Later the world would bow at his feet.

***

Yun-Qui and Quon had to fly east at first to avoid the arrows, then to escape the wicked storm that seemed to come out of nowhere. They had seen tens of thousands of soldiers to the north and the south of them, as well as a thousand or so blocking the route east. They had to fly higher to avoid the arrows launched from that group in an attempt to bring the two of them down.

Survival instincts kept them heading east. Once far enough away that there was no enemy in sight and the storm was safely behind, Quon, feeling intense loyalty to Ju-Long, suggested they turn south then double back east. Yun-Qui argued that the mighty Ju-Long would not do them the same favor. Besides, they were lucky to survive themselves. Ju-long and the rest were stuck in the heart of the battle. Both knew that if anyone could find their way out of that impossible situation, it would be Ju-Long. Even if he could save no one else, he would save himself. Quon wondered how they would fare without their master. He truly worshipped Ju-Long. As they blazed through the night sky and into unknown territory with an uncertain future, Quon wandered why it was that the things that supposedly brought fear were suddenly afraid?

***

Ju-Long and the remnants of his invincible army followed a wide southbound pass that they had stumbled upon a half-hour ago.Utter disbelief in the night's proceedings kept him mentally off balance. He had to regain his grip, his edge, clear his thoughts of all the frustration and confusion that swept through his mind. He could not be anything but focused on the current objective. There could be forces waiting on this side of the Wall. Certainly there would be military camps housing Jin soldiers on the other side.

He needed to accomplish three things: get over the wall, feed, and find refuge before dawn. All other problems, goals and plans would wait until tomorrow. He could not believe they were on the run. Just a short time ago he had believed his army was invincible. Now, until they could regain the numbers they had lost, they would have to hide. Hiding from the humans, running from their prey! It did not sit well with Ju-Long.

"Master! Master! The wall is just ahead!"

"Quiet!" Ju-Long ordered. "Everyone stay put! We shall not blunder into this." Wait here and watch yourselves. I am going to take a look." Ju-Long glided into the air, rising high enough that he could see everything with little chance of being spotted. He flew toward the wall, noticing a number of guards on watch duty scattered around here and there. Getting by them wouldn't be hard. He floated over the wall silently, searching and finding the things he dreaded.

There were campfires burning as far as he could see in either direction. There was a mixture of permanent structures and tents. The Jin must have reinforced their border guard to keep the problems of the north from spilling into their territory. Ju-Long flew westward, searching. He had to find a weak spot, somewhere he could sneak his men through. After a few minutes he spotted it. *There, that will do nicely.* There was a large gap between two camps that would give them the space to pass through undetected. All they had to do was quietly take out the guards on the wall that were in that vicinity.

Ju-Long made his way back to his men. "Quickly and silently we move west. There is a crease we can get through. Everybody focus on my lead. Do exactly as I say. We are crippled in number, but we shall prevail. We must find a safe haven for tonight. As far south as we can get. Tomorrow we rethink everything and rebuild our army."

"We will have to move in unison. There are a dozen guards in the vicinity we need to get through. We will take them, share the blood, and move along without delay. If we prolong our stay we will be in jeopardy of an alarm being sounded, and the Jin are in great numbers in this area. I do not want to lose a single one of you. Now my wicked warriors, let's move."

The small band moved as quickly and quietly as the woodland creatures that dwelled here. Ju-Long stopped behind a large gathering of rocks and waited for his warriors to catch up. The distance to the wall was sizeable, and there was little to no cover for them to move through. As humans they would be spotted for sure. Thankfully they weren't. Timing, speed and fluidity would be the key.

"On my mark you run to the wall as one using all the speed you possess. Once I give the second signal you will spring onto the wall, grab any guard within your reach making sure to muffle their screams, and proceed over the wall and southward until I stop you. We must be quick and quiet." Ju-Long had another thought. He had brought on a monsoon a little while ago. *How did I do thatt? Can I do it again it again?   Was it an undiscovered power I have always had? Or was it….a power gained from the dragon? Or . . . yes, the Naga.* He marveled at the fact that it appeared feeding on the blood of other supernatural creatures allowed him to steal some of their powers. He must seek out and feed on as many such creatures as he could. An army of his own might not even be necessary if he gained in power by feeding on every different kind of preternatural creature out there. Added to mission goals—find other freaks of nature and eat them.

"Hold on. Same plan, different signal. I am going to try to call the rains again. Just heavy rain, no wind or lightening. When the downpour starts and the humans are virtually blinded we move as one. This time straight to the top of the wall. Muffle their screams, but feed on the guards...sharing if you must. Then over the wall when I say and south as far as we can. Understood?" His men nodded. "Spread out."

Ju-long whispered to the skies. "Bring me rain. Bring me rain hard enough to cover our movements." He watched as clouds began to gather. "Bring me a downpour." He felt sprinkles fall on his face as he continued to stare skyward. It was not enough. His anger built inside him and the rain picked up. Still not enough. Through his mind he screamed *I said RAIN!* The drops came heavy and fast. He could barely see the wall from this distance even with his superior vision. This, along with the noise it brought would do. His men, including the servants, were already on the move. Ju-Long took to the air and followed.

***

By mid-day the caravan was over halfway back to the monastery. Zhan pressed them onward though many of them had gotten a mere couple hours of sleep before they were awakened and told they would depart immediately. Xiong rode up from his rear guard spot to the front with Zhan.

"Eldest one, I believe the men can make it without sleep until we reach our home, but we must eat soon."

"I know. I sometimes forget the need for food. I haven't had much of an appetite recently. Funny, when I used to drink I seemed to eat more regularly than I do now."

"When these nightmares first started we all thought you were going insane. And then the drinking. It was as if you were trying to drown out the world with all the wine you consumed."

"My strength grows again. I embarrassed myself with my actions before. I just didn't know what to do. There were only problems, never answers. I was afraid that I would fail you all, and terrible things would happen. I feared all of China would suffer because of my inability to foresee a way to stop the oncoming evil. Even now as I remember the terror, the darkness that consumed my thoughts, I wish to pick up a flask and drink until it's all over."

"But did the wine make the dreams go away?"

"No, they did not. It made them even more intense, while at the same time clouding my mind so I could never see the answers. I stay sober partly for myself, but mainly for you, your brothers, these people, and Gan. I could not bear it if Gan fell into the hands of these demons. I love him like he was my own, Xiong. Do you understand? Do you have any idea how much I wish I had a son of my own? Don't you ever wish--"

"Yes, Zhan, of course I do. But the young boys we teach, we raise. They are enough for me. They are not so much different than having children of our own."

"I disagree. By the time you were born, mother and father were older. They were tired and had lived the most active years of their life. They certainly weren't any less proud or in love with you than they were us, but they were not as involved with your childhood as they would have liked to have been. By the time you were old enough to get around on your own you were at the monastery."

"It was us, your older brothers that raised you and Biao. Your upbringing was not so much different than that of the boys we now instruct. But when it was just me, and then just Wei and I it was much different. Father looked at us knowing his legacy would be carried on. No matter what happened to him, his sons would live on. And maybe, just maybe, if things worked out right, his next existence would bring him back close to them." Zhan paused, a tear welling up.

"Mother. Sweet mother. She provided love and care that only a mother can. She held us when we needed it, knew all the right things to say when anything upset us. Sometimes she would tell us the story of how our father and she met. How he would make up poems about her beauty or how much he loved her. He memorized every word, every line. He could still recite them verbatim before he passed."

"It is these things that we do not have. It is these things that the boys are deprived of. They are certainly wonderful young men, and a joy to have around at all times, but they are not our own flesh and blood. It is different, Xiong."

"Eldest one, you wish for things we cannot have. You sadden me with this knowledge. I do have memories of mother and father. They were involved with me as much as they physically could be all the way up to their passing. Our gifts make us different. I know we are no better than our fellow man, but there are things we must deny ourselves personally for the betterment of others. I do feel for our young men. Some of the boys' parents are still alive and live in the village. For the others we do the best we can. You don't have to be blood to be family. Even if we are never blood, we are always family."

"You are wise beyond your year's young one. I do understand this, but you have not lived over seventy years. Have you never thought of settling down with a woman you love? Raise a family, live a normal life?" Zhan wiped his eyes with his sleeve. "Oh, I'm just babbling like I always do. I am just a foolish old prophet, drowning in his own sorrows. I know I want what we cannot have. I often dread my own existence because I realize that there will always be a need, a problem somewhere we must deal with. Our gifts are a blessing and a curse."

"Zhan, you think too much. I guess it is part of your powers that make you think in such a way."

"No, Xiong. It is the part of me that is just like the people of our village that provide these thoughts. Someday I know you will feel what I feel."

"What? When I am older? I do not hear Wei talking in such a manner."

"True, but Wei is Wei. As Ling would put it, Wei is a walking violation of the laws of nature."

"Aren't we all eldest one?" The two laughed. It felt good for them to laugh again. Lately, even Ling hadn't been his typically jovial self. They guessed even for jokesters like him humor was harder and harder to come by these days.

"Eldest Brother, it has been enlightening talking with you, but I am hungry. Let's eat."

***

The hot liquid slipped down his throat, filling him with power and life. Such a delicate young girl. Her skin was so soft and supple. He enjoyed stroking her body as he fed. He caressed her still developing breast. She couldn't be any more than fourteen. Most girls her age would be married and defiled by now. She was still pure. What a wonderful gift.

How could he thank Yue-Yan? The virginal blood of this girl was sweeter than he had ever experienced. Alas, however, this too must end. Tung could feel her heartbeat fading as he drew her life out to replenish his. He saw his lover out of the corner of his eye. She made her meal out of the girl's father. Yue-Yan fed with far less care than Tung. She had clawed the man to pieces as if he reminded her of someone she once held great hatred for. His victim had passed out early on and did not resist. Her father had slapped and punched at Yue-Yan until he no longer could.

Tung stood, stretching with the crack of bones as once stiff joints snapped back to life. He thought of hiding the girl's body but then decided against it. They would be nowhere near here by tomorrow night.

"Finished my dear?" he asked playfully.

"Always wishing there were more."

"We have a whole world at our disposal. Simply point the way, beautiful one, and there we will go."

"I want to experience something new, something different. I want to know what lies beyond this place, beyond these barbaric lands."

"South then, into a more civilized China?"

"No. I want to go west. I want to see places we have never heard or dreamed about. I want to experience everything. I want to see everything!"

"As long as I am with you, I don't care where we go. To the west then, for my love." Tung smiled at first, and then gave Yue a confused look. "Uh, I was never good at this, especially at night."

What's that?" She asked.

"West? Which way would that be?"

CHAPTER 13

There was stillness to the night. This was something Ju-Long had not enjoyed for a while. Two of his servants carried away the lifeless body from which he had fed. That was the last of the prisoners they had taken the night before. Their little band had been feeding off nearby villages, going out from the small encampment they had taken over. The first night they had hidden inside the huts, covering themselves with blankets and trusting their guardians to defend them from any danger.

The following night Ju-Long came up with a plan. He ordered his servants to gather wood and other materials and construct man-sized crates, built in such a way as to block the sun from its inner contents. They built nine the first day. Not the highest quality of craftsmanship, but the gaps in the wood were well packed with a combination of mud and grass. They weren't pretty, but they were highly functional. Ju-long expressed his pleasure, and returned the kindness by bringing back a feast for his hard workers. Along with a few prisoners he had also brought horses and carts, stolen from a small village they had left barren.

He believed that there was no reason to restrict their travel to night. With the crates, carts and horses, their servants could move them by day. He had their numbers built back up to twenty-one. In a couple of days his servants would outnumber his warriors. If you couldn't make your own kind, might as well stock up on the next best thing.

He had turned two young, attractive women into servants. He wasn't sure why he had, maybe in hopes that someday he would once again desire the company of a female. He had not had a single sexual urge since he had become the immortal being he now was. His drive was for blood, for power. Quenching his thirst was what brought him pleasure. Especially when the blood came from a mystical creature.

The other prisoners he just studied, trying to figure out how to turn them into xiang shi. That was a term he was using more and more lately. He enjoyed the sound of it as it rolled off his tongue. He had been enamored by it the first time he heard those miserable thieves cry it out in their terror stricken voices as they ran for their lives. Xiang shi. They would be the ones mothers warned their children about. *You had better be back by dark, or the xiang shi will get you!* The thought made Ju-Long grin.

Certainly when he unlocked the secret to create more like himself, it would be simple. That would infuriate him even more. Over the next couple of days his servants had completed the crates. Twenty-nine of them. The craftsmanship improved and the functionality remained impeccable. He took the number of human servants up to thirty-two. It was taxing, and he himself fed more than once per night. He continued to bring back carts, horses, and prisoners. Tonight would be their last night here. Before dawn he and his men would lie inside the crates. His servants would load them onto the carts, cover the crates in blankets, and away they would go.

When Ju-Long and his men awakened, they would be close to the next set of settlements. He was putting a lot of faith in his servants and their ability to defend them while he and his men were at their most vulnerable. It was one thing for them to guard their rest while they were hidden, but to rely on them as they traveled out in the open was an entirely different matter. They could easily run into trouble. A band of thieves looking for a quick score, a patrol of Jin soldiers, or a nomadic band of mercenaries could cross their path. His servants were well armed and certainly physically outclassed anyone they might run into. Cheng, the smallest of his warriors had trained the servants, including the women, in the art of combat. Cheng was short and frail looking clothed, but one of the most deadly he had. There was good reason why he was one of the survivors. With that idiot Kong gone, Piao nowhere to be found, and the survival of Quon and Yun-Qui unknown, Cheng had been promoted to his second in command.

If a larger force engaged them that could spell trouble, but alas this area would be hot soon. Word would eventually spread about abandoned villages and missing people. Then the hunt for them would be on. Best to move and keep moving for now.

The Jin had a presence here, but not like on the Wall and in the major cities. There was little threat of an uprising among these poor, unorganized peasants. There was also nothing here that was so valuable it need be defended by a large force. Ju-Long had definitely made the right move.

Ju-Long could sense another presence. He whirled around searching for someone. He didn't know who, but he scanned the area just the same. He saw only his men and his servants. Something though made him uneasy. He leapt off the rock he was perched upon and searched from hut to hut. Just as suddenly as he had felt the presence, it vanished. Something was watching them. He intended to find out what.

***

Zhan jerked, letting out a gasp of air. "Fool! How could you be so stupid?"

"What is it Master?" Gan said quietly as he hovered over his mentor with a cup of water. "Here"

"Thank you, Gan. There wouldn't be anything a little stronger around here, would there?"

"You know your brothers have taken all the wine from here for fear you would start drinking again."

"You are right. But this is different my boy. I merely need a little to calm my nerves and settle my stomach. Believe me—drunkenness is far from my plan."

Gan paused. He shook his head and frowned. "Wait here master." Gan hurried out of the room, checking the hall for others as he went. Zhan just sat there, trying to regain his composure. Within a few moments Gan returned with something tucked under his shirt. He entered the room and closed the door.

"Gan, you look like you have committed a crime and fear being caught."

"Here, master, drink the water then hand me your cup." Zhan gulped down the water and held out the cup in his shaking hand. Gan slipped a flask from under his shirt and took the cup. He nervously eyed the door as he poured the wine.

"One cup, master. If you become drunk it will not be hard for them to figure out who gave you the wine, and if they ask I cannot lie to them."

"Gan, you are truly an amazing young man. You will always hold your own special place in my heart. Thank you." Zhan greedily took the cup and tilted his head back, downing its contents in a single draw. "Ahhh. Wonderful."

"I hid one flask back for you, in case of such a time as this. Had I not truly believed it would do you good, I would not have let you know I possessed it."

"I don't blame you for your caution in bringing it to me. I assure you that I simply needed to take the edge off." Zhan held the cup back out, his hand steadier this time. "Now just a half cup more, and then put it away before somebody comes." Gan filled the cup a little over half, then tucked the flask back under his shirt and headed for the door.

Zhan sat in the same place sipping on the wine when Gan returned. "Sit down my son."

Gan sat cross-legged facing Zhan, leaving a respectful distance between them. "I was very careless tonight, young one. I can't believe how stupid I was." Zhan breathed in deeply enjoying the mild effects of the wine. "This week I have found my way into the mind of the one called Ju-Long. You know the one I speak of?"

Gan nodded.

"I carefully watched through his eyes tonight, read his thoughts while remaining hidden in his recesses of his mind. I learned more about him in a single night than all the other nights I was observing him through the eyes of others. This one is powerful. More powerful than I ever imagined. You understand, right? Of course you do. You are the brightest of pupils. Anyways, each night I watch and learn. Watch. Oh, how awful to watch these demons rob people of their lives. It is truly a horror you can never get used to." Zhan took down the last swallow of wine and put the cup down. "Tonight, little one. Ha, little one! That is how my father used to call me. How

I miss him. And mother too. Such simpler times then, even with the troubles we had that seemed so, so . . . paramount. Good word. It is one Te loves to use. Ahh, but I digress . . . hee, hee . . . another word Te would be pleased by! Are you following me alright? The wine has made me a little light-headed but I am still at full capacity. Not drunk. No, not I."

"Where was we? Yes, yes, those times held no horrors compared to today. Ju-Long could quite possibly take our village all by himself. That is were we not prepared. But, we are. Or shall be. We shall defeat him soundly, Gan, do not fret. I will never let anything harm you, dear boy."

"I feel safe here with you and your brothers. I do not worry."

"Good, good, very well then." Zhan reached out and patted Gan's knee. "So as I was saying, tonight I was careless. How could I be so stupid? I allowed him to detect my presence. Not on purpose, of course! It was as if I became so wrapped up in his thoughts that I began to slide further and further in. That is until he jumped, spinning around and searching for me with his eyes. He knows something was with him, but not who or what. He hasn't a clue that it was I. He believes he was being watched from the outside, not the opposite. I fear I may have spoiled it. He had become distracted with the multitude of problems he faces. That is how I got to him in the first place. He let his guard down." Zhan picked up the cup again, raised it to his lips and found it empty. He sat it back down, more than a little disappointed.

"Now, even as I hurried to withdraw from him, I felt the walls go back up. I may never be able to tap into him again. I know they are moving again. They are headed our way, but are still a couple of days off even if they traveled full speed ahead. They will be here and I will not have to worry about tapping into his mind anymore. Never again will I ever have to see any of his kind again. Never again have to witness them kill the innocent without mercy. He is coming and we shall end this game."

"Help me to bed, Gan. I need to rest. I'm afraid the wine is drawing me under," he said with a yawn. "Help me up." Gan jumped to his feet and reached out a hand. Zhan took it and slowly stood. His legs were a little wobbly, but the bed was not far. "You should get rest too, little one. Thank you for everything." Gan helped him to a sitting position on the edge of the bed, gave a bow, and scurried out the door.

Zhan listened as Gan's footsteps faded away down the hall. He waited a moment, and then got to his feet. *Thank you, Gan. I am sorry.* Zhan shuffled to the door, checked the hall, and moved in the direction Gan had gone. He had touched his young apprentice's mind long enough to see where the flask was hidden, and that there were four of them. He grabbed them all and hurried back to his room, shutting the door. He threw three down beside the bed and emptied the partial one left in his hand. He sat back on the bed and remembered the vision. When Ju-Long arrived it would be the last time he had to see these demons. Ju-long's warriors would be wiped out. The devil himself would be wounded. He would feed on one of the young boys to regain his strength. Another young one would come to the aid of the other. Ju-Long would drop the nearly dead one and grab the new prize. That young man was Gan. Zhan grabbed a second flask and took a draw. He was rushing toward the demon and his boy. His son. He drew the attention of the man-devil unto himself. Ju-Long dropped Gan's limp body on the ground. Ju-Long, the great dragon, sinking fangs into his neck is where the vision ended.

The vision had been consistent for the last five nights. Zhan emptied the second flask without even realizing it and flung it aside, grabbing a third one. Some of the events leading up to that moment varied, but the ending was always the same. Gan still had life in him when it ended. His own fate was a meal. And what happened to Ju-Long and Zhan's brothers was unknown to him.

It would be the last time he had to see these demons. It would be the last time he had to see such terrible atrocities. It would be the last time because he was dead.

***

Hu and Niu walked side by side on a trail partially shaded by the trees. Every time he looked at her, especially when she stepped into a spot of sun, he felt love renewed. She was so beautiful. The past week had been crazy.

They traveled constantly, heading in a northerly direction. Their second day reunited Niu had gone into heat. This drew the attention of not one, but two young adult male tigers in the area. They were brothers. Old enough to be on their own, but still young enough to want to be together. Mother had probably driven them away as she began to deal with a new litter of cubs. They weren't particularly large, but they were determined. And adolescent. And horny.

They were confused, yet curious as to why they had been drawn to a human female, when the scent they followed was tiger. Uncertainty kept them at a distance for several hours, as Niu and Hu looked for ways to drive them away in human form. It didn't work. The youngsters weren't smart enough to know they were outmatched. They kept circling closer. The last thing Hu wanted to have to do was kill them. What he really wanted to do was take Niu himself, as he had several times since the moment he found out she too held the tiger's curse within her. These meddling kids were standing in his way. The tiger inside him didn't like it.

The pair of tigers had lay down near a bush together several meters away. They yawned, and looked around, but still gave off the feel that an attack was coming. Take Hu out and then take the girl. *Not today, kiddos,* Hu thought. *Not today.* He moved closer to Niu. "Be watchful of our visitors. I am going to try to force the change and scare them off." Niu nodded. Hu slipped into the tree line behind them. As he went out of sight, the twins came up on their front paws, staring at Niu. She gripped the sword beside her a little tighter.

From behind her there was silence. Then the sound of agony and pain, Hu's screams came from the trees. Both tigers stood, on the alert. The one on her left took a couple of cautious steps to his right. Niu stood, bringing the sword in front of her and taking a defensive stance her husband had taught her. A roar sounded and a huge shadow went over her head. Hu, in tiger form, landed between her and the young ones. The pair of tigers fell back, hissing and baring fangs. Hu let out another roar. If the first was a warning, this one was a promise. He slowly edged toward them, puffing and gesturing as much as he could. They backed further away. In his human voice he bellowed "Run! Run Now!" There was a look of both terror and confusion in their eyes. He feigned a charge and the two turned tail and ran. He trotted behind them far enough to keep them moving, but not fast enough to make them turn and defend themselves. Once he was confident that they had received his message, that this tigress was spoken for, he turned to head back to Niu. She had followed and was only a few meters behind.

"My big protector. Chasing my suitors away. C'mon tiger, let's keep heading north, put some more distance between us and those cute little boys." And so the woman and her big orange and black pet moved on. They made love several times over the next few days, sometimes as humans, sometimes as animals. They fed and frolicked, and enjoyed being together again.

Today, he not only looked at his beautiful wife as they walked on, hand in hand, moving in and out of the sunlight and up the trail, but the mother of his child. Or children. Niu told him she was pregnant. He asked since when. She answered just in the past few days. "Are you sure?" He had asked.

"Yes, because the tiger inside me is sure."

***

Zhan awoke with a headache and a fierce need to pee. He got to his feet, still about half drunk, and saw that he had indeed emptied all four flasks. He shook his head and sighed at his stupidity. At the same time the thought of another drink started to come forefront in his mind. Gan and his brothers would be disappointed. They just didn't understand the pressure on him. The horrors he faced nightly. The doom that would soon befall him. Why couldn't he just drink a little when he wanted to? That was the real problem. They expected too much of him. They relied on him too much. They'd see how hard things were when he was gone and they couldn't turn to him anymore. Then they'd appreciate him. Then they'd understand.

Zhan moved over to the pot in the corner of the room. It wasn't a large pot, but it was easy to carry even when full. He was pretty sure it was going to be filled to the rim by the time he was done. Leaning on the wall with his left hand, and trying to aim with his right, Zhan proceeded to relieve himself, mostly on the floor and wall, with very little making the pot itself. He went back to his thoughts of self pity. *Why can't I just be myself? Why do I always have to hide who I am so I will not offend them? Who are they to judge me? Who do they think they are?*

He finished, stumbled back from the puddle he was standing in, and put himself away. A hand touched his shoulder and he felt calm. The hand stayed there and his mind began to clear from the alcohol and the headache disappeared. Te was right behind him. He wondered how long his brother had been there. He had not detected his presence.

"Our presence," he heard Xiong's voice.

"How long have you been in the room?"

"Two hours. Sitting in the opposite corner."

"Where is Gan?"

"He got us a few hours ago at dawn, right after he discovered you. He feels awful. But that is another matter. Right now we need you. How do you feel?"

"Besides the need for a bath and a drink of water, I feel much better now, Xiong. Thank you, Te."

"Done with the self loathing for a moment I hope, eldest one?"

"Yes."

"Good. That also is a matter for another time. For all of us. For now I will stay with you while you get ready." Xiong sounded calm, but there was an edge of anger and disappointment in his voice. Te removed his hand from Zhan and went over and picked the empty flasks up from the floor. As he moved to exit the room he stopped and gently placed a hand on Xiong's arm.

"Peace be with you, youngest one." Xiong didn't want to be calmed, but there was no choice. "I will gather the others while you help Zhan."

"You are right. We must all talk. If my drunken dreams are true, the demons will be here soon. Te, when you find Ling, send him to me." Te bowed and went out.

***

Zhan counseled with Ling and Xiong, then sent them north as fast as they could travel to warn the villages there of what would be upon them by nightfall. Most of the communities were preparing for the worst, banding together already. Zhan had urged them to come south to the monastery. They refused to leave their homes and their lands. Zhan respected their decision, and promised to give them as much advance warning as he could before the demons arrived. He had already touched their minds and let them know that the demons would soon be at their doorstep. He sent Xiong and Ling to try to persuade them once again to come south—and to help escort any who were willing.

Wei and Biao had only been asleep a short while. They had done the night watch. There was more to guard against than the demons. Thieves and rogue bands of overzealous Jin soldiers were still in existence as well. While they seemed insignificant right now, they still had to be dealt with. They were not awakened until Ling and Xiong had been gone for two hours. The others had already received the full report. Now Zhan explained to the next to oldest and next to youngest everything that was happening, except the mission Xiong and Ling were on. He merely told them they were on an errand to a neighboring village and moved on. He knew they would be angered that they had not gone as well. Biao would have been able to make the trip without slowing the other two down. Wei however was too slow of foot. Even a cart and a team of horses would not get him there as fast as his brothers.

Cai had heard the entire plan earlier. He realized that he, by himself, would not be any more help in battle than one of the villagers. He never planned on going it alone. He had reached out and called several tigers into the area, as well as a number of Amur and clouded leopards. He sent them to the area of the central village north of them where Xiong and Ling headed. It took effort to keep that many big cats in the same vicinity without fights breaking out. He solved the problem with the tigers by turning them into a hunting party. It was not common, but an occasional natural occurrence.

The leopards were another matter. They just never operated like that. Only during mating season did even the males and females come together. They were very solitary creatures.

He knew the real problem lay ahead. Orchestrating them in even closer quarters, around each other and humans, would be tricky. Just keeping them from attacking the wrong side would be a task in itself. He needed to be as close as possible to them if a battle broke out. He would need to guide them individually, yet simultaneously. He had been practicing this for a while off and on since he first learned of the existence of the demons. Especially after his trip via his rat friend. The real test would come soon enough, and he had no idea if he would be able to pull it off.

Cai gathered rations and water, planning to slip away and head north as soon as he could. If Zhan knew of his plan he would try to stop him.

***

"You are good, Biao, but not there yet."

"It is not done, Wei."

"You'll give. You might as well. You are beaten. Your speed and strength are still no substitute for my superior power and combat skills."

"Braggart."

"Sissy-boy."

"You'll pay for that, fat man!"

"Ha, ha! You so funny. Almost as funny as Ling!"

"I'll show you funny!"

"How? You're not going anywhere until I let you up. Your arms are pinned behind your back and I have your legs locked up with mine. I told you leverage is everything. If Te had you in this position he could hold you as long as he wanted."

"I doubt it. I'm almost free of you now."

"Really?"

"No. So could you please just get your oversized carcass off me?"

"You give then?"

"Yes."

"Say it."

"Just get off, Wei!"

"No. Say it."

"O.K., I give, now let me up!" Wei began to slowly get up, watching Biao carefully. "I said I give. I'm not going to try anything."

"I was kinda hoping you would. There's a new move I've been working on I'd like to try."

"Another time perhaps. I promised Zhan I'd see to it that the horses were fed and watered. Now get off, you big oaf."

Wei got to his feet. "It was fun brother."

"For you maybe. I just got whooped."

"But it was good training, no?"

"Of course, Wei. I needed to blow off some steam anyway. I want to face those demons and get it over with. I'm tired of sitting around waiting."

"I feel the same way. I think Zhan is wrong in waiting, especially at this point. But he is eldest, and he has the visions, so I will not go against him. Despite my occasional anger with his choices, now is not the time to fight amongst ourselves. As hard-headed as I can be, even I know that." Wei let out a groan as he rubbed his belly.

"What's wrong, Buddha? One of my fists of fury to that belly leave you a little sore?"

"Buddha is fine, little brother. However, Confucius say—*Smart man walk away before big man let one rip.*"

"Let what rip?" Then the smell hit him like a brick to the face. "What the?"

Wei chuckled deeply, his big belly shaking with laughter. "Silent, but deadly."

Biao walked down to the stables and the large pasture behind it where the horses were held. He would find Xiong, who should be back from his errand with Ling by then, and have lunch with him. He hadn't spent much time talking to Xiong lately. They had both been busy, and he had been training daily with Wei and the villagers. He loved Wei, but his big brother was not always easy to talk to. Xiong listened. Wei just gave his opinion. If yours was different from his, or Zhan's, he didn't want to hear it.

Biao saw someone duck behind a storage bin as he entered the stables. "Who's there?" No answer. "Come out now or I will have to come get you. You will not like that, I promise."

A head popped up. The corner of the stable was too dark to make out anything but an outline. "Come out from behind there. Step into the light."

"Biao, it's me."

"Cai? Why are you sneaking around?"

"If I tell you, do you swear you won't try and stop me?"

"That depends."

"Xiong and Ling are gone."

"Yes, but they should be back soon."

"It's more than a little errand to a neighboring village. That neighboring village is to the north."

"What for?"

"To try and sway the villagers to come here."

"So that is where they are headed. And what if the villagers refuse?"

"Then they are to return alone, immediately."

Biao shook his head. "You know that won't happen. Xiong will stay and Ling will not abandon his brother. What was Zhan thinking?"

"He believes Xiong will make the right decision."

"Did he make Xiong give his word to return?"

"I don't think--"

"Cai, you know you can't assume with Xiong. If he didn't give his word than he is under no obligation to return. His heart will go out to the foolish people who refuse to budge, not truly understanding these demons. They don't understand what they are up against. Xiong does, and he will not leave them to die. And Ling will not leave Xiong."

"I know that. It is why I am going and taking some animal friends with me."

"Does Zhan know of this?"

"No. And if you tell him before I am far enough away that someone could catch me and bring me back, then I will never speak to you again."

"Tell me, Cai, if you're on a fast horse with a head start, who would be fast enough to catch you? Xiong and Ling are gone."

"You."

"And why would I need to catch you when I am running right along beside you?"

"Should we tell Wei?" Cai asked. "He will have both our butts when he finds out we left him out of this."

"No. If something happens to us, he will be the last shot we have at defeating these demons. He can lead these people against the demons. Zhan, with all his wisdom, and Te, as intelligent as he may be, are not knowledgeable enough to orchestrate a battle plan. No. He must stay."

"Then help me finish getting this horse ready, and we will be on our way."

"First help me feed these horses. I gave my word. Then we go."

CHAPTER 14

Ju-Long awakened in completely dark surroundings. He lay there for a moment listening. All was quiet. Too quiet. They were not moving. Either they had reached the point he had instructed them to travel to, or something had gone wrong.

Quietly he lifted the lid and slid it aside. He was still bothered by the presence he had felt earlier. Maybe it had been Niu T'ou, come back to look in on his creation. If it was, Ju-Long had some questions for him. That is if he showed himself.

Ju-Long began to see this whole thing as some sort of game between the gods of the heavens and the gods of the underworld. They would soon find out that Ju-Long was not a pawn to be toyed with. But that he could think about later. Right now, as he eased from his resting place, he needed to find out what was going on with his caravan.

"Master, you are awake."

Nothing was going on. They had simply reached their destination a little ahead of schedule. They were still a way from the next settlement he intended to target. He was pleased that his servants had done exactly as they were told. He didn't want them to ride right into the village while he and his soldiers slept. He had suffered enough losses over the past month, he didn't need some nosy village elders to insist upon knowing what was in the crates his servants carried. It was getting harder to keep his soldiers alive when they were awake and aware of the danger around them. To lose them during a time when he was defenseless would be disaster.

"You have done well. Any problems?"

"No, master. We ran into no one on our journey."

"Have any of the others arisen?"

"No master."

"Is the prisoner I had you bind and bring with us still alive?"

"Yes, master."

"Bring him. I want to be at full strength before this night truly begins." The servant rushed off. Ju-Long stretched and walked around for a moment. Kai returned with the prisoner and Li Na, one of the twin sisters he had made into his first female servants.

Ju-Long took the man and fed furiously. Kai walked away to attend to other business, but Li Na remained, watching him as he drained the man of life. He finished and dropped the body to the earth. He stared into Li Na's eyes, not bothering to wipe the blood from his mouth. "Does it horrify you to watch me feed? Do you find my ways vile, young girl?"

Li Na remained silent, keeping her gaze fixed on his face. "Answer me, woman. I order you." Li Na paced gracefully toward him. *What kind of game does this child think she is playing? I will remind her of who I am if need be. I will not allow her to believe for very long that she may disobey me,* he thought.

Li Na moved tight in against him, her body pressed to his. She carefully placed a hand on his shoulder and rose up on her tip toes. Her tongue flicked out, licking the blood from his lips. Ju-Long felt something stir inside him. Old feelings arose within, as if awakened from a long, dormant sleep. He lifted the girl into his arms and engaged her in a kiss. Passion erupted inside. He accepted her tongue into his mouth and ran his hand down her back, gripping her firm buttocks. He wanted to take her right there. Power washed through him into her and from her back into him. She withdrew her mouth from his and kissed his cheek, then slid down to his neck. He looked around and saw the others rising. He put Li Na back on the ground.

"You stir things in me that have not been there for a while. When our work is done tonight, I will see you and your sister in private to finish what you have started."

"My only wish is to serve you well, master."

"And you shall. Now go. Tell Kai to get the horses moving as soon as all of my men are out of their resting places." Li-Na nodded and slowly turned away, smiling.

Cheng approached as Li Na walked away. "Master, I will gather the others and bring them to you."

"Good, Cheng. There is still a considerable distance to travel before we reach the settlements. Tell them the quicker we assemble and leave, the sooner they will feed."

***

The villagers had heard Xiong and Ling out, but still refused to go. The entire village was alive with people getting ready for the attack. The women and children were being escorted a safe distance south of the village by a small but well armed guard. Swords were carried in their sheaves, but wooded spears and bows were the weapons in hand.

Three of the other five villages were gathered in the main, larger settlement. The other two had either ignored the warning or were still on their way. Zhan believed that the central, largest village would be hit first. It also held the greatest number of sturdy buildings for the demons to hide during the day.

Ling had decided that he wasn't even going to try to talk Xiong out of staying with the villagers. He knew that would be wasted breath. There was no surprise when Xiong had told the villagers he would stand amongst them in battle. He had already started a battle plan with the elders of the four villages present. The chiefs offered some insight, but surrendered control to Xiong. They knew his plan would be best, and it allowed them to set aside their individual pride. This allowed Xiong to do what he had unknowingly trained for all his life. He was preparing to fight the forces of darkness that now plagued China. A part of him wished Biao or Wei was here to help.

"Take the men of your village and go to the line of trees at the far west end of this village. No fires and as little talking as possible. Have your men ready there with bows. The demons will come from the north. They will not be expecting a lot of resistance. They have no idea that we are aware of their coming. As soon as you judge them to be in range, give the command to fire. Remember you must compensate for their speed. Picture them as a herd of deer running full out towards the village, and make proper aim adjustments. You will probably only get off one round before they are upon us, so make it count. Have half your men reload in case they switch directions and come towards you. The rest should grab spears and do the best they can."

"Many of you will die tonight. You will be afraid. Very afraid. Gazing upon these creatures is like looking into the face of hell itself. You will want to run. You will want to hide. You will want to save yourself. I do not blame you. However, you're being here is of your own choosing. You chose to take a stand. Running from these beasts is futile. They are far too fast and determined to be deprived of the one thing which they seek from all of us. Blood."

"It is one thing to be brave right now. It will be another to remain so when they are upon us. Face your fears. Remember if we fail, if we do not stop them here, it will be your women and children who die next. Harsh words, but true nonetheless." Xiong turned to face the others.

"What about us?"

"Your men will hide in the huts with the remainder of Chief Wu-Kongs' men. The rest of his men, Ling, and me will be here and there." He pointed to two spots on the crude makeshift replica of the village he had made on the ground. It will look like a relaxed guard. I want them to feel it is business as usual. You will enter the battle when the demons are within the village perimeter. We won't have speed or strength on our side, so we will have to rely on surprise and numbers. We would have had no chance when they numbered five-hundred. Now, while not a great chance, these demons can bleed. These demons's can die. There is hope."

"How do you decide who hides in the huts, and who offers themselves up as the sacrificial goats standing guard in the open?" Chief Wu-Kong asked.

"Ling and I will change into outfits befitting of the people of your village. We will be two of the dozen 'sacrificial goats'. The others will not be chosen. Your men hear me as well as you do. The bravest of them will step forward. I look into their eyes now and know the men I speak of are among them."

***

Just ahead he could see the night watch with their torches. Maybe fourteen men total, talking and not paying attention to a damn thing. The village held around nine hundred, including women and children, who made up more than two thirds of the population. That left maybe two hundred men capable of putting up a fight. Ju-Long considered waiting for his human servants with the carts to catch up. The added firepower would be nice.

But his men, unlike he, had not fed and saw no reason to wait. They had risen a while ago and the thirst burned inside them. He would not prolong their thirst. If they had become so weak that they couldn't overrun a small village of peasant farmers, then there were larger problems to consider than the numbers game.

"Chang."

"Yes, master?"

"You will lead the men into the village. Stay low and silent until you are upon the guard. Surprise will be key. If they do not know what is upon them until the very last second, they will not be able to sound an alarm."

"Yes, master."

"I will be above, watching for any who might escape. We must work quickly." Ju-Long turned to his other men. "Feed only after the battle has been decided. Everybody watches everybody else's' back. I will not lose any of men to a bunch of farmers."

"Get them moving Cheng. I want this village under our control by the time the servants arrive." Cheng nodded in understanding as Ju-Long rose into the air.

***

"Be ready, but do nothing until you hear the snaps of our allies' bowstrings."

"I suddenly wish to run and hide, Xiong," one of the men said.

"A part of me does as well," Xiong lied. "We cannot let our fears rule us tonight. There is no escape from these demons. We must stand together. Right here. Right now."

"I will not run. If it be my time to die, I hope to drag at least one of them with me."

"Just remember their speed. Anticipate and strike where they will be. If you try to fight them like they are human, every move will be too late. Fight them like an animal." Xiong looked at the brave young man he was talking to. He had been among the first to step forward and volunteer to be a goat. He was physically mature, but had the eyes of an adolescent. He probably should have been taken with the women and children to a place out of harm's way.

Xiong looked deeper into his eyes, connecting with his mind. He was here to protect his mother and younger siblings. His father had passed, so being the eldest of seven children he had taken over the role of protector. Xiong would do everything he could to see this one lived till morning. If there had been more time, he would have sent the boy away from battle. Alas, there was not. "Stay close, kid."

***

Ju-Long planned to fly to the southern edge of the village, then circle overhead as his men engaged the peasants. No one could be allowed to escape. The longer they could remain a secret to the people of these lands, the better. The last thing he needed was a regiment of the Jin army to be sent here to put down whatever had the farmers running for their lives and screaming *Xiang shi.*

Movement in the trees to his right. *What the?* There were fifty or more men in the tree line. "Trap!" Ju-Long cried. "Retreat!" Arrows whistled through the night. They came from both sides. "No!" It was too late. His men were charging and some of the arrows were finding their marks.

***

Xiong heard the yell from above. One of the demons was airborne. Zhan had mentioned that a few of them, including Ju-Long, had the ability to fly. He had forgotten. A potentially deadly oversight. "Ling!"

"Already there, my brother!" The two dropped their spears and knocked arrows into place. "Just hold still creature and I'll cure your ills." Ling released his arrow and watched it go screaming into the demon's thigh.

Ju-Long watched as a third of his men howled in pain. "Damn you humans! You will pay for this! I will rip your hearts from your chests! I will twist your necks from the wretched bodies they rest upon!"

Something slammed into his thigh with such force it sent him flailing through the sky. A second arrow sailed by him. He righted himself, pulled the wooden projectile from his leg, and searched for its source.

Ling reloaded and took aim. Men were pouring from the huts, rushing to meet the enemy. He saw the airborne demon staring down at him. "That's right. It was me! Come to papa. I got your travel arrangements made! One way ticket back to hell!" The wind picked up as he let the arrow fly. Dark clouds rolled in overhead. His arrow sailed wide. Ling slung his bow over his back and looked for his spear.

Xiong led the charge. The sight of so many soldiers wielding spears sent the demons running. Finish their wounded. Tell my brother I follow the ones running north!" A couple had turned east and met a volley of arrows. Three of the beasts had turned west, meeting the same fate. A dozen were in full retreat.

Xiong knew he was outnumbered. He knew that save Ling none would be able to keep up with him or the northbound demons. Ling had hit the one in the sky. His own arrow had missed. He glanced upward looking for the beast, but only saw a storm brewing. He couldn't take them all, but maybe if he kept them in sight and observed where they hid, he could bring the men to them and finish this after dawn.

Ling grasped just below the business end of the spear and turned. A hand caught him by the throat and lifted him off the ground. The rain was coming down hard now, but he could make out the face, with its fangs.

"Game over! You lose!"

"Not quite, fly boy!" Ling shoved about a foot of the spear into the demon's side too quickly for it to defend. He could see the look of shock and pain fill the creature's eyes. "Speed kills!"

Ju-Long shoved him backward, sending Ling and his spear to the ground. "You are a more formidable opponent that I thought. Your blood will be a pleasure to drink."

Ling jumped to his feet only to have to roll away from the oncoming attack. He came up on the balls of his feet, his arms ready to fend off an oncoming blow. The demon was gone. *But how?* Ju-Long smiled as he wrapped his arms around Ling from behind.

"It appears speed does kill. You are exceptional, and fast, but still merely mortal. Did you really believe you could face the great Ju-Long and live to tell about it?"

"Xiong!" Ling cried. Ju-Long twisted Ling's head to reveal the large vein in his neck. "Xiong!" Ling tried to fight, but the demon was too strong. "Xiong!"

"No, my friend. Xiang shi!" Pain ripped through Ju-Long's back. He dropped Ling and spun around to meet his attacker. "You will die, boy!" He grabbed the young warrior, palming his head in one huge claw. He used his other hand to punch through the boy's chest, ripping his heart out.

"Look closely, child. This is your life ending." The young soldier choked, coughing blood from his mouth as he fell to the ground.

"Die!" Ling yelled as he drove a small, hand-held stake into Ju-long neck. Ju-Long howled, clutching at the wooden dagger. He yanked it out with a loud cry. The rain and winds had slowed. He was feeling weak. Others were coming. He looked around to see a score of men bearing down on him. He shot upward, fighting to maintain his grip on reality. He must feed. He was uncertain of his own ability to heal this many wounds without the help of fresh blood.

The rains had all but dissipated as Xiong gave chase. He could see wagons coming from the north. The demons were running for them. He glanced skyward again, looking for Ju-Long. He hoped his brother had finished him.

Loud roars filled the night. A number of large cats sprang from hiding places, pouncing on the demons. *Cai! But how?* He knew it was his brother's work. He reached out with his mind, but could not detect his sibling.

Xiong watched as the pack of tigers from one side, and a dozen leopards from the other tore into the demons. At least five of the creatures had dodged the big cats and kept running for the caravan. *Thanks for evening the score, brother. I will finish this fight!*

Xiong circled around the big cats, not wishing to become a meal himself, and headed for the wagons. He increased his speed. One of them had fallen behind. He was large, but slower than the others. Xiong closed on him and tackled the beast to the ground. "Help me!" the creature cried to his fleeing comrades. Xiong pulled a stake from his belt and drove it through the back of the demon's neck. The beast convulsed, gurgling but unable to scream. He rolled the demon over and drove a second stake through its heart.

An open hand slap drove Xiong sideways. He could feel the sting of the cuts claws had delivered to the side of his face. He rolled away from the force of the blow, coming to his feet just as a second demon leapt onto him. The hard landing knocked the wind from him as he fought to keep the beast's talons from tearing into him.

He could see the creature that had slapped him coming over to join the fight. Zhan had warned him that the demons were as strong as he was. He was finding out how right his brother had been. The approaching beast howled in pain, an arrow lay deep in the demon's chest. It drew the attention of the one on him, and Xiong took advantage. He pushed the beast off him and sprung to his feet. He had barely gotten his sword out when the creature came at him again. Xiong side-stepped, swinging the blade and cleaving away an arm. The monster roared, groping for his lost limb. Xiong stepped to him, swung the blade again, and relieved the demon of its head.

"You alright?"

Xiong turned, trembling. "Biao! Man am I glad to see you."

"I couldn't let you get all the glory. You've been stealing the show since the day you were born. Besides, someone had to save your ass!"

"I was just getting started. I had them right where I wanted them!"

"Glad to hear you're grateful."

"There's still more. At least three headed for that caravan."

You know, Xiong, if we finish this Wei will kick the shit out of both of us for not letting him in on the action."

"Biao, if we make it through the night, Wei can beat me senseless everyday for the rest of my life."

***

Cheng stumbled through the weeds, most of his thigh gone from the vicious bite of the tiger that had jumped him. A panther owned a chunk of his forearm. He had clawed his way out, killing two other cats, but couldn't save the other men. He needed to reach the servants. It was his only chance. He fell to his hands and knees. His head was swimming and he could not find his bearings. He crawled through the tall grass, unsure if he was headed for help or hell.

***

The people were unhitching the horses from the carts as Xiong and Biao approached. "What are they doing?" Biao asked. "Why aren't the demons attacking them?"

They must be the servants Zhan spoke of. I was afraid of this! We must turn back! There are too many!"

"Help us! Help us please! The xiang shi are going to kill us!" Two young women came screaming and crying toward them. Three men chased them, swords drawn.

"We can't leave them!"

"I know, Xiong." Xiong and Biao moved toward the girls. "Get behind us and keep running!"

Swords clashed, steel biting steel. Biao held one sword off while kicking a second attacker to the ground. Xiong met his opponent's sword, ripping down its blade and driving his sword into the man's torso. He drew his sword back, thrusting it into his attacker's chest. These weren't demons, but they weren't totally human either.

Biao wrestled with the other two, playing them off with defensive moves. His upper arm bled from a strike that had grazed him.

Xiong noticed the girls had not left. "Run! Get away from here! Run and don't stop!" Xiong turned his attention to the ones attacking Biao. Xiong rammed his blade through the side of one man, ripping upward. Biao drove his sword home, burying his sword through the other one's neck. Xiong swept the area. No one else was coming, yet the horses were free of the carts and the remaining people were riding off. The two brothers turned to find the girls standing there. "You should be running. C'mon let's get you out of here!"

"But we haven't thanked you yet." With a blur of speed, the girls kicked upward, planting their feet into the brothers' groins. Biao bowed forward, bellowing in pain. A flurry of fists and elbows drove Xiong to the ground, his sword falling from his hand. The other girl delivered a roundhouse kick that sent Biao sprawling sideways. "Don't kill them just yet, sister. The master may find use for them. A nice meal if nothing else."

Xiong grabbed the talking girl's foot. Her confidence and chatter would be her downfall. He gave it a hard jerk and sent her falling flat on her back. The girl rolled out of his reach as soon as she hit the ground. The brothers heard horses coming, hard and fast. Ling bolted out of nowhere, tackling the second girl to the ground. *Ling led the villagers here!*

"The ones fleeing are not human! They serve the demons!" Xiong looked around. The girl was running, managing to stay ahead of the horses. A storm followed them, and Xiong knew that Ju-Long was still alive. "Where is the other girl?" he asked, helping Ling to his feet."

"I don't know. I tackled her, then she punched me! Is my eye black? Man, I hope not. She hits like a mule!"

"She kicks like one, too." Biao groaned.

"You OK?" Xiong asked as he helped Biao up next.

"Other than my pride? Sore but still intact."

"C'mon! We must run down these devils!" Xiong yelled. "Keep one eye to the sky! No one escapes!"

CHAPTER 15

It was almost morning by the time they made it back to Chief Wu-Kong's village. They had delivered a serious blow to the demon's army. The game was not over yet. The villagers, along with Ling, Biao, and Xiong had chased the creatures a great distance, catching some of the human servants. There had been several small, but bloody skirmishes along the way. The demons sacrificed some of their servants to buy time for their own escape.

The only demon that dared to show himself during any of the fights was the one called Ju-Long. He would swoop in, snatch a villager from their horse, then fly away quickly. He took at least a half dozen men before he was through. After he had taken the last one, a great storm erupted, far more furious than the one that had gone on most of the night. It made travel impossible for the villagers, who turned back. The three brothers continued on, only to lose the trail of their enemy.

The journey back was a somber one. The storm had cleared, the sun came out, but despite the victory there was also great loss. Almost seventy five dead or unaccounted for. Xiong walked the village, hoping to find the young man among the survivors. He found him lying face down no more than twenty meter s from where they had spoken before the battle began. Tears filled his eyes. The young man was just a little older than Gan.

"That's the one that saved me last night."

"He was just a child, Ling. I should have been there. "What happened?" Xiong asked, wiping away the water that threatened to run down his cheeks."

"The flying one, Ju-Long attacked me as you and the others made your charge against the demons. I fought him hard, wounding him, but he was too strong. Maybe even faster than I. He had me from behind, ready to sink his fangs into my neck, when the boy came to my aid. He drove a wooden stake into the demon's back. The beast released me, turned, and killed the boy before I could stop him. I am sorry Xiong. It should be me lying there in his place."

"It is not your fault, Ling. I must see to it the boy is sent on to his next existence with proper care."

"I will help you. I owe the boy that much."

"No, you should return to the monastery. I will remain here with the villagers for a day or so. I will do what I can for the boy's mother and siblings. His father has already passed on. This will not be easy for them. I only hope there is an uncle or grandfather left for them."

"What shall I tell Zhan?"

"Zhan already knows everything." Xiong hesitated. "Has anyone seen Cai? He was at work last night. I never saw him, but the large cats joining in the fight wasn't mere chance."

"I have not, but I will find him if he is here."

"Good. I will help with the dead, then speak with the chiefs. Let me know what you find out."

***

Feng, Kang, and Shen had taken shelter in a small village that had been abandoned. The storm had driven them to cover. For whatever reason it had been the first night that they had not shifted into rat form with the coming of night. They could feel their animal counterpart within them, but it seemed to have resided a bit.

Just a couple of hours before dawn the door to their shelter burst open. A small band entered. A short fight ensued, but the demon men and their helpers were too strong. The one who had knocked Feng senseless, then drank his blood, was unbelievably powerful. Just when Feng thought he and his comrades would surely die, an enormous amount of energy transferred between the demon and him. It was a mixture of pleasure and pain. And then something seemed to click. A bond formed between the two as like creatures found each other.

The fanged man drew away from him laughing hysterically, as if drunk. The power subsided within Feng and he blacked out. He hadn't been sure what happened to his companions until he woke up. All three of them had been bound securely with thick rope. Four men stood guard over them, swords in hand. He tried to speak with them, reason with the men, but they stood silent without expression, as if they couldn't even hear him.

Feng glanced around the room. His friends were still out. He saw no sign of the demons, but there were what appeared to be three bodies, covered in blankets and hides lying on the other side of the room. His body was weak and feverish. His clothes were torn and spattered with blood. His anger rose, but he could not bring on the change and escape these ropes. It was probably for the best. Kang laid closest to him. Feng spoke to him, trying to wake him. Kang was alive. He was still badly bruised and swollen from the beating, but alive.

With no one to talk to, and no way to leave, Feng made another plea to his captors. "Please untie me. I am too injured to fight. My friends and I need food, water. I will not run. I give you my word." The guards didn't even bat an eye. "Please. I'm begging." The rat inside him began pacing. It was hungry, injured, and feeling trapped. These men were about to find out that nothing fights harder than a cornered rat!

"You could at least say something! Yes, no, go to hell! Untie me, you cowards, and I'll kill you all!" Feng struggled against the ropes, kicking wildly. A boot met the side of his face, hard, and the lights went out again.

***

"Wake up!" Ju-long ordered, slapping Feng's face. "Jia-Li, fetch some water and bring it to me."

Feng looked up at the demon who had fed on him last night. His vision was blurry, and he could feel the fever had gotten worse. His strength was minimal and his mouth was so dry he struggled to speak. "Water." He coughed.

"It is on the way my peculiar friend. I am not sure why I spared the three of you, but when you are strong enough, we will find out much about each other." Jia-Li returned with a large but leaky pail. She dipped a cup of it, leaned down, and put it to Feng's lips. He greedily emptied it and she filled it again. He took it down in three gulps, almost choking.

"Thank you. My friends, they need water, too. Please help them." Jia-Li looked at Ju-Long, who nodded. She went to the others, waking them and letting them drink.

"Please untie me. I will not run. I haven't the strength to fight. I give you my word."

"I will honor your request, but know that I am Death, and any treachery will lead to yours. Are we clear?"

"Yes."

"Kai, cut his ropes." Without a word Kai followed orders. He sliced the ropes that bound Feng's feet first. He roughly rolled Feng over, who let out a groan, and cut through those that bound his hands. Feng let out a moan and struggled to push himself up.

"It might be best to sit up for a while before you try to stand. Kai help him. Then free the others. Gently Kai. I don't want them damaged any further until I find out if they possess usefulness to me." Kai carefully helped Feng into a sitting position against the wall.

"Thank you."

"You're welcome. Are you hungry?"

"Yes."

"Of course. You must be starving. What do you eat?"

"I prefer a fresh kill, but I can eat the same as any human."

""Li Na, find some food for these gentleman." Ju-Long twirled one end of his long moustache between his fore finger and thumb. He crouched down so he was closer to Feng's eyelevel. "You can eat like a human, but you're not quite human, now are you?" You share your body with another creature."

"Yes. We all three do."

"So I have ascertained. In time you will explain it all in detail. However, allow me to introduce myself. I am Ju-Long, immortal god. I have no equal, only subordinates, servants, and prey. Once we have discovered just what you are, I will allow you to choose which of these you shall be." Ju-long stood, towering over Feng. "I am master of the xiang shi. Are you familiar with that term?"

"Yes. It means blood sucker."

Ju- Long chuckled. Suddenly Feng remembered the demons that had attacked them that night. It should have been easy pickings for the large band of thieves he rode with then. Instead it turned into a blood bath that Feng and his friends were lucky to escape. He almost mentioned it, then thought better of it.

"Good. I am glad you are at least somewhat educated. I can fly. I am able to control the winds and rain. I can bring on a storm with a mere thought. You probably saw and heard some of my handiwork last night. My power grows stronger each time I feed on another preternatural creature like you. I have drunk the blood of a mighty dragon, consumed the blood of the Naga, and now dined on whatever it is you are. Feel honored to have fed me, and be grateful that unlike everything else I have feasted on until you, I have killed. Somehow, with you and your friends, there seems to be some familiarity. A bond if you will. As if there is something that links us together. Did you feel the same thing as I drank from you last night?"

"Strangely, yes. I cannot describe it in words, but I felt a connection. There was an energy flow between us."

"Indeed. It is that very sensation that led me to spare you."

Li Na returned carrying three large cuts of meat. "Fresh enough for you?" She smiled sarcastically.

"Perfect." Feng's mouth watered. "Thank you."

The smile faded as she handed a slab to him. "We're down one horse, master. I would have hunted for some wild beast, but I did not wish to keep you waiting."

"You have done well, beautiful one. Now go with your sister and fetch some more water for these men. As soon as they have finished eating we will ride out of here. I must find food for my warriors."

"They have taken a little blood from your other servants. Just enough to quell their pangs."

"And from you, also?"

"No. They wished to, but I told them that my sister and I were off limits, per your orders, master."

"Very well then. I hope before this night is over to taste you both in many different ways."

***

Cai and Ling were headed back to the monastery. Xiong, and Biao, who refused to leave his brothers side, helped bury the dead and repair some of the damage to the huts caused by the storm. The women and children were brought back to the village just before nightfall. The four villages that were present agreed to stay together for at least a few days. The threat was still out there. They all doubted the demons would return here anytime soon. The question was where would they turn up next?"

Their need for blood would force them to another human settlement. They had a chance to end the nightmare, but had fallen short. More innocent people would die because of it. If only he knew where they were headed. Zhan could find out where they were.

Zhan. He had not been happy with the decisions Xiong had made. He had reluctantly answered his eldest brother's call earlier. He knew he was in for an ear, or rather a mind full. However, not everything Zhan had to say was bad. He refused to give up any information on the demon's whereabouts, except that they were a safe distance from the village and he did not foresee them coming back.

Zhan encouraged Xiong and Ling to finish their business and return home in the morning. Xiong made no promises, but did agree that both of them should return soon.

***

"You look as if your heart has been broken in two, brother."

"I'll be fine."

"Are you so sure, Xiong? It is the boy's death that troubles you?"

"Yes. He wasn't even supposed to be there. He should have been with the women and children."

"You must not blame yourself. Did you not tell Ling those exact same words?"

"Such a brave young man. He insisted on fighting. His mother told me that his father had been a great hunter, and the strongest warrior in their village. When he died, the boy tried to become just like him."

"I believe he did."

"But Biao, now he is dead, too. One day he might have been a mightier man than his father. He might have raised a strong family of his own. Now, no one will ever know."

"His bravery to stay, his courage to step forward, and his actions in battle last night more than proved he was every bit worthy to walk in his father's shoes.. He honored his father, his family, his village, and himself. He did not die in vain. He saved Ling from certain death. We will see to it that his death does not go unavenged."

"You are right about the first part. I only wish I could be so certain about the latter."

"Is there anything else troubling you?"

"Just a conversation Zhan and I had."

"Pretty pissed, isn't he?"

"Not today. Several days ago."

"And it still bothers you?"

"Yep."

"What was it about?"

"Family. Having a family of your own." Xiong shrugged. "You ever thought about marrying, having kids?"

"The last two women we dealt with kicked us in the family jewels and stomped the shit out of us. I'll pass. No thanks." They both grinned.

***

"So you were attacked by some pack of crazed rats? They passed a curse onto you, corrupted your blood so that you were no longer just you, but also them?"

"It sounds unbelievable, I know."

"Look closely into my eyes, Feng. I am the unbelievable. I was once merely human. Superior to all others, but human."

"Do you think that is why we appear to have this bond? The fact that we were transformed from our human state into something more fantastic?"

"Maybe a part of it, maybe not. When I fed from you, tasted your power, I also tasted some of my own. Not coming from me to you, then back again. It was coming directly from you, as if your blood possessed a part of me. I am not sure how this connection was formed, but it exists."

"So whatever made you also had a hand in making us?"

"I was forged by a devil from hell itself, not some fucking rats!"

Feng saw the anger flash in Ju-Long's eyes. "I am sorry. I did not mean to offend or suggest. Maybe the rats were lesser demons from hell sent to create us. Sent to aid you in your quest."

Ju-Long sighed. "I have my theories on many things. I believed that I had been created to rule all of China and beyond. I believed my victories would come easy. I believed that city after city would fall to me. Now, my army that once numbered over five-hundred is reduced to myself and two more. I am beginning to believe that we are all here for the sole purpose of amusing the gods of the heavens and the gods of the underworld. The devils below created us to use as their game pieces on earth. The gods of the heavens created them to fight against us."

"Them? Who are them?"

"Ahh. I am not surprised you have not met our counterparts yet. It wasn't until last night that I discovered them myself. Or at least three of their kind. I am certain there are more.

"So what are they?"

"Supernatural beings like us, only they have retained their human souls, where I have not. They are not as powerful as we are, but they are formidable opponents. I am sure their blood contains a wonderful kick."

"So, if all of this is just a game, where do the humans fall in?"

"They are not unlike the harvest. We try to send as many of their souls to hell as we can. The other side tries to save them from us. Our opposition is like the farmer, doing all he can to keep the crop healthy and strong so that they will produce what is expected of them. We, my friend, are the locust. We were sent to destroy and ruin the crop, using it up to fulfill our own needs."

"But I have no need for human blood or flesh. We can survive without that."

"Yes, but if you try to coexist with the humans, you will not last long. They despise anything different. Once they discover what you are, if they find you killing and eating their livestock, they will treat you as they treat all predators. They will hunt you down and kill you." Ju-Long shook his head. "Don't you get it Feng? Creatures like us were made to put fear in their hearts. Human kind was once the top of the food chain. Our presence has changed that. We threaten their existence. For certain they have worshipped their gods, paying respect to those they have never seen, but believe to exist. On the other hand they have become accustomed to ruling the things of this earth, and battle each other for that very right. I know, I once engaged in the same pattern of thought."

"With respect, great one, I must say that It appears you still think along those same lines. From what you have said, you wish to hold the same authority the humans now possess."

"Quite right. I like you Feng. You do listen well to what is said, and you seem intelligent, but you are still missing the point. Humans believe themselves to be powerful, yet they are not. Among the animal kingdom there are far more physically powerful creatures. The tiger, the leopard, and the elephant are all mightier than the human. Without man's weapons and intelligence they would be unable to defeat any of the creatures one on one. Sometimes even that is not enough to save them from those beasts."

"Humans are far too pathetic to rule as they do. They are fit to serve. You see Feng, it is our kind that are meant to rule. We are the perfect combination of both. We possess not only the superior human intellect, but also the strength of the mightiest creatures in the animal kingdom. And instead of worshipping gods they cannot see or touch, and doing their bidding, it is creatures like us, gods in human form, they should worship and serve."

Ju-Long rose from his sitting position. "Why should we merely coexist with the humans? We are more powerful. The only thing we lack are numbers. Once we have built an army large enough to put down all resistance, the humans will have no choice but to serve us or die."

"But, Ju-Long, without human blood to feed yourselves, would you not perish as well?"

"I could not go for a long period of time without it. That is true. Feng, my friend you underestimate the human will to survive. They will choose to serve once we are firmly in power. They already serve others of their own kind. Their emperors, their kings, and are we not more than they? Of course. Most humans are born into a life of servitude already. Who is more worthy of their services than us?"

"I guess I have just never looked at it in that manner before."

"Were you ever in a position of power before the change? Or were you merely one who followed orders?"

"I was not one to respect the laws of kings or emperors, but I did not lead men myself."

Ju-Long let a devilish grin cross his face. "I suspected as much. What you fail to comprehend Feng, is that the game has now changed for you. You have the power to rule, but lack the vision and drive. In the short time we have been together, I noticed how your friends look to you for guidance. You lead them without even knowing it."

"Kang and Shen are free to make their own choices. I have no say in what they do."

"Really?" Ju-Long shook his head. "Then explain to me why it is they have you do all the talking?" If they were your equal, or assumed a leadership role themselves, would they not be interested in hearing what I have to say? Of course they would. However they have entrusted you to do the talking, make the decisions, and lead them. They are counting on you to keep them alive when they know I can bring them death. Whether you accept it or not, whether you want it or not, they have given it to you."

"Then what is next?"

"We can play the game for the devils that made us, or we can say to hell with them and make our own way. We can become so powerful, so strong in number that even those who created us will fear us. To do this we must accomplish three things. First, we must survive. We should be the hunters, but for now we are the hunted. That leads to the second part, eradicating the supernatural ones sent against us. Once they are destroyed, there will be no one left to even come close to matching us in battle. Lastly, we must find a way to create more like us."

"I have already discovered how to share my power with the humans, turning them into my servants. I will find a way to turn them into warriors like my remaining two."

"How can you be sure?" Feng asked, hoping he had worded the question in a non offensive manner. It was clear this man was insane, but too dangerous to piss off.

"For, I was created by one of the devils of the underworld personally. When he made me, he told me that what I destroyed would be destroyed, but what I kissed, as he put it, would become like me. However, this kiss has evaded me. It is much more complicated that he made it out to be. I know it can be done. I will find the way!"

Ju-Long began to pace back and forth. "I believed, when he made me what I am, he was truly interested in making me to rule over the earth. I know now that his only concern was to fill his hell with more souls to torture. I could care less if I handed even one more soul over to him and his kind. If doing his bidding was my only goal, than I would have not hesitated in sending him yours."

"What?" Feng asked in surprise.

"Your soul. It has not left you as mine has abandoned me. My transformation was a true one, all my humanity taken. Your change, like you have referred to it, is just a curse. The beast lies within you, but it does not totally own you. Your humanity is not truly lost."

"How do you know this?"

"When I drank your blood I could taste the human soul within you. You are both man and beast, unlike me. There is no more human left in me than the one who made me what I am."

"So, and I am not sure why I dare even ask, why do you bother with us? We are part human, as you said, and certainly not as powerful or as worthy to rule as yourself."

"You know when to be humble. We must work on your self image. I am fully aware you are not my equal, but yet you would make a powerful ally. As we uncover the mysteries of ourselves, we would make a powerful team. You would always remain subordinate to me, but you would rule over your kind as well as the merely human. I would demand obedience as I do of all my men, but you would not go without compensation."

"Once we have control over the humans, I would give you your own kingdom to rule. You would be the Rat King, if you will. It would still be my world, but you would have your piece of it. Besides, you felt the ties that bind us just like I did. I believe you can make me more powerful than I already am. Otherwise you would not be here. I know I can make you more powerful."

"I see. And so I must make a choice?"

"My offer is not truly a choice, Feng. Consider it an ultimatum. Your friends up there, riding alongside my two men, are counting on you to make the right decision. My warriors will kill them the second I give the command. You do understand the gravity of this conversation now, don't you?"

"Yes."

"Good. Then I will expect your answer before the sun rises."

CHAPTER 16

Xiong and Biao rode through the night as fast as the horses could go. The two traveled northwest, then due west from the village. They had discussed the different routes their enemy might take to both find food and avoid conflict. The chiefs, elders, and others who knew well the territory agreed this would be the path of least resistance. Xiong hoped he could reach out with his mind if they got close enough and discover the demons location. If the girs that had beaten them were still alive they would be the easiest to locate. Both their faces were fresh in his mind. However, he was not Zhan. It was uncertain if his powers were enough to make that link.

"I would follow you into hell itself if that was where you were going, Xiong. Not because I respect your judgment. This idea is both crazy and foolish, but because you are my brother."

"You are my back, Biao. With you there, I have no fear of what is behind me."

"But you should, Xiong. These are not bandits or thieves we are fighting, these demons are equal to us. Maybe even better. I would sooner face a tribe of headhunters than one of these beasts, and we chase more than one. And who knows how many servants. We nearly lost last night, but Ling and the villagers saved us. When we find them this time there will be no Calvary to come to our rescue."

"I fully realize that, Biao. I am not without a plan. It is not my intention to rush into battle the moment we find them. We will simply watch them until dawn. When the xiang shi rest, we will make our move. That will leave only the servants. We take them out, then kill the devils while they rest."

"Biao laughed. That is your plan? I am sorry, Xiong, but obviously you forget about the strength and speed those two girls possessed. Taking out their servants is not as easy as you saying it. Had it not been for Ling, we might both be dead."

"They will not have the element of surprise on us this time. That luxury will be ours. And I am sure if we send our arrows true, we will be able to decrease the odds against us before they even know we are there. Biao, brother, we must end this. You know it. I know it. Even Zhan knows it. Our eldest brother is simply avoiding the inevitable because he fears them, especially Ju-Long. The time to finish this is now! If Zhan refuses to get involved, then we will do it on our own! Every day we waste, every day we let them exist, we run the risk of them discovering how to create their own. There can be no more waiting. No more hesitation. I do not want to be responsible for the blood of our fellow Chinamen anymore!"

"I am with you Xiong. I just hope you don't let your emotions interfere with your judgment. That boy is still not your fault."

Xiong slowed his horse to a trot, then stopped. "Would you say such a thing if that boy were Gan? If he had been one of the others that we have raised in the monastery? No, you would not. You would not rest until these demons were dead. You would not rest."

Biao paced his horse backed to Xiong. He saw his brother was near tears. Biao knew they would probably die if they carried out his brother's plan. It mattered not. "Xiong, my apologies. I said I would follow you into hell itself. Lead the way!"

***

Li Na rode Ju-Long hard. His right hand was clamped on her left ass cheek, driving her down as she slid from the tip of him all the way to where the bottom of her lips brushed his balls. Jia-Li was mounted on Ju-Long's mouth, facing her sister. She had one hand buried in her womanhood as her master explored her backside with his tongue. Li Na leaned forward into her sister's breasts. Jia-Li wrapped her free arm around her and held her as the strokes slowed and her body convulsed wildly. Li Na panted against her sister's chest as her body continued to shudder.

Soaking wet with sweat, she rolled off her master's still stiff member and lay on the ground beside him. Without missing a beat in his own work, Ju-

Long reached up aand grabbed a handful of Jia-Li's hair, pulling her forward and down to his manhood. As her mouth took him in he laid his head back and let out a moan. She worked her one hand and lips up and down his length in unison, still flicking the fingers of her other hand over herself. Ju-Long could feel himself getting close.

Jia-Li Raised her head, but continued to furiously work him with her hand. "Is the master ready to come for me?"

"Yes! He roared out.

Li Na joined her sister at his groin. Ju-Long grabbed Jia-Li's ass and shook as he exploded. The girls took turns catching his seed. They smiled and giggled, exchanging him in between their mouths.

"Do we please the master?"

"Yes, Jia-Li. I have never experienced such an intense sexual encounter. Truthfully, until I made you two my servants, I did not believe sex would ever be a part of my existence again."

Jia-Li moved up to rest her head on his shoulder and rubbed her inner thigh along his leg. She gently kissed his cheek as he stroked her silky hair. Li-Na played below his navel, hovering over his groin as she prepared to go down on him once again. "No more, my loves. Dawn is not far away and I must speak with the others before then." Ju-Long sat up, reaching for his clothes and gently moving Li Na away from his still erect manhood. "I would love nothing more than to continue our play, but there is work to be done. You two get dressed and fetch me one of the bandits we captured. You have awakened another hunger in me."

Ju-Long moved through the tree line. The girls would go to the small cave where Kai guarded the five prisoners and fetch his meal. Somehow, even though he knew his soul was gone, the reintroduction of sex in his life gave him a warm feeling inside.

***

"We have no choice at this point. If we wish to live we will let him believe we are with him. I do not trust this demon. He is a raving lunatic. I do not plan to go along with him for any longer than necessary."

"Feng, lest you forget, he killed our brethren. I do not wish to ride with him for even another day."

"It is the only way right now, Kang. Do you think that I do not feel the same anger as you? Especially after seeing those demons brutally murder that band tonight. We will make our split as soon as possible. For now, I need more time to think. Ju-Long told me it was follow him or meet death. What I need to know from you both is will you trust me, and go along while I figure out what to do next."

"I will," Shen answered. "I know we cannot fight these men and win. And I believe you are smart enough to make the right choices and get us out of this alive."

Kang sat silently, head down. "Kang, how about you? I need an answer before Ju-Long returns. Kang?"

"Of course I trust you. I will do whatever you ask. But I don't like it. Get us away from these demons as soon as you can."

"I will."

* * *

It was afternoon before Zhan crawled out of bed. He pushed aside his hunger, washed up, and went to gather Wei, Cai, Te and Ling. He already knew Xiong and Biao had not returned. Cai and Te were in the monastery. "Do you know where Wei and Ling are?"

"Wei is in the courtyard with Gan and several of the other boys. Ling is in the village somewhere."

"Come with me to the courtyard." The threesome moved silently down the halls. Wei was practicing the long staff with the boys. The small class straightened, then bowed as Zhan and the others entered.

"I thought you said Biao and Xiong would be back by today? They aren't coming back are they?"

"I am afraid not. Not by choice at least. Gan, boys, go and fetch Ling. Tell him to meet us here immediately."

"I'm going after them, Zhan. Nothing you can say will stop me. When I find them, and you will help me find them with those mind tricks of yours, I'm gonna beat them both within an inch of their lives, then drag their sorry asses back here."

"No, Wei. You will not go after them. You will wait here with the rest of us."

"The hell I will, Zhan. I'm not going to stand around here doing nothing while they go and get themselves killed."

If you leave, you'll miss them. They will be on their way back by dawn tomorrow, I promise you that."

"I don't believe you. You are just stalling, like usual. Why, I don't know. What I do know is what must be done, even if you refuse to see it. Now stand aside Zhan, or you'll end up getting hurt."

"What's going on?"

"Ling. Glad you're here. I'm going after Xiong and Biao. You in or what?"

Ling looked from his huge brother to his eldest brother. "I thought they were on their way back, Zhan."

"They will be. Help me talk this hot-head into hearing me out."

"Te moved around Wei, coming up behind him. Te laid his hands across his big brothers shoulders. "Not now, Te. I am pissed and want to stay that...aaaaaahhhhh." Wei slumped to his knees. "Why did you have to go and do that?" Te knelt with him, pouring calm, healing energy into Wei's body. There was no use fighting it. Te was good at this. He had brought down Wei from his rage too many times before.

"Alright Te, that's enough. I'll be good. I'll listen to what the old goat has to say. Just stop it. You're about to put me to sleep." Te lifted his hands and took a step back. "You know I'd whoop your ass, but you don't fight fair, Te."

"Thank you, Te." Zhan bowed to him. "Now I need you all to listen. Pay close attention. What I am about to do will change everything, and I don't know that we will have much time to prepare."

Gan crept down the hallway, sneaking like an intruder trying not to be discovered. He peeked around the corner, ensuring the coast was clear before he made the turn. It was. He bolted to the door and quietly pushed it open. He shut it carefully after he was inside. "I got it." Gan pulled the oversized wine flask from under his robe.

"Thank you, my boy. Now fetch my cup from the stand, then leave me."

"Are you sure? You might need me."

"Do not worry for me. I'll be just fine. I need solitude for what is next."

"Yes, master." Gan brought the cup to him, bowed, and turned to exit.

"You may wait outside the door, guarding it if you will."

"Yes, master. Gladly."

"Gan, I don't care what you hear coming from this room, you, or anyone else, must remain out there. Do you understand?"

"But--"

"No buts, Gan. No one enters. For any reason. I will emerge from the room when it is finished."

"Yes, Master Zhan."

"I will be alright little one."

"Gan exited the room, shutting the door tight. Zhan tossed the cup aside and took three long draws from the flask. Soon the trembling in his hands would quiet, and false courage would start to swell inside him. At least he hoped it would. He was not afraid. He was petrified. What he was about to do though, must be done. There was no more time to wait. Xiong and Biao would die going it on their own. Xiong did not realize just how dangerous Ju-Long was. Zhan did, and that is what terrified him.

***

The young man's eyes grew wide and he let out a muffled scream through the gag in his mouth. The slurping, sucking and gulping sounds pounded in his ears, along with his heart beat. It had been racing, but now slowed and began to fade. Ju-Long fed furiously, enjoying the rush, but yearning for another taste of Feng.

The vampire threw his head back, licking his lips. The man slid down the rock wall, falling to a heap on the floor.

"Master."

"Yes, Li Na."

"Kai located a cart. The others built the new strong boxes."

"And what have you and your sister been up to?"

"Watching and caring for your pet rats as you requested. They have been fed and watered. The one called Feng wishes an audience with you. All three of them have been whining to be untied."

"I can't blame them. However, I suppose they will blame me. Once Cheng has awakened, send him to me. I go to speak with our pets as you call them." He exited the cavern, pulling aside the furs that covered the entranceway. Kai and the other male servants had formed a half moon perimeter around the small cave. Jia-Li stood over Feng, Shen, and Kang, who were tied to a large tree inside the perimeter.

"Ju-Long! This was not part of the deal! I pledged our allegiance to you! This is our reward?"

"Feng, Feng, Feng, easy now. It might not have been part of your deal, but it was part of mine. I mean really, did you expect me to just take your word? Surely you understand that I couldn't allow you to run free while I rested. My servants had errands to take care of. You might have decided to take advantage of me when I am at my weakest. So, tying you up was the smart solution, don't you agree?"

"Well, how about now. You are awake. Untie us."

"First, I would watch my tone and be careful not to make demands. Second, you and your little pack need to understand that until I am confident you will not betray me, this is the way it shall be. Do not feel sorry for yourselves. You have it no worse than I. You are free by night, but bound by day. It is the same way I am bound by death during the hours of sunlight."

The three rats looked at each other puzzled. Ju-long realized he had just let them in on a little secret they did not know. *Damn it!* he thought. He was really slipping lately.

"How do we gain that trust. How may we convince you we are men of our word?"

"In time, Feng. In time. For now, make no demands. Do no more whining. These things will only bring your death. There is something I like about you, but not enough to spare your life if you cross me in the slightest."

Feng stared back into Ju-Long's eyes wanting to say something more. Instead, he lowered his head and accepted this defeat. "I understand, my friend."

"Oh, and for your information, we are no longer friends. You will call me master whenever you address me."

"Master!" Cheng called from behind him. Ju-Long turned to see his warriors on either side of a third man. They were struggling to keep him under control. It was the man Li Na and Jia-Li had brought him just before dawn this morning.

"I killed you boy! How is it you live tonight?"

"Master, he was feeding off the last prisoner. Came right up on us as we fed on the others! We had to drag him off. He fought us like crazy! He hits like we do!"

Ju-Long paused. *Could it be? Had he finally done it?* "He hits like we do because he is one of us! Release him!"

"What?"

"Release him, Cheng. Now!"

"Yes, master." His warriors let the man go and backed away, staying at the ready.

"What is your name, boy?"

"Qing-Nian."

"Who am I?"

"The one who attacked my people last night."

"No, I want to know who I am now."

"You are the one who made me."

"And what are you?"

"I am you."

"So then, I ask once more, who am I to you?"

"Master."

"Yes! I am master. Go and finish your meal, then report back to me."

"Yes, master." The young man, turned blood sucker, moved back into the cavern in a flash.

"Cheng! Ladies and gentleman, a new era has begun! I have created! There will be no stopping us now!"

"But how, master? How did you do it?" Cheng asked.

"I'm not sure. Come, we will discuss this when our new born returns. Kai, untie the rats. My mood has lightened and I have a good feeling about what the night will hold!"

***

"Xiong, come take a look at this." Biao shouted as he leapt from his steed. Xiong dropped from his mount and hurried over to his brother's side.

"What is it?"

"A dead horse. Let's take a look around."

"I'm with you. Look at the claw marks on its neck and chest."

"I know," Biao replied, already searching the area. "I think I found its rider."

Xiong stood, moving toward Biao.

"Look here at the bite marks. And here, his heart has been torn from the rib cage."

"You thinking what I'm thinking, big bro?"

"Yes. We are on the right trail."

"They can't be that far ahead us. We can catch them Biao!"

"Just hold on a second. Think. If we go any further we run the risk of stumbling into them blindly. If they are close, you should be able to find out where. Try and find the mind of one of the girls, like you said. Remember your plan only works if we surprise them, and make our assault after the sun rises."

"Yes, you are right. Keep looking around. I'll see what I can do."

***

Zhan felt his heart sink back in his own body. They had created another of their kind. He had waited too long. Maybe his brothers were right. He had sat idly by until the inevitable happened.

He looked through the one called Cheng's eyes upon the face of Ju-Long. It frightened him to even think about what came next. He had felt Ju-Long's power before. Now was not the time for panic. Zhan pushed himself into Ju-Long, slamming into a wall immediately. The mental barriers were in full force. It made no difference. Zhan was not trying to hide himself this trip. It was time to turn up the pressure.

***

"What did you say to me?"

"I have not spoken, master."

Ju-Long stood and turned to see Kai was still untying the rats.

"What is wrong, master?"

"Nothing. Get everyone here. I am going to take a little walk. Just keep everyone here. And be on the alert."

"Yes, master. Is there a problem?"

"Nothing I can't handle. I'll deal with this one personally." Ju-Long moved through the trees. The presence he felt was back. This time he would not allow whatever it was to escape.

***

"There are several more bodies and tracks leading west. Any luck on your end?"

"I am afraid not. I can feel Zhan, and that is all. He won't talk to me, but he is blocking my abilities. I don't know what he is up to. He is probably trying to force us home."

"Well, maybe he is right. I'm not suggesting we turn back, Xiong, but maybe we should hold up for a little while. Give this plan a little more thought. I want to end this as much as you do, but it is night. This is the most dangerous time."

"I am aware. Is there any food left?"

"Yes, I still have quite a bit."

"Good. We shall discuss this over supper. After that we will proceed cautiously. But we follow those tracks."

"Agreed."

***

Ju-Long continued his search, going further and further away from camp. The presence felt so strong, it had to be close.

"You fool. You search for me where I am not."

"What? Where are you? Show yourself and die like a man!" Ju-Long's head was on a swivel, scanning the area.

"I am not hiding. I am right here. Can you not feel me?"

"I can feel you alright! And when I can see you, I'm gonna rip your heart out!"

"You can feel me, but you don't know where I am? I guess I gave you too much credit. You are not the all powerful one I thought you were. Let me help you."

Ju-Long let out a roar as he fell to his knees. His head felt as if it were going to explode.

"Feel me now, great one?"

"Get out of my head!"

"Hurts, doesn't it?" I wasn't so sure it would work on you, but apparently it does just fine. The great dragon does have his weakness."

"You are a coward! Meet me face to face and I will feast on your blood!"

"Ju-Long, do not try to shut me out. Your resistance at this point only increases your pain. If you lived long enough you might someday possess the power to stop my intrusions, but I don't foresee you living much longer."

"I am immortal! You may cause me discomfort, but you'll never stop me!"

"Strong words from a man whom I have brought to his knees with just a portion of my power!"

"My words are strong, but my bite is stronger. Why don't you come feel it for yourself! Arghhh!" Ju-Long fell forward as the pain intensified again.

"Oh, I have watched you work. I know all about you. I have followed you since the night that devil made you."

"Are you a god, then?"

Zhan let out an echoing chuckle throughout Ju-Long's mind. "I own you."

"Then you must be a god. A god of the heavens I presume? I do not care where human souls go. I do not obey Yen-Lo or any of the other lords of the underworld. I live for Ju-Long alone!"

"I am flattered you think I am a god. Alas, I am not. I merely have a gift. How do you like my present so far?"

Ju-Long fought to his feet. No matter how intense the pain, he would not collapse again. This he vowed. "What is it you want?"

"Your death, Ju-Long! The death of your kind. Why don't you save us both the trouble, grab a large branch, shove it through your heart and be done with it."

"Never!"

"Really, Ju-Long? The game has been amusing, but I grow bored with it. I have you now. You will never escape me. There is nowhere to run. There is nowhere to hide. There is no place you can rest that I won't find you."

"If you want me dead you will have to do it in person. No matter how powerful your mind tricks may be, you'll never force me to take my own life."

"Now we're talking. Give me what I want. Deliver yourself to me."

"What? Walk right into a trap you have set for me? I don't think so! You want me, come get me, coward!"

"A trap? Of course I will have prepared for your arrival. Of course I have a plan. You have already escaped two of our plans. You might even escape this one."

"It was you!"

"The She-Le and the Xia? Correct. The village lying in wait? You know it. You say what I ask you to do is a trap? More like a challenge, coward!"

"A challenge? A fool's challenge! I am no fool!"

"It's the best offer you are going to get. If you make me chase you, I will simply arrive during the day. My men will slay your human servants, and then we'll take care of you. Oh, that's right," Zhan laughed, "days are bad for you. You rest all day. Say so long to your companions. Enjoy tonight and tomorrow, for on the third night you shall rise no more. You're dead Ju-Long. I'm just giving you an option as to how it all ends."

"Damn you! Damn you whoever you are!"

"You can call me master."

Ju-long fought the pain in his head, and the truth that rang through the man's words. It was so hard to think. "Wait a second." He hesitated. "If you think it is so easy to just come here and kill me while I rest, then why haven't you already done it?"

"That is a good question, deserving of an answer even coming from the likes of you. Let me explain. Up until now, watching mere humans destroy your army was fun enough for me. I couldn't believe the devils in hell would send something so powerful, yet so weak as their representatives on earth. How pathetic this whole thing has turned out to be. I was hoping for more of a challenge, but it looks like my task is easy. It's almost a shame that I have to waste my powers on you. Hell, we took a hundred of your mighty army using rats in Fanzhou!"

Rats? Ju-Long thought, but the thought went as quickly as it came. "A shame? I'll show you a shake! I don't believe you are nearly as powerful as you say you are! If you were you'd already have taken me out!"

"I told you Ju-Long, I was trying to make some sport of it. However, maybe you are right. Maybe I can't just run up there and take you out as I have said. Then again, maybe I can. You're right, don't worry about it at the break of dawn every day. 'Will it be today? Will it be today that Zhan and his men bring my death?'"

"Words! How about some action?"

"You mean like this?"

Ju-Long fought to remain upright. The pain in his head was excruciating! His knees began to buckle, his vision blurred, and his ears popped."

"I grow tired of you, Ju-Long. Maybe I'll just dispatch a legion of the Jin army on your location and let them finish my light work!"

"Enough! Just tell me where you are and I will be there!"

"Good choice. I would have taken the easy way out if you hadn't. Yet, I know it will be much more exciting to kill you in battle. While you have been a disappointment thus far, I'm sure you are capable of providing some entertainment. This works to your advantage as well. At least you will get to look into the eyes of the one who brings you death!"

"Enough talk! Tell me where!"

"From where you are, travel southeast. Further south than the village you had to run from two nights ago. You will find a monastery. A very large monastery with a village and farm land all around it. I'll give you a night to plan. I'm generous like that. But don't keep me waiting long. I may revoke my offer to let you die with honor, and simply drive a stake through your heart while you sleep."

Ju-Long laughed hysterically. "My friend, I just met the real you."

"How do you mean that? Laugh now, but not for long." There was a quiver in Zhan's last statement.

"You almost had me. Then I smelt it. It is unmistakable. Unfortunately, the pain you caused did not totally leave me without senses. Oh, I am coming alright. Don't worry yourself, Zhan. I am too excited! My appetite is wet for the taste of that which you reek! I will feast on you and make your powers mine!"

"What do you think you smell, Ju-Long?" Zhan tried to sound strong. "What is it?"

"Fear!"

Xiang Shi

***

"Gan, come quickly!" Gan burst through the door, rushing to Zhan.

"What is it master?"

"Get the others! I must contact Xiong and Biao immediately!"

"What has happened?"

"We have company coming, Gan. The kind of company nightmares are made of!" Gan turned and bolted out the door and into the hallway. Zhan breathlessly reached for the empty flask. He turned it up but found nothing but the scent of wine as he brought it to his lips. He tossed the useless thing across the room.

Zhan closed his eyes fighting back the fear, fighting off the urge to run screaming from the room. *How could I be so stupid?* Surely he should have realized a creature as powerful as Ju-Long could walk the channel back to him. Whenever you deal with a supernatural being you must assume they possess some psychic ability. It is the first rule of mental warfare!

"Xiong, hear me. Hear me now! You must return to our home immediately. I am exhausted. I cannot go into detail. Return because I have sent the enemy an invitation to our place, and he is coming!"

Zhan fell onto his back. His breath came in gasps. The ceiling swirled, his body and mind trembled. Underneath all the pain he could feel something. No—more like hear a faint, but recognizable voice. 'Who owns who?'

***

"Did you hear that?"

"What, Xiong?"

"No, of course you didn't. He was only talking to me."

"What? What already?"

"It was Zhan. His voice was faint, but desperate."

"What did he say?"

"I can't believe it. It might just be a trick to bring us back."

"Brother, what the hell are you talking about?"

"That is exactly what I am talking about, Biao! Zhan has invited hell to our home!"

"What does that mean?"

"He revealed himself to Ju-Long, challenged him to a fight."

"What? Not Zhan!"

"Yes. If what he says is true, Ju-Long and his small minion have accepted the challenge. That must have been what Zhan was up to."

"Then we head back?"

"Not necessarily, Biao. If we stop them, finish them off before they reach our village, maybe no one else will have to die."

"Xiong, if we fail on our own, that weakens the strength of the others. If we die trying to stop these demons, what happens to the others?"

"Biao--"

"No, Xiong. There is no way you are going to get me to agree to chasing these creatures any further. We are needed at home. Home is where we will make our stand. Together. Only when we work as one will we be able to conquer our enemy."

"But--"

"No. No buts. We turn back now. As elder brother I am pulling rank."

Xiong let out a huff. "I am not happy. I thought you would want to end this as badly as I do."

"I do. But let us be sure. Let us band with our brothers and do this right."

"What if it is just a trick by Zhan to get us to return?"

"I don't think so. I am not psychic, nor do I pretend to be. I believe Zhan is on the level with this."

"What makes you so sure?"

"I knew this moment was coming. I could see it growing in Zhan's eyes more and more lately."

"And what is it you see, Biao?"

"He has plunged into the fight. It has taken him long enough, but he has stepped up to end this. One way or another."

CHAPTER 17

"Master, are you alright?"

"Yes Cheng. I am fine. We have a new mission. A new goal. There is a new plague that threatens our existence. We shall wipe it from the face of the earth."

"Yes, master."

"Where is my creation?"

"Gathered with the others as you requested."

"Let us go to them. There is much to do, yet little time. We must make haste."

"What troubles you so, master?"

"Nothing. At least not for long. We will find out just how I created Qing-Nian, then we will duplicate the process as many times as possible over the next few days as we travel towards our enemy."

"Who is that, master?"

"His name is Zhan. I have only just met him, but he has known us all along. He knows our weaknesses, our time of vulnerability. He possesses powers that are not human."

"Can we defeat him, master?"

"I will feast on his blood before the week is out. He is powerful, yes, but not immortal. I have tasted his fear, felt his mortal soul. Zhan challenged me to a fight. Fool! I will bring death to his door step."

***

"We should turn back."

"That is crazy Quon. Ju-Long and the others are dead. If they are not, then Ju-Long will surely kill us on sight for deserters."

"Then what do we do now? We have reached the ocean. We can travel no further in this direction. These lands are too dangerous for us to stay in. The people here will hunt us down eventually."

"We will find a place to rest for this day, Quon. At next nightfall we shall feed, then cross this great water to the land on the other side. There, no one knows of us, so we can live safely for a while. Until we figure out what to do next."

"Yun-Qui, what if we do not find land and the sun rises while we are still over water?"

"We will find land. There is a country there. I have heard of it. Sailors have traveled there for trade, and sometimes war. They call it the country surrounded by water. It is like a great island."

"Yes, but can we make it in one night?"

"If we can feed quickly and leave right after. We will have to fly as fast as we can, but we can make it. We'll have to make it."

"I hope you are right."

"Faith, Quon. We will make a home there for as long as necessary. We will create our own servants to help us and protect us by day. This place, I believe they call it Japan, is like an overloaded fruit tree just waiting for us to harvest what we need."

***

"Tie these four up with the rest, Kai, and give me a total."

Kai nodded and pushed the men toward the cavern. "What is the plan now, master?"

"We have the four of us, Chang, plus nine servants left. We will make a half dozen more servants before dawn. The rest we will turn into ones like ourselves."

"I still do not understand the process, exactly, master."

"Quite simple, really. Our bite Cheng, is the kiss." Ju-Long wrapped a long arm around his much shorter warrior's shoulder. "If we just feed, drain the life from our victims without destroying them, that is the key. Before we were merciless, ripping out their hearts and shredding their bodies with our claws. We destroyed them, so they could not come back to us as our own."

"Now, my good man, we have learned better. If we just feed, then protect their body from the sun, the next night when we rise, so will they. We now possess the ability to turn whoever we choose into one of our own."

Kai came back. Li Na and Jai-Li were with him. "There are forty-six, master."

"But master--" Li Na interjected.

"Yes, beautiful one?"

"Three of them are women. You do not plan to turn them as well?"

"Why not? Women make wonderful servants. Look at you and your sister." Li Na and Jai-Li both lowered their heads. "What? What is wrong? I thought you both might enjoy more company of the female persuasion?"

"Yes, master."

"You sound less than thrilled by the notion, my loves." Ju-Long reached over, cupping the girls' chins in the palms of his hand, and gently forcing them to meet his gaze. "Do I detect jealousy?"

"What if you come to enjoy one of them more than us? You might forget about us. You might hand us off to one of your men. We are yours, master. We do not wish to be replaced." Li Na said with a tear forming in her eye. Jia-Li nodded in agreement.

"Li Na. Jia-Li. Your fears are unwarranted. You will always hold a special place of your own with me. Forever will you be mine, and mine alone. You are forbidden fruit for any amongst my ranks. I do not share like that. However, you must understand a man with an appetite like mine must have a variety to choose from. One of my powers cannot be bound like a commoner to a single woman. Even two women. It cannot be."

"Besides, maybe my men would someday like to have the pleasure of a woman. I cannot deny them that forever. Since they may never possess either of you, I must make more. On the other hand, I am more than satisfied with my present company. I will turn no more women for now. Set them aside till tomorrow. They will make a good first meal for some of our newborns."

"Yes, master. Thank you for your graciousness." The twins turned and went back into the cavern.

"Cheng, get the others. We have work to do. The sun will be up in a couple of hours and we must deliver our kiss to these men."

"You wish for us to help?"

"Yes, Chang. There is a limit to the amount of blood even I can consume in one night." Ju-Long thought for a moment. He hoped his men could create others in the same way as he. If they could, then they could turn at least two each tonight, for a total of eight. Then, if the four from their earlier feeding arose as well, that would make twelve. Add that to Ju-Long and the current three, and there would be sixteen. If they did the same with sixteen more upon rising, there would be thirty-two, and if that thirty two could do the same to sixty-four more. Ah, the possibilities. Zhan would be the first to face his new army. By the time they reached the monestary, Ju-Long's warriors would number in the hundreds, with three score of servants.

"Kai, come here."

"Yes, master?"

"After the break of dawn, you and a few of the others will scout out a village along a southeastern route. I want the location as soon as I wake. I know we have two carts, and horses for them. Find me three more. We will be transporting prisoners both alive and dead with us tomorrow night, and the dead ones won't walk themselves. A new dawn, sort to speak, is upon us. I want an army when we arrive at our enemies gates."

"Yes, master."

***

"Cai, Te, and Ling." Zhan motioned to them. "You three will begin passing the word amongst the village elders and warriors that the women and children are to be moved to the safe place, along with their guard, at dawn tomorrow. Then, the rest of us will meet when the sun reaches its highest point. Hopefully Xiong and Biao will be back by dark tonight. We will

254

finalize our plan then, and share it with the villagers at the meeting tomorrow."

"Yes, eldest one," Ling replied. "Who should I send to escort and guard the women and children? We discussed this, but never assigned the people to do it."

Zhan thought for a moment. He knew his decision would not go over well with the ones that were chosen. However, it was the best way. It was the way he could be sure that the one he loved the most would be out of harm's way. "The apprentices. Our apprentices. They are skilled and sufficient enough in number to handle the task. Gan will lead them."

Wei, who had been listening to be sure he would not be one of the ones handed the chore of escort and guardian, was even more appalled by the decision Zhan had made if he had been chosen. "What? Have you lost the last scrap of sanity you had holding you together? You cannot send the boys as guards! They're just, just, well, they're just boys!"

"Am I the only one who sees how absurd this is?" Wei continued his rant. "What if a band of thieves attacks the group while they travel? What if a rogue band of Jin soldiers decides to take the women for their own pleasure? Then what Zhan!"

"Every woman and child who can carry a spear, or a stake will be armed, Wei. Anyone of them that can shoot a bow will have one. Plus there are almost two hundred apprentices, average age is fourteen, who will be well armed and have been trained by the best. That would be you Wei! You even brag what fine warriors they have become. That is unless you have become as big of a braggart as you have a pain in my ass! Plus, while it is dangerous, it will be far safer than being here!"

"They are good! Yet they are boys! The training field is one thing! They are not battle tested! They have never had to kill before!"

"Battle tested! Oh, what a novel idea! You are right, they have never had to take another life before. I hope they never will! Battle tested?" He could see Te moving towards them both. "Not now, brother. We need to settle this!" Te bowed and stepped back as both of his eldest brothers stared holes through him. Zhan took another step towards Wei. "So you are telling me that you think it is a better idea to have them battle tested against the demons who come for us then to send them on what hopefully will be the uneventful chore of staying in a safe place with the women?"

"No, that is not what I meant." His voice was a low growl.

Zhan rapped his staff on Wei's huge arm. "You are the strongest man I know, and not just physically, but of heart." He moved the staff upward, tapping his brother's head. "But this, this is my forte. Let me do the thinking. I am always open to a bright suggestion from any of my brothers, but consider all the possibilities before you speak."

Wei pushed the staff aside, gritting his teeth.

"We have no time to fight amongst ourselves. There is way too much at stake in the very near future. I can see how badly you wish to hit me. I am not a strong physical specimen like you, but I am not without my defenses. There will be no more bickering from anyone involved. Not even you Wei. They draw even closer to us. Fight them, not me.

Te stepped between them, reaching out toward them both. "No, Te. Do not lay hands on him. I need to know right now if he can control his temper. Keep his ego in check. If his pride means more to him than anything else, he will prove to be more of a hindrance than a help."

Wei opened and closed his fists over and over again. "I can control my temper. You're still upright aren't you?" Ling chuckled in the background, drawing a stare from all. "I did not mean the boys should stay here and fight. I just think we need to send some adult males with them. At least twenty to twenty five."

"Done. You pick them. Then go over our battle plan again to make sure it is the best possible. In that I have total faith in you."

"Well, that's a new look, Zhan." Wei rolled his neck till it cracked.

"What's that?"

"No fear. Not even a twinkle of it in your eyes. That's a first in a long, long time. It makes me feel like following you, listening to what you have to say, and acting upon it."

"Unfortunately, I waited too long, let the wrong person sense that fear. I have made up my mind that Ju-Long will not see that fear when he arrives."

"As soon as this is over, I will go back to squabbling with you. I would truly miss it if we did not argue. It is in my nature. For now though I will follow." Wei bowed.

"I don't need you to follow. Just stand with me. With all of us. When we win this fight, we shall renew our natural way of differences."

"Agreed."

***

Ju-Long had been up for almost a half hour. Only Cheng had risen thus far. They had both drained one man each. Kai was loading their bodies into a cart. Ju-Long was tired of waiting. He watched from the entryway, hoping more would soon rise. His new creations lay lifeless. They had to rise. He knew he was right about this. They were deep in the cavern and true dark was moments away. *Patience.* It was not a quality he readily possessed. Nor did he wish for it. Twelve new warriors, six new servants, all in a single night. As soon as he defeated Zhan there would be nothing to stop him. He could rebuild an army in a matter of weeks. As long as he lived, the xiang shi lived. They were now the master race.

Two sat up, then another. Three more followed. *They are alive! They were alive and they were his!* No matter how much they despised him last night, they belonged to him now. So simple. So easy were they to create. If only it had not taken so long to discover, the Xia army would already be bowed before him.

After he answered this fool's challenge, which would be his next mission, he would go back to the lands of the She-Li and turn enough of them to finally conquer those who cursed and exiled him. How delightful that would be. The Xia council would die slowly. He might even turn a couple of them into servants, just so he could make them grovel at his feet for all eternity.

Ju-Long looked over his new creation. *How beautiful, wonderful, exciting.* "I am Ju-Long. I made you in my image. I have given you the gift of eternal life. I have passed to you more power than you have ever known. You will forever be indebted to me for it."

"To you I am ruler, chief, master, and god. You will do exactly as I say, when I say. You will be subordinates to me, but together we will rule over all other creation. There are two main rules to your eternal life. One is obeying me. The second—feed. The hunger you feel inside you now is not for food as you have known it. Search deep inside yourselves. That hunger is for blood. Human blood. It is all you may consume. It is all you will ever need."

Ju-Long's new warriors gathered closer as he spoke. He could see the need in their eyes. The mere mention of blood increased their hunger tenfold. "That is enough talk for now. There is much more for you to learn, but we will discuss that after dinner. It is time to go and quench that thirst. Follow me."

Ju-Long turned to lead them. Last night he had made history. The first of the new xiang shi was born. Tonight they would make the future. From now on the future belonged to the blood suckers.

Ju-Long could feel the energy that their hunger produced all around him. It was strange, yet exhilarating. Funny, since Zhan had played mind games with him yesterday, it had somehow sharpened his senses. It was as if a channel never before known to him opened in his mind. He wondered what powers Zhan's blood would hold for him. The thought was almost erotic.

"Kai, once they have finished feeding, load the dead and start moving towards the next village. We shall be along shortly. I have to give some instructions to our newly risen. We shall meet you on the outskirts."

"What about our pets?" Li Na asked, joining the conversation.

"Why yes. I almost forgot about them. Release them. If they wish they are free to go."

"Yes, master. Why the sudden change of heart?"

"I have not the time right now to worry about their loyalty. This next week will prove to be the most important in our history. I would just kill them, but they may have a use in time. Somehow, I believe I will be able to call them to me if I wish."

"Yes, master."

***

The monastery. Their home. A sight for sore eyes. They had traveled nearly non-stop. A part of Xiong still wished they had stayed on the trail. Mostly, though, he and his brother were glad to be home. "It is good."

"A beautiful thing, Xiong. Hell is coming, but right now all I see is heaven."

"I agree, Biao. Zhan will want to council with us immediately."

"He isn't saying squat until I have food in front of me. He can talk while we eat if he likes, little brother, but I will hear nothing until I am nourished."

"You sound like Wei."

"I feel as if I could eat like Wei tonight."

"Speaking of Wei, you think he's going to make us pay for our sins?"

"You mean running off to fight the demons without him, Xiong?"

"Yep."

"Oh, he's going to take a piece of our hides for it. But later. He knows business comes first. He will be focused on the enemy until the battle is over."

"Business, Biao? He's made a business out of kicking our butts since we were old enough to train."

"That's not business lil' bro. For Wei it's a pleasure." The two laughed as they stepped up the pace. They had ridden the horses until they were exhausted. They left them with a farmer on their way back. Since then they had been on foot.

"Race ya!"

"You'll just loose again, Biao."

"Bring it!"

The two brothers accelerated to full speed. In these times of trouble it was nice to act like boys without a care in the world. Maybe he would let Biao win for the first time in a long, long time.

Nah.

Ju-Long rode into the village on horseback, watching as his men fed for a second time tonight. The power flowed around him. Their power. It was almost as if he could feed off their rush without taking in a drop of blood for himself.

"Master?"

"Yes, Chang."

"Isn't it amazing?'

"You feel their power, too?"

Cheng let a puzzled look cross his face. "A little. What I mean is, isn't it amazing—that look in their eyes. The thrill of the kill. To them it is fresh, new, exciting. It is not just a means, but a magic."

"Yes. Funny how a little of the luster wears off over time. It is still exhilarating, but not like when we were them."

"I shall rally them, master."

"Have them load the ones they drained on the carts."

"And the prisoners?"

"There are no survivors, so there are no prisoners."

"But, master--"

"Cheng, there are no survivors."

"Oh. As you wish, master."

"This little village was just a stepping stone to the next." Ju-long dismounted and handed the reins to Cheng. "Take my horse. Keep everyone moving at a good pace. I am going to fly ahead and scout things out. I don't want any surprises tonight. There is much to be done, and the moonlight is burning."

***

Biao pushed his bowl aside. He had eaten too much. Even after he was full he kept packing it in. The boys had prepared a feast in honor of their return, and real food tasted so good. Xiong had finished long ago. Wei obligingly took the leftovers and began scarping them down.

"Better to my waist, than to waste," Wei said with a chuckle.

Biao noticed how light and friendly Wei had been since they returned. It was a pleasant change. Too pleasant. He must be planning something. "So, Wei, you're not even going to yell at us?"

"For what?"

"For running off and having all the fun without you?"

"You mean battling the demons? Taking off and trying to steal all the glory for yourselves?"

"Yes."

"Oh, I forgot. Besides, my time for fun is coming."

"So you are going to beat our asses?"

"You both place too high of an importance on yourselves. I speak of the devils whom will soon be here."

"So, you're not going to beat our asses?" Xiong interjected.

"No. I'm still going to stomp the shit out of both of you when this is over."

"See, Xiong? I told you!"

"True, Biao."

The three laughed heartily. It was not something they had done together lately. Actually, Biao couldn't remember the last time the three of them had laughed together at all. He and Xiong had their share of laughs, but Wei was so damn serious all the time.

Zhan entered, along with Cai, Te and Ling. "Well you boys seem to be having a good time."

"We were all making fun of you, Zhan," Wei said. The three of them laughed even harder. "Just kidding."

"I know. Usually you probably would have been. For now, I know different."

"Can anyone tell me where Wei is? And who this imposter is sitting across from me?" Biao laughed.

Zhan gave them a moment to settle down, then motioned for everyone to sit in a circle.

"So what is the plan eldest one?"

"It is not that simple, Xiong. Certainly I have ideas in mind. Some things are already being put into action. However, the battle itself will require us to work and think as a collective."

"So tell us what you got, and we'll go from there."

The dining hall was about to become the war room. What they planned here tonight would decide their fates. Zhan knew Ju-Long would show up soon, yet take just long enough to create a sizeable force to bring with him. The fields and the village would be littered with dead bodies. Both demon and human alike.

"The villagers are moving barriers into place around the northern part of the monastery and village. These barriers are made of long wooden shafts, sharpened at the end. It will not stop them, but it should slow them down. There will be strategic gaps between them to funnel our enemy, making it easier to take them out with arrows. Beyond those gaps there are pits, loosely covered with netting and brush and loaded with wooden stakes embedded in the earth." Wei explained as he rolled out a sketch of the battle field. "There will be archers all along the rooftops of the monestary. We will also have them four deep on the ground. Two lines will fire, and if there is time, so shall the next two. With any luck their forces will be decimated before things go hand to hand."

"Ling and Biao, you will watch the skies for Ju-Long and any airborne assault. A dozen archers will be assigned to you, Cai. Well you and Te are freelancers. Do what you do and go wherever you see need. Zhan will be inside the monastery doing his thing. Apparently Ju-Long can control the winds and weather. That could ruin our bow attack. So our eldest one will be keeping his mind occupied to prevent that from happening."

"What about the rest of the village?" Te asked.

"The rest of the village will be empty. With the women and the children gone, protecting it is unnecessary. Huts can be rebuilt."

"So can the monastery."

"True, Te, but we are not actually defending the monastery. It has a significant value to mount our defense, and gives the enemy a focal point. Plus we would have to spread ourselves thinner to defend a larger area. This will help force them into our hands."

"What if they don't come straight at us? With the monastery so heavily defended, would it not be wise to flank us from either side?"

"The entire monastery will be defended from all points. The goal is to have at least the majority of their forces attack from the north, but it is not the only plan," Wei explained.

"And as I can add, Te" Zhan spoke up "I will be in the monastery. Ju-Long wants me. His thirst requires my blood. I have challenged him. Plus, with his discovery of procreation, his arrogance is at a high right now. He could care less how many of his own are going to be sacrificed, he will make more. All he wants is me, and the rest of you, dead."

"I've heard every name but mine," Xiong spoke up "I'm starting to feel like I am not loved."

"Oh, but you are. You have the most important job of all."

"What would that be?"

"You're going to be my personal bodyguard. We will be in the courtyard in the center of the monastery."

"You're telling me that while these goofs are fighting the bad guys, you and I will be sitting in our own little sanctuary doing nothing? I ain't having it!"

"I will be doing plenty. And you will be making sure I have every opportunity to do it. If it is action you want, you'll get it. I just hope we're both enough to handle the action we are going to get."

"You mean Ju-Long?"

"Yes, Xiong."

"He might not even make it that far."

"Perhaps. I would be extremely surprised if he does not. Ju-Long is a survivor. He will not be stopped as easily as the others. He is very determined and will stop at nothing once his mind is set. He will see to it, despite our best efforts, he gets to me. That is when I will need you the most. While I'm no longer afraid of him, I do not believe I can defeat him one on one either."

"I like your plan a little better now. But if he ain't all that, and he doesn't survive the gauntlet awaiting him, then I'm gonna--"

"Be grateful that not even one more human will perish at his hands."

***

Huang-Fu slipped quietly into the hut. His half of the night watch was over. He tip-toed over to the room and saw his two angels fast asleep, his mother-in-law curled up beside them. As he walked to his room he noticed lights coming from it. He stepped inside to see a half dozen candles burning. Lin-Yao was awake, lying under a thin blanket smiling at him from their bed. "I figured you'd be asleep."

"Are you tired?" She grinned as she pulled the cover down far enough to expose her left breast.

"Not that tired." He smiled. Huang sat down on a stool and removed his boots. "They will be escorting the women and children to a safe place in the morning, a village south of here."

"They? You said they?"

"I am not one of the ones that were chosen to guard the group. My part of the battle is here."

"Why? You have risked more than most already! You deserve to sit this one out!"

"No man deserves to be put in this fight, my love. No man asked for this." He stood, lifting his shirt over his head and tossing it on the floor. He moved over to his wife, leaned down and gave her a gentle kiss.

"Let's just go. Grab the children and our family and run right now. You don't have to do this!"

"It must end somewhere. If we run, if others run, and the demons prevail, it will be our children and children's children who will truly suffer. I vowed to stand with good men and fight this evil." Lin-Yao went to say something, but he placed a single finger over her lips. A tear slid from her eye. "Not tonight. I just want to enjoy us."

He stood, grabbing the blanket and pulling it off her. He pulled the stool closer to the bed and sat down.

"What are you doing?"

"I just want to admire the perfection that is you."

"Are you afraid you will never see me again?"

"No. I just want to remember all that I am fighting for. I want to take in the reason I will make it through tomorrow night."

"Will you come for us when it is finished?"

"Nothing will stop me from doing that. I will always come for you."

"Will you come to bed with me?"

Huang stood, pushing his pants to the floor and stepping out of them. He started crawling to her at the foot of the bed, rubbing and kissing her feet. He slid his hands under her calves, massaging them as he kissed his way up to her knees. Scooting higher he moved his hands up umtil he cupped her ass. He lifted her hips slightly until her stared at her womanhood. She had never particularly had much more than a tuft of hair above her opening. He loved the view. He nuzzled his face against her thighs, gently kissing each one. Lin-Yao let out a coo as she spread her legs, inviting him to explore further. Huang blew gently over her vagina, bringing a soft moan from his wife.

"Tomorrow night, I will pray to any and every god that will listen." He ran his nose along her opening, taking in her beautiful scent. "But tonight, I worship just one goddess." Huang buried his face into her sweetness.

***

Ju-Long circled above the next village, scanning the surrounding area for any sign of danger. There were plenty of people that was for sure. He would divide them into three groups—those to be converted, those to be servants, and food. They drew closer to their enemy. It was important to create more of his kind, but also to add reinforcements to their daytime guard. He wasn't sure how close they were. Kai had ridden to the two villages they took tonight, and to three smaller ones further south. He found no sign of a huge monastery like the one called Zhan had shown Ju-Long during his mental intrusion. At dawn Ju-Long would have Kai ride again to try and locate the monastery. He did not want to be within easy striking distance for the enemy while he was at rest. That would be a fatal mistake.

He landed behind a hut, out of sight. His men would be here soon. He was anxious to see what powers he had transferred to those he had personally created. Could they fly? Could they bring a storm? How exciting was this new age."

***

"Xiong."

"Yes, eldest one."

"We have another problem."

"So what's new, Zhan? This whole dilemma is really just one big problem isn't it?" Ling joined in.

"True, but during our busy preparations, I have made an oversight that must be corrected. Many are already lost, but those who remain can be saved."

"What is it?"

"Ju-Long is coming."

"Duh," Ling said, expecting much more of an epiphany from his wise brother.

"He is coming, and he is hitting all the villages along the way. He builds his forces quicker than I thought. That is not good."

"So we gather an army and go on the offensive?" Xiong got excited.

"Hardly. There is an easier way."

"And what would that be?" Xiong huffed.

"I have contacted the chiefs of the three villages that remain between us and them. I have shown them what is coming. They have agreed to come to us for refuge. They are moving out now, but they are short horses, and to

266

travel that distance by foot would take them over a day, leaving them open to attack by the demons."

"So you want us to take them steeds and escort them in?" Cai asked.

"Correct. Take Biao, ten men from our village, and yourselves. Cai you will lead all the horses we can spare."

"When do we leave?"

"Now. Right now."

***

Ju-Long discovered that the ones he had personally created could all fly. They also could make it rain, but weren't able to make it storm. Ah, but they were still young. There strength and speed were as remarkable as the men in his original army. By sunset this evening they would number ninety-three. Respectable, but if Ju-Long could manage two more nights, the numbers he would have would be well over four hundred, along with nearly a hundred servants. He, and the larger of his new creations, had converted even more than his goal of having each man turn two per night.

He had also allowed Chang to create servants. As he expected, they were loyal to Chang. However, Chang was loyal to him, so it would suffice for now. There were three villages they could hit when they next arose, and hopefully Kai would find a couple more before the monastery. *Yes, that would be helpful.*

His warriors stormed the village. The people put up little resistance after they saw the speed and power of their adversaries. Ju-Long divided the peasants into his three groups and got his men to work.

"Chang!"

"I am here, master."

"Get these huts reinforced. Dawn comes soon."

"Yes, master."

"I will be retiring with my companions now. See to it the work is done. And that all are in before first light. I have already given Kai his instructions for the day."

"As you wish."

"Li Na! Jai-Li!

"Yes, master?"

"Come."

CHAPTER 18

The three friends had quit running. They now moved due east, once again in human form. Ju-Long had released them, but let them know he could find them again any time he wished. While that might be true, Feng and company had no intention of making it easy for him.

"Are you certain this is the best path of travel?"

"I don't know if there is a best path, but this is a logical choice, Shen."

"How so?"

"Ju-Long heads southeast."

"Yes, but that is half of the direction we travel. It still keeps us in line with those demons, Feng."

"For now it does. Ju-Long plans to rebuild his army after he takes out some adversary down south that he keeps rambling on about. After that he will head north to conquer the people that betrayed him. He was exiled by the Xia even before he became this demon. He wants revenge."

"How do you know all this?"

"Some things he told me. Other things I overheard, Shen. Do you two not use your new heightened sense of hearing?"

"Obviously not as effectively as you do."

"Then you should start. We are not different. Your powers are equal to mine. Our beasts are the same. It will take all of our abilities combined if we are to survive. Do you understand?" They both nodded.

The trio walked on silently for a while. The moon was bright and the skies were clear. Only a small shadow of the moon was missing. Soon, it would be full again.

"So I know we are heading east, but to where?"

"Shen, my friend, the only thing I can say for certain is that we are heading into the heart of the Jin's rule. It will be quite some time, if ever, before Ju-Long has a powerful enough force to take on their armies. By that time, we will be elsewhere."

***

"We will have these people back to the monastery well before dark," Xiong said as he trotted alongside Ling.

"That is a good thing. But what do we do with the women and children?" Zhan supposedly sent ours away this morning."

"I know, Ling. I imagine we will have to hide them in the monastery for tonight. There aren't that many of them." Xiong slowed down. "Shh."

"What is it?"

"Zhan reaches out to me. I must stop. Tell the others to continue. I will catch up."

Xiong found a spot off the trail and knelt down. *I am here, Zhan.*

A male servant heads to the third village. He has already found the other two abandoned. After that he seeks out our location.

What do you want me to do?

You and Ling turn back and find him. This is what he looks like. Zhan gave Xiong a mental image.

He's a big old boy. This should be fun.

Don't kill him unless he gives you no choice. I want you to send him back to Ju-Long with a message.

What message do you wish to relay?

Come tonight and end this game one way or another. If he does not, then at dawn we will come find him. Game over.

Then we wait no more?

That is correct. It is time to end it. Go now, and hurry back. You won't want to miss the battle.

Xiong quickly caught the others, grabbed Ling, and told the others to continue. He had an errand to run for Zhan.

"What's going down?"

"We are going to catch us a messenger pigeon, Ling. Then we are going to send him back to Ju-Long with an ultimatum."

***

Kai had reached the first two villages only to find them empty. That would not be the news the master wanted to hear. He was in sight of the third village, and it was looking just as empty. He would ride in just to be sure, but something must have tipped them off as to what was coming their way."

***

"Wait until he is all the way inside the village, then I'll take him from the front, you grab him from behind."

"No problem, Xiong."

"Oh, and try not to kill him. We are sending a message, remember? Hard to deliver a message when you are dead."

"We could write it out, attach it to him, and send the horse back with him on it."

"No guarantee the horse would go back." Xiong paused for a moment. "Damn, we should have brought Cai! He could have told the horse to go back."

A whisper came from behind them "Never fear, Cai is here."

"Where did you come from?"

"Mother and father, same as you!"

"Quit stealing my lines."

"Sorry, Ling. Biao thought one more wouldn't hurt. An extra set of eyes to watch your backs, and an extra sword if you need it."

"So what are you doing here?"

"So funny, Ling! You make me laugh." All three let out a low chuckle. "Biao wanted to come himself, but I persuaded him otherwise."

"How's that?"

"Easy, Xiong. Biao can be reasonable. I made his horse buck him. By the time he got his butt off the ground and realized what I'd done, I was already racing back to you guys."

"I'd love to have seen that. Good work, Cai."

"Well, thank you, Ling."

"That changes the game plan. We don't need your sword, Cai, but if you could find a writing utensil and some parchment, that would be great. Ling, knock in an arrow and take him out when he is in range."

Cai was off fetching the items and then writing the message.

"I can see him. Almost in range, Xiong. C'mon boy, we're the local welcoming party and we are going to show you a real good time."

"When this is all over, I think I'd like to do some traveling, see some new places. Take a little break, you know?"

"Gonna try to slip outta town before Wei beats the shit out of you, huh?"

"You know it, Ling. Want to come with?"

"I'm already there."

"And so is our friend. Now, Ling"

***

Kai felt the first arrow take him square in the chest. A heartbeat later a second lodged in his neck. The horse bucked wildly and he fell to the ground. *I am sorry, master. I have failed you.* All he could do was think the words, as blood filled his mouth, choking him. Everything swam around him, growing dark even as he stared into the bright afternoon sun.

***

"Carefully now, Xiong. I think he's dead, but best to be sure."

"Exactly what I was thinking." Xiong drew his sword up above his head in a two handed grip, then swung down hard, cleaving the head from the body just above his arrow."

272

"Well, if he wasn't dead, he is now." Ling said, poking the limp body with the end of his bow."

Cai had ridden up, holding the paper. "Let's tie him to the horse, attach the message, and I'll send the mare on her way."

Two men raced into the village, followed by a third on horseback. They were careful to enter from the west to avoid some of the pitfalls. As Cai tied up his horse, they spoke for the first time since heading back.

"Just a few hours of sun left."

"Getting nervous, Ling?"

"More like anxious, Xiong."

"I know the feeling."

"Do you two think the way we tied that man to the horse was really necessary?"

"Don't look at me, Cai. It was his idea."

"Well, Ling?"

"Are you serious? Did you see the size of his nose? I mean it just made sense." Ling laughed. "I just figured if we tied his head face down in the crack of his ass, the nose would help keep it from slipping off."

"Very funny."

"That's our Ling."

***

"Are the men in place?"

"Yes, Zhan."

I don't want to make the place look defenseless. That will only raise their suspicion and ruin our trap."

"We have a sufficient show of force without giving away our actual numbers."

"Excellent. You had enough volunteer to be in the open? I was afraid no one would want to take such a dangerous position."

"They are scared. But they do not lack courage in the face of fear. These are some of the bravest men I have ever met."

"Then they will do their jobs and we shall do ours." Zhan stood "Brothers, man your posts. Wei, lead us. Xiong with me."

"Yeah, big fella, lead us." Ling said. "What is your job, exactly?"

"I'm the one man wrecking crew. My job is to fuck demons up!"

"Fair enough."

"One moment Zhan, please."

"What is it Cai?"

"The tigers and the leopards I used to aid Xiong and the others?"

"Yes."

"I can reach them still, but they are tough to control. I think they have gone mad."

"Really? What do you think is wrong?"

"I'm not sure, but it might be related to the vampires they fought. Some of them consumed the demon's flesh. Maybe it transferred some of the essence of the xiang shi into them."

Zhan scratched his chin. "Possible. Besides being hard to control, what else are they doing?"

"Not all of them, but most of them, they crave something. I mean, sure, if they are really hungry they will go after whatever prey they can find. This—this is far too deliberate."

"What are you talking about, Cai?"

"Humans. They are deliberately hunting humans."

"Then tomorrow, if there be one for us, we will have to hunt them down and destroy them."

"I understand."

***

Ju-Long was awakened with a message running through his head that kept repeating. 'I am sorry, master. I have failed you.' It was Kai's voice. If

274

the enemy had taken him prisoner, then they must be closer than he thought.

"Master?"

"Yes, Li Na."

"You are needed outside."

"Kai has not returned, has he?"

"His body has, but he is no more."

"What?" Rage began to build inside him.

"Someone has killed him. They beheaded him, master. And they have sent a message as well, only none of us can read."

"Where is it?"

"Outside. Jia-Li has it."

"Let us go." He stormed past Li Na and went out into the village. He saw Kai tied to the horse in a most dishonorable manner.

"What kind of insult is this? How dare they mock me! How dare they send my servant back to me like this!" The skies darkened and a distant thunder began to roll. "Where is the message? Hand it to me, Jia-Li! And you two men, cut him loose and burn his remains in the fire! Now!"

Ju-Long snatched the scroll from her hand and paced away from the others. He read the note once, and then again. Some of his warriors had awakened. Others were on the rise. They would feed, and then, then they would end this!

"Game over?" Do you hear me, Zhan? I know you are listening! I will suck the life from you! I Will Kill You!"

***

"What is it, Zhan? What's wrong? Xiong asked.

"They're coming."

"Did you hear that?" Biao turned to Ling, who was busy making a few wise cracks to lighten the mood of the men around him. Ling turned to face him. His smile left him as he gazed upon his brother's serious expression.

275

"What is it?" Now the other men were turning to look at Biao. He could see their faces go from levity to fear."

"It was Zhan's voice. Let us ready ourselves. Hell will soon be upon us."

"They're coming?"

"Yes, Ling, they are coming!"

CHAPTER 19

The clouds and rain he had caused over the village did not follow him. He had calmed himself, wanting clear visibility as he scouted his target. He would bring the storm when he needed it. He climbed a little higher, wanting to make sure he was out of range of any arrow that might be aimed toward him. With the full moon and clear skies, he had no problem seeing the monastery and its surroundings.

There were archers on the roof tops, maybe a hundred. There were more archers on the ground. There was a wall of barricades across the northern border, made from sharpened wooden poles. It had gaps here and there, and looked unfinished. Most of his men could leap over them. Surprise, several would be flying in. The surrounding village appeared empty, and probably was. Defending it would spread the enemies forces thin. However, it would also be a good place to hide reinforcements inside the walls of its huts. Best to be sure it was empty.

Ju-Long went east of the village, lowered himself down to a meter off the ground. Had he actually been touching the earth, he would have been lying in a prone position. Cautiously he made his way in and peered through cracks and open windows. All the huts he looked in were empty. He was satisfied that the others were the same.

An ambush wasn't likely anyway. Everyone knew he was coming. He had been invited. Apparently the enemy was arrogant enough to believe they could defeat him in battle, head on. That would be their downfall. The one called Zhan and his allies would soon see the error of their ways, much to their demise. The two most important things in battle were to know your plan, and your men's ability to carry out that plan. Then it was just a matter of bringing on your opponents destruction. His men were not carrying weapons in hand. Instead, they had shields on each arm as defense against the archers. Once they were inside the enemy's perimeter, those would be shed, and the claws would come out. When his warriors were fully engaged, then the servants would ride in for support and clean up.

Time to fly back to where his men were waiting. He fired skyward, high enough to be out of range of any missiles. He looked down on the monastery and thought about how appropriate it would be for the devil to make his home there while he built his army. Soon he would be feasting on the blood of his enemy. *Yes, Zhan, the game over.*

***

Ling saw the figure jettison up from the village. It was too late to fire by the time he had the shot lined up. He was sure it was Ju-Long. Ling turned his gaze and scanned the village. *What if there were others? The attack might be on. Why hadn't Zhan contacted them?*

He is alone. Merely scouting. The war party has not arrived. Ling could hear Zhan's voice echo in his head. *I did not pry into his mind, but merely tracked his presence. Ju-Long is no fool, but he is beyond arrogant. It will be his downfall tonight.*

You will let us know when they are coming in force?

I will alert all when the time is upon us. Within the hour I believe. His forces are close. I must go. I am going to listen in on his conversation with his men through one named Cheng.

***

As he descended, he could see his men were awaiting his return. With a mere thought he had started a nice cloud cover their way. He would send it ahead of them, and just as they began their assault, he would create a storm with winds and rain that would make the enemies arrows useless. That would make the battle hand to hand, and he knew his men could win that one in a landslide.

Cheng fell to one knee in front of Ju-Long. "We await your command, master."

Ju-Long set to giving a quick, yet detailed description of the monastery turned stronghold. His men listened intently, asking no questions as he spoke. Cheng had wisely forewarned them that it would be a really bad idea to do so. With the layout of the objective fully described, it was time to divide the forces and reveal the plan.

"Cheng, you will take twenty of the men and circle east. You will attack via the village. The place is empty and the defenses on that side of the monastery are weak. You will cut off any attempt to escape by our foe. If there is none, than penetrate the monestary itself. Gather your force, but leave me the flyers, and depart now. You will need a head start to get into position just outside the village. Do not begin your assault until you see my fliers and I begin our attack on the monastery from above.

"Yes, master."

"My flighted fighters will gather unto me. A dozen warriors came forward. "The rest of you will storm the monastery head on. Once we have breached the outer defense, my servants will all ride in as reinforcement." He looked around and saw that his young, hungry warriors were focused and ready.

"Li Na, Jia –Li, come." The sisters were close to him already, and knelt before him almost immediately.

"Yes, master?" They answered in unison.

"You will return to the last village and wait there until I send for you."

Jia-Li spoke up. "Humbly, master, we beg you to let us fight for you. We will not be a burden in battle."

"Stand, ladies, and look me in the eyes." Ju-Long paused, taking in the beauty of both women. "As surely as I know we will be victorious tonight without you, I also realize you would fight with every ounce of your being for me. I know you would not be a burden in battle. You both handle yourselves well. However, I will not risk losing either of my treasures for any cause. You will go to the village and wait as I have commanded. It is your other services, not your ability to fight, that make you my most valuable assets."

The sisters gave a smile, then bowed. "As you wish, master."

Ju-Long turned to his airborne assault team. "We shall fly above the clouds as cover. I will bring rain and wind as we descend upon them from above and our ground force attacks from the north. Let us ride the night sky."

***

Can everyone hear me?

The six brothers answered Zhan's call almost in unison.

There will be a score entering the village from the east. Send the reserves to the huts closest to the monastery and ready them. Cai, are you ready on your end?

Moving the last of mine into place in the middle of the village. We will be ready, eldest one.

Good. They have a dozen, plus Ju-Long who can fly. They will be descending from the clouds above us. Have the second line of archers on the roof, and the fourth line on the ground look to the skies. Everything else is as planned for now. I will be occupied here shortly, as I prepare my personal attack on Ju-Long. He plans on bringing a storm with him to counter our archers. My job is to stop that if I can.

***

Ju-Long and his men hovered just above the clouds that covered the monastery. "As soon as we break the clouds, I will bring the storm. Fly fast into them, but spread out and do not take a simple straight line. Swerve to and fro'. Do not allow them to lock onto you with their arrows." He peeked through a gap in the clouds and saw his ground troops approaching.

"Now!" he screamed and plunged through the clouds. As he broke through he felt a presence. He knew it was his adversary, Zhan. "Get out of my head!"

"Now, Ju-long, is that anyway to greet an old friend? Your manners need correcting. Allow me!"

Ju-Long screamed as Zhan forced his way deep into his mind. Zhan searched for weaknesses, anything he could use to turn up the already intense pain. More importantly, he had found and temporarily shielded Ju-Long's ability to call the storm.

Ju-Long, clasping his hands over his ears in an attempt to keep his head from exploding, as it surely seemed it would, spiraled out of control toward the earth.

The flying demons were harder to hit than any of them had imagined. With over sixty men firing into the skies, the first round of arrows had only stuck around six or seven. Ling's shot had definitely been a kill, but the others plummeted to the ground screaming. The ones that remained were upon them quickly, flying into the roof top ranks. Ling had heard the bowstrings of the front line send their missiles towards the xiang shi approaching from the ground, but then the hand to hand fight was on. The demons ripped and tore into the men while they still held useless empty bows. It was a slaughterhouse that would not stop if they didn't think of something fast.

Huang-Fu lie face down in the trench with others. There were three of these trenches about forty meters outside of the wooden barrier. Each trench held twenty men lying side by side. Their mission had originally been to wait for the demons to pass over, then rise up and attack from the rear. That had changed with a message from the one named Zhan. Once the demon's passed over, they were to stand fast and wait for the sound of horses approaching from the north. These would be carrying Ju-Long's servants. Their job was to take them out.

The demons had passed what seemed like forever ago. They could hear the screams, cries, and wails of the battle to their south. Then hooves shook the ground before them. It was time. "Now!" Huang-Fu yelled. The men stood, flipping the light, but sturdy bamboo lid that covered the trench behind them. The men knocked in their arrows and let them fly into horse and rider alike.

Chang led the charge from the east, through the road that fed through the center of the village. A few of the men were ahead of him when the ground gave way and they disappeared into the earth. Chang and several others leapt over the pit. The rest swerved to one side or the other avoiding it. As Chang passed over, he saw the unfortunate ones that were impaled on wooden stakes at the bottom of the pit. They all slowed down their approach. Surely there were other traps set.

A bird, and then another flew by his head. He looked forward and saw a mass of birds coming for them. *Really? Tigers and leopards the last time. Now I have to battle birds?"*

Te could see the havoc being wreaked on the rooftop. He focused in from his hidden position and channeled his energy into one of the demons. This time it was not to heal, but to bring pain. It slowed the demon enough, made him pause, and allowed the much slower humans around him to send their stakes home.

Biao and Ling combined to take out one of the demons that had come from above. The humans had just taken out a second. There were three left and they were making short work of the village warriors. They saw another buckle in pain, then get staked by three humans around him. Biao ran and leapt on another, both of them disappearing over the wall and to the ground inside the monastery. Ling raced for the last one, a stake in each hand. Before he could get there, the demon flew upward. He dropped his stakes and grabbed a bow off the roof and drew an arrow from his quiver. The beast writhed in the air, thrashing about and clawing itself as if it were being attacked from the inside. Ling took aim and put the beast out of its misery.

Wei watched as the arrows flew into the enemy coming from the north. The second wave, sent by the third line rang out. A number of the demons fell, despite carrying shields. Others met their end in the pits. There were still more. Wei rose from his crouching position. One of the devils ran straight for him. He extended a large arm, and the fist at the end of it met the beast dead in the face, sending it flying backwards. Two more leapt at him. He caught one in each huge hand and crushed their necks. He tossed them to the side. "Next!"

Jie stared down on the battlefield from the second floor window. He ached to be in the action, but that was not his assignment. There were archers all over the second floor, posted in twos at each window. If the outer defense was defeated, then they were to open fire on any remaining demons. There were more ground forces hidden on the first floor. Together they were the last line of defense.

Jie had his bow ready, arrow in hand, but there were no clear shots. Somehow, the forces outside the monastery were holding their own. The large one, named Wei, was knocking demons around like it was an art form. He had never seen a man that size move with such grace and ease.

Chang fought off the birds, but not without a price. He watched as they flew away, heading east, away from the village. He looked to either side, having to turn his head fully to the left to see that way. A bird now held that eye in his belly. All the other men either lay on the ground moaning, or had been ripped completely to shreds by thousands of beaks. He turned in the direction of the monastery. There were fifty or more men, armed with spears, two meters from him. "Wll ain't this some shit." He groaned as one of them stepped forward and rammed the weapon through his chest.

Huang-Fu had taken a hard punch to his ribs, and another to the head. The man-demon on top of him now had locked hands on his throat and was quickly squeezing the life from him. His hand was on a stake, but his arm was pinned under the crazed man's leg. The night was growing darker. Huang-Fu knew he was dying.

Then the beast above him coughed, and blood spewed from its mouth. His body convulsed and his grip loosened. Huang-Fu took advantage, freed his arm, and drove the stake into his opponent's neck. He rolled the beast off, and saw several of his comrades also shoving their attackers off them. Some men were still fighting the remaining three servants, who were alive and well. The newly freed men, including Huang-Fu, rushed to their aid. Moments later the fight was over. They had lost plenty on their side, but the victory was theirs'.

"What happened?" One of the others asked.

"The gods themselves must have intervened." Huang answered.

"What next?"

"To the monastery! That battle wages on!"

***

Ju-Long woke. Unable to stop his plummet to the earth under Zhan's attack, he had slammed into the ground. The impact had rendered him unconscious. *How long have I been out? Is the battle over? Have my men claimed victory?*

No. He could still hear the war cries, and the screams of men dying. He could not feel Zhan's presence any longer. Maybe the fool actually believed he had killed the great Ju-Long. He would soon find out differently.

He tried to push his way to his feet, but his left shoulder screamed at him in agony. Obviously, along with his head, it had taken the brunt of the blow when he hit the ground. Ju-Long grimaced, then rolled to his right side and made his way to feet. Gingerly he ran his right hand over his left shoulder. The impact had moved that shoulder out of its natural position. If he could move it back into place, maybe he could use it again.

Out of habit, he took a deep breath, then gripped the dislocated shoulder with his right hand and began to pull it forward. He cried out, but continued the motion until he heard it pop back into place. It still throbbed, but he could use it again. He surveyed his surroundings. He had ended up southwest of the monastery. He could not see the battle from where he stood. His left shoulder let out another groan as he moved it. He thought about going skyward to observe how his warriors were faring. The last image in his head before he was knocked out came to him. It was a bald monk, sitting in a courtyard inside the monastery. Another monk, sword in hand stood guard next to him. It was Zhan sitting there. His shoulder rebelled against him again. He needed blood, and he knew whose blood he was about to drink.

Ling surveyed the ground battle between Biao and the demon. It was a stale mate. Both were bleeding but continuing to deliver blows. *Gotta save him for the second time in a week.* Ling strung an arrow into his bow, waited for a moment of separation, and sent the missile to the demon's heart. Biao watched as the beast fell lifeless. His eyes then searched upward, where he saw Ling smiling of all things. "That's two you owe me, Biao."

"Thanks, bro."

Ling caught something out of the corner of his eye bound over the southwest wall of the monastery. "Biao! Go to Zhan and Xiong! I'm right behind you!"

Zhan had lost contact with Ju-Long during his period of unconsciousness. He did not see him coming, nor did Xiong. Ju-Long leapt from the second story balcony and landed a hard right to the back of Xiong's head. Zhan turned with a scream as Xiong rolled by him. Before he could mind meld with his enemy, the devil was on top of him.

"I can taste your fear even before I tap your vein, Zhan. Sweet victory!" Ju-long drew back and sank his fangs in as he grasped Zhan's collar in both hands. He heard the missile a fraction of a second before it drove thru his left shoulder. Ju-Long let out a roar as a second landed just to the right of the first. He released Zhan, rolled to the right and onto his feet just in time to see his assailant drop from the same balcony he was just on. He recognized the face. It was the same one that had gotten away from him in the village several nights ago.

"You!" He yelled, just as a blur tackled him head on. This one was bulkier and stronger, and the hard impact on the ground broke and twisted the arrows inside Ju-Long.

"I see you've met my brother!" Biao yelled as he landed atop the struggling demon and began pummeling him with his fists. Caught by surprise, and in pain, Ju-Long absorbed blow after blow until he blocked a right with his bad arm, and caught a left with his right hand.

"My turn!" Ju-Long crushed a wrist in his grip, and head butted Biao three times before rolling right again and tossing his opponent across the courtyard. He leapt to his feet. He had sampled Zhan's blood, it was incredible, but he had not time to enjoy it. A stake took him in the left abdomen and Ju-Long cried out in agony.

"Just little ole me!" Ling said as he plunged the stake in several more times with lightening speed. He was on the attack, but failed to defend as Ju-Long drove an elbow back into his face. Blood gushed from Ling's crumpled nose as he flew backwards into a wall.

Ju-Long tore pieces of arrow from his shoulder. Some would have to wait. A pain exploded in his right thigh. He looked down to see the business end of a quarrel protruding through the front. He whirled and faced a boy who was doing his best to reload the crossbow he held. He heard men entering the courtyard from the north. A quick glance let him know they were not his, and they were armed with wooden weapons. Another glance and he saw archers gathering on the balcony. He picked the child up in a blur and leapt onto the south end of the balcony, disappearing down a corridor. He heard a cry from below as he moved through the monastery's second floor.

"Gan!"

Wei stood in the middle of the battlefield twirling a long staff sharpened on each end. There were moans all around him from dying men. Many were already dead. The big man looked to his left, then his right, staring briefly at the last demons standing against him. He readied himself to add two more to the bodies of both man and devil that littered the ground. A light rain had begun to fall, so that the blood Wei was covered in was being washed away. He could hear men from the village coming from the east, and the cries of others running back from the trenches in the north, successful in their missions. He would end this before they got here.

The one on the left sprang first. He caught the beast square in the chest, impaling it through the heart. Wei slammed the demon to the ground and crouched slightly, bringing the empty right end of the spear into the air. The second devil impaled himself on it through the abdomen. It clawed at Wei's back breaking three long nails as it barely broke skin. Wei let the spear drop from his hand and whirled around.

"I'd love to see if your fangs would break before they penetrated my hide, but I'm gonna just bust them out the old-fashioned way!" Wei said as he punched the demon in the face shattering teeth and bone. He drew a stake and drove it through the unconscious beast's heart. Then a voice boomed in his head. It was Zhan.

Gan!

Temporarily sated and almost healed, Ju-Long dropped the lifeless body aside and worked his way down a set of stairs. He could feel the presence in his head, but it was too busy sobbing and urging those around him to save the boy, to bother him. He could feel the shields that protected his mind full and in place. The little bit of blood that he had taken from Zhan had made him more aware of the inner recesses of his own mind. *How much power would I gain from a full feeding?* He reached out trying to see if he could sense any of his own. There was nothing. He could feel his twins in the distance, both distraught and crying, but nothing and no one else. Something far to the east, but that was all.

For tonight, he was on his own. He would escape this place when he was ready, but not until he had finished doing what he came for. *Your night is not over, Zhan. But it will be soon.*

"Find Gan! He is on the second floor with that devil. Save him! Save him!" Ling and Biao were on the move already, and via Te's arrival and touch, Xiong had recovered. The blow to the back of his head and neck had snapped two vertebrate, paralyzing him. "Go, Xiong! Find Gan!"

Te moved over to Zhan. "Your neck is bleeding eldest one."

"I'm fine! Get to Gan. His heart beat is faint, but he lives! Save him! Please save him Te!"

Jie and the men on the balcony were already running along the hall in the direction the demon had taken the boy. The men on the first floor followed the four brothers into the halls at the south end of the courtyard. "Second floor, near the rear stairwell." Zhan touched the minds of everyone in pursuit "Hurry!"

Ju-Long slipped out the east side of the monastery and shot skyward. The rain was light, but soon he would bring the worst storm this place had ever seen. That is after he attended to unfinished business. He confirmed that all his men, including Chang, who had attacked from the village, were dead. The northern battlefield was filled with celebrating humans, and in the distance he could see that his servants had fallen. His anger built, as did the rain, but he would hold it back. The last of the men had cleared out of the courtyard, save one. The only one he wanted. For now.

He felt the presence, stronger now, in his head.

"That's right. I'm here. I'm alone. Let's finish this!"

Ju-Long peered down to see Zhan staring up at him.

"Fool!"

Wei was surrounded by the villagers who were in various states of joy, relief, and sorrow as they hugged each other, happy to be alive but grief stricken at their fallen brothers and friends. Wei peered into the sky over the monastery. He saw a figure hover above the courtyard for a moment, then shoot downward. It wasn't over yet. The big man began pushing his way toward the north entrance.

Zhan pushed hard into Ju-Long's mind, throwing the demon off course and giving himself a chance to roll out of his path. Ju-Long skidded across the ground, his arms empty of the prize he had had in his sights. The pain in his head grew. The war of the minds was on, only this time he was armed.

Zhan threw mental blows, and Ju-Long blocked them. Not enough to totally stop them, but shunt their effects. *A sip of your blood has made me stronger. Imagine the power I will possess when I drain you dry, monk!*

Zhan concentrated his strikes on Ju-Long's vision center and balance as he moved in a wide circle around his opponent. Ju-Long fought the effects as he saw three to twelve versions of his opponent all around him. Each time he leapt forward his arms only caught air.

"You can only hide for so long, monk!" Ju-Long yelled. He stopped for a moment, trying to clear his mind. He shook his head, but the blurring only got worse.

"Your defenses are not enough. You will be blind soon." Zhan watched as Ju-Long continued to fight, and at the right moment drove a stake into his enemy's chest, just missing the heart. As he attempted to back away quickly, Ju-Long lashed out with a back fist that caught him flush on the jaw. He flew sideways, feeling bone snap.

Ju-Long yanked the stake from his body. The pain was intense, but his vision was clear. As clear as his target lying sprawled out to his right. Ju-Long was mounted on top of him in an instant. "That jaw does look painful. Wake up!" He hissed. "You're going to miss the best part!"

Zhan rolled his eyes upward and met Ju-Long's gaze. A moment later, his foe sank fangs into his neck for the second time tonight.

Wei entered the courtyard and saw the demon bite into his brother's neck. His thudding footsteps went unnoticed as he ran to Zhan's aid. He only hoped he would get there in time.

Ju-Long was lost in the rush from Zhan's blood. The image of the boy he had just fed on kept rolling through his mind. He transferred a thought as he felt his latest victim's heart beat weaken. *First, I broke your heart. Next I will remove it entirely.*

A strong hand grabbed him by the hair, another by his left arm. There were still splinters inside that shoulder, and he winced as he was ripped forcefully from his meal. He was easily twelve feet off the ground, staring at the sky, when he felt the shift in momentum and braced himself for what came next.

The impact was vicious as he met the ground hard for the second time tonight. It jarred every bone in his body, but he was still conscious. Kudos to him. "Shit!" he exclaimed, catching a glimpse of the behemoth that was jerking him back into the air. He grabbed the big man's wrist with his right hand and clamped down hard, but even his long fingers were not enough to encircle it. He heard his opponent chuckle as he was slammed down once again.

Wei saw his opponent was completely stunned. He lifted a large leg and stomped down, feeling ribs crack underfoot.

Ju-long roared, as the giant lifted his foot again, he had to move and move now.

The demon rolled away from him as his foot met the ground where the beast's head should have been. He saw Ju-Long come to his feet, then stumble into the wall, still dazed. Wei started his charge.

Ju-Long took a big side step to the right as the gargantuan blasted into the wall to his left, caving it partway out. This one wasn't fast, but he was strong, and impervious to pain. Like a raging bull, his opponent came off the wall and was on the attack.Only Ju-Long's superior speed, degraded by a multitude of broken and cracked bones, kept him just out of reach.

Everyone had a weakness, and was he at full strength, he would find it. But right now, even after the power he drew from Zhan's blood, he needed to escape and feed. He was certain this one wasn't going to offer up a vein any time soon. He sprung upward, attempting to fly out of danger, but his opponent caught his foot and sent him sailing across the courtyard. *This is getting old.* He thought as his body slammed into the north wall.

Wei glanced back and saw his eldest brother still lying motionless on the ground. He drew a stake from either side of his belt, and began to move purposely towards Ju-Long. "Time to end this!"

Ju-Long gathered himself and got to his feet. His foe was coming, stakes in hand. He was still fifteen meters away, not running, but coming. Ju-Long shook his head, trying to clear the cob webs. Then it came to him! His head! He had to use his head!

Wei was closing and the demon just stood there, glaring at him. "I will be quick now, devil." Then it hit. The pain in his head was excruciating. He dropped to his knees, the stakes dropping from his hands as he clamped them on either side of his head. He yelled out, unable to stand as agony shot through his entire body.

Ju-Long grinned as the big man fell forward, bowed three meters in front him. "As it should be!" He delighted in his new found power, but only for a moment. Men were pouring in from the south corridor. Archers lined the southern balcony, bows loaded. He delivered one last mental blow and saw his fallen giant curl into a fetal position on the ground. "Until we meet again!" He shot skyward, but a moment too late. A flurry of arrows was coming at him. Two found pay dirt. One caught him through the abdomen, a second drove into his left thigh. He spiraled right, barely clearing the west wall as he temporarily lost control.

Ling, the only one of the three with a bow as they entered through the east of the courtyard, took aim and fired as Ju-Long sailed over the west wall. The missile pierced deep into the right foot. He heard the roar of pain as Ju-Long disappeared into the rainy dark. "I hope that stings like my broken nose you poopyhead!"

"Poopyhead? Really? That's the best you got?" Biao shook his head. "Asshole!"

∗∗∗

Ju-Long reached out with his mind as he flew west. He could feel he twins, distraught and afraid. "I am headed west. Move quickly. Bring food. I will guide you too me. Get to me before dawn!"

CHAPTER 20

Zhan was on a table. Gan lay motionless on the one to his right. There was candle light, but the windows were completely covered with heavy blankets and furs. Te was slumped in the corner, sound asleep. "You are awake, eldest one?" Wei's voice came from the other side of the room.

"Yes." He coughed through a dry mouth. "Water." Wei helped him sit up and handed him an already filled cup. He gulped it down, then went into a coughing fit as he nearly choked on it. Wei took the cup and refilled it.

"Sip on this one."

"Yes. Thank you." Zhan took a small swig, rinsed it around his mouth, and then swallowed. "How long have I been out? Days? Weeks?"

"Not quite. Several hours."

"Gan lives. I can feel him as well as see him. How is he?"

"Stable. Te asked me to wake him in an hour. It is nearly time. He will be able to explain much better than I."

Zhan followed Wei's right arm down to his huge hand that was gripping an oversized stake on his belt. "You are expecting that kind of company by day?"

"It's been a long night and morning. This, and the one on my left were meant for Ju-Long. They never got delivered."

"He lives?" Zhan took another sip. "But of course he does. I should already know that. The only thought I have had since I was out has been about the one that lies on the table next to me."

"We believe so. He took a lot of damage, more than I have ever seen anyone, or anything take and still live. Let alone have the strength left to escape. He is hard to kill. If he managed to feed before the sunrise, then he probably lives. I was feet away from him when he attacked me the only way he could."

"Your mind. Power that he stole from me."

"It was not unlike the mental slaps you have delivered to me from time to time. This was intense. It dropped me instantly."

"The same way I used it to initially drop him. Did any others make it out with him?"

"He was the only one. Not even one of his servants remained alive. We lost many ourselves."

"Our brothers?" Zhan asked anxiously.

"Still alive. But many good men on our side perished last night."

"Of course." Zhan felt shame that his first thought went strictly to his own. Wei was right. Many were lost that deserved to still be alive. Brave men. Men that were far better than he.

"And you? How are you?"

"My head is still pounding, but I am fine."

"Te has not attended to something so simple yet?"

"There were far greater needs, inside and outside this room, then mine. He is drained."

"Yes. I would imagine so." Zhan took a larger swig from the cup. "Your still gripping that stake like you might have to use it at any moment. Does it hold another purpose?"

"It did. It does."

"And?"

"If you woke, but were no longer you--"

"You were the one that was elected to take me out?"

"No. All of us volunteered. I just pulled seniority."

Zhan gave him a look of surprise.

"Just kidding." Wei smiled. "It was determined that I was the only one with the inner strength to follow through with what must be done."

"And, am I still me?"

"I believe so. Te will know for sure."

"And after that?"

"I'll take my hand off. Until tonight."

"You believe Ju-Long will return tonight?"

"It's not impossible. But no." Wei glanced over at Gan. "If he awakens, and the worst has happened, I too am the only one with the inner strength to do what must be done."

"You can't kill him!"

"His request. It is what he made me promise him during his brief period of consciousness just before dawn."

"He spoke?"

"Weakly, but yes."

"What did he say?" Zhan put his feet over the side of the table facing the one Gan was on.

"He asked how you were. Fine we told him, but resting. Then he asked Te if he was going to become a demon. We told him we did not know yet, but we were doing everything we could. Then he looked at me and said 'Master Wei, if I have been turned, than my soul will already be moving into its next existence. What you see, won't be me. Promise you'll kill it.'"

Tears trickled down Zhan's cheeks. "So brave. So smart." Zhan stood, a little wobbly, then knelt by Gan's bed, holding the boy's hand in both of his. What has been done for him? What can be done?"

"I had better wake--"

"I am already awake, Wei." Te got to his feet and moved towards them.

"What can we do for Gan?"

"First you, then him." Te reached out and placed one hand on Zhan's forehead, and the other on the back of his neck. "I will need you to let go of Gan's hand during this. I want no possible interference." He closed his eyes and began the examination.

Zhan could feel Te's energy slowly moving through him, searching. It seemed to take forever. Te left no organ, no vein, and no tissue unchecked. When he finally finished, he removed his hands and spoke. "He is completely clear. Not even a trace remains."

"No trace of what?" Zhan asked.

"The demon's bite transferred something into your blood stream. It was spreading very slowly when you were at your weakest. I helped your blood cells multiple and rejuvenate. It stopped the spread of whatever was in you.

The stronger you got, the harder your body fought. It actually began to take out the—the—the infection we will call it. It seems your blood has now totally removed any remnant from your system."

"That's good to hear." Zhan glanced back at Wei. "You can take your hand off the stake now."

"Gladly."

"What about Gan?"

"Gan had the same infection as you. His was spreading much more rapidly. I came up with an idea after I saw how your blood was fighting it."

"So you gave him some of my blood?"

"Hardly. You were still weak at the time. But I figured, since we are all brothers, and we all share the same bloodline, maybe ours would work. Long story short, we gave him our blood. We started with Xiong, then Biao. Their blood slowed the progress. Then Cai's and Wei's did the same. It was slowing, but not stopping. Ling refused until I fixed his nose."

"Yeah, until he made our little princess beautiful again." Wei chuckled.

"Yes. He is all pretty again. His donation slowed it even further. When I gave Gan mine, the spread of the infection stopped. You were much better at that time, so we added yours to the mix."

"And?"

"Same as mine. The spread had stopped, but there was no sign of reversal."

Zhan's heart sank even lower. "Give him more! Give him all my blood!"

"That has been done. We gave him more of yours before I fell asleep."

"And?"

"And we're about to find out if anything has changed." Te moved around the table and up to Gan's head. He placed his hands on the boy, closed his eyes, and began.

Zhan watched in nervous silence. A puzzled look came across Te's face several times. When he opened his eyes and removed his hands, he just stood there saying nothing. Zhan couldn't stand the silence.

"Say something! Is he better? The same? Worse? Speak damn it!"

"I don't know."

"What don't you mean you don't know?""

"When I checked last, I could detect the distinct differences in the blood. I could recognize each of our bloods, surrounding the infection and protecting what was left of Gan's own blood." He scratched his head and moved a couple of steps away from the table."

"And?" Zhan snorted.

"I can detect our blood, his blood, the infection still. But they are no longer individual. They are no longer separate. Everything is combining."

"Is that good? Bad?"

"I don't know Zhan. No one will know, until he wakes."

***

It had been over a week since Ju-Long lost the last remnants of his old army, all of his new army, and every human servant save the ones he lay between. It was a strange feeling, to not even care if he led an army. He knew he would again someday, but for now life was good. He had selected and created a dozen human servants. All male, all large, and all skilled Jin soldiers. They traveled by day with him safely tucked into an eight foot long crate.

He had not created another of his own. Not that he kept anyway. On the third night of this new life, he drained the life of a beautiful female. She was tossed into the spare crate and taken with them. When she rose the next moonlight and had been fed, she became a part of a sexual foursome that lasted on and off until the approach of dawn. He repeated this with a new, different woman each night. Even his wonderful twins found ways to enjoy the new girls in bed. What they really enjoyed, he believed, was bringing the girl true death after dawn each day.

Daybreak was near. The group continued to head west, but at no particular pace. He had not felt Zhan's presence trying to pry his mind. He, via his own powers, knew that the monk was still alive. He knew no one from the monastery had left to try to find his trail and hunt him. His band would travel to other lands, but one day he would be back. One day he would rule

China. For now his mission had changed. Instead of building a powerful army, his interest was in expanding his own powers. The hunt was for other supernatural creatures to feed upon.

***

"When, Zhan? When do we go?"

"Soon, Xiong. You are almost ready."

"He gets further away every day. He could have built another army by now. Tomorrow will be three weeks he has had to run. Three weeks to kill, create, plot, and plan!"

"It is not as if I haven't been keeping track of days, or what he is up to. He has built no army. He travels light, more interested in exploring his own powers, and young women. He still must be dealt with. He is far more dangerous than before he drank my blood. We had him twice, and he still survived. You, Biao, and Ling must all be ready. I have worked with you all on your ability to block an attack of the mind. He brought the strongest man any of us know to his knees with a thought. He will learn how to use it to track you when he realizes we have started to actively hunt him. There will be no surprise, there will only be preparation. Yes, preparing for anything the enemy may throw at you. I can offer shielding for us here from his prying, but out there, when you are on the road getting further away from me, it will be yourselves you have to rely on."

"He nearly took five of us out that night, and we had an army with us. There will only be the three of you this time. There will be no army at your side. Patience young one. Soon. I promise. The time is near."

"Yes, eldest one."

The final meeting before Xiong, Biao, and Ling left was called. Everyone knew Xiong was going. Only Xiong and Zhan knew who would be joining him. The village chiefs and elders were invited, because the plan for how they moved forward here at home was going to be discussed as well.

"So who goes and who stays?" Wei asked, knowing his name was not going to be on the 'go' list.

"Xiong, Biao, and Ling. That is unless one of them objects."

"Well, I object, Zhan!" Wei groaned.

"Wei, your importance here is paramount. If you are not here, who will protect this place if we came under attack again? Who would train the boys? "

"Yeah, and who'd eat all the leftovers!"

Wei shot an evil look at Ling. "Quiet, boy. Your two brothers over there already have a beating comin'. Wanna join them?"

"I'm good." Ling looked away, whistling.

"Wei, I owe you my life. I do not keep you here to punish you. My reasoning is much more selfish than that. Your mere presence makes me feel safe. That has been the truth since you were four years old. Having you at my side, I fear no enemy."

"You just had to go and get all sappy and sentimental on me."

"Not to mention that right now, Gan needs you. Outside of me, and occasionally Te, you are the only other he is not afraid to be around."

"Ok, ok. I get it. You win."

"Hey, speaking of Gan, do we get to see him before we go? Outside of you three, no one has seen him since that night. You have kept him sequestered from the world for a month." Xiong asked.

"I will answer that in a moment. There is other business first."

One of the villagers stood. "Most of you know me. I am Jie. I realize I possess no qualities that com-compare to your brothers. However, I can fight, and I can shoot an arrow as tr-true as any man. I was born and bred a Fanzhou wa-warrior. I have nothing left here to st-stay for. I feel as if I have no purpose. This, th-this would give me life again. I would rather da-die with purpose, than spend my remaining days living out a miserable existence."

"I object. This is no mission for normal humans," Zhan answered.

"I object as well," Xiong added "You are a brave man, and a true warrior, but you will only slow us down."

"I can ride a horse. Surely you don't plan on sprinting the entire way? Certainly you must sleep? As strong as you are, you must get exhausted at some pa-point?" Jie hesitated. The silence and stares around him were deafening. "You have to eat right? Did I mention that I am the best campfire ch-chef in all of China?"

"Objections overruled!"

Everyone turned to look at Biao. Zhan said, "How do you figure?"

"Well, Zhan, the way I see it, you ain't going so that rules out your objection. I'm pulling seniority on the kid over here," he said and pointed a thumb in Xiong's direction, "since I'm elder to him. And if Ling objects, I'll beat the shit out of him. Besides, if this man can cook, we need him to help us keep our strength up. Making meals is not my forte, Ling couldn't boil water to save his life, and not even Wei would eat that mess Xiong calls cooking."

"Ouch!" Ling laughed, elbowing Xiong.

"I second that," Wei spoke up. "This man has survived the demons before. From the talks we have had, he is a warrior after my own heart. He has made a decision. His past actions, courage, and bravery speak for themselves. He goes. Any further objections will have to go straight through me."

Silence.

"Well, that settles it. And Jie makes four. Welcome aboard the wierdo wagon my friend, destination lunacy," Ling chimed in. A chuckle flowed through the crowd.

"Ok, objection withdrawn," Xiong said. "My apologies, Jie." The two nodded at each other. Then Xiong turned to Zhan. "Now answer my other question. Can we see Gan?"

"No."

"Why?"

"I told you, he is afraid."

"Of us?"

"Not of you. For you."

Everyone stared at Zhan, falling silent, all joviality suddenly gone. *What, exactly, has Gan become?* They all thought the question, but none of them could muster the nerve to ask.

They feared the answer.

About the Author

Shawn Boyd was born and raised in Whitehall, Ohio, where he still resides. Shawn served as a combat communications specialist in the U.S. Army Reserves. He has been a Deputy Sheriff for over twenty-four years, spending time working in the jail, court services, community relations, and as the Deputy assigned to the Children's Services Intake building. He helped create and taught a program about gangs and gang awareness for almost ten years.

Shawn and his wife Kathy have been married for twenty-five years and have three children, Ashley, Andrew and Shawn Ryan. They are also blessed with two granddaughters and four grandsons. The publishing of Shawn's book The Evolution of the Vampire: Xiang Shi, culminates Shawn's life-long dream.

Thank you for your purchase. If you would like to read more by this or other fine TT authors, please visit our website at:

www.tell-talepublishing.com

****

****